OWL

and the

TIGER
Thieves

Volumes in Kristi Charish's Owl Series

Owl and the Japanese Circus
Owl and the City of Angels
Owl and the Electric Samurai
Owl and the Tiger Thieves

For Cindy — I seriously doubt this book
would have been finished without
your support and unwavering help.

OWL

and the

TIGER
Thieves

1

WE GET WHAT WE DESERVE

St. Albinus of Angers Prison, Peru.
Time? Beats me. I haven't seen the sun in a week.

I swore—loudly—and sat up with a start as ice water drenched me, shocking me out of whatever semblance of sleep my brain had managed to achieve, huddling against the stone wall in the corner I'd eked out to the left of the cell door. I'd reasoned the guards would be less likely to single me out if I was absent from their line of sight.

So much for that idea.

I bit down on the sides of my mouth to hold back the tirade of curses threatening to unleash at the guard standing over me, his features vague in the dim torchlight. Still, I caught the flash of gold teeth. I'd wondered more than once whether they were trophies from inmates—the mismatched sizes indicated as much.

He hissed and I cast my eyes down, focusing on the flashlight glow reflecting off his black boots. Fear. That was something they expected from us—and if you didn't deliver . . .

Besides, this wasn't the first or last time a guard would drench me with a bucket of frozen water. That was one of the first things I'd learned in this Peruvian hellhole. The second? Keep your mouth shut. Letting the guards see you sweat is like tossing a bucket of entrails at a pack of jackals. They don't care if you're already dead; they still move in for the kill.

I blinked as he passed the flashlight over me, willing my eyes to adjust to the light faster as I kept them on the dirt floor. For the most part we were left in darkness, no lamps, no candles—no electricity either. Didn't want anyone with an engineering bent getting any ideas.

"*Levántate. ¡Ahora!*" the guard barked in Spanish, adding a hard kick to my leg just to be clear the message carried across the language barrier. Get up. Now!

Again I bit my tongue as I used the wall to balance, pushing myself to stand on underused leg muscles as quickly as possible, the memories of the last few weeks coming back in an unwelcome rush.

How long had it been since one of them had stopped by? A day? Two? I guessed it had been almost a full day since we'd seen the light pass by underneath the door—the anonymous deaf and mute Peruvian woman who walked the halls with her cart, sliding something reminiscent of food under the bolted and iron-reinforced door.

Another brand of torture they'd cooked up—not the food but the latch: large enough to fit your arm through, small enough that your shoulder inevitably got caught. I should know—I'd gotten stuck twice, each time earning me a kick from the guard who'd found me.

"*¡Ahora!*" Now!

"Yeah, yeah, Kujo." My nickname for our gold-toothed guard since he seemed to be more interested in using his mouth to growl than speak. "Getting up." Not wanting to elicit another kick, I pushed myself off the wall, wincing at the resulting aches and pains. The guards didn't strike me as particularly concerned with whether or not we were dead or maimed, and Albinus hadn't been designed with long-term inmate survival in mind. More along the lines of "We stuck you here to rot away and die a horrible death, so get on with it already."

The prison I was in wasn't Virgen de Fátima, the notorious Peruvian women's prison, nor was I stuck in the desert in Ancón. No, this place was much worse. No virgins or scavengers circling overhead with a permanent offer of relief.

This was the Albino Prison—St. Albinus of Angers, to be precise. The patron saint against pirates. The prison had been built in the 1600s to house the pirates that preyed upon the Spanish along the Peruvian coast. It was repurposed in the early 1900s by the International Archaeology Association and promptly scrubbed from the history books. Ancient pirate jail? What pirate jail? They used it to get rid of the odd thief who was stupid enough or unlucky enough to get caught pilfering goods out of the more . . . exotic South American sites, shall we say—the ones where the supernaturals hang out. Occasionally they just wanted their goods back, but mostly they just wanted us forgotten.

Which begged the question, to what did I owe today's honor? I tried again to calculate in my head how long I'd been down here. Without the sun or anything resembling a routine, day and night melded together, taking all sense of time with them. A week? Maybe.

I stumbled as Kujo shoved me towards the door, my aching back protesting. That was another thing about the Albino, after a day or so you drifted off into a state between waking and sleep. It was a dark place, the one that waited in the back of your mind, a low pit of despair and boredom where the only things that seemed to play out were all the wrong choices that had landed you here.

And if your mistakes were the sound track, your regrets were the script playing out in Technicolor, burning a permanent hole in your retinas.

I wondered if that was on purpose—part of the Albino's plan to keep the pirates imprisoned by stone and deep despair.

Despite the iron shackles around my ankles and my wrists, I straightened and did my best to walk upright, back straight. I still had some standards to maintain.

Funny thing was, irrespective of the prison, the questionable company, and the even more questionable guards, I didn't need St. Albino's help to wallow in the deep dark pit I'd sunken into of late—I'd found that place all on my own.

"Pssst." The sound, little more than a high-pitched, forceful hiss, came from the corner nearest the door.

Kujo barked a command in Spanish—something in the local dialect that I didn't quite catch—and kicked the lavatory bucket towards the disturbance.

The cell I'd been locked up in was nine by nine feet, carved out of the cliffs with no seams to speak of; I'd checked every inch of it. Four of us shared it at the moment—and usually we had the sense to keep to ourselves.

Out of the corner of my eye I glanced at the woman who'd risked drawing the ire of Kujo. It was Mathilda, a French archaeology graduate student who'd been on an IAA excavation of Písac—Incan ruins that *weren't* Machu Picchu. She'd been caught lifting diagrams from one of the burial chambers, using rice paper and charcoal, and selling them online to discerning collectors.

Mathilda was the youngest and most inexperienced of the four of us when it came to IAA's extreme crackdowns. She I actually felt bad for. She really didn't deserve to be here.

The rest of us? Grave robbers of some stripe, every last one of us.

The light from Kujo's flashlight barely reached her; still, I could make out her face and the direction in which she jerked her chin—the slightest nod. Towards the cell door, now open.

But it wasn't escape she was hinting at. Faint footsteps echoed down the hall. One long, the second short, jarring, and uneven—as if one leg were shorter than the other or, as in this case, the knee were unable to bend.

Shit. Miguelito.

I hazarded a second sideways glance at my other two cellmates, Cora and Lucinda, but they kept their heads down, not wanting to have anything to do with whatever was about to come. I offered Mathilda a silent nod of thanks as Kujo shoved me out of the cell onto the jail's slippery stone hallway just as our warden extraordinaire turned the corner.

Miguelito was a small man, and not just in stature; he was the kind of small man who is so threatened by his size that he hones himself into a particular kind of bully, one that's driven solely by his need to make everyone around him feel inferior. His features were pinched, as if he were permanently angry, and there was an involuntary twitch to his lip that reached all the way to his nose. His features were otherwise unremarkable: dark hair shaved to disguise a receding hairline and failing, a rounded face, long ears, and disproportionate long front teeth—a mangy, lop-eared rabbit comes to mind, though the comparison was unkind to sick bunnies.

As for the leg? According to Miguelito, his right knee had picked up shrapnel during a local eruption of Peru's ongoing civil war. He struck me as too much of a coward, and my cellmates agreed. Mathilda figured he'd fallen drunk down a flight of stairs, and the two other women, Cora and Lucinda, guessed he'd been caught sleeping with someone's wife and subsequently been beaten with a baseball bat.

My money was on a disgruntled partner shooting it off in a dispute.

As Kujo shoved me into the light, I noted that Miguelito's nose was red and swollen and set off at a slight angle. I'd slammed him in the face with an old wood beam on my last escape attempt.

He hadn't liked that.

"Miguelito," I said, wary. Our warden had a couple of faces—or, well, two: volatile and semireasonable. The second only occasionally reared its head.

"Charity," he said.

I flinched at the spittle that landed on my face but didn't dare wipe it off. Miguelito offered me a forced smile that would have been right at home on a loan shark or pimp. "We have much to discuss today."

I returned the forced smile, showing my own teeth. "As long as it doesn't involve any misplaced treasure. I've really bought into the IAA rehabilitation program, hook, line, and sink—*oomph!*" I doubled over with the shot to my kidneys, then glared over my shoulder at Kujo, who was grinning and hitting the palm of his hand with the billy stick.

I did my best not to puke or pass out. "I guess that's a no for talking to my IAA student representative?" I managed.

Miguelito snickered.

Now . . . that was out of the norm. Miguelito didn't have much patience for my particular brand of contempt. Normally I'd be thrown back in the cell by now.

"*¡Vamos!*" Miguelito barked, clapping his hands and setting off at a clipped pace down the corridor. Like a good guard dog, Kujo shoved me in the back with his stick, sending me stumbling over the slick stones after the warden.

Did I mention these assholes were corrupt? A jail for thieves and pirates who are a thorn in the IAA's side was a great idea on paper, but in practice, sticking the best—or worst—archaeology thieves on the South American continent into a single jail and paying the staff a minimum wage breeds an entirely different relationship. One that most definitely didn't involve containing the problem.

Being the entrepreneurial sort, Miguelito had figured out that right here, under his dictatorial thumb, were the locations to restricted digs, little-known tombs, secret temples—a gold mine of treasure all over South America and the channels to off-load it. The kind of information network that takes a lot of time, sweat, blood, and tears to build. Only Miguelito hadn't been the one doing the shedding.

Oh, mark my words, Miguelito would get his reckoning from the IAA one of these days. *When* they caught him. Despite being a greedy waste of otherwise vacant human space, he had a talent for institutional thieving and a good system—a rat warren of a system, but a good one.

Why was it that the IAA always left the fat sewer rats in charge?

A question for another day—once I got the hell out of here.

Speaking of warrens . . . I counted the stones off silently as I followed Miguelito down the ever-branching cell-lined corridors. I had it memorized now: ten unevenly sized stones to the left, then a right turn, then another twenty stones until we reached his office door. Kujo's breath was warm and rancid on my neck as he followed close behind, ready to prod me with the end of his baton should I slow. He'd learned to stay close right after escape attempt number two.

"*Para,*" Kujo hissed. *Stop.* The command was followed by a sharp jab in the small of my back that had me stumbling in my shackles.

Eyes still down, I heard Miguelito's iron keys jingling against their key chain before the correct one was inserted into the old door lock. Again, electric and computer-derived locking systems might look high-tech and work in a regular prison system, but not when you were housing world-class thieves—and I wasn't including myself in that estimation. I barely rated a petty thug.

The door creaked open, the hinges shrieking, protesting the sorely lacking oil. Another shove in the center of my back sent me into the office. I swore as my bare feet scraped into the wood floor, picking up a splinter or two. Out of all the Albino's cold stone interior, this was the one room where wood floors had been laid. I'd wondered at that—why bother when the stone served so well?—but then I had seen the blood and various other bodily fluids that had seeped into the cracks, years' worth of stains concentrated around the plain wooden chair placed in the center of the room, a few feet away from an oak desk—an assortment of books and papers scattered across its surface in a haphazard order—or lack thereof.

"*Póngala en la silla,*" Miguelito said, nodding at me as he maneuvered himself into his own comfortable seat. Get her in the chair.

Did I mention Miguelito's office smelled? Of people—the kind of lingering scent beaten into the very wood itself. Cramming a few centuries' worth of human misery into a confined space. Not unlike when I had taken Captain to the vet's and the very scent of the room had warned him that other cats had not had a good time there.

Kujo shoved me again and another guard, taller than Kujo and leaner, stepped out of a darkened corner. He jammed the butt of his gun into my chest and pushed me towards the chair, just in case I hadn't understood.

I did what any self-respecting thief would do in the same situation: I sat, doing my best not to stare at the bloodstains on the floor.

"Tell me, Charity, how are you enjoying your stay at the Albino?"

I lifted my head to stare at Miguelito, who was smiling and regarding me like the rat he was from behind his large desk.

Shit. He knew—or knew something. I decided to gamble and see just how much. "I'm disappointed in the room service," I said.

Miguelito chuckled before repeating what I had said in Spanish, eliciting snickers from Kujo and the new guard. "Room service," he said to me, still smiling amiably. "Funny. What was it last time? You wanted cable TV, no? And before that, you asked to see a lawyer, yes?" He dropped the feigned smile. "You think you are a comedian, Charity?"

I jerked my chin at his chuckling goons. "Not really, but from the sounds of it, those two do," I said.

Miguelito barked a command in Spanish I didn't quite catch.
Crack.

"Ow!" I shouted as a blinding pain spread across the back of my head. I was rewarded with a sharp kick to my calf. I glared at Miguelito, but kept silent.

Miguelito casually pulled a folder he'd been worrying out of the pile and flipped the cover open before sliding it my way.

It was a collection of photos. Of me, but not just from my stint in Peru as Charity. *Shit.* Still, I stayed silent and gave Miguelito a blank stare.

The first chinks in Miguelito's pleasant facade showed. "*Míralo!*" Look at it! he bellowed, in Spanish, then English.

My chair was dragged to the desk, and Kujo "helped" me look, forcing my face down until my nose was pressed against the cheaply printed matte photos. I flinched, though it wasn't as though I had much to worry about from paper—except maybe death by gangrened paper cuts . . .

"And here I thought we were coming to an understanding about the business I am running in this prison, Charity—or should I say Owl?" One of his sparse eyebrows shot up. "Oh, yes, I know who you are. I am not the idiot you have mistaken me for. How did the notorious Owl end up in *my* prison?"

That was the first intelligent question I'd heard Miguelito ask. My stomach churned. Well, this certainly changed things—and bumped up my timeline—

I screamed as Kujo's club met my shoulder blade in just the wrong spot.

Miguelito smiled viciously down at me. "We continue in English, no?" he said.

I hazarded a glance over my shoulder at Kujo and his shadow of a bookend. They both wore slightly confused expressions now, and even exchanged a glance. Not wanting the muscle listening in was never a good sign.

Goddamn it, I hate it when my plans get rushed.

Some might say that if there is a golden rule for thieves, it's "Don't get caught," a close second might be "Know where the treasure is before breaking in," and a third would be "Have an escape route planned out before you start."

As I'd had none of those when I'd set out three weeks ago, I'd decided to challenge accepted wisdom and wing it. I mean, I *sort* of had the second one . . . The treasure was in here somewhere, I didn't know *exactly* where, but still . . .

And as for the other two? I was working on them—*Hello.*

Sitting on the edge of Miguelito's desk, peeking out from underneath a pile of papers, was another set of keys. This one heavier, antique, *old.* This trip to the warden's office was already looking up.

"Well?" Miguelito prompted, voice rising as he leaned his small frame across the desk, using it to make himself appear bigger and meaner, wearing his insecure Napoleon complex for the world to see, let alone his prisoner. "What do you have to say for yourself?"

Well, the gig was at least partly up. And this was going to get messy real fast if I couldn't manage some damage control. I set my jaw, pulled my backbone out of hiding, and stared right back. "What do you really want, Miguelito?"

That caught him off guard. "It's the logical question," I continued. "I mean, we're left in here to rot. Who cares who I am? Well, the IAA does but you haven't handed me over to them, so I'll ask you again." I nodded at the pictures scattered across the desk. "What is it you want?"

He narrowed his eyes and watched me for a long moment before producing a squat, coffee-cup-sized gold idol inlaid with lines of red and blue dyed stones from his pocket. "What is it and how much is it worth?"

It was an Incan artifact, a relic from a long-dead religion, reminiscent of a female fertility idol; I'd located it at an IAA dig site as part of my master plan to buy myself a ticket through the Albino's front door and into the warden's office, as Miguelito's coveting of rare artifacts was famed in the antiquities community. I suppose it had worked . . . in a roundabout way. The intricacy, the color . . . Not even an idiot like Miguelito would miss that it was magic.

The rusty wheels in my head churned as Miguelito and his guards watched me. Miguelito had asked me about the idol a few times now. It was supposed to imbue weapons with poison—the magic kind that could down anything, including the supernatural. Mr. Kurosawa had wanted it for his armory, part of his arms race with the other side of the supernatural war. Like hell was I telling the warden that thought.

Miguelito could simply call his IAA bosses and ask them what the idol was, but he didn't want to; they'd take it away. He'd rather sell it on the black market. Meaning if he was desperate enough to confront me about my alias, he probably had a buyer. He needed the details and a price tag, and he needed it now. That's what this visit was about.

I licked my lips, the dry cracks distracting my sluggish brain. It was still bad but not quite the clusterfuck I'd feared. Miguelito was so distracted by the idol that he hadn't bothered to wonder how someone good enough to sneak into an IAA dig and find it had managed to get caught. Greed did that to people, made them miss what was right underneath their noses. As Mr. Kurosawa had once said to me, greed was something I could work with. If Miguelito had any inkling of what I was *really* in here for I'd be talking to black-suited IAA, not a corrupt prison warden.

I shrugged as cavalierly as I could manage. "Beats me. I'm a thief, I just find things. I don't bother asking questions—*oomph!*" The punch was to my arm this time—enough to smart but not hard enough to cause any damage. Still I glared at Kujo. No need to advertise that they really did need to hit harder if the goal was to put the fear of St. Albinus into me . . .

"Now let's try that again," Miguelito said, holding up the idol. I couldn't help wincing—the acid on his fingers was destined to damage the inlaid dyes. Idiot . . . "*What is it?*"

I knew there was a smart answer and a dumb answer to Miguelito's question . . . "For sacrificing the blood of puppies and kittens to long lost Incan gods— Ow!" Another smack, this time to the back of my head.

"St. Albinus can be a dangerous place," Miguelito said mildly, and I saw where his eyes darted: to the small table Peruvian thug number two was hovering over.

On it was laid out a variety of barbaric-looking instruments that didn't belong in the most sadistic dentist's office. He smiled and fondled one of the sharper-looking instruments, its edge rusted. Like Kujo, Miguelito's second man-at-arms was a local who had no interest in going about his prison duties in a genial manner, but unlike Kujo, who struck me as taking some form of pride in his work, Bookend wasn't the type who looked like he was interested in results. He looked like the type who got off being mean.

I glared back at Miguelito. The last smack to my head had set my ears ringing. His upper lip twitched in amusement. "I am being a reasonable man. This is your last chance. Tell me what this artifact does, or you will shortly find out just how dangerous this prison can be."

There's a line somewhere about never believing a man who starts negotiations off by telling you that he's the reasonable one . . . And the novelty of my prison detour had worn off.

"If I tell you the truth and you hit me for it, then really, all I have left are the lies you might believe. You realize that's why intimidation and torture are so fucking inefficient?"

"What does the idol do? And don't try telling me it's not magic. You wouldn't be after it otherwise. I will not ask you again."

But he would. Only under the prompting of Kujo and Bookend's ungentle hands . . .

I chewed my lip as I forced my gray matter out of its self-imposed sabbatical.

Come on, brain, don't fail me now . . . The seconds ticked by—one, two, three, four, five. Metal sang as Bookend began sharpening two of the more conspicuous table knives.

"What do I get out of it?" I blurted out—unintentionally. *A little less warning than I would have liked there, brain, but at least you're back on the job.*

To judge from the confused glances I earned, it had worked—at least to derail the conversation on torture. Miguelito seemed to think about that. "Cooperate, and we don't torture you for hours. I thought the implication was very clear."

I shrugged as much as I dared under Kujo's watchful eye. "Say I cooperate and tell you what the idol does. Then what? You let me go? Give me an outstanding inmate door prize?"

Miguelito gave me a terse smile. "I'm afraid the IAA frowns on that sort of thing. But there are things we could do to make your stay more—accommodating."

I snorted. "In the form of a pine box or just dropping me into a deeper, darker pit headfirst?" I shook my head. "Here's the thing, Miguelito, if I knew what that idol did—which I'm not saying I do—I have no confidence that you plan on doing anything but kill me. Now, a smart interrogator might say that there's the chance you might not kill me versus the certainty; the more pessimistic might say that at the very least I'll be dead faster." I *tsk*ed. "Either way I see it, I end up dead. Only one way ends up with everyone pissed off about it, including you."

I must have come across as sincere, because Miguelito didn't immediately yell for Kujo and Bookend to beat me. "What do you want?" he finally spat out.

The keys to the cordoned-off lower levels, idiot. "A bed?" I asked. "The floor doesn't exactly lend itself to restful sleep. Neither does the lack of a lavatory."

Miguelito leaned across the table. "You can have all of that and more. All you need to do is tell me what the idol does and what it's worth. The great Owl does not chase after trinkets, no?"

A fourth golden rule for thieves? No one ever believes you, so don't bother telling the truth. Lie, and lie well. I shrugged again. "Something really valuable to a buyer interested in South American relics and ancient art. They approached me—*oomph!*" I was interrupted in midsentence by a heavy jab to the back of my rib cage. I doubled over onto the table, my face planted into the matte photo of myself.

I winced. That felt like it would leave a mark . . .

"No liar survives in St. Albino. And no more warnings."

"What kind of a lousy deal is— Son of a bitch!" I arched my back as it reeled in pain. It took a moment for the muscles to stop spasming enough for me to sit straight.

Miguelito shrugged, unfazed. "If you give me an answer I like, *maybe* he won't hit you again. There is the *possibility* you won't be permanently disfigured." He nodded at Bookend. "If I like what I hear, maybe we don't give you to Jesús. People he works with often find religion."

I snorted as I pushed the pain smarting along my spine out of my mind. Jesús was watching me now like a predator waits for prey to stop moving—so it can start eating it alive.

Time to switch my tactics. "Ever heard the phrase 'Don't gut the golden goose'?" That made Miguelito pause. I licked my lips. "*Tu piensas que solo conozco una cámara del tesoro,*" I said as clearly as I could. *You think I only know about one treasure chamber.*

It had the effect I wanted: Despite my poor Spanish Jesús and Kujo exchanged a glance.

Miguelito was unfazed, though. He kept his smile and waved at the room. "Take a good look at your surroundings, *mija*. This entire prison is a golden goose. Maybe we can afford to let the odd one go. ¿*Verdad?*" True? Miguelito asked the other two. Jesús and Kujo exchanged a wary glance before nodding.

While the three of them faced off uncomfortably, I scanned the room, searching for something I could use as a distraction—anything to get those keys.

By accident my eyes fell back on Jesús's eclectic dental implements. Miguelito saw where I looked and smiled. He flicked his wrist, and I felt Kujo's calloused hands close around my face, prying my neck back. I couldn't see but heard the clink of metal utensils.

I gagged as gloved fingers were jammed into my mouth, prying my teeth apart, and something cold and metal traced along my jaw before I felt the retractors jammed inside. The smell of rancid sweat was strong now, and I caught a glimpse of a rusted dental pick that looked like an antique for excavating cavities from the 1930s.

Jesús spoke, though I didn't catch all the words. Miguelito filled me in.

"Jesús says people tend to scream his name when he works on their smiles—he says to try not to, the tongue gets in the way and there is a shake in his right hand."

The retractors were opened wider.

I'd made a mistake. I'd tried to take away Miguelito's muscle. And now it just might cost me. I didn't have to pretend I was desperate. I was.

"*¡Espera!*" Wait! I shouted, though it came out muffled and garbled. Another piece of wisdom? Don't wait until the damage starts to beg. Seems counterintuitive, but people are funny. Add in the right mix of adrenaline, and the rush that comes from screams of pain that aren't your own—

The rusted dental pick halted centimeters from my mouth, and a satisfied smile parted Miguelito's thin lips, making his features look even more rabbitlike. "See? I knew we would come to an understanding." The metal was removed from my mouth.

Greed and ego. Men like Miguelito were servants to them.

"Look, I have no idea what the idol does—seriously!" I added as Jesús turned back to the dental implements. "But there's more back in the temple—a lot more. Caches of them."

Miguelito leaned back in the chair, steepling his fingers over the idol. "Tell me about these caches. More magical trinkets? Like this?"

I nodded—slowly. Fun fact: I had no idea if there were any more caches of magic treasure. There couldn't be many—not after a few hundred years of conquest. But what I believed didn't matter, because the three of them certainly did. More important, if Jesús got a chance to start in on me, I'd tell them everything I *didn't* want them to know—and then some.

"Even the IAA can't uncover every nook and cranny," I continued. "Grave robbing isn't exactly a new pastime—the Incans hid their burial valuables well."

Miguelito eyed me. He wasn't an idiot, and he probably knew that if it sounded too good to be true, it probably was. But even as the skepticism wove its way through his mind, his greed took over. "Where are these caches? Exactly?"

Lying, don't betray me now . . . There were no maps—I'd had one, the one Mr. Kurosawa had given me to find the idol, but I hadn't brought it here. I shrugged. "There isn't one book of maps. Random notes from various grave robbers and archaeologists over the years—mostly, left for themselves to find the caches once again. You need to know what to look for."

Miguelito's lips curled up. I could practically taste the greed ebbing off of him. Incan gold: the downfall of many a man. "Which I suppose is where you come in? Is that it?"

I shook my head. "That's the thing about trust, Miguelito. It goes both ways." I thought about giving him a freebie, telling him where one of the other caches I knew about was located, one I'd come across. But I decided against it. Despite his protests to the contrary, he really did strike me as the type to gut the golden goose to see what was inside.

"We could torture it out of you," he said with the kind of offhand casualness that could only come from a sickening level of familiarity.

I licked my lips and gambled. "You could. But do you really want to bet a few millions' worth of Incan gold caches that I won't be able to hold out and lie? Trust me, I'm petty enough to do just that."

I glanced at the other two, who were exchanging looks. Incan gold was a universally understandable term—and they were as greed driven as Miguelito—more so, maybe, considering their casual and curious disposition towards torture.

Miguelito weighed his options. He wanted to know what the idol's significance was, but the treasure was a tempting consolation prize. "*Where?*" he finally demanded, pulling out a map of the ruins and tapping it. There was a fingerprint stain on the page the color of iodine. "A location, *Charity*," he added, emphasizing my alias in a warning that promised violence.

I tried to not think about where the stain had come from.

What to give them? Not an actual cache—a clue then? Which one?

I stared at the map. There were a number of side tunnels leading off the main excavation site. Most of them had been thoroughly mapped. If they knew much about the site, they'd know those were empty—or had been emptied over the past fifty years. The lower levels? As tempting as it was, I didn't think they'd fall for the traps that lined the old sacrificial chambers . . .

A shove from behind, followed by "*Rápido*" and something less than complimentary in the local dialect, I imagined.

Come on, Owl, fast. I spotted the side tunnel off the main chute, near the bottom. It was in a section of the temple that had been used to house slaves—not the ones destined for hard labor but the ones destined for sacrifice. The historical records were vague on the details, but during the heyday of the temple's reign, the popular thought had been that if you managed to sacrifice enough people to the temple and gods, you'd earn yourself the Incan version of a sainthood . . . brings new meaning to the idea "We only ask for your heart" . . . no wonder the culture had been on its way out a hundred years before the conquistadors showed up.

It was also one of the least excavated sections of the ruins. I mean, even the IAA figured the slaves didn't know anything useful, particularly the ones who were destined to end up living sacrifices. Ironic, considering that was about how the IAA treated its army of graduate students and postdocs . . .

The point was, what better place to hide clues to treasure?

I heard the scrape of metal on stone and hazarded a glance to where it was coming from—Jesús was sharpening another utensil from his table, bigger, pointier than before . . . A gold tooth glinted back at me in the lantern light as he smiled.

"Marco and Jesús are impatient men, particularly when it comes to the gold of their forebears—and with foreigner women who lie," Miguelito offered.

Hunh, Kujo was Marco. Wouldn't have guessed that one. And if Marco and Jesús were Incan descendants, I'd eat my cat. My eyes found a plausible place, and my fingers followed.

"There," I said, pointing at a series of passages that wove around the burial chamber. If memory served, the entire wing of the temple had been written off as looted by early conquistadors.

"The slave quarters?" Miguelito said, sounding surprised—which was better than accusatory.

"Empty!" came the angry reply from Kujo, who was staring at the map from behind me.

"*No.*" I tapped the spot again. "*Hidden.* Probably another compartment the Incans hid behind the wall." They'd had a talent for that—hiding entire wings of temples from everyone, from kings to archaeologists.

"A passage the IAA has yet to uncover?" Miguelito asked, arching a thin eyebrow at me. The skepticism was still there, but under it I could hear he was willing to buy the lie. So was Kujo.

Jesús, however, proved to be not so gullible. Torture implement in hand, he checked the map and the location the other two were now discussing in low Spanish, before leveling a skeptical stare at me.

"And you believe it, so all we need is a door?" he asked, in surprisingly passable English. "The Incans didn't suffer thieves."

Point to him for intelligence.

But here's the thing—thieves don't trust one another. Even if they figured I was bluffing, they'd still chase after it.

I leveled a stare at Miguelito, not the hired help. Always go up the chain of command. "No. You're supposed to believe that you need me alive and cooperative," I said, and held Miguelito's gaze as I waited for him to make his call.

He stared greedily back down at the map while Jesús and Marco argued quietly amongst themselves. Seeing my chance, and not daring to breathe, I slipped the black ring of keys off the desk and tucked them under the sleeve of my shirt.

Miguelito turned his eyes back on me. "How do we get inside?"

Greed. It brings people together and keeps the world turning around, and around, and around . . .

"Let me go, and I'll make sure you get out alive. I'll even walk you through the tunnel myself."

Miguelito's mouth twitched. "You'll do it from the cell."

"No faith in the word of thieves?"

Miguelito leaned across the table. "No faith you won't try to kill me the first chance you get."

I reached for the map and just as quickly retracted my manacled hands. "Hey, hey, now!" I said as Kujo's knife came down on the parchment. "Remember what I said about trust being a two-way street, Miguelito."

"And you'll be begging Jesús for a new religious experience if you don't tell me." I waited until they'd relaxed their various sharp instruments before taking the map and sinking back into the chair. "Ah—pen? Pencil?"

After a moment's hesitation, Miguelito rolled me a pencil. Freshly sharpened. I quieted my mind as to what I could do with it, Miguelito sitting just across from me. I had a much, much better way . . .

"Here," I said, making an *X* with the pencil on one of the temple holding cells, paying particular attention to Jesús's ominous-looking nail spear.

Miguelito and Jesús studied the map while Kujo intimidated me.

It was Jesús who snorted. "Press the patterns in the right order, and a door opens?" he said to me. "Miguelito, she's lying. I can smell it on her."

More arguing in Spanish. Jesús was skeptical, I could see that clearly as he glanced back at me. "Why are you so certain we won't go back on our word?" Jesús asked me, his lip curling into a sneer. "Send you back to your cell beaten and bloody."

I smiled. "Call it remedial faith in humanity. The way I see it, you have two choices: send me back to my cell beaten and bloody or worse and hope I've told you where the traps are, or play ball." I made a show of thinking about it. "Or I suppose there's a third option: the three of you could forget the whole thing, stick me in some forgotten pit here, and subsist on whatever the IAA pays you. Now, how about that soft bed and three square meals?"

Often the truth is a lie's best alibi. I saw Jesús's resolve waver.

For a moment, as the three eyed one another, I worried that I'd overestimated their greed. That they'd cave to my demands. I needn't have concerned myself. Miguelito laughed, and the other three followed.

The last rule you should always remember about thieves is that the really good ones like their honor. Once their word is given, they go out of their way to keep it. After all, a deal with a thief is only as good as their word. And these three didn't even merit an entry-level card.

"We give the orders here, not little girls with delusions of thievery."

As expected, there was my double cross. Couldn't say I was surprised. And I definitely wasn't going to be treating any of them with something even resembling honor. "There are two types of people who become prison guards, Miguelito. The ones who genuinely want to usher criminals towards a better life and the ones who enjoy having unlimited power over other humans and the chance to exploit them. I'm guessing you're not here because you wish you could have helped your sister avoid that prostitution charge."

Miguelito's self-satisfied expression faded to something more sinister, *violent*. Oh, he fumed, but as I'd expected, he didn't hit me. He wasn't in a rush to give me an excuse to usher him towards his own mortality.

"I'm the one holding all the cards," Miguelito growled. He was trying to convince me less than himself and his two goons. If trust amongst thieves is gold, then respect is platinum. And Miguelito was a broke amateur.

"Just remember that when you're deciding which tiles to step on."

Miguelito and I stared at each other for the count of four. Then, without any warning, he reached out and slapped my face. Kujo grabbed the back of my neck, and once again my face was driven down onto the table.

Maybe I shouldn't have added that comment about his sister . . .

Miguelito leaned in until he was eye level with me, his face a twisted mix of anger. "Where are the traps?"

"Beats me, Miguelito," I managed. "I was too busy running from the IAA."

"The traps!"

I noticed something silver reflecting the light over my eyes. Jesús's sharpened spatula.

"Tell me, or it's your eye."

"That thing so much as *scratches* my eye, mark my words, I'll make sure you fall down the first trap I can find—and I'll make certain it's a doozy."

I held his gaze. Every ounce of feigned civility was gone. It reminded me of an expression someone else had looked at me with recently. I pushed that unwelcome memory aside. I did not need to be thinking about Rynn—not now, not while I was in here.

Come on. Do it.

I don't know where the voice that wanted me to goad Miguelito came from, but some part of me, wedged in the back of my mind, begged him to let Jesús do it—dole out some kind of permanent pain that I wouldn't be able to brush off or forget. The part of me that knew I deserved worse than the deck I'd stumbled out of Shangri-La with.

It still counts as bad luck when you don't want the good, right?

For a second I thought Miguelito would do it, tell Jesús to take my eye out. It'd be so easy, so simple.

Maybe I'd feel something besides the numbness that had followed me down here and bred.

But he didn't. Self-preservation and something resembling logic came back into play. Or he realized he was losing it in front of his two goons. Didn't know, didn't care.

Miguelito *tsk*ed, and the sharpened spatula disappeared out of my limited line of sight.

He sat back down in his chair, and the grip on my neck loosened. Slowly I lifted my head.

"Here is what you will do, *mija*. You will tell us exactly where the traps are from the corner of your cell, and if you do anything we do not like, or Jesús or Marco thinks you are lying"—a smile spread slowly across his lips—"well, Jesús is not the only name you'll be calling."

Now to barter for that phone call . . . Lady Siyu would be pissed I hadn't checked in, but if I timed things right, I'd be out of the lower dungeons and boarding a plane before they realized the traps started fifty meters before they ever reached the puzzle.

But then I noticed something: the draft that constantly wound its way through the old fortress from the ocean and cliffs outside had stopped. It was quiet in here, except for our own breathing.

There was only one supernatural I knew of who could do that. Must have gotten wind I'd ended up in here—not the best timing, but then again I hadn't exactly discussed my tentative plan with the Onorio— when your plan consists of getting thrown into prison and figuring the rest out as you go—well, Oricho likely would have had some issues . . .

The real question was, what would Oricho want me to do?

Stall for time. And for the love of God, not to let my big, fat mouth pick a fight.

"Fine." I spat the word out through clenched teeth, earning a smile from Miguelito.

"Take her back to her cell," Miguelito said in Spanish, tossing the ring of cell keys to Kujo, who caught them easily. Kujo then kicked the back of my chair, knocking me to the floor. Jesús came up beside me and hoisted me up by my shackled arm none too gently. Kujo in the lead and Jesús beside me, I was led out of Miguelito's office and back towards my cell.

I kept my eyes and ears peeled as Kujo and Jesús spoke in low voices. I'd done my part, I'd stalled. Now, where the hell was Oricho?

"You hold up your end of the bargain, we'll try to make Miguelito hold up his," Jesús said.

Yeah, I wasn't about to hold my breath for that one. I nodded absently and meekly, keeping my head down so I could count the stone slabs. Ten, eleven, twelve . . .

We turned the corner. I counted another ten stone slabs, all the way back to my cell.

Still no Oricho. A brief panic coursed through me as the iron ring of keys jingled against the lock; a moment later the door swung open. Was it possible that my own desperate imagination had concocted Oricho? Shit.

I heard the first body drop to the stone floor, bringing to mind a sack of potatoes. Kujo and I both turned to see Jesús crumpled against the stone wall, his large physique looking oddly like a discarded rag doll, the way his limbs were angled in odd directions. Kujo swore and went for his knife—but there was no one there besides the unconscious Jesús. No sound, no breathing, no scrapes, no Pacific Ocean draft running through the hall; even the lamps seemed to dim in the darkness.

Still he brandished his knife, as if it might chase off a ghost. I stepped out of the way, towards my open cell door. He didn't notice, sweat collecting on his face as he scanned the darkened hall. "*¡Muéstrate!*" Show yourself.

There was no response. Instead he gasped, clutching at his throat. I know it was a cowardly thing to do—but I'd seen enough violence over the past year. I flinched and turned my face away. I heard Kujo choke and drop to the cold stones but was spared having to watch. Not that I felt bad for him. Of late I had just preferred to avoid being a spectator.

"Just had to wait until I was right outside my goddamned cell, didn't you?" I said as I wiped off my hands and stood. "And by the way, I had everything perfectly under control." I hadn't expected Oricho to know I was in the Albino, let alone lift a hair to help me, but I wasn't looking this gift horse in the mouth. Now all I needed to do was convince Oricho that we should hang around for another hour or so—I mean, since the guards were unconscious . . .

Oh God, I hoped he'd only knocked them unconscious. Not that they didn't deserve it, just the idea of letting a supernatural with dubious morals loose in here to kill even evil guards at will left a bad taste in my mouth.

I supposed I could always tell Oricho the truth. Hey, Oricho, I know we agreed I wouldn't do anything brash without conferring with you, but I came across a story that referenced the Tiger Thieves in some old Peruvian church archives and figured I'd check it out. How about we take a quick tour of the dungeons downstairs, won't take more than an hour, promise.

Dangerous? Oh . . . a couple stories about cursed pirates, but I'm sure it's nothing I can't handle. Probably not even real.

I turned around—slowly—Oricho was still a supernatural after all. "You know they were probably a few seconds away from beating me up? Would have been a lot harder to drag me out of here uncon—"

My voice caught in my throat.

I'd expected to turn around and see a tall Japanese man dressed in an expensive suit with a dragon tattoo winding around his neck looming menacingly over the guards' bodies. Instead, a blond man stood in the hallway—tall, lean, his features obscured by the shadows but still familiar.

I couldn't speak, though I wanted to. It couldn't be, there was no way . . . yet I wasn't imagining him standing there, watching me . . .

Unless I was dreaming.

"Rynn?" I whispered, letting more hope scratch my voice than I had any right to.

But the optimism was short-lived as the man angled his flashlight beam into his face. Even if the features were similar, the sardonic smirk he gave me shattered what little illusion there'd been.

My own temper and months of pent-up anger boiled right up to replace it. Of all the lousy, no-good—it wasn't Rynn—or Oricho, not even close. I balled my hands into fists.

"*You?*" I managed, hearing cruel disdain dripping from my voice. "What the hell are *you* doing here?"

Artemis, Rynn's cousin, washed-up musician from the eighties and all-around low-life incubus, was the blond man standing before me. Blocking my exit.

Not Rynn. Not Oricho. *Him.* If the guards hadn't cleaned out the lavatory buckets, I'd have thrown one at him. And I wouldn't have missed.

As it was, all I could do was glare as he *tsk*ed and stepped over the downed Kujo. "Apparently we have a great deal of catching up to do," he said, the eastern-tinged accent reminding me even more of Rynn though the attitude did not. He stuck the flashlight into my cell, looking more curious than anything else.

What was that saying? Out of the frying pan and into the fire. I might as well be dead. Because if Artemis was any sign, that's where this was heading.

2

THE MORE THINGS CHANGE . . .

Time? Still have no clue on account of no lights.
I'm about ready to toss an incubus over the cliffs, though . . .

I'm not one who's usually lost for words, and generally only for a few seconds. I have no filter at the best of times and I tend to revert to my old habits under stress.

Which is what I was doing now. "How the hell did you find me?" I asked. I had the good sense to keep my voice low, but man, did it take effort. I clenched my hands instead, ignoring my nails digging into my palms. It was all I could do to keep myself from punching him—or throwing something at him—or pushing him into a dark, empty cell and throwing the key away . . .

Artemis. The last person—scratch that—*not-person*—I ever wanted to see again, let alone find here.

His smile only widened. Just as cold and cruel as I remembered—no, more so. "Aw, Charity, now, is that any way to greet an old friend?"

"We are most definitely not friends, nor will we ever be." Where was a deep, dark Incan pit when you needed one?

Artemis rolled his eyes. "Fine—not friends." He made a show of examining his fingernails. "Though I assumed you'd be more pleasant to someone who might let you out."

I fantasized about shoving him into the empty cell behind him. The problem was that snakes like Artemis always managed to crawl out of whatever cage you stuck them in. They thrived when you sent them to rot with the other bottom-feeders.

To his credit, Artemis's smile didn't falter, even as he *tsk*ed. "Why don't you tell me how you really feel, Owl, instead of standing there fuming?"

Because Artemis knew exactly what I thought of him. He, like Rynn, was an incubus—but that's where the comparisons ended. Unlike Rynn, Artemis was the asshole version—the kind who figured humans were there for entertainment, who used humans . . . the kind who couldn't damn well be bothered to *attempt* to blend in . . . Now that my eyes had adjusted to the light, I got a better look at Artemis's outfit. He'd broken into the prison wearing a reflective gold T-shirt, a metal-studded leather jacket that belonged back in LA, and boots that were easily worth more than the average Peruvian's monthly salary. Not the kind of outfit you broke into any prison wearing, let alone one of the IAA's. It was a wonder he hadn't set off the alarms from the outskirts of the town.

It was also a wonder he'd managed to sneak up behind both Jesús and Kujo.

Artemis pulled the loop of keys from Kujo's hand and held them up in front of me and raised his eyebrows. He then held them up for my cellmates. Still shackled to the walls, all three had watched the goings-on outside the cell with extreme interest but stopped short of bringing attention to themselves.

I held out my hands, then my feet for Artemis to unlock. I have pride. But not enough to stick around here.

"It might just be your lucky day, ladies," Artemis said, his voice raised, as he unlocked my manacles, their iron hinges creaking as they dropped to the floor. My three cellmates shielded their eyes as Artemis's flashlight danced about their cell. Lucinda, I think it was, swore a blue streak.

"None other than the infamous Owl has been your cellmate these two weeks past and is currently breaking out," Artemis continued. "You should feel honored. Normally she's responsible for burying people—*oomph!*"

I derived a small sense of satisfaction as I elbowed the air out of Artemis's chest with a sharp jab to his rib cage.

"Ignore him," I said, rubbing the raw skin where the metal had chafed it over the past two weeks. Artemis gave me a questioning glance and nodded at my cellmates. I nodded back. A more prudent and cautious thief might have left them in there—the fewer chances of alerting any wayward guards, the better—but I wasn't even going to pretend to entertain the idea. Besides, they were professionals.

Artemis made quick work unlocking their shackles, each woman testing her cramped legs and arms. While the three of them rubbed their wrists and ankles, sore from the chains and what I gathered had been months of disuse, I set about seeing exactly what Jesús and Kujo had been hoarding. More keys, a flashlight, cash—good for getting a train ticket out of here, if nothing else—a cell phone, two pocketknives, a baton . . . I also grabbed Kujo's jacket; it had enough large pockets to carry everything as well as protect me from the draft.

"Charity, is it true?" Mathilda asked in her timid voice. I turned around; the acknowledgment seemed to give her bravery a boost. "You are the Owl, yes?"

To be honest, the question stumped me. How did one answer something like that? And really, at the end of the day, did it even matter? Who cared who let them out? I shook my head. "Just—get out of Dodge fast—before someone wakes up or another guard comes down." She nodded, eyes wide.

I don't know what inspired me to keep going, but I did. "And don't use any of your ID cards or your bank accounts, not even ones you have stashed. Otherwise the IAA will have you back in here faster than you can access an ATM." I divided the money I'd looted from Jesús and pressed some of the bills into her hand. The rest I offered to the other two. "Let her follow you out, at the very least to the train station." I wasn't being completely altruistic either, I reasoned. Mathilda on her own might end up alerting the IAA that there'd been a prison break, but the other two were career criminals and knew how to stay under the radar. If they got Mathilda to the train station and she didn't access any of her accounts, I figured she would be fine—at least until I was finished in here and well out of Peru.

"What about you?" Lucinda asked in a gruff voice.

I glanced back over my shoulder. Artemis, after outing me, had apparently lost interest and was once again leaning against the wall and checking his manicure.

"Up the stairs, take a right, then a left," Artemis told them, not bothering to look up from his nails. "Watch out for the night watchman. He spends his evenings streaming soap operas and porn on his phone, but every now and then he gets up to grab another beer and relieve himself." To me he added, "Given someone that incompetent at his security job, it seemed a shame to interfere."

Cora and Lucinda. Both gave me a narrowed sideways glance.

I shook my head. I knew what they were asking: maybe we weren't that far off on our codes of thieving as I'd thought. "No catch. It's just seriously your lucky day."

"You're not leaving as well?" Cora this time.

Not that far off in the thieving world, but definitely not that close. I pointed down the hall. "Do you three really need an invitation to vamoose? Get while the going is still fucking good, and don't ask so many questions."

They needed no more prompting. Once they had disappeared down the hall and no screams, alarms, or shouting had ensued, I turned my attention towards my more immediate problem. The one in a ridiculous leather jacket and T-shirt.

"I'll ask you one more time, Artemis. What the hell are you doing here?"

Artemis's veneer faltered and his irritation and impatience shone through. "You know, for someone who just narrowly escaped being tortured, you might want to be more grateful."

Yeah, right. For all I knew, Artemis had been sent here to drop me into a deeper, darker, more bottomless pit. "Let me guess. You're here out of the goodness of your magnanimous black heart?"

If the powers that be on the other side of the supernatural war had gotten wind that I was here and decided a cell in the Albino wasn't permanent enough . . . I'd already thrown enough wrenches into their plans—inadvertently, I might add, and accidentally, but the fact still remained that I'd been a nuisance in their recent ploy for supernatural world domination.

Artemis made a derisive noise, then pretended to take a first look around. "Oh, my—look, a prison." He frowned. "I remember hearing about this place. It's the one where they throw away little thieves and pirates to rot for all eternity, no? I'd think you'd be a little more concerned about getting out."

"I would have found my own way. Eventually." Besides, I *needed* to be in here.

Artemis glanced pointedly at the unconscious forms of Jesús and Kujo. "Tell me, where did you hide the key? Lift a weapon? No, the other two in your cell, the dangerous ones, would have taken it from you if they'd thought for one moment you had something that could put distance between them and this place." He gave me a once-over. "You aren't exactly the intimidating type. No, please," he said, as I fumed. "I'm dying to hear how the infamous Owl planned to get out of here. Please, continue."

Half the problem had been getting into the Albino. The other half—locating the pirate I'd read about and finding the Tiger Thieves pendant—had been the other half, which I'd still been working out. Was still working out. Though I now had the keys that would let me into the lower levels. In other words, I'd had no fucking clue. Not that I was going to tell Artemis that . . .

I crossed my arms. "I had everything under control." *Lie,* came the accusation from the back of my thoughts.

Artemis didn't back down. "Fine. Step back in the cell, I'll shut the door, and you can go back to whatever it is thieves who get caught in dungeons do, exactly."

We stood there, staring at each other for the count of five. *Oh, nuts to this.* I broke the standoff first. Artemis knew I wasn't getting back into that cell, and so did I.

The clock was also ticking, and I could use a map to the lower levels. "You took care of the warden, right?" I asked him.

"Yes, I dropped him in a storage room, along with a number of other guards I came across. Trust me, I had much better things to do than come here rescuing you— Hey! Where the hell do you think you're going?" he said as I shoved past him, heading in the opposite direction my cellmates had taken, back to Miguelito's office.

Artemis didn't take the hint; instead, he fell in step beside me, much like how an irritating fly follows you through a swamp. "Go away," I told him.

"No, I don't think so. I was told to get you out. In one piece." His smile had faltered now and there was something cold behind his eyes.

I snorted. That was laughable. "Whose orders?" Oricho wouldn't have roped Artemis into this. He might be Rynn's cousin but the comparison ended at familial resemblance. Artemis was about as rotten to the core as an incubus could get, Oricho had to know that.

He fell a step back as the already cramped corridor narrowed. "If you must know, Lady Siyu called in a favor—or threatened me. Take your pick, the point is that Naga isn't to be slighted lightly."

Well. Wonder of wonders, we agreed on Lady Siyu. And the fact that Lady Siyu had ordered Artemis to spring me out just made it all the more suspect. Lady Siyu and I didn't see eye to eye. On anything.

As if sensing my suspicion, which was entirely likely, he added, "I think it's prudent to point out that Lady Siyu didn't exactly emphasize the value of your particular skill set. I believe her exact words were 'No one tortures and kills the thief except me.'"

Well, that at least made more sense as far as Lady Siyu's motivations were concerned. And she knew how much I hated Artemis. If she was going to send anyone to rescue me out of a prison, it would be him.

"And for a thief you're a lousy pickpocket. I would have had the key off the large man on my first day."

I felt the baton in my pocket, hoping Artemis wouldn't pick up on my intentions. After all, they really hadn't changed since he'd shown up, despite his letting me out of my cell and shackles.

"And speaking of my orchestrating your prison escape, *this* is the wrong way."

We'd reached Miguelito's office, and, true to Artemis's word, there was no sign of the warden or any more guards. I hoped that meant the others had gotten out unscathed.

I sighed as I surveyed the shelves stuffed with boxes and papers. A veritable treasure trove of confiscated goods and maps over the years. If Miguelito possessed a map to the lower levels, it would be somewhere in here. It was my best chance of finding my pirate. Not that I was telling Artemis that. "Look, if Lady Siyu sent you to find me, then what she really wants is Mr. Kurosawa's idol. I'm not leaving without it." And it was true enough. Regardless of my ulterior motives for coming to Peru, Mr. Kurosawa and Lady Siyu would be expecting their treasure, and there would be hell to pay if I left empty handed. For me and Artemis.

Now, where the hell would Miguelito have stashed the prison maps?

Ah, there they were. Upper levels, men's quarters, storage rooms—I wondered just how many artifacts he and his counterparts had stashed in here over the years. If I had more time and the Peruvian equivalent of a U-Haul...

Underneath the various blueprints, right at the bottom, yellowed with decades' worth of neglect, were the maps of the lower levels. The pirate cells—the original ones from the 1700s.

I'll bet Miguelito hadn't had a clue what was lying a few stories underneath him—or if he had, he hadn't realized the significance.

The Albino in Peru was far from the only prison built to deal with the New World's blossoming pirate problem, but it was the first that meant business. Whereas in most prisons, chances were good you'd earn yourself a fast hanging, the Albino was where they'd stuck pirates to rot. Forever. The fact that the prison had been built over Incan burial chambers had led to all sorts of speculation about what had happened to the pirates who had been buried alive in the cells rumored to lie below us. There was the usual mess of contradictory local legends: ghosts of pirates haunting the cliffs, strange howls heard throughout stormy nights, stories of an ancient Incan curse . . . all bolstered by the rumors that no one who ventured into the lower levels ever returned.

The last I was hoping was due more to a wide assortment of ancient Incan booby traps than an assortment of cursed undead. Contrary to popular myth, undead monsters and curses were rare and hard to come by—despite my own recent run-ins.

The fact that no one in recent history had escaped the lower levels had left me with a small dilemma after I'd come across the reference to the Tiger Thieves, namely that I needed a reliable map to find my way to the right cell. Which I wouldn't find until I was inside the prison. Those trips to Miguelito's office had paid off. The maps had been where I'd figured—along with everything else.

I smoothed the prison map out on top of the desk, blocking it from Artemis's view. Carefully, I traced the cell wings—1700s, 1750s, 1800s . . . Now, where was the entrance, and more important, where had they locked the Mad Hatter up?

Artemis cleared his throat.

"Will you give me a minute? There's no telling where they hid it." All the corridors had been marked with numbers at regular intervals. I traced one of the corridors that branched off into the cliffs—1780, 1790, 1800— They were dates, they had to be. I'd found my pirate.

Artemis cleared his throat again, louder.

I glanced up from the map. He was leaning against the doorframe, arms crossed, watching me with narrowed eyes. "The drawer," he said, nodding towards the desk. "I believe what you are looking for is in the desk drawer, not hidden amongst those papers. I distinctly remember seeing the warden put it there. Which you know, since you were in the room at the time."

I frowned at him, forgetting the map for a moment. How? How had he seen that? He hadn't been in the room—or I didn't think he had.

Artemis only gave me one of his cruel smiles. "Ah, ah, ah. Not all of us supernaturals like giving away our tricks of the trade." His expression hardened. "What is it you're really looking for?"

I tensed, acutely aware the incubus could tell if I was lying. "I'm a thief," I said carefully, and held up the map. "I'm always on the lookout for treasure. This is a pirate prison, ergo—"

"Jesus fucking Christ. You weren't fucking caught, were you? You *planned* on ending up here—"

I had two choices: to try to lie through my teeth, which was idiocy—Artemis was an incubus, he'd be able to tell—or not say anything at all. I went with the latter.

Artemis took that as an affirmative. He swore again. "You broke in with no fucking idea how to break out, didn't you?" he said.

"No, I had an idea." And in my defense, I'd planned on sneaking into the Albino, not being thrown in a cell with the rest of the thieves. And it had seemed a great idea a couple of weeks before. That's the problem with desperation—you tend not to think things through entirely.

Artemis snorted.

"I would have figured a way out. Eventually." At the face Artemis made I added, "I was close."

In a fluid movement faster than I would have liked, Artemis crossed the cell-like office until he was on the other side of the desk, looming over me. The light caught his green eyes, giving them a sinister air. I swallowed. The last time I'd been in this kind of proximity to Artemis—well, let's just say he hadn't been the good guy or on our side.

"What is it you're really after, Owl?" he asked, letting a veiled threat hang in the air.

I pressed my hand down on the map, ready to grab it and run. With my other I felt for the baton in Kujo's oversized jacket. I'd spent a lot of blood, sweat, and tears over the past month tracking down the Tiger Thieves. I was tired of all the dead ends Oricho had sent me chasing. This three-hundred-year-old lead was the first real break I'd had. I wasn't about to abandon it now, not after spending a week in this hellhole.

My fingers closed around the baton and I shifted my weight. I was too close to turn around and run now.

Artemis either didn't care or didn't notice; he was too busy looking exasperated. "I don't have time for this. You may not want me here but I *definitely* don't want to be here. And I doubt Lady Siyu does either." He nodded towards the hall. "Come on. Before you do something you regret."

Yeah. This was one time I was not going to feel bad about my imminent actions. Sorry, Artemis, but I have a dungeon to crawl, pirates to see . . . I slid the baton out from under my jacket and swung it at his head.

Rynn would have been proud of me. I didn't telegraph, no windup, conserved my motion.

Only Artemis caught it, snatching my wrist out of the air before I could connect.

Shit.

He smirked, cold and calculating—the amused look gone. "I'm not an idiot," he said, and squeezed my wrist until the muscles released. The baton clattered to the floor.

He pulled me in and trapped my arms, holding me tight facing away so I couldn't even spit in his face, though it didn't stop me from trying.

"Now, we can do this two ways," he hissed in my ear as I struggled against him. "The easy way, which is you tell me what it is you're really in here after—or the hard way, where I *make* you tell me."

That made me pause. Artemis, I knew, would follow through on that threat, and the result would be neither subtle nor painless.

I licked my lips as I gauged how much to share. "I'm after a pendant—one that was last seen on a British pirate imprisoned here in 1758."

"What kind of pendant? Magic? Cursed? It can't be another trinket for Mr. Kurosawa, they would have mentioned it."

I kept my mouth shut. I was not going to give Artemis that much.

In a smooth motion he switched from pinning my arms to a choke hold that he sunk in deep. Artemis *tsk*ed. "It's not too late for the hard way, Owl."

Goddamn it. "I'm telling the truth! Just treasure hunting after a pirate."

"Hard way it is," Artemis said, and I caught his eyes flash an unnatural green.

If he knocked me unconscious and dragged me out of here, I'd never find it—which meant I'd have to tell the truth. "It's called a Tiger Thieves pendant, all right?" I managed. "I need its map."

Artemis let me go. I backed up and covered my neck.

"The *Tiger Thieves*? Are you out of your mind?"

I shrugged. In a manner of speaking. "I don't have it yet. It's still on the pirate." I pointed to the map of the cells below. "It should be in this wing—two levels down, the entrance is down the hall—"

Artemis swore again. "Oh, I'm putting a stop to this now. Tiger Thief tokens given to pirates? You have gone daft."

"How do you know who the Tiger Thieves are?"

He snorted. "Every supernatural knows who the Tiger Thieves are. Self-righteous assassins, the lot of them. Be glad you haven't found them yet; they'd find somewhere worse to stick you than in here."

He took a step towards me. I played my last card. "I think they can help Rynn."

That made Artemis pause. I rushed to continue, "Ori—someone thinks the Tiger Thieves might know a way to get him out of the armor, but I haven't been able to find them. I've been looking for months. This is the first concrete lead I have." There were stories about the Tiger Thieves in esoteric history books—a thieves' guild with political power, attempting to run interference between humans and supernaturals. Take your pick, but the stories all added up to the same thing: they had ways of dealing with big, bad supernatural problems. And they didn't want to be found. By anyone—Oricho, the IAA, recruits, *me* . . .

Artemis watched me, but whether he guessed who my source might be, he didn't say anything. Regardless, his expression didn't change. "I'll admit I admire your loyalty and tenacity when it comes to helping my cousin," he said more carefully than he'd phrased anything else to me.

"Great. See you later, I'll make sure to tell Lady Siyu you got me out," I said, and started for the door.

Artemis snorted and blocked my way. "Not a chance."

That had been the answer I'd expected. Artemis and Rynn might be cousins, but like a lot of families they weren't exactly on good terms. "An hour is all I need, tops. Look, think of it this way, Rynn is dangerous— not just to humans but to supernaturals." Reports and sightings of Rynn had said as much. He'd been acquiring a small army. Lady Siyu and Mr. Kurosawa considered him undirected, a chaotic variable, and therefore not nearly as great a concern as their war. What none of them seemed to realize was that that made Rynn the most dangerous part of their war—for both sides. From the look on Artemis's face, he knew it too. The question was, how much did he really not care?

Artemis narrowed his eyes at me. Still blocking my exit. "I make it no secret that I occasionally like to sit back and watch Rome burn."

I nodded. "Yeah, but I don't think Rynn plans on just burning things down. I think the new Rynn plans on taking over." That's more or less what the rumors had said. Rynn had been seeking out both supernaturals and humans, giving them an ultimatum: follow him of their own free will or lose their free will and follow him anyway. The reliable whispers at any rate. The unreliable rumors were much worse.

Artemis narrowed his eyes at me. "Are you certain about the medallion?" he finally asked.

I nodded. I'd come across a mention of it in the journal of a Spanish galleon officer. In 1758, it had been attacked by a British pirate, the

Mad Hatter. It was neither out of the ordinary nor spectacular by pirate encounter standards of the time except for the officer's reference to the Mad Hatter's flamboyant nature and the mention of a worthless stone pendant the pirate had insisted on keeping; he had gone half mad when they'd tried to take it from him. An old pendant made of stone and leather, with primitive drawings, golden dashes and lines, and the ghostly image of a Tiger's head overlaid only visible in certain light.

The Tiger Thief medallion. It had to be it.

"They probably took it from him when they threw him in here," opined Artemis, though he was less certain than he had been.

I shook my head. "Every account I can find of the Tiger Thieves medallions says they were often mistaken for a worthless piece of stone on leather."

"That's far from a certainty."

"Then let me check. Downstairs, two flights. That's it. All the pirates who were ever locked in here were left to rot, all the cell keys thrown into the ocean—"

"Well, that's just fucking fantastic."

"It means his body has to be down there."

"Which is exactly the problem."

I frowned. "Dead bodies? Not to be morbid or macabr—"

"No, for a human you spend an inordinate amount of time around dead bodies. It's the pirate ghouls I'm worried about—the living dead kind, not the supernatural."

The bottom dropped out of my stomach.

"Ghouls?" I said. "You mean pirate ghosts." Ghosts weren't exactly a walk in the park, but they could be outmaneuvered. Nowhere in my research on Albino had I seen a goddamn thing about ghouls.

"This was an Incan burial site, yes? Well, if you'd bothered to look up the old conquistador legends, you'd know that the locals weren't exactly thrilled to have the Spanish move in."

"The conquistadors killed them all—"

"*Most* of them. And they still had some magic left when they tried."

Shit. Malicious ghosts I'd been prepared for, but ghouls?

"They aren't your run-of-the-mill zombies either," Artemis added. "For one, they retain some semblance of intelligence. They also don't eat flesh."

Well . . . that had to be a good thing. Not eating flesh was a surprising improvement over zombies. I'd had the misfortune of running into some a few months back.

"They prefer bone marrow."

Oh, fuck . . .

Artemis gave me a look of contempt. He was still blocking my way. "Ah, and now she sees the predicament she's wandered into."

"You're bluffing."

He arched a blond eyebrow at me. "Maybe you manage to get past me, knock me out, get into the lower levels." He loomed over me. "But do you really want to find out firsthand whether the bone marrow–eating pirates are a figment of my imagination?"

Goddamn it. Much as the warden hadn't wanted to risk calling my bluff, neither could I call Artemis on his. And I trusted him even less.

"What do you want? Treasure? A favor? I'd offer to put in a good word with Lady Siyu, but I think we both know that would do more damage than good."

For a moment—a very brief one—something flickered across Artemis's face that struck me as regret, or maybe shame.

"Simple," he said, the discomfort showing through now. "I want you to forgive my—indiscretions."

"*Indiscretions?*" He said it as if the whole fiasco in LA had been nothing more than a faux pas at a dinner party.

"Ah—yes," he said, looking even more uncomfortable, if that were possible. "Forgive the incident—and accept my apology."

There was a formality to it that struck me as very supernatural—the supernaturals had more social rituals than attendants at a debutante ball. Even so, I didn't get the impression that he was particularly remorseful. About anything. Ever.

I snorted. "Not a chance."

A flash of anger worked its way across Artemis's face. Now, that looked more at home on his features. "Why the hell not?"

I started counting my reasons off on my fingers. "Because I don't trust you, you're despicable, the definition of a misogynist, I don't like you, and I don't for one second think you mean it. And that's the polite version."

Artemis's nostrils flared, and I could see him bite back a retort. Instead of lashing out, though, he let his breath out between his teeth, making a soft hissing sound. After a moment he said, "Agree to forgive me for my indiscretions, and I'll let you go on your suicidal venture below. But I'm coming with you. As I said, Lady Siyu specified alive."

I laughed at that. I couldn't help it.

He narrowed his eyes at me. "Laugh all you like. I might not be my cousin, but I did just take out all three guards and infiltrate an IAA prison without having to get myself thrown in. As much as you hate to admit it, you need me."

That was the crux of it. I did need help. There was some kind of supernatural bullshit going on—there was no way Artemis wanted my forgiveness out of the bottom of his rotten black heart—but I didn't see that I had much of a choice. Not if I wanted to find the Tiger Thieves and save Rynn and everyone else from the Electric Samurai.

"*Fine,*" I said, my hands clenched by my sides.

Artemis crossed his arms and didn't move out of the doorway. "*Say* it."

Of all the stupid supernatural bullshit to run into down here . . . "*Fine.* I forgive you for being a psychopathic supernatural." At Artemis's prompting I sighed and added, "Who tried to turn me into some kind of monster."

"Wraith, actually. But that should do."

I shook my head. Artemis. Who with enough alcohol and/or dim light was Rynn's green-eyed doppelgänger. Yet another reminder that it should have been me in that armor. Not Rynn.

I shoved my emotions down lest Artemis pick up on them as I grabbed the map to the lower dungeons and pocketed the idol. He was the last damn supernatural—no, make that *entity*—on the planet I wanted watching my back in a dungeon. If I'd been looking for another way to complicate my side project . . .

"Let's get this the hell under way before more guards show up," I told him. "And there'd damn well better be ghouls down there," I said as I pushed past him. I heard his footsteps fall into line behind me.

"For your sake, I hope I am wrong."

Even I had to admit he sounded sincere. A shiver ran down my spine as I took a left down an unlit, little-used corridor. Time to find me a pirate. And hopefully not his ghost.

3

PIRATES OF THE PERUVIAN COAST

The Albino Prison, going down.
For eighteenth-century pirates, get off on the third floor . . .

"Artemis, shine the flashlight over here, will you?" I said as I examined the door we'd found at the end of the corridor. Old wood reinforced with iron rails, then fitted over the top with an iron grate, spikes facing inwards. It certainly looked like a serious attempt to keep ghosts and other scary things out—or in, as the case might be.

The grate was newer. I'd wager it had been installed only a hundred or so years ago. Sure enough, once Artemis managed to angle the light properly, I found the divots where the posts had been drilled into the rock.

That meant I'd be looking for a newer key. I crouched down in front of the lock and started going through Miguelito's collection. There were only three newer-looking keys. I tried to fit the first into the lock. No go. On to the second . . .

"How about *Curse of the Incan Princess*?" Artemis said from behind me.

I shook my head and jiggled the second key, doing my absolute best to tune him out.

"Fine, what about *The Pirates of Patagonia*, then?" It wasn't working. For one, he was right behind me; for the other, he was an incubus. He could feel just how frustrated I felt every time he opened up his mouth. Key number two was also a no-go. This time I had to wrench it back out, swearing as the metal stripped away.

The third time was a charm.

The key fit, but it didn't want to turn. Where was a can of WD-40 when I needed it?

"Fine, what about *Pirates of the Peruvian Coast*? That has a nice ring to it."

The key turned, then stuck. I wrenched it and gained only a fraction of a turn for my efforts.

"Well?"

If I didn't answer, he'd just keep going. I spun around, shielding my eyes from his flashlight beam, which was conveniently aimed right at my face. "*No*, all right? The movie's been done. You can't just change the titles and hope people won't figure it out. It doesn't work like that." For the past five minutes he hadn't shut up about his great plan to remake the pirate movies in this place.

Artemis arched an eyebrow. "Actually, depending on what part of the movie industry you're in, that's exactly how it works. Granted, those movies tend to show a lot more skin and not be so concerned with scripts." He glanced around. "But the scenery and costumes—or lack thereof—are important. Separate the amateurs from the professionals."

I shook my head and went back to the lock. Of course Artemis would go straight to the porno industry. Somehow that seemed fitting for an incubus. Filming a porno in a haunted prison . . . sorry, allegedly ghoul-infested prison. There! Finally. The lock gave with a shriek of metal and swung open. Careful to avoid the spikes, I started on the door lock. It was older, and I had to try more keys. A label or two would have been nice. The keyhole was large, so I started by size.

"For a smart girl, Alix, you have very little understanding of how the entertainment industry works."

I made a face as I counted off the keys, trying not to mix them up. "Enough to know you can't just put a coat of paint over something and pass it off as something completely new."

Artemis *tsk*ed. "Which one of us is the expert?"

That was debatable. And a moot point. "People aren't that stupid."

"No, *you're* not that stupid. The vast majority of the human race rather enjoys being fooled. It's probably why you find yourself in so much trouble," Artemis mused.

Four keys down, half a dozen to go—let's hope five was the charmer—there! It clicked, and the lock began to turn. Not wanting to jam it, and without any oil handy . . .

I found myself in trouble because I didn't know when to say no or keep my mouth shut, not because I refused to swallow all the regurgitated bullshit the world at large tries to cram down your throat. "Not everyone wants to stuff their faces with junk food."

"No, but the world would really prefer it if you did."

I cranked the key gently, ever so gently, and was rewarded with the sound of the ball bearings clicking into place. I held my breath as I eased it along, until finally the lock gave and the door cracked open, eased by air on the other side trying to escape—a mix of fresh sea mixed with stale, cavernlike smells I was used to. For that much sea air to accumulate, there had to be a sizable number of drafts—maybe even another few exits.

I waited, listening for the sounds of anything moving on the other side. Artemis had the good sense to keep still and quiet as well. Maybe I'd get lucky and anything that might be waiting would eat Artemis first.

I glanced up at him.

He let out a long-drawn-out sigh and peeked around the doorway with his flashlight. "Let me guess, send the supernatural in first? Sadly, I agree with you on that point—but thank you for thinking to throw me to the proverbial wolves first. I'm starting to see why you like your Charity alias so much. Now, out of the way, before something not human figures out we're here."

My instinct was to snap, but instead I swallowed my pride and got out of the way. Artemis eased the door open, its hinges shrieking and making me wince.

Still nothing happened. He angled the flashlight through the door, illuminating a stone staircase covered with dust that wound its way in a tight circle downwards.

Still no noise—not unless you counted a faint breeze whistling through the corridors below.

I flinched as the flashlight was aimed right at my eyes.

"There's still time to turn back," Artemis said in an offhand manner. I made a face and took his flashlight, shining it down the stairs. I spotted the door below us, twenty or so steps down, about three or four turns of the stone down the pit. There were no railings to prevent one from falling off. I continued with the flashlight beam, but though the steps continued I didn't see another landing.

That had to be it. I stepped through.

"Thought you wanted me to go first?"

"I decided I'd rather keep your flashlight," I said as I ran the beam over the wall where the stairs were anchored into carved grooves. Looked stable enough . . . carefully I eased myself onto the first step of the staircase. It held, even as I eased my weight onto its center.

I breathed a sigh of relief. That could have gone a lot worse . . .

Then I made the mistake of shining the flashlight into the black pit below. A black, bottomless-looking pit.

"Well, now we know where the breeze is coming from." I kicked a loose rock over the edge and waited, listening for it to hit bottom. It didn't. Shit. Fantastic.

Seriously, where was a set of decent climbing gear when I needed it? Oh yeah, sitting in a locked, unlabeled closet—or on one of the guards' eBay pages . . .

"Stay a few steps behind me and hug the wall," I told Artemis, easing my way onto the second step, waiting and watching for signs of instability.

And doing my damn best not to look down . . . maybe the stone pebbles had hit water or enough sand that it had muffled the crash?

I tried not to think of it as I counted our way down the spiral steps.

"You realize this depressing place was built over a very old Incan temple?" Artemis finally said.

We were halfway down now, and so far the steps were holding. As much as I detested the idea of making small talk with Artemis, it beat thinking of careening into the black abyss below.

"Tell me more about these cursed pirates, Artemis."

"Not much to tell."

I glanced over my shoulder at him, two steps above me, hugging the wall as I'd told him to do.

"Well, start with what you heard and where you heard it." For one, I needed the distraction from the black pit, and two, I was genuinely interested. Four hundred years of Peruvian/Spanish colonial history had yielded very little about the pirate prison and its inmates, which was odd. Pirates loved their superstitions—especially the ones that had anything to do with them. A story of a cursed pirate prison, however far-fetched, should have been too good for the debauched miscreants to pass up, especially once they were into the rum kegs. There should have been more mentions of it, and the fact that Artemis had uncovered more than I had . . .

"More legends than anything else, mostly from the locals while I was taking stock of the town. You'd be surprised how much little old ladies gossip. That's something that certainly hasn't changed in a few thousand years." I shot him an impatient glance.

"A jaded little thing, aren't you?"

"Kettle calling the pot black, Artemis." Despite my best efforts I couldn't help looking down once more. *For Christ's sake, Owl, just hug the walls, will you?* It was bad enough that I didn't have any climbing gear, but with Artemis as a dubious backup . . .

"Considering I've had a few thousand–odd years for my jaded disposition to really sink in, and you've had, what? Twenty-seven, maybe twenty-eight, years of existence?"

Then again, I was the one carrying the idol. Something told me he'd be reluctant to let it go over the edge. Despite his protests to the contrary, I didn't think he was stupid enough to cross the Dragon Lady.

Shit.

I halted my descent as the staircase groaned and the stone slab under me shifted, sending bits of sandstone dust down into the bottomless pit. Artemis stopped as well. The acrid taste of panic filled my mouth as neither of us made a sound.

But despite the show, the stone step held under my weight. I counted to ten. Nothing happened. I gauged the distance to the doorway. We were halfway there, just needed to go slowly . . . ten more steps, and we'd be home free.

I held my breath as I placed my foot on the next step. It held. I let the breath out. "More local legends, less bullshit," I said to Artemis, as I continued my slow descent, though this time I kept my voice to a whisper.

"Well, first off, they're stories, so take them like everything, with a grain of salt—but you'd be surprised what you pick up passing through town and listening to the locals."

"I did, and the locals didn't say anything about pirates."

"Rule of thumb, Alix, when mixing with the locals, actually mix with the locals. Not the ones who speak English and are university educated. In this case, I found some interesting conversations at a café outside the local church. Just happened the old Peruvian ladies were hanging out having their coffee."

"Seriously?" I shot Artemis a glance over my shoulder, but there was no guile on his face.

He shrugged. "It might have been spiked with a little hooch, but who am I to judge what a tiny ninety-year-old great-grandmother sticks in her morning coffee?"

"Not that. I meant what did you hear, exactly. And how did you learn to speak—"

I was about to say "the local dialect," which I'd been having problems with, despite it being mostly Spanish . . .

But I didn't have a chance—the breath was knocked out of me as the stone step keeled sharply to the right, downwards and towards the pit. I lost my balance and hit the slab on my chest. It was a miracle I managed to stick the flashlight into my mouth before I crashed down.

My momentum didn't help any. The step groaned against its stone anchor and shifted again, I slid another inch, my feet hanging off the side now. I searched for something to grab onto—

And spotted Artemis's hand.

Of all the lousy times for a trust game . . .

Sensing my hesitation, his face twisted. "Don't be an idiot, take my hand."

The stone shifted again, this time sandstone from its anchoring point in the wall careening down.

I reached for Artemis's hand. He caught it and quickly made a double grip, which I latched on to with my other hand.

No sooner did he try dragging me back up than the stone step beneath me collapsed, crashing down into the abyss and taking the next three steps with it.

Artemis looked down and then at me. "All right. I'll admit it, I'm glad you told me to stay behind," he said as the three stone slabs continued their descent.

I glared at Artemis and shone the flashlight back down at what remained of the stone staircase.

Only three steps had fallen away—not an insurmountable gap.

More important, the doorway was only five steps below the gap. Five short steps.

I wondered if there was ever such a thing as going far enough.

I drew in a deep breath. I could make the jump; it was downwards, I wouldn't even need a running start. Just had to hope to hell these had been a fluke and the rest wouldn't collapse.

Artemis's face went white as it dawned on him what I planned to do. "You can't possibly—"

I didn't let him finish. I leapt while the adrenaline still coursed through me—into the air, over the black pit, as the flashlight beam wavered, Artemis swearing behind me. I hit the step—and braced.

No cracking, no shaking, no tilting. Just the sound of my feet hitting the stone and my own loud exhale of breath.

The stone had held.

"Of all the stupid—"

I glanced back to where Artemis was cursing at me from the other side of the gap. "Yet here I am."

"What the hell do you expect me to do?"

Me? I was the one with the flashlight. I made my way down the last four steps to the landing and the sole door. Much like the one upstairs, the wood had been creosote-soaked and reinforced with iron, along with a spiked grate that was a duplicate of the one above. Yup, this was definitely the place . . . "Stay there if you want," I called back as I set to work examining the door. Much like the one upstairs and despite the iron grate, it had every look of a normal door and entranceway, still locked, covered with dust that had burrowed its way into the creosote. Not a hint of the supernatural to speak of.

Then why the hell were the hairs on my neck bristling?

Methodically I began fitting the keys on the ring into the grate lock. I found the right one on the second try, and thankfully this one opened without the screeching protest of iron I'd been greeted with upstairs.

There was another stream of swearing, then Artemis hit the stairs above me.

"You're an idiot. You could have gotten the both of us killed," he said as he joined me outside the door.

"Someone once told me that only I could take responsibility for my own actions."

"It was probably my cousin—and he's an idiot as well."

Again I found the right key, and with minimal effort the second lock clicked open. Adrenaline coursed through me again as I pushed the door open a crack and a gust of air rushed out, this one staler and carrying something I couldn't quite place, a metallic sweet scent that wasn't altogether in place in the stone caverns.

Tentatively I shone the flashlight through. No movement, nothing hiding in the shadows, no moaning, shambling, growling. Just a deserted, dusty stone hall that hadn't seen a footstep inside in well over a hundred years. Looks could be deceiving, however.

I shone the flashlight into Artemis's face. He swore and shielded his eyes.

"Well? Any input from the supernatural peanut gallery?" I asked him.

"No sense of anything magic down here, though I'm not entirely certain I'd recognize it if there were. And get that thing out of my face."

Straight ahead it was. I pushed the door open another few inches, and more stale air rushed out. I covered my mouth and nose with the sleeve of my jacket, getting a mouthful of dust. I hated when that happened. There hadn't been an airtight seal around the door, but that didn't mean air was flowing smoothly—not down here.

I took the sleeve of my stolen jacket away and carefully inhaled. The strange scent wasn't poisonous gas or anything dangerous like that, more like a rot I couldn't place hanging on the stale air. Goose bumps rose along my arms, but, as Artemis had said, there was nothing I identified as overtly dangerous.

Artemis nodded at the now-open door, the one I was standing in front of like a scared undergrad. "Shall you or shall I?" he asked.

I shouldn't be scared; there was nothing concrete to be scared of . . . then why the hell couldn't I shake the feeling? "Still no sense of anything?"

This time he turned in his pensive look for a smile. "No," he said, and bracing against the stone wall loomed over me. I gave him about as dirty a look as I could muster. He was probably enjoying the fact that he could tell I was scared. "And to be honest, that has me even more worried. Still, there's nowhere to go now but forward."

He pushed the door. Its iron hinges creaked in protest, but it swung open wide.

I wrapped the sleeves of my stolen jacket around my hands to hide how much they were shaking as I aimed the flashlight through.

A long stone hall with a low ceiling carved out of the rock, only six feet high or so, stretched out in front of us. The floors, made of the same carved stone tiles that lined the upper levels of the prison, were covered with a thick layer of dust, one that hadn't been disturbed in well over a hundred years—not until now.

I slowly let out the breath I'd been holding as my heightened nerves acclimatized to the idea that there wasn't a monster on the other side waiting to eat me.

Slowly I started down the silent hall, watching my footing on the uneven stones.

"So how does this dungeon rate on the tomb-raiding scale? One star for tame, five for terrifying, or ten for certifiable? Potential off-the-beaten-track travelers are dying to know."

"Either finish telling me about the pirates or keep quiet while the archaeologist in the hall works. And you can start with how you got the locals to talk." I'd tried and been met with derision and more than a few chastising stares.

He gave me a terse, insincere smile. "I have a charming face and demeanor little old ladies love."

Probably used his powers . . .

I shivered, thinking about Artemis turning his green incubus eyes at the defenseless old ladies.

"Contrary to popular belief, I don't spend my time flashing my powers around. Not when a simple solution will do. Do you have any idea how few people pay the elderly any mind at all? Why the hell bother using my powers when showing a simple interest in their stories will do?"

I didn't answer him; I didn't want to. I was familiar with Artemis at his worst.

"Point is, they were more than happy to share. Now, I'm not familiar with all the names and language nuances, but apparently the caverns under this mountain were the last major stronghold of a minor Incan kingdom. One of the ladies even bragged about being one of their blood descendants—" He trailed off, and I could have sworn his nostrils flared. I knew Artemis's sense of smell was much stronger than a human's, but I'd never noticed him using it quite like that.

"What?"

He shook his head, snapping out of it. "Honestly? Don't know," he said. "It doesn't smell right, but not entirely wrong either. Not yet, anyway, which is why I suggest we get on with this. Now where was I? Ah, yes—the local Incans. Apparently they didn't need the conquistadors to help their little kingdom hasten itself towards ruin. That happened when the local priests started sacrificing too many of their flock, who decided that they'd rather not—"

"Get to the point." Again, it was nothing I didn't already know. Contrary to popular belief, human sacrifice wasn't nearly as big of a hit with the local Incan peasant populations as the history books make it out to be. Oh sure, it's interesting to watch when you're sacrificing criminals and prisoners of war, but when the priests turn on the locals? Oddly enough, I'd argue that despite their reputation, the European Christians were much more prone to human sacrifice than the South American civilizations ever were—witch trials and Inquisition, anyone? Torturing people to death to appease your God is the same regardless of what religion you ascribe to.

Artemis made a face at me over his shoulder. "Well, one of their witch-priests—a young one not nearly as well versed in magic as she should have been—decided to cast a spell as a last act of defiance before the locals overran this temple. Probably wasn't planning on cursing or killing anyone; probably meant to protect the place or weed out her enemies, but like most every other time supernatural magic gets in the hands of humans, things went horribly, horribly wrong."

If it even worked. "So what? Magic explosion?"

Artemis shook his head. "Nothing so drastic. In fact, after a bit of wind whirling around the woman, everyone figured that the spell had failed; the peasants won the fortress and promptly set about punishing the priests, priestesses, and the rest of the ruling class." He glanced back at me. "I wonder what it feels like to have the tables turned like that? To go from spectator to sacrificial lamb? Can't imagine it's a pleasant contemplation while your innards are being spilled over a holy rock."

"Still not hearing anything about a curse," I said. I could see where the lamp casings had been left mounted on the wall along with odds and ends: buckets, tools with the untreated wood more or less rotted off. People had obviously left here in a hurry.

"I'm getting to it."

"You're telling a story," I said as I examined a doorway to my left. A quick pass showed it had been used for storage, not as a cell. If the map was right, I still had a way to go before we reached the cell wings.

"For context," Artemis continued. "Something you woefully ignore. Now, according to the half-cut little old biddies, no one knew there was anything wrong, least of all the peasants who took over the place. They sacrificed a few hearts, locked the priests and priestesses in this very dungeon into which we're descending. It wasn't until the priests and nobility who had been entombed alive started dying from dehydration and starvation that the warnings began."

Before I could stop him Artemis took my flashlight and shone it on his own face, giving it a sinister glow. "Moaning and shrieking in the middle of the night, rattling of chains and bones in the corridors."

I snatched my flashlight back. "They must have checked."

"That's the interesting part. No one who went to check on the priests and priestesses ever returned. Though they did find the odd human bones washed up below the cliffs, covered in human tooth marks, bone marrow removed."

I waited for more, but apparently Artemis's recounting of his dalliance with the local knitting club was over. "And that's it? It sounds like an old wives' tale, no pun intended."

"Maybe," he said with a shrug. "But you know more than most that there's often a bit of truth to the old legends that survive for centuries—especially the ones that march out ancient curses, misused magic, and monsters."

Yeah, yeah. I was an outright expert on how to stumble into a curse, a recent feat I hoped never to repeat. The problem was, besides the reported hauntings, the gates, and Artemis's tale, there was no sign of anything supernatural here. No markings, no scent of blood, no magic-laced scriptures. Just centuries of superstitions, and those tended to feed themselves.

I wrested control over my misgivings and pushed away the chill that flooded my senses as I continued down the hall. Ever since the disaster in Shangri-La I'd been jumpy, more paranoid. It came on in waves, taking over and sending me into a panic, but usually never amounted to anything more than an empty corner or shadow. I couldn't trust my senses and hunches right now—not entirely. I needed proof, not Artemis's stories.

"Oh, I have no doubt something horrible happened here." Kill that many people, even with only remnants of ritual magics disguised as religion, and you were bound to have some kind of magical misfire. "My problem is, if this place is cursed, then how the hell didn't the conquistadors and Spanish only ever tell the odd ghost story? They ran this part of the prison for almost three centuries. And for that matter, why no stories amongst the pirates? They loved that kind of stuff, especially once they got into their rum. Ravenous undead Incan priests or priestesses that devoured bones? I mean, that's hard to miss."

Artemis inclined his head. "Magic is sometimes tricky," he said, stealing back the flashlight and angling it up ahead where the hall curved to the left before handing it back. "Sometimes magic waits until the most inopportune moment to wreak havoc. It leans towards chaos, a bit of a bitch like that and not unlike supernaturals."

"Some of you, anyway." I noticed the dust had changed from gray to a white crystallized powder. I moved it with my toe, then collected it between my fingers. Salt. I wondered how that had gotten in here.

"*All* of us are—we're an affront to nature. Some of us are just better at hiding it. Me? I prefer to be more honest in my dealings with humans."

We reached the corner and stopped to inspect what we hadn't been able to see a moment before. It was a narrower hall with a lower ceiling—not enough to force either of us to hunch over, but I imagined it would have been claustrophobia-inducing in a prison population who'd never see a glimpse of sunlight again. It wasn't in nearly as good a condition as the hall we'd entered through. A cursory look showed a number of collapsed wooden beams blocking the way, but nothing that indicated structural concerns. Unlike the walls in the upper levels, these hadn't been so much built as dug out of the cliffs that lined the ocean town, then reinforced with the odd arch of masonry and wood. The corridor itself stretched farther than the flashlight could illuminate—as did the cells that lined the long corridor walls, a mix of what looked like Latin and Spanish carved into the stone around them.

Cautiously, I approached the first set of collapsed beams. Rotted through, despite its being unusually dry down here. Maybe the water had managed to wind its way in . . .

"Termites," Artemis opined.

When I frowned, he added, "The collapsed beams. Live a few hundred years without any pesticides or other insect repellents, and you get very familiar with the pests of humanity."

"Takes one to know one."

Artemis gave me a terse smile. "Will you do the honors, or shall I?"

I crawled under the beams and made my way to the first cell. Its wooden door had been treated with creosote and reinforced with thick slats of iron that were large enough to prevent anyone inside leaving. Ever. They were still solid even if they'd rusted along the edges.

Carved into the adjacent wall were names and dates, and the wood itself had been branded with a number one. Checking the surrounding wall, I hovered my light over a series of much older carvings, Incan, a series of murals carved into the length of the hall, worn by the years but the details still visible, albeit interrupted by broken and worn tiles—a progression of slabs with people lying prostrate in various poses, detailing an ominous progression: sacrifice. Out of all the artwork that could have survived . . .

I glanced back at Artemis with a questioning look. He caught on and sniffed at the air, his nostrils flaring and his lips parting much like a cat's. When he was done, he shrugged. "A little more carbon monoxide than I like, and a higher number of particles and dust particulates than at the entrance—molds, bacteria." He shrugged again. "Not pleasant to breathe but nothing that will outright kill you—quickly. Still no magic I can sense," he said.

That would have to do.

It was time to see what was behind door number one. I stood on my tiptoes in the too-large boots and shone the flashlight through the small grate.

Stone, dust, shackles—I sucked in a sharp breath as my flashlight fell on something white.

"What?" Artemis said, tensing behind me.

I shook my head. Son of a bitch, it wasn't even moving, not even a rodent, or a gust of wind to give me an excuse . . . "It's just a skeleton—hey!"

Artemis took my flashlight and angled it back into the cell for his own look. "Well, will you look at that? I wonder who this poor fellow was?" he said.

I checked the carving in the stone outside the door. "Diego de Santiago," I said, reading the name off. "They even bothered listing his crimes: pillaging, rape, stealing from the Crown—pretty well what you'd expect from a pirate."

"Well, hopefully it was a long, fun-filled run, because from the looks of it so was his imprisonment."

I took the flashlight back and looked into the cell. Artemis was right; it looked as though he'd starved to death, shackled to the wall . . . no shoes, the bones of bowed legs visible through what was left of his pants—burlap that had crumbled away into dust, probably bag scraps fashioned into pants after the original pair he'd entered with had rotted. The bowed legs were common enough for the times. Before the early 1900s, rickets had been a European epidemic in the lower classes, the malnutrition and lack of vitamin D inherent from city living. Whatever shirt he'd had—if he'd been given the dignity of a shirt—was long gone.

There was only one set of shackles in the seven-by-seven-foot cell. He'd been confined in here by himself—left to either waste away from lack of food and water or to die of loneliness. "Guess the prison guards weren't worried about wasting space," I said. I noticed the scratches in the sandstone: days counted, years' worth from the sheer number. I couldn't help wondering when he'd given up carving them.

"Or more likely ran out of space in their rush to catch pirates—they did love their gold and bullion."

He took the flashlight from me again and aimed it at the far wall. "See?"

Sure enough, fixed into the sandstone amongst the familiar four lines with a fifth dashed through were the old bolt holes and grooves where storage shelves had likely once been.

I shuddered. It was sad, pitiable, morbid, whatever description you could come up with. But this wasn't the pirate I was looking for.

The Mad Hatter, also known as Timid Jack, had been English, not Spanish. I turned to the next cell, then the next, checking the names carved into the walls beside the doors. None of them were Timid Jack's.

Beyond more fallen beams, there looked to be another set of cells and what looked like another hall, likely leading to more cells.

The space between the beams and the floor was too tight to crawl over or under this time; I'd have to move them—but if the Mad Hatter were still here, along with his pendant, it'd be past here.

Artemis brushed his hands over one of the beams. "And wood rot." He turned his light on the ceiling, examining where the wood had been fixed. "Probably added this near the end, when the place fell into disuse. Didn't know enough to use tar to preserve and temper it. See how the edges began to crumble around the original arches? If that had happened earlier, the stonemasons would have been brought in to fix it properly. No, this was done by peasants."

By that point I'll bet no one remembered what the prison had been used for—and I doubt any prisoners left alive would have been sane enough to tell them.

The fact that Artemis could speculate on the decline of this place was not what I expected from him and a far sight removed from the debauched rock star image he'd cultivated—or the reckless, dangerous incubus . . .

"You forget," he said, "I'm the kind of supernatural who gets a good seat when Rome starts to burn. You start to recognize the signs. The little and big."

That figured. Carefully I tested what was left of the rotten wood beams, checking to see how fragile they were, while Artemis leaned against the wall and watched. As I pushed, one of the beams gave a little, sending a shower of sandstone down, but otherwise the ceiling and walls held.

Something occurred to me regarding Artemis's motivation, Lady Siyu aside. "Is that what you're doing here?" I asked as one of the beams groaned as it loosened. "Getting a good seat so you can watch the supernatural world burn down?"

The corner of his mouth and left eye twitched in a decidedly unfriendly expression. "Be thankful the skeletons in the cells weren't moving," he said.

I snorted as I dropped the beam to one side. The one nice thing about rotten, termite-eaten wood is that it's light.

"I'm starting to think those knitting club stories were overblown."

"Then how do you explain all the people who've disappeared in here?"

I shrugged and looked at the name on the next cell. Three inmates, a Smith, Diego, and one that loosely translated to Mateo the Bone-legged. Curiosity got the better of me, and I shone the flashlight through the grate. "There are an awful lot of ways people die in tombs that don't involve supernatural monsters and magic. Traps, poisonous gas, collapsing tunnels, that pit—hell, there's good old-fashioned getting lost." . . . Hunh . . . the name had been accurate . . . I was surprised that they'd left him with the bone leg . . . then again, maybe he'd carved it from an unfortunate cellmate . . . I angled the flashlight around. Sure enough, one of his cellmates was missing a femur.

Morbid creativity in desperate times. Not to be macabre, but I was tempted. It wasn't every day you ran across something like that.

"Maybe," Artemis said, checking the door opposite mine, me working the left and he the right. "But I'd rather be cautious than caught unaware—and besides, you're forgetting one thing."

"Which is?" Next cell. A few more skeletons with the skin hanging off their bones like rice paper. Yet again, not what I was looking for.

"That legends like that don't last hundreds of years without a little bit of truth."

I snorted. No—there was nothing in the cell that indicated anything but a bunch of pirates who'd had their heads bashed in, apparently by the one who'd managed to slip his shackles. Maybe he'd gotten tired of dealing with the others and listening to them whine? Or just gone mad . . . or hungry.

"When did you say your pirate was incarcerated here?"

"Mid–eighteen hundreds." Goddamn it, where the hell was my pirate? If the remaining guards weren't onto the prison break yet, it wouldn't be long.

Artemis checked the door again. "These dates are all wrong. Late eighteen hundreds—petty thieves and minor-league pirates. I'm guessing the one you're looking for was more of a contender?"

I inclined my head. "You could say that." Timid Jack, the Mad Hatter, had certainly made a name for himself along the coast. I aimed my flashlight down one of the two offshoot halls that were more akin to tunnels, twisting farther into the cliffs.

"My guess? If we head down one of these, we'll reach the sections where the real pirates were kept—well away from any chance of escape.

The old Spanish who built this place weren't afraid of a few ghosts and a dark cave, not when it meant they could do Isabella's and God's work torturing the evil out," Artemis offered.

If I jumped at every dungeon that gave me the heebie-jeebies . . . "Still not picking anything up?" I asked Artemis.

"I'm starting to resent being treated like a supernatural bloodhound."

"Yeah, yeah. Start sniffing."

He shot me a dirty look, but his nostrils flared once again. "From what I can smell and taste in the air, there's still nothing setting off alarm bells. Yet. Happy?"

"Very. You go left, I go right. Yell if you find anything, scream if it's a monster." I found an old torch left in the wall and, using the prison guard's lighter I'd pocketed, lit the end. I shoved it to Artemis and started down the right. It didn't take long to reach the cells. They were larger this time and fitted with reinforced bars. I checked the date on the wall beside the cell: 1852. Michael Smithy, William Bonny, Black Roberts . . . this was where they'd stuck the English pirates. And from the reinforced spikes and solid iron grates fitted over the cell door slot, apparently the Spanish had decided that they deserved special treatment.

Something scraped against the stone in the hall.

Shit. I froze and listened. The sound didn't repeat itself, not even as I counted to a slow ten in time with my pounding heart. It could have been anything, I reasoned. A fallen beam, a piece of sandstone giving way . . .

Anything. Anything at all.

Setting my nerves aside, I moved on to the next cell.

Whereas all the previous doors had angry black letters etched deep into the wood, this one was different. On one of the doors, the one farthest to the left of me at the end of the hall, the burnt, grooved letters and numbers had been filled in with bright green.

I peered through the grate; at least Artemis wasn't here to see my hands shaking the beam of light. Obscured by the shadows I saw something green—

I heard another scrape against the stone floor, then felt a brush of air against my ear.

I spun, knife out, only to find Artemis standing behind me.

He smiled unpleasantly. "Still think those old wives' tales are a waste?"

I shook my head and put the knife back into my pocket. "I think you like scaring me."

Artemis inclined his head and began examining the green-lettered door. He brushed his hand against the grooves, tracing the still bright letters with his fingers and holding perfectly still. For a moment I wondered if he sensed something, but when he caught me looking at him, he said, "It's nothing—I would have smelled something by now. I'm one of the monsters, remember?"

I couldn't fucking forget . . . "Give me a boost, will you?"

Artemis obliged, kneeling down and bracing his hands.

I placed my flashlight in my mouth before stepping up. Now, why the hell had I thought there was something green in there?

"I was impressed you let them go."

I glanced down at Artemis as I angled the flashlight into the cell, not bothering to hide my confusion. For once he actually looked uncomfortable. "Your three wayward cellmates," he clarified. "Not everyone would have. Let them go."

Yeah, and if they managed to get caught by the security guard Artemis had decided to leave watching Spanish soap operas, I'd be regretting it. I turned my attention back to the cell. Sure enough, there was something green in the corner . . . "I had the good fortune to be leaving. I figured I might as well spread the love around."

"And it doesn't hurt to have them chasing four people instead of one. Worst-case scenario," Artemis added.

What the hell was the green? Leftover green furniture? Maybe oxidized copper? Though I had a hard time believing anyone would leave oxidized copper lying around on purpose— *Jesus.*

Sure enough, tucked into the corner and shackled to the wall with irons was a husk of a body, traces of clothing scraps still clinging to the bones and tattered skin of the corpse. It wasn't too different from the others we'd seen—with one exception.

It was green—all of him—the same shade as the paint outside the cell. Under other circumstances the color might have evoked grass or new leaves—a picture of the healthy outdoors and spring. Up close, though, in conjunction with the tar-soaked wood door and under the blue glow of my flashlight, it looked more putrid than fresh, lending the corpse a garish, sickly appearance—not that corpses normally evoke good health. It wasn't every day you saw paint like that hold. Jesus, even his fingers were dyed that color . . .

"You realize you might have made things worse for them?"

Hunh? I looked hard at Artemis, taking my eyes off the green dead man.

"The mousy French girl in particular. She didn't strike me as a career thief," Artemis said.

Yeah, and a lot of people would have said the same thing about me a few years back. I started on the lock. The corpse wasn't moving, and if Artemis wasn't worried . . . A cursory look at the key ring I'd lifted from Miguelito showed that none of the keys would fit the jail cell lock—at the very best they'd be stashed away down here in an abandoned office, or more likely they were in some Peruvian attic as part of old family antiques. Shit. "See if you can find something to pick a lock with," I said to Artemis.

He frowned at me. "I have no intention of sitting here twiddling my thumbs while you try to get an old, rusted lock open."

"I won't know if it's rusted through until I try to open it—hey!"

Before I could stop him, Artemis picked up a broken piece of stone off the floor and smashed it into the lock. I cringed, expecting it to ring out. It rang—but the sound was low and muted, like bending metal. I opened my eyes. Artemis was holding two pieces in his hands. "See? Rusted through."

Asshole . . .

"And that girl could be dead in a week."

I doubted it. She had to be resourceful to have survived this long in the IAA. "Maybe," I said as I tried the cell door. Regardless of the state of the lock, the hinges worked. With a creak of rusted metal the door to the pirate's cell swung open. I aimed the flashlight inside—again, nothing out of the ordinary, except for the green hue of my dead pirate. "But rotting in a cage because it's a known quantity isn't safer. It just means you rot. And I didn't put her in here in the first place." At some point, everyone had to stop looking for something and someone else to blame and start taking responsibility for their own fucking disasters. Mathilda had grasped that one—faster than most archaeology students I'd known who'd run afoul of the IAA. "She'll be fine," I said, and mostly I believed it. "I could have done without your telling them who I was," I said to Artemis.

"Trust me, I'm helping."

"How? By making sure the IAA and any supernaturals out looking for me have a trail?" Algorithms were a bitch these days. If online retailers could tell whether someone was pregnant from how many times she bought moisturizer, I'd hate to see what the vampires could do with a handful of confirmed sightings.

"No, by getting you some fucking credit."

I turned on him. "I don't need credit! I'm a thief. The point is *not* to take credit—for anything! Ever." I turned my attention back to checking the corners and ceiling of the cell. "Look, can we change the topic?"

"Fine. You spent an inordinate amount of time with my cousin over the past six months. Tell me, did you ever have any inkling he had a warlord in him? I mean, I certainly didn't, but I'll be the first to admit we haven't really spoken in decades. I suppose even us supernaturals have the potential for change."

Why did I even try? I clenched my teeth and read the name carved into the stone. The Mad Hatter. I'd found my pirate. "How's Violet?" She was a woman I'd met—both before and after Artemis had turned her into a wraith, right before he'd tried to do the same thing to me.

Artemis let out a low whistle. "Ouch—that hurt. And Violet is just fine. Doesn't remember a thing. She's even enjoying a newfound career on daytime TV. It suits her well."

I made a derisive noise. There were no traps, no obvious structural faults, the skeleton looked sturdy enough. I didn't think it would crumble into dust . . .

"What?" Artemis said.

"Nothing." There was no point saying anything. Artemis was the kind of supernatural that wouldn't get it.

"Oh, for—" He turned me around and held the torch near my face, a disconcerted expression on his face. "No, I'm actually curious."

I sighed. "You can't just make things better by giving people things," I said.

Instead of offering me a snarky comment, he laughed. "Why not? Violet doesn't have any complaints about her new lot in life. And who the hell are you to tell her she should?"

I turned my attention back to the Mad Hatter. Of course Artemis was wrong, but a small part of me wondered if he didn't have a point—a very small point, but still, it was unsettling.

"For someone who hates being told what she must or must not do, you're certainly a hypocrite to hop on the bandwagon of judgment."

"Not the same thing," I replied. What Artemis had done had been abusive, cruel, evil. Not seeing anything that elicited warning bells, I stepped inside the cell.

I waited three breaths for something to happen, an ancient trap to be sprung. Still nothing.

"Well?" Artemis called from outside.

I crouched down in front of the Mad Hatter. His wrists were still chained to the wall overhead with old irons, scraps of bright green cloth clinging to the desiccated and partially mummified limbs. "Nothing in here except a skeleton in chains." It smelled like death in here—along with the faint trace of something I recognized . . . garlic.

Arsenic—and lots of it.

Well, now I knew where the green color came from.

"What the hell did that to him?" I turned to find Artemis crouching less than a foot behind me. I couldn't help but jump. Goddamn it, how did he keep doing that?

"Artemis, say hello to Timid Jack, aka the Mad Hatter. And the healthy green shade is a mark of Jack's life before he took up a lucrative and short career of rape and pillage along the Peruvian coast."

"Failed artist chased out of town? If his hands are a sign of his skill, I agree with them."

It really was amazing how well the color had been preserved, if not the fabric and skin. "Close. Jack here owned a clothing shop in London, one that was doing well until a shipment of cotton and furs was pilfered by pirates on its way across the Atlantic."

"A tailor?" Artemis asked dubiously.

I made a *tsk*ing sound as I tentatively began searching through the scraps that remained of the Mad Hatter's clothes. "You make him sound so mundane. Our deceased friend Jack here owned a *dress* and *hat* shop for ladies and men of high fashion. Our friend Jack here was a master hatmaker." And that had been his downfall.

"A hatter and dressmaker for the high-fashion set during the eighteen hundreds was an unenviably dangerous profession courtesy of arsenic and mercury."

I spotted what I'd been looking for in the corner. It reflected some of the light back off its smooth, slick surface—like fur. A black rabbit-fur top hat like the ones that had been worn by well-to-do gentlemen or ones who wanted people to think they were well to do. One that still retained its shine, despite the dust, due to the mercury paint.

Jack had never been seen without one of his mercury-laced top hats. I guess the prison guards at the time couldn't be bothered taking it from him.

"You are familiar with Lewis Carroll, the author of *Alice in Wonderland*?" I asked Artemis.

"The debauched author who drank too much absinthe?"

"And smoked way too much opium—but as far as the Mad Hatter is concerned, Lewis Carroll had the nuances right."

"Hatters of the eighteen hundreds went stark raving mad by the time they hit thirty from the mercury used to coat these," I said, holding up the well-preserved rabbit-fur hat. "The paranoia, shyness, and manic tendencies of the Mad Hatter in *Alice*? Accurate portrayal."

"That certainly puts *Alice in Wonderland* in a whole new light."

"I imagine the arsenic and aniline dyes used for the dresses didn't help much either."

"So he goes from hatter and dressmaker to pirate?"

I inclined my head as I crouched back down before the shackled remains of Timid Jack. "Guess he was really upset about those pillaged furs and cotton. The mercury likely ate his brain into a paranoid delusional mess years before. The poisons we expose ourselves to . . ."

"That still doesn't explain the green skeleton."

"Ah, but it does. Dresses, lace, and artificial flowers, especially the flowers, were all painted with arsenic. It was the only way to get the green shade. Shame it eventually took its toll on the dyers' livers and lungs. Puts a new spin on the expression 'dying for beauty,' doesn't it?"

Artemis didn't answer me. Instead, he let out a low hiss. When I looked he was holding up his hand, the universal signal for "stop."

All of a sudden I was very conscious just how much breathing echoed in the deserted stone cell. "What?"

Artemis went silent for a moment, then seemed to shake it off. "I keep scenting something, then it vanishes—probably this place and your mercury-addled pirate." He nodded at the cell again. "So, did he discard the traditional garb in favor of high fashion on the high seas?"

I shrugged. "It's the unexpected that scares us. I don't know about you, but having a pirate dock at the side of my ship wearing a ridiculous top hat and green frock coat would have terrified the hell out of me. Who knows? Maybe he made hats for all his crew as well." Hard to give up habits, even if you weren't poisoning yourself with mercury.

It brought whole new meaning to the phrase "Pick your poison."

A small stone medallion on a chain of leather with markings on the back—that was what I was looking for. Nothing flashy . . .

I ran my flashlight over the corpse before pushing the remains of his bright green frock coat and the overgrown length of dried hair to the side. I braced myself and with the end of my flashlight pushed aside the tatters of green material that had once formed the lace of his shirt.

Shit. It wasn't there around his neck. I searched but there was no medallion—not under the remains of the green frock coat, not on the floor. For all I knew, he could have pawned it off to the locals or the guards in exchange for food or whatever passed for vice down here.

I stood and did another sweep of the cell, then the walls, searching for any nook or cranny that could have been used as a hiding spot.

"It's not here, is it?"

"Just because I haven't found it doesn't mean it isn't here." Come on, now, where would a Tiger Thief medallion have been hidden? *Think like a mad, mercury-addled hatter, Owl . . .*

"Oh, for the love of—" Artemis added a few more choice phrases that translated in context if not words.

I gave him a long, hard look. He was agitated; upset and focused down the hallway that led farther into the prison's depths, a far cry from the way he'd been a moment before. It couldn't just be the fact that he was losing patience—not that fast. "What are you not telling me?"

"Less questions, more searching." He stepped outside the cell.

"Where are you going?"

"To the old guards' room I passed, I think I saw some weapons."

Shit. He really was hiding something. I followed him out. "Artemis?" I whispered at his back down the hall.

He ignored me.

"Artemis!" I called out, louder this time.

He turned, hands open at his side. "I may have—been quick to dismiss my misgivings earlier."

Shit. I spun on my heels, searching the hall, my ears open for something, anything. But there was no movement or sound, not a trace of anyone there. I spun back around on Artemis.

"It's hard to describe, but the scent's changed, like death—and there's something electric in the air, I can feel it on my skin. As if someone plugged in every appliance they could find and turned things on high. Imagine you could hear the fuse box," he added at my confused expression. "Now imagine it's screaming, as if it's about to blow."

Shit. I needed to find the medallion and get out. "Go—" I said to Artemis as I skidded back into the Hatter's cell, checking it over with my flashlight once again, anywhere Jack could have reached from his irons. There were no loose stones, no dug-out mortar; nowhere to hide an inmate's valuables . . .

Why the hell did pirates have to be so damn good at hiding their treasure? As bad as the Dragon—

Scratch that. Dragons might build a bitch of a warren or death maze, but they left their treasure fortresses out where everyone could see them.

"Owl?" Artemis called. He stopped just outside the cell, bracing himself on the entrance, eyes wide, a single age-dulled sword gripped in his hand.

"Find anything?"

He shook his head. "And it's getting stronger."

I swore and fell back on my ass as the stone fortress's foundations shook. Thankfully only a few bits of loose mortar rained down on us. Please say Jack hadn't bartered it away.

"We need to go now," Artemis said, backing out of the cell, his voice worried.

"I need another minute!" Maybe it really wasn't here; maybe I'd spent the last two months on one giant, useless goose chase . . .

The fortress shook again—this time not as strongly, but carrying with it the pungent smell of a dank, stagnant cave.

"Remember what I said about there not being any magic in this place? I take it all back."

Think, Owl—shit! I dropped back to the floor as the dungeon shook for a third time, longer and stronger than it had either time before. When the dungeon once again came to a rest, I picked up the distant sound of clicking—faint, like teeth chattering.

Artemis heard it too. "Now!" he said, gripping the sword he'd found. "Or I'm leaving you to fend off whatever that magic is heralding."

"What the hell do you plan to tell Lady Siyu?"

"Whatever the hell I want. You'll be dead—or worse."

Artemis might be right. If I didn't cut my losses now—

I caught the glint of something gold and metallic hiding by the mercury-laced top hat, which had been knocked on its side by the shaking of the fortress.

I scrambled over and grabbed the hat, turning it over in my hands. Tucked inside the green velvet lining that folded inside its brim was a stone medallion painted with gold.

I wrapped my hand in my sleeve before pulling it out, coarse leather rope and all.

"Got it," I said, and held it up for Artemis to see.

He wasn't looking at me, though; he was staring at something behind me in the cell. But before I could see what had Artemis speechless, something gripped my arm, the one that was holding the medallion. It spun me around until I was facing a set of grimacing green teeth set into a skull covered with paper-thin skin. One of the shackles had come loose, freeing the arm that now gripped mine.

Its green teeth parted as its grip on my hand tightened, and it let out a dry, off-kilter laugh as it lunged for me. All that kept me safe from its chomping green teeth were the three chains still securing him to the wall. And the anchors were crumbling.

"Artemis!" I shouted, "now would be a good time to use that sword!" There was no answer. I hazarded a glimpse back at the door, but Artemis was nowhere to be seen.

Fucking fantastic. True to his word, he'd abandoned me. Leaving me with the pirate. I swallowed. "I don't suppose you'd consider letting me go?" I asked the Mad Hatter.

In answer Jack's teeth chattered, his vocal cords long since dried out. He wrenched his left hand free.

"Guess that's a no," I said, ducking a nasty left hook and braining the Mad Hatter with my flashlight.

It didn't slow him one bit. He squeezed the wrist he had, trying to force me to drop the pendant. Like hell. I fought, trying to pull away, but all that did was make him grip my wrist tighter. The Mad Hatter pulled me towards him, the garlic scent of arsenic wafting off him, as his teeth chattered towards my face.

I almost closed my eyes—I would have if not for the silver arc that came down between us, a hairbreadth close to my face before sinking into the Hatter's arm. Like a pair of scissors through paper, dried tissues and skin gave way as the sword embedded itself into the tendons and muscles. The Hatter's grip loosened and my hand came free.

Artemis stood beside us, wielding the blunt sword.

Where the hell had he been hiding?

"Stop playing with the dead pirate so we can get out of here!" he shouted.

Didn't need to tell me twice. I shoved the medallion into my jacket as the Hatter swiped at my head with his other arm. He laughed—a dry, low guttural laugh, empty green eye sockets fixed on me.

I shook my head as I backed towards the cell door. Humans and magic. Every goddamned time, they had to raise violent dead things. Why, oh why, couldn't we aim for anything else? Like an army of harmless bunnies?

"Owl!" Artemis called.

Seriously—weapons, spontaneous bunnies, changing weather patterns, endless supplies of clean water—there were *millions* of things we could try to do with magic, but oh no. Dead things.

The Hatter's right foot broke free and he lurched for me. I danced back out of the cell. Only one shackle remained and not for long if the way the rusted exterior crumbling against its braces was any indication.

I slammed the cell door in The Hatter's face. "Run!" I said to Artemis, and bolted for the prison proper. But Artemis grabbed my sleeve, stopping me. "Not that way," he said. "There are more of them."

Sure enough, more chattering noises reached us—echoing not from below but from the way we'd already come.

That was how everyone else had been trapped in here. The ghouls didn't animate until you made it past a point of no return.

"Come on," Artemis said, pushing me towards the stone steps leading farther down. "This way. I can smell fresh air coming from below."

I did my best to keep up as he took two stone steps at a time. I could have sworn the sounds of clicking teeth and rattling of chains were gaining on us.

"Hurry up!" Artemis called, hazarding a glance over his shoulder.

Son of a bitch, he was already five steps ahead of me. I squeezed the medallion in my pocket and picked up speed. I needed to get it out of here—this was the closest I'd come.

I hit the bottom in time to see Artemis bolting down another row of dungeon doors, each one rattling against its rusted hinges, the clicking of bones behind them.

One of the doors gave—not fully but an inch—enough to let a skeletal arm shoot out. It caught my hair and pulled, while another pirate tried to reach me through the grate.

Like hell. I gripped my hair and pulled. Some I won back, some came out by its roots in a painful clump. Either way, I was back to running.

And Artemis was near the end, still running at full speed.

"Hey! Wait for me!" I shouted. The banging on the doors went up in volume and intensity as soon as I did. I ducked another door as it rattled off its hinges, pushed by a group of pirates clawing for a grip, and yelped as the hinges on yet another cell gave. A skull wearing an eye patch and covered with thin, rice-paper skin wedged its way through, its teeth chattering at me. I kicked the door hard, severing the head right off the skeleton. It rolled to the ground and I jumped over it, just in case.

A bone-chilling howl echoed down the stairs we'd descended moments before.

I made the mistake of glancing back.

The Hatter, in his arsenic-and-mercury-laced glory, stood at the bottom.

He lifted a shaking hand and pointed it at me, and his teeth began chattering out a new, sharp tempo.

As if in reply the cells around me rattled back.

"Run faster!" Artemis called from somewhere down the hall, where I could no longer see him.

Right, because I'd been running at a Sunday sightseeing pace.

I ran. The doors were rattling incessantly now, as if the pirates behind them could taste fresh meat or a potential mark. I'd made deals with vampires, a Naga, and a Japanese Red Dragon; I fit the sucker bill perfectly.

I caught up to Artemis. He'd reached a heavy grate that had been fitted at the end of the corridor. He was trying to force it open. From the dirt and tears on his shirt, I figured he'd also had to deal with some of the celled pirates.

As I reached him, I grabbed the nearest piece of loose stone and brought it down on the lock. It wrenched and bent at an odd angle; the rust, having damaged the integrity, made the iron malleable.

I hit it again before Artemis grabbed the piece of broken stone from me. "Let me."

The third time was the charm. The lock snapped in two, and I swung the grate open. "You go first," I said. I preferred the supernatural to take the lead—especially if we'd woken up any more pirates. I followed and slammed the grate behind me, then scanned the other side for something, anything, that I could block it with—a stone, a fallen piece of wood . . . I settled on a piece of broken rebar, wedging it through at an odd angle. Not that it was the most secure blockade; I imagined it'd hold them only for a while.

"Oh, for the love of—" Artemis spun me around. "Let the IAA deal with it! They set up shop over a haunted pirate dungeon, they can deal with the aftermath. Besides, it'll mean they won't have time to worry about who set them off."

He had a point there—one I might have echoed a year ago—but I didn't trust the IAA to save anyone, let alone the locals in the surrounding area. Cover up? Certainly. Just not go out of their way to help anyone.

But under the circumstances it'd have to do. Just in time, as the first pirate thrust himself at the grate. I was not sticking around to have a deep and meaningful conversation with the Mad Hatter and his friends . . .

I gave the rebar one last shove before following Artemis.

This new tunnel wasn't the same kind of finished product as the halls above, polished and reinforced to look something akin to civilized. Its walls were rough and uneven, as if they'd been excavated only enough to allow passage. On top of that, we were heading down, towards the ocean, if the puddles on the ground and dampness running down the sides of the tunnel were any indication. That the trickling water and the echo of our feet drowned out any chance of hearing the rattling chains and chattering teeth was oddly comforting.

I did my best to keep up with the jog Artemis set, refusing to look back and see if the pirates had made their way through. Sometimes it's better not to know.

The tunnel widened and leveled out, turning into a shallow pond. I skidded to a stop at the edge. Artemis was already up to his knees.

"What?"

"I haven't had the best luck with stagnant water and tombs."

"Fine, stay here with the pirates," he said before jumping in.

Yeah, that wasn't going to happen. I covered my mouth with my sleeve and waded in after him.

My boots, the ones I'd stolen, sloshed with water as I reached the other side of the pool and broke into a clumsy run. I could see light up ahead: moonlight and the lamps from the exterior of the prison above, maybe a lighthouse. It was a sight better than what was down here.

And I could hear something: the crashing waves that for the last two weeks had been only a faint whisper in the dead of night. I picked up my pace as I spotted the ocean outside—only to skid to a stop when Artemis held up his hand.

Fighting against my need to get the hell away from here, I stopped.

It was the sirens that warned me there was something afoot outside—that and the floodlight that was sweeping over the beach, not the lighthouse light, as I'd initially thought. When the light had passed over, I took a look out the cavern entrance.

Above in the prison and the road leading up to it were fire trucks and a number of black SUVs, the kind IAA agents were fond of terrorizing archaeology students in.

Past the trucks I could see smoke and the tips of red-orange flames.

"See? The IAA is already taking care of it. By morning the prison interior will be burned to the ground. I doubt the skeleton ghouls will survive that."

I spun on him. "There aren't any ambulances!" There were at least a hundred IAA prisoners in there; there was no way they could have gotten them all out before striking the match.

Artemis only shrugged. "Means they aren't concerned about accounting for the prisoners—oh, don't look so scandalized. Consider yourself lucky. Besides, you didn't light the place on fire, so it's hardly your fault. You even let a handful of wayward archaeologists out. A good deed."

Over a hundred people could die, all to cover up a supernatural snafu, and I should congratulate myself for getting three people out? It wasn't a good deed. It was disgusting. And it was Artemis's fault. I should have let them out, if he hadn't stopped me . . .

I turned on Artemis, fists clenched, barely able to control my rage. "You are the worst supernatural I have ever met!" The floodlight passed over the beach twice more. I got its timing down and left the cave, keeping to the cliff face where the beam couldn't strike. With the slippery rocks and poor-fitting boots it was slow going but I had no intention of spending another minute in Artemis's company.

He didn't see it that way. "You need me," he shouted.

I kept my eyes on the rocks and beam. "I don't want your kind of help."

He didn't take the hint, catching up and shadowing me along the cliff. I ignored him. Chances were good the run-down jeep I'd bought from a gas station was only a few miles down the coast. I'd left it hidden on the outskirts of town, keys hidden in the undercarriage, where I'd figured it'd be safe. Not that anything is a certainty. It might take me a few hours to get there, but get there I would. Worst-case scenario, the jeep would be gone . . . I'd figure something out.

Artemis pulled a pair of keys out of his pocket and jingled them in front of me like one of Captain's cat toys.

I started to tell him to go to hell. Then I noticed the metallic cat and the fossilized shark's tooth. Oh, for fuck's sake . . . they were mine—unmistakably mine.

"Give me those!" I hissed, and made a grab for them, almost face-planting in the sharp shale.

"No," he said, easily holding them out of my reach.

"I don't need your help—"

"*Yes, you do.*"

I opened my mouth to argue but stopped at the hostile expression on his face.

Artemis continued, "You need my help because you didn't just come back from Shangri-La reckless. You've stopped caring whether you live or die; that makes you dangerous."

I fell into silence. Thank God, so did Artemis.

He wasn't wrong . . .

"Mr. Kurosawa and Lady Siyu haven't figured it out yet. Though I'd wager Oricho has. He's dealt with enough humans over the centuries that he can tell when your kind goes suicidal—so can I, for that matter. You've still got yourself some time. Oricho isn't inclined to say anything to the Dragon or the Snake out of Onorio spite, and as for myself? Well, I just plain don't care." He glanced back at me. "But they will figure it out. Dragons know when an asset becomes a loss. Consider it one of their talents."

"Give me my keys back," I said, my fists clenched.

"Certainly," he said, and tossed them at me. I scrambled to catch them before they hit the surf coming in.

"But I'll be accompanying you back to the Japanese Circus. Consider it my ensuring that I fulfill my bargain with Lady Siyu."

I maybe should have argued. Normally I'd argue. I was not suicidal.

But after two weeks in a prison with three thieves and only my own thoughts to keep me company, I knew as well as he did that he had a point.

I didn't need to be an incubus to figure that one out.

I felt for the pendant in my jacket pocket and held on to it. It was still there, warm against my skin. At least I'd gotten what I'd come for—that and the idol. Two weeks in the Albino, and I was none the worse for wear—more or less.

My recklessness as of late was just a temporary glitch, a result of my desperation to find the Tiger Thieves.

I told myself that over and over again as we continued down the shore, watching for the floodlights, which quickly faded into the burning background that was the Albino Prison as the IAA continued its morbid cleanup.

I wondered who was worse; Miguelito for his abuses of the prisoners and his position with the IAA, the IAA for their willingness to burn their mistakes to the ground, or me for not realizing that just about any quest I set myself on seems to end in disaster and ruin for someone.

It was a hard choice.

4

THE DEFINITION OF MADNESS

4:00 p.m. two days later: The Japanese Circus, Las Vegas.

Madness is defined by some as repeating an action over and over, expecting to get a different result.

That was exactly what I felt like I was doing as the glass doors slid back, opening the way to the Japanese Circus much like the gaping maw of a monstrous whale about to swallow a man whole.

Like Captain begging for a treat, there was a hardwired routine to this madness; he'd complain for half an hour while I tried to put my things away and ignore him. He'd progressively get louder and more annoying. Eventually I'd tire of the noise and give in.

We both knew the script and what our resulting behaviors would amount to. He'd spend half an hour begging, and I'd eventually give in.

At no point did either of us attempt to alter our behavior for a more efficient and satisfactory outcome. We were caught in a continuous loop of repetitive behavior that neither of us was particularly happy about.

The point was that I knew exactly what kind of reception was waiting for me in the Dragon's private casino upstairs. Lady Siyu would level baseless accusations at me, tell me I didn't know how to do my job; then Mr. Kurosawa would make up his own damn mind.

I knew it, they knew it, Captain probably knew it.

Still, every time I walked in there, I hoped for something different, some modicum of respect, an interaction in which Lady Siyu wasn't trying to weasel permission to kill me.

Maybe I was mad, or maybe it was just another symptom of the human condition. Either way, I wasn't in a rush.

I made my way across the mezzanine to the ornate glass elevators without checking the front desk or my phone. I needed an hour to think and didn't want distractions.

I unlocked my suite door to a baleful Captain, who stood in my way and let me know exactly what he thought of my two-week absence. I maneuvered past him. "Yes, I'm sorry. But you'd have hated the Peruvian prison," I said, patting his head. "No mice, and we had to run through water." That wasn't exactly true. I would have preferred to take Captain with me, but I'd been worried about being recognized. Captain and I together were a little too well known in IAA circles now. Considering the fact that I'd spent two weeks in prison, it was probably a good thing I hadn't taken him. What if I'd never gotten out?

And I hadn't abandoned him here; I'd had one of the nymphs stop by and feed him with instructions to contact Nadya if the worst happened to me. That didn't stop the pangs of guilt as he bellowed at me, tail straight up in the air, as he followed me through my home away from home, the luxury suite on the penthouse floor at the Japanese Circus. The floor no guests ever stayed on and that Mr. Kurosawa appeared to keep for his own use. Originally it had been filled with carefully chosen antiques, but Lady Siyu had removed most of them, replacing them with things Captain couldn't destroy. No dishes, no dust, no signs of life beyond Captain . . . looking around my empty apartment, it felt as if I'd been gone for much longer than two weeks.

Rynn was no longer here and it seemed empty now, and strange. Yet another mistake added to my long list. How the hell had I not seen the elves' plot coming? Of course they'd wanted Rynn. He was their wayward soldier, the warrior; I was a damnable thief.

Captain didn't care about my musings on the changing nature of our living arrangements or Rynn's absence. Not done with his lecture yet, he stood in the kitchen and made a noise that was a cross between a mew and a growl.

Once I'd ditched my bag, and removed the sweats and sneakers I'd been wearing the past two days, acquired before stepping foot on a plane, I finally picked up my cat. He spent all of two seconds appeased until he caught the scent of something that interested him—something supernatural. He twisted around in my arms until he zeroed in on my bag and clothes.

I used the reprieve from his attention to see to the condition of my kitchenette. It wasn't pretty; Captain had upended his kibble since it had last been filled—which normally wouldn't be a problem except that he'd followed with his water dish, leaving a soft, squishy, wholly unappetizing mess on the floor. I wiped it up and set the dishes right side up before refilling. Captain strolled in, as I was filling his water dish, having finished with his inspection. He snorted three times as he sat in the middle of the floor, tail curled around him, as if he were waiting for an explanation.

"Yeah, I wasn't happy about having to work with him either," I said as I put the filled kibble bowl on the floor.

He mewed one last time before shoving his face into his dinner.

Now that I was back in civilization and caught up with a few hours' sleep, I noticed the smell. It was coming from me. I badly needed a shower and a change of clothes. I took my time under the hot water, washing off two weeks' worth of grime. I'd been able to clean up a bit on Mr. Kurosawa's plane, but it wasn't the same thing. After a long shower and a change of clothes, I grabbed a beer from the fridge and retreated to my desk and laptop, Tiger Thief medallion safely in hand.

The Tiger Thieves, as Oricho had told it, were a secret society that had originated out of the ancient Silk Road trade routes. More assassins than thieves, they'd started by hiring themselves out to caravans as guards and guides, protecting wealthy merchants and their wares from opportunistic bandits and local armies looking for a payoff.

They'd also been the first of their kind for another reason: they were the first recorded attempt at protection from the supernatural. Why and, more important, how was foggier. Some of the stories said they had been formed by a group who had been grievously wronged by supernaturals; others claimed they were supernaturals themselves; still other more fairy-tale versions claimed it was their sacred duty to protect humans from the supernatural, which I didn't buy one bit.

Though the Tiger Thieves had surrounded themselves in secrecy, Oricho had been certain on one detail: that they'd had ways of dealing with supernaturals who got in their way, from the weakest to the most powerful. During a time when supernaturals had roamed free, eating and enslaving people as they saw fit, the Tiger Thieves had become their version of the bogeyman. And any group powerful enough to take out a dragon were the only ones who stood a chance against Rynn.

The other details he'd gleaned were less concrete, more legend and myth: the Tiger Thieves had kept to themselves and vanished a few hundred years ago; the only way to find the Tiger Thieves was by invitation or possession of one of their medallions.

Did they still exist or had they gone the way of most secret societies—extinct? All I might uncover would be a few ancient buildings and objects hastily discarded, never to be returned for. Or maybe I'd find them.

Whether the medallion brought me to them or them to me was also up for interpretation, if it worked. The details were sparse, and the medallion wasn't giving up any of its secrets.

I'd had a chance now to look over the gold markings decorating the stone for almost two days. Nothing. There was no code, no magic, no hints. I had the key to finding the Tiger Thieves right in my hand, yet after two days I still had no idea how to use it.

I opened my laptop and scanned an image of the medallion, then sent it off to both Nadya and Oricho. Hopefully they'd have better luck—or maybe Oricho would see something I hadn't. Captain took it upon himself to curl up in my lap, apparently having forgiven my lapse in judgment leaving him behind.

Even though I'd done the same online searches before, I searched again for "Tiger Thieves" and the markings on the medallion on the faint hope that I'd missed some obscure line or reference.

Artemis's words came back to me as I sipped my beer and patted Captain, trying not to let my mind wander as I skimmed through all the references I'd seen before.

Had I come back from Shangri-La reckless? Possibly, but this time I wasn't being reckless for myself; it was to save someone else. That had to count for something.

And I wasn't about to let anyone else I cared about end up on the supernatural serving platter. Not again.

An hour or so passed of doing online research and waiting for a response from Nadya or Oricho that didn't come. When I checked the time, I was a half hour away from my meeting with Mr. Kurosawa and Lady Siyu, organized on the plane back without anything resembling my input. From experience I knew it was best to be early rather than late when it came to Lady Siyu. I closed down my laptop and wound the medallion's strip of leather around my wrist before tucking it into a pouch that I hid in a concealed pocket under my shirt. I wasn't about to let it out of my sight.

I stood up from my desk, gently dumping the protesting Captain on the floor, and tied my hair up in a loose ponytail before slipping on a leather jacket and a pair of boots. There was something else Artemis had said that had rung true; Mr. Kurosawa and Lady Siyu would eventually wise up to the fact that I was playing two games—their quest for supernatural weapons to use in their war and my own to save Rynn. I didn't think either of them would be happy about it.

Well, I'd deal with that when the time came. I grabbed the Incan idol from my backpack and tucked it under my arm before heading to the door.

"Time to go see Mr. Kurosawa, Captain," I said, letting my cat into the hall. "And let's hope Lady Siyu hasn't finally convinced him to let her eat me alive."

Captain, happy not to be left out, darted ahead to the elevator. Everything else might have changed these past weeks but at least my cat hadn't. Be thankful for the small things, eh?

—⁓—

I was starting to think that Captain liked to growl at Lady Siyu.

The elevator chimed brightly and cheerfully when we reached the twenty-fourth floor, the penthouse. As the elevator doors slid open, Captain mewed and darted out ahead of me, setting a fast pace down the vaulted hallway to Mr. Kurosawa's private casino, the large doors looming black, gold, and ominous up ahead. Mr. Kurosawa's architects hadn't skimped on space up here, combining two floors into one, I figured. The decor was also designed to make an impact; gold-leaf plates adorned the arched hallway ceiling, and black walls with white wood accents highlighted the artwork on display.

And then there was the plush carpet sinking under my boots. Whereas the walls, ceiling, and detailed wood had been done in black, gold, and white, respectively, the carpets were a disconcerting bright red, the color of freshly oxygenated blood.

I didn't think they were there for the aesthetic appeal and to set off the artwork . . .

There were decidedly more pieces of art displayed on the walls and in the mounted glass cabinets—nothing supernatural as far as I could tell, but there were a number of expensive pieces I'd retrieved over the past few months. They were not to be pegged to a specific time frame or theme, but they complemented one another in an intangible way—a style. My eyes paused on a piece I'd acquired for Mr. Kurosawa recently, a painting on wood now restored and protected behind glass. I realized why the changes to the art had bothered me. It was a trophy hall, everything a piece I'd acquired for the Dragon. I didn't take the display as a compliment. Not from those two. More like a reminder of just who had my leash.

I knocked on the casino's black doors and watched as they swung open of their own volition. Captain lost no time dashing through.

"Captain, stop," I said.

He halted at the edge of the carpet that denoted the start of the casino's smoky marble floors, sniffing at the rows of slot machines, everything from Hayes early-1900s antiques to modern electronics. All of them stretching out into an endless maze, Mr. Kurosawa's evil enchanted forest of whirring lights and sounds.

The slot machines were all possessed with the ghosts of everyone who had ever crossed the Dragon—mostly thieves but also those who'd had the bad luck to be in his way. They were trapped forever, his eternal slaves condemned to guard his treasure.

The maze had the power to entrap any human who entered uninvited, but whether that courtesy extended to cats and other small animals . . . ?

As if sensing that something was there, a handful of machines began to chime, their lights flickering and gold coins clinking as they fell out and struck the marble floor.

Captain edged forwards, sniffing a coin that rolled his way. I scrambled to pick him up before he could be accused of stealing Mr. Kurosawa's treasure. Captain might be a Mau, a breed of cats hardwired to seek out vampires, but even he couldn't resist the lure of a shiny toy.

I noticed a scent drifting our way—smoke, but not from a fireplace. Mr. Kurosawa must already have his dragon panties in a bunch about something. "Best to get this over with," I told Captain, despite what my stomach argued as it flipped.

It was yet another symptom of madness, I suppose: talking to my cat and assuming he understood . . . "Hello?" I called out into the maze. My voice echoed back at me off the wood-paneled walls stained a deep gray, and I could have sworn the flecks that looked like smoke in the black floor tiles swirled.

I waited and had to readjust my grip on Captain as one of the nearby machines began to blink its lights enticingly. Another slot machine farther into the maze chimed, followed by the sound of more gold coins striking the floor.

"Assholes." I'd decided that most of the ghosts were belligerent jerks. They might also have been mindless from years of imprisonment—or just stupid for thinking I'd fall for the lure of gold coins and lights. My cat, however . . .

I attached his leash to his collar as he strained to investigate the slot-derived stimuli.

The scent of smoke intensified, this time bringing with it the smell of burnt cedar. I shuddered as I stood there, waiting for whatever game Mr. Kurosawa and Lady Siyu were playing with me to unfold.

Finally, after what seemed like minutes had passed with only the deranged slot machines to keep me and Captain company, I heard the *click-clack* of Lady Siyu's designer heels striking the marble floor. A moment later she emerged from the maze.

Unlike her usual black business suit attire—a dark jacket, white shirt, and pencil skirt paired with dark sunglasses that obscured her eyes— today she was dressed much like the first time I'd been dragged unwittingly into the casino, in a modern version of a Japanese kimono, the silk a bloodred, decorated with tiny white, black, and green flowers and fashioned into a minidress that hit just above her knees, exposing pale bare legs that ended in a pair of patent spiked heels the same bloodred color as her dress. Her face was decorated with a modern take on Kabuki makeup: skin pale but natural paired with bloodred lips and deep black winged eye liner—all the better to set off the golden, snakelike slits that were her eyes.

Captain's ears laid back and he let out a guttural hiss, straining at his leash.

Captain didn't like Lady Siyu. A few months back he'd been interned with her as an idiotic idea of payment for removing a curse.

I picked him up with the intention of restraining him. He didn't like that much and squirmed until he fixed his eyes right back on hers, hissing and growling warning all over again.

Lady Siyu's red-lacquered lips peeled back in her own snarl, and then off-white fangs extended down, dark yellow venom dripping from the tips. She hissed right back, and Captain backed down to a low growl. The feeling of extreme dislike was mutual. Captain hadn't made their few short months together easy for Lady Siyu and had done so in a form she could understand, rending antiques and designer shoes.

Mau cats had been bred by the Egyptians to sniff out and hunt down vampires. Their saliva was venomous to them, eliciting a severe allergic reaction reminiscent of anaphylactic shock. It shed a whole new light on the idea of cats being the guardians of the underworld. The same trait also allowed Captain to sniff out other supernaturals—though the reactions were varied and . . . unpredictable.

I might suck at identifying the supernatural, but my cat had been earning his assistant cat status lately and making up for my shortcomings.

As I wrangled my cat, I noted Lady Siyu was carrying something under her arm but didn't get a chance to get a good look at it before Captain renewed his efforts at Naga evisceration. I shortened his leash as he launched another round of claws into the air as a warning, then shoved his head under my leather jacket. He bleated in complaint but otherwise quieted down.

Captain successfully subdued, I got a better look at what was tucked under Lady Siyu's arm: a tablet.

Nothing good ever came of Lady Siyu bearing electronics . . .

"Thief," Lady Siyu spat as she stopped three feet away, her nose crinkling, whether at me or Captain I decided was a moot point.

"Lady Siyu." I nodded as well as I could with Captain still making a valiant effort to get free from under my coat. "And I prefer 'Owl' over 'thief.'"

Her upper lip curled in an amused sneer. "I am certain you do."

With that she held out the tablet—or shoved it under my nose might be a more accurate description.

I frowned. This was usually the point where Lady Siyu demanded I hand over the loot, then led me through the maze to see Mr. Kurosawa at a breakneck pace that could only be in the hope that I'd fall behind and take a wrong turn.

Keeping an eye on Lady Siyu, I looked at the tablet, aware of both Captain and the idol wrapped in sheets of three-month-old gossip rags. It had turned into a game for me, a dangerous one. My irreverence for the way I packaged and delivered the goods I acquired for Mr. Kurosawa offended Lady Siyu more than seemed reasonable. Who cared what the package was? A jeweled box couldn't make a fake artifact any more real than newspaper could make the authentic a fake.

Lady Siyu gave me an unfriendly smile as I glanced down at the tablet, as if the change in routine had been designed to set me on edge. If she was anything like her snake brethren, she could smell the fear wafting off of me.

On the tablet was a report, not from a news source like Reuters but a curated report like what you'd get from someone paid to do research.

Sweat began to collect at the back of my neck. What if they'd found out about my contact with Oricho? I'd been careful, but even I knew it was only a matter of time before they realized I was half-assing their acquisition of weapons and started to wonder why.

My panic subsided as I read. There was no mention of Oricho, the Tiger Thieves—not even Rynn. It was an account of my imprisonment in the Albino as Charity, the alias I'd given to the IAA dig guards when I'd been caught—on purpose. Also included was a photo—a bad one as I'd put up a fight to make my imprisonment look more plausible.

My relief that I hadn't been caught doing something worse was short lived as I looked back up at Lady Siyu. A fang now protruded from underneath her curled and sneering lip. "I am curious what excuses you have for your egregious misstep in Peru."

Egregious misstep? I handed her back the tablet and, negotiating past a growling Captain, reached into my leather jacket and removed the cheaply wrapped Incan idol. "I have your treasure for you, right here."

"That is not the point," Lady Siyu hissed.

I nodded at the tablet, sincerely at a loss. "Then what is? My picture? Is that what you're pissed about?"

She tucked the tablet back under her arm with a violent flourish of her wrist. "The point is you were *caught*. While working for Mr. Kurosawa."

Oh, for the love of— "As I said, I got out—*with* the idol. Are you worried about the photo being on record? That my alias got out? This isn't my first rodeo. I can scrub the photo, and there's a drawer full of aliases I haven't touched."

If anything, that only made Lady Siyu angrier. Her eyes narrowed into slits. I got the distinct impression she was about to explode, all the way from the ornate hair piled on top of her head down to the tips of her red patent heels. "You were *caught* retrieving items for Mr. Kurosawa. Do you have any idea how that looks to the supernatural community?"

Oh, for fuck's sake. I so did not have time for this . . . "That's what you're upset about? That I was caught? What is this, a supernatural pissing match?" I sighed. "Look, just take me to Mr. Kurosawa." He was usually more reasonable about these kinds of problems. Usually.

"Mr. Kurosawa has sent me to deal with you. He has other, more pressing concerns."

Great. Fantastic. But I'd learned the hard way not to press when the Dragon did not deign to see me. I took a breath and went for reasonable. "I'm a thief, a specialized one, and sometimes things don't go as planned. It's not like I have security watching my back anymore," I added. I'd noted over the last two months that Mr. Kurosawa and Lady Siyu had said disconcertingly little over the elves' fuckup that had gotten Rynn possessed by a suit of armor and running around playing warlord . . . and not a damn peep about a solution.

"*Clearly.*" Lady Siyu's fingernails had extended into long lacquered claws that now poked between the fingers of her clenched fists.

I held up the gossip rag–wrapped idol again. "And as I already said, I got what you wanted. Contract complete."

Still fuming, Lady Siyu snatched it out of my hand like a cobra striking prey. Surprised at the flash of movement, I couldn't help but jump back. Captain redoubled his hissing efforts, hackles on end.

Oddly enough, my show of fear seemed to mollify her a fraction. The fangs rescinded back into her jaw, and the claws receded.

"Which is the only reason you are still alive. I am here to pass on a message from Mr. Kurosawa: if you dishonor this house again, regardless of whether you retrieve the artifact, I strongly suggest you run."

"I can't. Contract, remember?" I said.

But Lady Siyu had already turned on her heels. Thick smoke that smelled of cedar billowed out of the maze and engulfed her. She did offer me a glance, every ounce of hate seeping into her smile. "Oh, not for you, little thief. I prefer my victims to offer chase."

Oh, for— Thank you for coming, Owl, now go get more useless artifacts while we try to bandage the problem of having a supernatural war spill into the human world.

The smart thing would be to keep my mouth shut. She'd already retreated into the smoke-filled maze.

Goddamn it, I couldn't leave it. "You realize this arsenal you're accumulating isn't going to do a damn thing? Not when both you and the Monsters Who Voted to Come Out of the Closet are doing the *exact* same damn thing, and that's not counting Rynn and his deranged band of mercenaries."

I heard rather than saw Lady Siyu stop her retreat. A moment later the quick click of heels striking the tiles sounded and yellow snake eyes burned through the smoke.

I went cold despite the sweat collecting on my skin. But I was right this time. I raced to make my case. Lady Siyu wasn't completely above reason. "Look, I'm not suggesting I abandon Mr. Kurosawa's list of weapons. I'm just saying there might be other ways, other avenues than chasing after ancient, dangerous magic weapons—shit." I stumbled back as Lady Siyu exited the smoke and came to stand a short foot away from me.

Her lips curled, exposing her fangs, as she gripped the front of my jacket with red-clawed hands and pulled me in. Captain hissed. I gulped. I'd never realized her venom had an acrid smell.

"Are you suggesting I'm in *error*?" she demanded, her voice laced with the threat of bodily harm.

I chose my next words very carefully. There was a dangerous edge to her voice, and considering I was as close to revolt as I'd ever been . . .

"What I'm *suggesting* is that a weapons race with Rynn and the Monsters Who Voted to Come Out of the Closet is the obvious path and the one of least resistance. Everyone is chasing after magic trinkets, including Rynn and his dark minions. It's sheer dumb luck I haven't run into any of them yet."

For a long, tense moment I thought Lady Siyu would kill me right there and then. Instead, she let me go.

"*Dumb*. That is an apt description for the luck that keeps your head attached to your neck. And as much as it pains me to admit it, for once, thief, we are in agreement," Lady Siyu said.

With my open mouth I must have looked like an indignant goldfish. She continued, "The others will be searching for many of the same artifacts. We are in a proverbial arms race, meaning we either increase the pace of acquisition—"

"That was not what I meant—" I stopped in midsentence as she turned her head inquisitively—not an entirely human gesture but cold, calculating.

"*Or* we alter the playing field. Possibly by reclaiming our mutual associate, the incubus? Isn't that right, Hiboux?" She smiled wide and venomously.

I clenched my fists and forced myself to keep silent. She knew I'd been up to something in Peru besides looking for the Incan idol, but if she had any idea just how much time I'd spent trying to find a way to get Rynn out of the suit . . .

As it was, the way her fangs were extended, venom glistening off the tips . . .

"*However*, as Mr. Kurosawa has pointed out, having two birds in the hand is useless if it equals an individual head and tail, and I do not care to press the issue of the incubus at the moment."

I held my tongue, wondering just how expensive this olive branch was going to be.

"I want our arsenal insurmountable, thief. If you please me, I will plead with Mr. Kurosawa on your behalf to investigate avenues to free the incubus." The corner of Lady Siyu's mouth turned up. "I recommend you try to acquire the Vatican artifacts. They're localized in one place and, as such, are an obvious target."

I snorted. It was piecemeal. "That's like telling Cinderella she can go to the ball if she can come up with a dress. I could find every artifact on this list and it still won't be enough—"

"Silence!"

I shut up. When faced with a furious Naga, options are limited.

"The pure impudence—you cannot fathom the gift I am giving you." She came in close, her face almost pressed against mine and her voice low, the scent of venom and floral perfume unifying in a terrifying mix. "You think I don't know all about your antics in Peru? I could have killed you the moment you walked in and been in my right. Listen well, thief. I'm *allowing* you to live because Mr. Kurosawa cannot see that being better armed will not win a battle on two fronts. Once we've defeated one side, the other will destroy us, but we still need an arsenal. *That* is the reason I do not carve you up into pieces and devour your heart."

I would have gulped, but I was afraid that even the slightest movement might entice her to bite me anyway and just get it the hell over with.

"Now do as you're told," she hissed. "And mark my words, if I *catch* you straying from your duties again, the day I kill you will be imminent."

With that last uncryptic statement, she disappeared into the maze of slot machines, which whirred and chimed in her wake.

A moment later, the cedar smoke retreated and once again I was standing at the entrance of a deserted casino, with only a warm breeze and a touch of smoke to remind me where I really was: in a dragon's lair—and that my presence was no longer requested. A hotter breeze with something less pleasant, like sulfur mixed in with the cedar, blew my way.

I didn't need to be told twice. Neither did Captain, who let out a quiet, forlorn mew and tugged on his leash in the direction of the exit. "I'm with you, Captain, there's just no pleasing the monsters."

We made a beeline for the elevator, which thankfully was waiting open for me. I didn't question why, not even after I was safely—or relatively safely—inside. I was just happy to be done. I pressed the main floor and waited as the elevator slid down to where the rest of humanity was corralled. It took me until the tenth floor to realize my hands were shaking and another long three seconds for it to set in that I'd be prudent to hide that. I shoved them back into my pockets.

I stared at myself in the mirrored artwork that Lady Siyu had installed in all the elevators: nature prints overlaid on the glass done with a modern Japanese aesthetic that she changed with the seasons. This one was a series of fruit trees that sprawled over the glass with the faintest trace of pastel colors. Each elevator had a slightly different version, though they all followed the same theme: late summer. I often wondered when the casino staff had time to change them since the elevators were in constant use. Another trick of management, or once again putting the supernatural talents of the casino's inhuman employees to use?

I was surprised by the gaunt face that stared back at me in the mirror's reflection. I didn't think it had been there before Peru. Or maybe it had and this was just the first time I'd decided to pull my head out of the Shangri-La hangover daze and look.

Well, if there was a bright side to all this, it was that Lady Siyu only suspected I was trying to save Rynn. If she'd had any idea I was working with Oricho . . .

Let's say I don't think I'd have left her presence.

The elevator reached the bottom floor, and the doors slid open. Captain strolled out into the crowd waiting for the elevators, earning me more than a few curious glances. My guess was that it wasn't due to

Captain; when people got over the initial shock of seeing a cat wandering around the casino, one who was polite enough to bleat at them to get the fuck out of his way, they usually reacted to him like everyone did to cute animals—by cooing and trying to pet him. Little did they know.

No. Despite Captain's gregarious nature, I figured my own disarray was the reason for the curiosity. Old leather jacket, hair tied in a messy ponytail out of convenience, and a pair of dirty, partially tied boots might be functional but didn't look nearly as cool in person as it did on the pages of a fashion magazine. A woman dressed like Lady Siyu in an expensive suit and well-coiffed hair? She could do whatever she wanted, but me? An explanation was demanded for not meeting enough ticks on a boxed-in checklist.

"Assistant pet," I said, and suffered another round of sidelong glances. Discreet ones this time, wondering what I needed an emotional support animal for.

The answer was vampires. Long story, worth the ten grand I'd had to bribe someone . . . a rip-off, really, considering that vampires was as good a reason as any for an anxiety disorder.

I ignored the glances and headed straight to the bar. The bartender would refresh my beer supply, even if only to get rid of me faster. I had earned myself a reputation amongst the supernaturals who worked the casino; half of it was deserved, but the other half was mostly speculation and my professional reputation.

The bartender on duty was a radish demon who gave me a surreptitious look as I approached. When I asked for the case of beer, he retrieved it and deposited it on the counter without the barest attempt at pleasantries.

On most days I cared, but lately I couldn't be bothered. I had more important things to deal with than starting petty squabbles with supernaturals who slighted me.

As an afterthought, I decided to swing by the front desk and see if there were any messages or mail for me.

Halfway across the mezzanine by the central fountain I stopped in my tracks. There near the entrance was a blond man wearing a jacket I recognized. One of Rynn's.

I grabbed onto the fountain's edge and steadied myself. There were two things that raced through my mind as the shock coursing through me settled: that I didn't think I'd been this happy to see anyone before and then fear. I knew what Rynn was now. He or the armor must know I was getting closer.

I stood perfectly still as he turned around . . .

But it wasn't Rynn.

It was Artemis, dressed as Rynn, standing in the Japanese Circus casino lobby talking to the front desk. He smiled and winked at me before going back to speaking to the supernatural personnel.

I fumed. How dare he show up here, dressed as Rynn, of all things? Because he certainly wasn't dressed in his own clothes—not nearly tacky and flashy enough.

"Come on, Captain," I said, and with the case of beer in hand stalked back to the elevator. I could call down to the front desk. Later.

I wasn't fast enough.

"Owl," came Artemis's voice, much closer behind me than made me comfortable.

I ignored the dirty looks I was getting from the casino patrons as I mowed past them on my way to the elevator. Damn it. And here I thought I'd ditched Artemis on that flight out of Lima . . .

"Owl," Artemis called louder this time, though no one around me bothered to look. They were all fixated on me, the angry cat lady who didn't belong in a casino and was furiously bulldozing her way to the elevator. I picked up my pace, Captain in tow on his leash, grumbling and fighting me now that he'd picked up the scent of an incubus—one he recognized.

Of course it had been Artemis. I chided myself for letting my guard down—again.

The elevator doors opened and for once no one wanted to get in with me and my cat.

Except Artemis, who darted in just as the doors were sliding closed. Captain let out a wary mew at him, part warning, part curiosity.

"Why, fancy running into you here, Alix," Artemis said as the elevator started its ascent. "How have you been since we parted ways?"

If I ignored him, he'd only keep coming back—and come up with more overt ways to mock me. I crossed my arms and let Captain's leash go so he could sniff out the incubus. "Fine," I said. "Never better. Busy, though."

He gave me a terse smile, deciding that pretending we were friends was too much, even for him. He held up a rolled gossip magazine. "I'm not in here," he said, unrolling the cover for me to see. "Leave town for a week and they forget I exist." He *tsk*ed and tucked the gossip rag back inside his jacket, the one that bore an uncanny resemblance to one Rynn owned. "That's the gratitude I get for selling millions of their shoddy magazines over the last decade—for one measly week."

He made a show of examining his outfit in the mirror. "Like the outfit? Personally I prefer something a bit flashier, more metallic, but I decided to try something new."

Captain let out a low growl from where he was sniffing Artemis's pant leg.

If ignoring Artemis would egg him on, so would outright blowing up at him, though I clenched my fists. "Cheap impression," I said.

Artemis laughed, apparently more amused than offended. "And here I expected you to give me the third degree on my reasons for being here."

"Fine. What brings you lurking around the Japanese Circus?"

He leaned against the mirror and made a show of smoothing his hair. He gave me a conspiratorial look. "Did you know incubi have fantastic hearing?"

I went cold. There was no way he could have been upstairs listening. For one, he wasn't that stupid.

"The walls have ears, and people talk." He went on to examine his nails. "Besides, I had to report in to Lady Siyu in person." The corner of his mouth twitched, a hint of his own frustrations when dealing with the

Naga. "So you failed to mention to the Dragon and his pet snake that you're after the Tiger Thieves."

Fuck . . .

I shook my head, and Captain let out a low growl. "Now, it would be a shame for those murderous two to find out what you were really doing in that prison. Though I suppose I have some obligation to tell them." The friendly sham of a smile he'd kept fixed to his face vanished, leaving the cold, calculating eyes I remembered from the last time I'd seen him. The ones I'd caught a glimpse of in Peru. "So what is it worth to you to keep your little Tiger Thief quest secret?"

I wondered how much of a push it'd take to break the elevator glass. I mean, he wasn't human, so chances were it wouldn't kill him, just get my point across. There were only so many supernaturals whose eyes I could pull the wool over, and Lady Siyu and Mr. Kurosawa were already a dangerous handful. I did not need to be watching over my shoulder for Artemis. "Let me assure you, talking to anyone about my little side trip into Albino would be very bad," I said.

He clicked his tongue. "Depends on your perspective, really."

"*Perspective*? You have no—"

"I wonder how many other thieves would be willing to get their hands dirty for an outcast supernatural? Who'd be willing to get themselves locked up in an infamous Peruvian prison?" Artemis had been keeping to his side of the elevator, but that changed as he closed the distance in a step to menace over me. I remembered just how terrifying Artemis could be. "One, say, who's hiding out in Tokyo with one of your known accomplices? Taking that logic a step further, I wonder how many thieves the Dragon could find to replace you."

I don't know how, I don't know why, but he knew about Oricho. Son of a bitch. It should have terrified me. All it did was strengthen my resolve. "Trust me, I'm a real bitch to replace," I said, each word clear and just as biting.

An inclination of his head. "So you say. In my estimation, part of anyone's value is her reputation—and yours isn't what it used to be."

The two of us glared at each other, me wanting to kill him and he calculating. He broke eye contact first and went back to studying the gossip rag. "You asked me what I want; here it is. I want to be included in your plans to find the Tiger Thieves."

I snorted. "*You?* Help *me?*"

He leaned back against the elevator glass. "In a manner of speaking."

I would have laughed, said that he was out of his mind, very funny—but the serious tone and expression were still there.

Shit, he was serious. Artemis was a supernatural—a *dangerous* one, despite his harmless exterior and antics. I'd seen just how dangerous and unpredictable he could be firsthand—and Rynn hadn't trusted him as far as he could throw him.

Rynn had also grossly underestimated his cousin, which had almost gotten me killed a few months ago. Which was why I stopped myself from laughing.

"*Why?*"

"My own reasons—and no, before you ask, I'm not sharing them with you."

I scoffed, "Then the answer is no."

"Fine. But you'll have to take it up with Oricho since I've already struck the deal with him. As you're aware, those kinds of arrangements are difficult to break."

Oh for the love of— I was going to have strong words with Oricho. The elevator chimed its arrival on the twenty-third floor. Finally. I ducked past him and set a fast pace for my room, Captain in the lead. We'd see what Oricho had to say about all this . . .

But Artemis managed to get in front of me and block my way. "You can use me. The Albino proved that. How long do you think you would have lasted on your own?"

"And wait until you stab me in the back? Not fucking likely." Captain hissed at Artemis, making him jump. I dodged past him and reached my door.

"I'm not asking you to trust me. You shouldn't trust me. You shouldn't trust any of us! I'm asking you to use me as Oricho's offered help—I may not be Rynn, but I have my uses."

"You mean by using people? Manipulating them, controlling them?" Goddamn it, of all the times for my lock to stick. I swiped the card again as Artemis continued to plead.

"Suggesting. You'd be surprised what most people are open to. It's been behind the fall of most of your civilizations. And we don't all express or use our talents in the same way. We make do with what we have." He leaned in until his face was close enough that I could smell his breath and a trace of amber—not unlike Rynn but a darker, more burnt version. "Not so unlike you."

I would have liked nothing better than to send him packing—but there was a problem with that: it was unlikely that he would lie about having struck a deal with Oricho.

And even though I was loath to admit it, I didn't believe for a second that Oricho would bring Artemis in unless he thought it essential to our success in breaking the armor's hold over Rynn. Oricho was a lot of things and I had issues with his methods, but he was sincere about stopping a supernatural war and trying to save humanity from the monsters. That necessitated removing Rynn's chaotic reign from the picture.

And screwing that up was something I wasn't willing to risk, even if it got me stabbed in the back. Not without talking to Oricho, at any rate.

Artemis smiled. He didn't need to be able to read my emotions to know I was trapped.

"Just don't let Lady Siyu find out you're still here," I told him. "It'll raise too many questions. They've got a blind spot for how humans react, but they're not stupid."

"I know how to make myself unseen. Even with my own kind. Trust me, it's one of my many talents."

A cold feeling spread over me again. *Trust* was a strong word, one I wouldn't apply to anything involving Artemis. I also got the distinct impression that Artemis's "talents" ran much darker than Rynn's.

"So do we have a deal?" he asked.

I must have had my head knocked around a few too many times in the Albino. "*Fine*," I said, holding out my hand. "*After* I talk to Oricho. If he says I have to deal with you, I'll deal with you."

Artemis grasped my offered hand in his, gripping it with a cold, isolating touch, again so unlike Rynn's.

What did I say the definition of madness was again? Doing the same thing over and over and expecting a different result? Making another goddamned deal with one of the monsters . . . if I hadn't been in the mad category before, this sure as hell put me square into it.

Artemis smiled, a self-satisfied expression full of the knowledge that he'd won this round—though, as I kept reminding myself, not the war. With a passing glance down the hall, as if just realizing where we were, he said, "Well, I know when and where I'm not wanted. Don't forget to send me our travel arrangements."

"Wouldn't dream of it." Despite the frustration and anger building inside me, I kept my voice calm and civil. Regardless of whether or not Oricho was on board, Artemis knew enough to be dangerous to me now. I had to tread carefully. Captain, picking up on subtler signals, flicked his tail and let out a tentative growl.

Artemis arched an eyebrow, looking again like Rynn's darker, evil shadow. Every expression he made was more a mockery of the human expression, devoid of any sincerity. "So many secrets," he *tsk*ed, shaking his head as he backed away.

I didn't open the door to my room until I heard the elevator doors hiss shut.

Captain let out a long, forlorn mew.

"Yeah, I don't trust him either, Captain." Much like Lady Siyu, I was certain Artemis was waiting to stab me in the back. I preferred Lady Siyu's methods. There was an honesty to her outright threats even I could appreciate.

Captain let out another loud, insistent meow as he planted himself in front of his food dish. I sighed and fished out a can. Choosing which battles you fought and when were things I'd been forcing myself to learn lately; I was fighting enough people and supernaturals on multiple fronts. At the moment, Captain begging for food and Artemis weaseling his way into my plans weren't the battles to pick. At least Captain knew it; so probably did Artemis.

"Cat-pain," I said, rubbing his head, as he began to scarf down the tuna now in his dish. I left him to gorge himself in peace and, after placing my new six-pack of beer in the fridge, relieving it of one, I sat down in front of my laptop. Again.

This time I opened my email, ignoring the World Quest icon at the bottom of my screen and the messaging box. No, that was a lie. I did look and once again felt the pang of emptiness that there wasn't anything from Carpe.

World Quest was the online role-playing game I subscribed to that was modeled after ruins and civilizations from the archaeological record—accurately, with monsters. It was also more than it seemed. I hadn't seen hide nor hair of Frank or Neil after the disaster in Shangri-La. We'd all gone our separate ways. I couldn't blame them. I had gotten a vampire to give us a ride out. I'd have hightailed it as far as possible away from me too.

There was comfort in the fact that I wasn't solely responsible for trashing the place. I'd had copious help—between the mercenaries, IAA, and the elves . . . I had barely touched Shangri-La while it had fallen to its ruin.

To be honest, I was surprised the game was still running. From what I'd gathered from the designers, Frank and Neil, it had been developed in a magically made city that had a will of its own if not an actual mind. As a result, it had woven its fingers into the makeup of the game. I couldn't help wondering how the game was still running if the servers in Shangri-La had been destroyed along with the city and the pocket dimension that had sustained the trading hub of the ancient world.

I pushed thoughts of Carpe aside. I was blaming myself for enough things as it was. Carpe—whatever had happened to him after he'd pushed me out of Shangri-La—wasn't something my brain could handle right now. I didn't know when I'd be able to process it. Yet another wonder of going through the numb stage of grief. By definition you didn't feel a hell of a lot.

Carpe had picked the wrong side. He'd known that and had done what he could to make it right. As Nadya had said, that had been his choice, not mine.

I hadn't thought I'd miss his meddling ways—not this much.

I drafted a quick email to Oricho. It was simple and to the point: *What the hell are you thinking letting that degenerate incubus in?*

I rewrote it to make it more polite, taking out *hell* and adding a *please* and *thank you*, but the point remained the same. Next I pulled out my phone. Time to fill Nadya in. *"You up?"* I texted.

A moment later my phone rang, Nadya's name flashing across the screen.

"You will not believe the couple weeks I've had," I answered, and began to recap my most recent adventures—beginning with Peru and finishing off with Artemis accosting me in the lobby. Nadya, being the generous best friend she was, listened patiently, interrupting only to ask for clarity.

"I don't know what game he's playing but it ends with a knife in my back."

"Mmmm, possibly," Nadya mused. "But Oricho is not reckless. If he's brought Artemis on, there must be a reason."

"Blackmail?" I'd gotten the distinct impression that Nadya had gotten to know Oricho better since the two of them had been working together in Tokyo trying to mitigate the antics of the Come-Out-of-the-Closet crowd. I wasn't entirely comfortable with it. Oricho might be one of the more sympathetic supernaturals I'd had the pleasure of meeting, but he was no Rynn and had screwed both Nadya and me over before.

But Nadya was an adult and could handle herself. I was the last person on the planet to shove unsolicited personal advice her way. She was a far sight from reckless and had a much better nose for trouble than I'd ever have. If she wanted to tangle with Oricho, professionally or otherwise, I wasn't about to chastise her about it.

At least not until it deteriorated into disaster. Good friends don't try to prevent every disaster; just the ones that will maim you.

"Though I do wonder what it is Artemis stands to gain from his involvement," Nadya continued.

I snorted. "That is the million-dollar question. My best guess? We won't know until I'm trying to pull the knife out of my back."

"Which is why I think Oricho must have a good reason. He wouldn't risk involving Artemis otherwise—not when you've had your first break on the Tiger Thieves in months, and with Rynn . . ." She let the thought trail off, and an uncomfortable silence filled the line. We both knew that Rynn had been stepping up his reign of chaos and violence amongst the supernatural and mercenary communities, building his own personal army and collecting supernatural weapons. I didn't need to be reminded, I had a hard time forgetting.

"One can hope" was all I said, and took a swig of my beer. "The enemy of my enemy is my friend," I continued. "The problem is, we have no idea who Artemis's enemies are."

"Maybe he just really does want a good seat to watch the world burn. Let's face it, a seat beside you isn't a bad choice—and people have switched sides for less," Nadya offered. "Look, I need to go. Club duties—I have a group of Japanese businessmen in, and Oricho has lent me a pair of succubae to watch over the club."

"So you put them to work?"

"Waste not, want not. I want to make sure they don't take things too far; they're"—Nadya paused as she searched for words—"not the kind of girls I would usually hire. Let's leave it at that."

Supernatural protection and staff rolled into one. My, how far we'd come. If someone had told either of us in grad school that in a few short years we'd both be knee-deep in supernatural bullshit . . . I wasn't about to complain. Another of my conditions for agreeing to work with Oricho had been to make sure Nadya didn't get caught up in the inevitable shit storm.

There was a brief pause in our conversation. I hadn't planned on asking, I'd in fact made a point of steering my mind away from it, but I couldn't help myself. "Any sign of Rynn over there?" I asked as casually as I could. It wasn't a question completely out of left field. Both Nadya and Rynn had run host/hostess bars in Tokyo. If anything, I was surprised that Rynn hadn't gone straight back to his old haunt.

"No, thank God. He is the last thing we need running around Tokyo right now."

A pit formed in my stomach. I didn't think for a moment that Rynn was ignoring Tokyo. I only hoped I could reach the Tiger Thieves before he turned his attention to it—and that there was something inside left to save.

"Good luck, Alix, you're going to need it," Nadya said, and sighed. I couldn't tell if it was for her own problems in Tokyo with supernaturals running amok or for me. I figured it was a bit of both.

"And try not to start a bar brawl with Artemis."

"Depends what he says to me first." Which was true. The supernaturals expected a certain level of hotheadedness from me. Wouldn't want to disappoint.

We said our good-byes and hung up.

With Nadya back in Tokyo and Rynn—well, running helter-skelter with his own personal army, to what end no one had yet figured out quite yet—things were lonely.

I refreshed my email to see if there was a response from Oricho yet. There was, and it was quick and to the point:

Received your message about the Tiger Thieves amulet. I have yet to decrypt its meaning but remain hopeful.

I swore and lifted my beer to my lips, finding it empty. Great. Oricho had no fucking clue what the gold markings on the Tiger Thieves amulet meant either. Why was I not surprised? One step forward, two steps back.

In the meantime I suggest you attempt to find the artifacts reported to be in Venice as Lady Siyu suggests. In your spare time, I recommend you seek

out da Vinci's lair. He had dealings with the Tiger Thieves and notes may
have been left.

RE Artemis: The benefits outweigh the risks.

I snorted. Oricho's benefits, my risks. Yup, that had the makings of
a supernatural deal.

I was about to close my laptop and head to bed when a flickering
message box in the lower left corner of my screen made me pause. It was
the message box I had used to talk to Carpe. I licked my lips and hovered
my cursor over the email, hesitating, but only for a moment.

It was only a message from World Quest, a generic email saying my
annual subscription would renew automatically in the next month. A
simple, generic, automatically generated email . . .

I frowned as I reached the bottom, where a single line was scrawled:
Hey asshole—we need to talk.

Frank must have drafted it. Neil would have attempted to be nicer—
or, if not nicer, at least more polite.

I stared at the computer screen, trying to focus on the message in
front of me, not the jumble of emotions crashing through my numbness.
The problem was that, just like before, I couldn't tune it out. Not one
damn bit of it. Despite what my brain knew, some small part of me had
hoped there would be a trace of Carpe in there. When you don't actually
see someone die, even though every ounce of your being says it's the only
logical conclusion, your mind still plays tricks on you.

With a sigh I hit Reply and kept my message to Frank and Neil suc-
cinct: *Fine—when and why?*

I closed my laptop. Carpe was dead, obliterated along with the
pocket universe that had been Shangri-La. It had been two months; if
he had miraculously survived, he'd have reared his head by now.

I passed by the kitchen to grab a new beer before heading to my
bedroom.

The other problem with not seeing him die was that there was another part of me that didn't want to know. The part of me that didn't hold
grudges and still wanted to hope.

It was a small part, I'll give you. I'd had too many people validate my grudges for me to be generous with that.

I left the door open a crack for Captain before climbing into bed. I flipped on the TV to the international news, trying to parse the supernatural-derived disasters from the normal ones.

I finished only half my beer before abandoning it on the nightstand. It left a dry taste in my mouth. I hit the lights and turned in early. I needed my sleep, I reasoned, I'd be dealing with Artemis in the morning.

I tried to drift off as fast as I could, more to forget how much things had changed over the past few months. Rynn, Nadya, Carpe—the only thing worse than being hunted by vampires, I'd come to realize, was finding out you were completely alone, especially after you've found out what it's like not to be.

I was grateful when Captain hopped up onto the bed and staked out his territory.

If change was supposed to be so good for you, why the hell did it feel so horrible?

5

LAIRS OF VENICE

*Twenty-four hours later: Venice, Italy,
the City of Romance—and vampires.*

The funny thing about Venice is its reputation as the City of Romance. I suppose it's true . . . if you consider vampire pheromones a valid substitute for love.

Oh vampires, you cockroaches of the supernatural world, is there any major city where you haven't dug yourselves into an unretractable hole? Like ship rats or new and interesting STDs landing in a fresh port . . .

Venice might not seem like an obvious haunt of vampires: an island city with no underground hideouts, lots of small spaces, and a naturally superstitious population courtesy of the Byzantines, who'd had a healthy fear of the supernatural. Through the Middle Ages and Renaissance, Venice was not a favorite stomping ground of the supernatural community. They preferred Florence and Rome, cities where you could eat a few people and ride to the next before anyone was the wiser.

That was before the buildings in Venice started to sink.

Throughout Venice today, you can find buildings where entire floors are hidden under the flooding water—but others? Nothing a few heavy-duty pumps can't manage, especially if you aren't concerned about molds and various diseases that breed down there. In that sense, modern Venice has become a veritable playground for supernaturals. And the tourists? It's like a sushi train at the all-you-can-eat Japanese place on the corner—the band is constantly turning, delivering yet another delectable morsel . . .

The supernaturals haunting the submerged levels of Venice added a layer of difficulty to retrieving and removing any artifacts. I'd avoided jobs in Venice for that very reason—unless the pay was substantial—and I'd been certain I could avoid the supernaturals.

I glanced over at Artemis, who was shadowing me down the narrow street. Oh, how times had changed. Hopefully he could smell any vampires or other supernaturals before we stumbled into them.

I'd held out hope at the Las Vegas airport that Artemis had decided to hell with torturing Owl under the pretense of help and decided to blow off the flight with a bachelorette party from Tallahassee—or wherever else bachelorette parties originated.

That hope was trounced when I stepped out of Italian customs and found Artemis lounging by a pillar. Shit. He had made the flight. And now we were here. Artemis my unwelcome shade . . .

"You could at least pretend not to hate being here," he whispered after a couple passed us by. Captain, for his part, shuffled around in my backpack to get a good look at the incubus before letting out a bleat. Captain couldn't figure out what to make of Artemis either.

"It's either pretend I don't hate you or keep my eyes out for vampires."

"You have me for the vampires."

Captain let out an excited bleat at the word *vampire*. "No offense, but I'll take his warnings over yours any day." Now . . . I thought this was the right street up ahead . . . had the right shape, though it was difficult to determine without any posted street signs. It was a Venetian thing; I suppose if you lived here you knew what all the streets were, so why use signs?

"So where to now, oh great explorer?" Artemis asked.

I turned down another street, at the end of which was a taxi stop.

I spotted a water taxi turning the corner. "First things first—blend in with the rest of the tourists, and get on a boat." I frowned as I gave Artemis's clothes a once-over. Whereas I'd donned my usual backpacking student gear, Artemis was wearing torn black jeans with gold paint with a leather jacket that stood out as expensive and opulent rather than subdued. It screamed "Look at me!" not "Just here for the sightseeing." He didn't stick out like a sore thumb, he was the sore thumb.

My expression must have been obvious because he said, "Don't worry, no one will even notice I'm here."

I made a face. "It's hard to see how not."

"I have my ways," he replied with a wink. We were out of time so I didn't push the point. The taxi pulled up to the stop, and we joined the line to get on.

Sure enough, as we made our way down the aisle to find seats, I noted that though I garnered the odd glance, no one paid attention to Artemis, who was unabashedly dressed like a movie-extra rock star.

I eyed him warily as we took two seats near the back. His sunglasses were firmly set over his eyes. "You're using your powers," I accused him.

He scoffed as he leaned back, resting his head against his hands. "Of course I'm using my powers. Otherwise I'd have to dress like you and slink around in the shadows, and it'll be a cold day in Hell before that happens."

"I thought incubi read and manipulated emotions."

It was Artemis's turn to make a face. "That's a baseline. It's not unusual for things to . . . branch off. Suffice it to say that I can make certain no one bothers to pay attention to us."

"Since when the hell can incubi make themselves invisible?"

Another face. "We can't—and I can't. I'm just making them not pay attention. I'm very good at it. It's not something that ever came easily to Rynn. He's too honest."

Sure enough, no one was looking at us, but neither did anyone try to sit down in our seats. We weren't invisible but about as close a facsimile as you could get . . .

"I will admit that this place wasn't the first one to come to mind for one of your infamous heists."

I bristled as I kept my eye on the canal stops. Should be coming up in two . . . "Venice is an ancient trade city that was part of the Byzantine Empire. The question isn't whether there is stuff worth taking lying around, it's what, where, how dangerous, and who originally stole it." It was astounding the number of things that got lost in some old merchant's warehouse, then were passed on for generations, until an army came in and sacked the place or a plague killed off everyone who knew the location of the vault . . . repeat that over a thousand and a bit years, and Venice has a number of interesting artifacts stowed away in its depths—dry and otherwise.

"Mmmm," he mused. "So tell me, what is it we're after? Don't worry, none of them can hear us." He glanced at the passengers sitting on either side of us. "Or more accurately won't bother remembering." At my expression, Artemis made a clucking sound. "That's right, you're a little shy around supernatural magic."

"I have good reason to be."

"I suppose. But you take it a little too personally, if you ask me."

Yeah, I had taken being attacked and almost included in an incubus's harem pretty fucking personally . . .

Artemis must have felt the round of emotions rolling off me—none of them complimentary—so we pulled into the next taxi stop. It took me a second to realize that he was staring at me, eyes narrowed in concentration. "Things aren't always what they seem, Owl. You of all people should know that" was all he said.

Yeah, and the world was full of misunderstandings . . . And this was definitely it. I jostled Artemis to get up as soon as the taxi came to a halt. I was worried that we might have to push our way off, but once again people didn't quite ignore us; they just didn't bother showing an ounce of interest. Like being invisible without the toe squishing. We alighted on the canal sidewalk and headed for the narrow streets. This section of Venice, for whatever reason, hadn't attracted the number of tourists that others had. It wasn't run down, more forgotten. Kind of like we were . . .

I got my bearings and headed towards the street where the church should be.

"It was either Venice or head to Norway and try to outwit a bunch of ice trolls," I told him. And both Oricho and Lady Siyu were keen on it, though for different reasons. Not that I was sharing with Artemis. I might have to take him with me, but Oricho hadn't said a damn thing about letting him know the details.

"So our current location is entirely due to being the less cold and lethal choice? I'm disappointed. I thought there would be more of a plan."

I kept my annoyance in check. "I have a hunch, Artemis. Let's leave it at that."

"How does the saying go? 'If you believe that, I have a magic bird to sell you'?"

I checked the front of the building. It was the right one, an almost exact match for the one in the drawing minus a few sunken feet. This was definitely one of Leonardo da Vinci's old secret storehouses—not that it was in any of the history books. The city had even been nice enough to include a street sign here. Wonder of wonders, would have been real useful earlier . . .

"The saying is 'Magic *beans*'—hello?" I called out, knocking loudly on the door and listening to the echo inside. There was no answer. "The birds are two in the bush versus one in your hand. Apparently, according to Lady Siyu, you guys have a bush that includes two dead birds."

The old building had been converted into a church, of all things. I tried the wooden double doors.

Odd . . .

The doors swung wide open, but not a soul was inside.

"A bit odd for a church to be this empty—during visiting hours, no less," Artemis said.

And it was low lit, even for a church. I pulled out my flashlight and aimed the beam inside, where I was greeted with an abundance of dust—on the wood floors, along the ledges, even on the dust sheets that had been used to cover a portion of the furniture before someone had given up. I even picked up dust suspended in the air, reflected in the thin beams of light that had managed to escape through the cracks of the boarded-up stained-glass windows.

Artemis examined the sign by the door. "It says it's open and these are the visiting hours," he said.

Somehow I didn't think it was due to the laissez-faire nature of Italians—that they'd simply forgotten to put up the "Closed for renovations" sign.

It could be a sign of something else . . .

"Well, Captain?" I said, and eased my backpack off my shoulder before opening his compartment. He crept out, carefully examining the area around him before creeping along the floor to survey the rest of the church.

"Looks like something has your cat being cautious."

Or he smelled mice and didn't want to scare off a potential snack . . .

I aimed my flashlight at a corner in the rafters, peering into the dusty darkness. I could have sworn I'd seen something—a flicker of movement.

I was about to chalk it up to pigeons and my brand of paranoia when Captain chirped. He was straining to sniff one of the covered pews. I stopped moving and held up a hand for Artemis to do the same. My paranoia might know no bounds, but Captain was immune to the machinations of my imagination.

I glanced back over my shoulder through the open door. It was early afternoon, but that didn't mean much when there were this many shadows. I did think it odd that on a midafternoon of a sunny day in Venice, no one was in the vicinity.

"You picking up anything, Artemis?" I asked as I continued to where Captain was nosing his way under a sheet.

"Nothing distinct," he said. He'd opened the visitors' book and was perusing the contents—signatures of people who had visited the church.

I waited for Captain to do something—growl, hiss, let out a battle cry. But all he did was sit back on his haunches and start cleaning himself. Apparently even the church mice weren't coming out to play.

"Find anything?" I called out to Artemis, my nerves relaxing a fraction.

"Signatures from all over, people stopping in to visit the church. A lot of comments about the dust and no one here to meet them, but other than that, nothing. I thought Leonardo spent most of his time in Florence?"

"Leonardo moved around—Florence, Milan, and Rome mostly— but he spent a stint here during the Italian war with the French when he worked as a military architect and engineer." It was also where he had built most of his supernatural devices, the vast majority of which had been lost to the ages—or the Illuminati—or the supernaturals themselves . . . it really depended on which conspiracy theory you subscribed to. "It wouldn't be much of a secret workshop if it was in schoolbooks." This one had been buried under centuries' worth of IAA archives. Might even have been courtesy of the Illuminati themselves.

"Tell me, Artemis, you were around during the fifteen hundreds, yes? What do you know of the Illuminati?"

He snorted. "Next you'll be telling me that the Masons were friends of the Tiger Thieves too."

"No, the Masons stayed the hell away from supernaturals. They were smart."

Captain, having given up on seeking mice, accompanied me while I began examining the church walls.

"Well," Artemis said, "the Illuminati were real enough, if that's what you mean. Less educated and more dangerous than the stories would have you believe. And they weren't chasing after the way to turn lead into gold, not the serious ones at any rate."

I tapped the wall at various intervals, searching for a hollow sound that would denote a passage of some sort.

Artemis continued, "Now, immortality through alchemy, that's a different story entirely. There are enough incubi and vampires who survived the Illuminati inquisitions and experiments to attest to that."

I nodded to myself as I examined a seam in the wall that struck me as out of place. It matched with what I'd learned about them at university: the Illuminati were one historic group the IAA didn't gloss over. It used them as a cautionary tale of why not to meddle with supernaturals. Scattered throughout the Middle Ages, their activities had consisted of bumbling over artifacts they had no right testing—dangerous, magic ones. They had been a nuisance to the supernaturals but manageable.

Then, around 1500, they got organized, some say because of Leonardo da Vinci's involvement. And his search for immortality.

"You ever run into any of them?" I asked.

Artemis gave me a serious look, one of the few he'd bothered with. "Today you might call them supernatural hunters, though *exterminators* is more accurate. Especially the more extreme factions that popped up over the centuries. They were particularly fond of capturing supernaturals without any proverbial teeth, and even the ones with teeth weren't immune to their attentions."

I followed the seam to a spot where, due to a difference in the wood stain, it looked to me as though an altar had been removed. I tapped it, and it echoed back hollow. Bingo.

"As I recall, the Illuminati and Leonardo took quite an interest in my vampire brethren."

That was not surprising, considering vampires were one of the only breed of supernaturals that started off human. If I were after the secrets of immortality, that's where I'd be inclined to begin.

Though the idea of humans being any real threat to supernaturals was dubious. It wasn't that Artemis was a liar—there were too many grains of truth in what he'd said—but humans hunting supernaturals? I held my hand up to one of the cracks. There was air coming from the other side—faint but definitely there.

"Don't believe me?" Artemis asked, from where he was still perusing the guest book.

Now, where the hell would I hide a release for a panel door in here? "I just don't see the supernatural community ever considering humans a real threat."

"The vampires would know more than I about the Illuminati's interest in supernaturals. I would have asked them."

I snorted. "Unfortunately, Alexander and the Paris boys aren't exactly returning my phone calls." I had tried to contact Alexander despite the fact that as a rule I avoided any dealings with vampires, particularly Alexander, since we'd had a substantial falling-out a few years ago, one that had involved me exposing one of the elders to sunlight—by accident, I might add, though that detail had been lost on him.

We'd briefly shelved our differences on account of the turmoil in the supernatural community. Vampires ate people, but the smart ones had no interest in coming out of the closet. They were too easy a target and had very well publicized weaknesses. They also weren't the hard hitters of the supernatural world that romance novelists make them out to be. Annoying and dangerous, certainly, but cockroaches compared to a dragon or a skin walker. Alexander had no interest in humans' knowing vampires were real.

Regardless of our truce, though, Alexander hadn't deigned to answer my queries on Venice or Leonardo da Vinci. He probably had enough to do keeping vampires in line and out of everyone's sights.

Now, door release. Come on, wouldn't it have to be here, somewhere . . . With my luck a tall person designed it and it'd be just out of my reach.

"Hey, I found something," Artemis called. When I looked his way, he nodded at the church guest book. "Did you know this place was being run as a vacation rental?" he asked.

I frowned. "A vacation rental?"

"Starting a few years back, through one of those online sites—there are even instructions here, see?" He picked up the book and brought it over. It occurred to me that out of all the items in the room, the book was the only thing that wasn't covered in dust. Sure enough, there were pages of check-ins, along with a pamphlet instructing people how to access the apartment, which was billed as a historic restoration.

"Surprises you?"

I shrugged. "Nothing really surprises me anymore." I supposed that if everything dated back a thousand years, the idea of an old building as a historic site wore off. Might as well make a few bucks off it—even a church.

"It says, 'To access the apartment, pull the lamp handle.'" That was a little clichéd—and nonspecific, considering that the church was filled with wall lamps of varying appearances and sizes. It took us a few minutes, but eventually, through trial and error, I found the right one. I pulled it, and sure enough, a set of pulleys churned behind the wall and the door opened, revealing a small, comfortable-looking apartment done in a mid-century modern style. There was a small desk to the side, a kitchenette done in a muted orange, an old chesterfield with a small coffee table, a sparsely occupied bookshelf, and two small bedrooms, the doors ajar enough for us to see the two single beds in each. The rooms were dark; they would have been pitch-black if not for three small windows, their glass dusty and purpled with lead.

"Hello?" I called out again. No response, only the musty air of a room that hadn't been aired in a while.

Odd for a vacation rental in Venice.

I glanced to see if Artemis had anything useful to offer. "After you" was all he said, nodding at the inner rooms.

I could have sworn I saw something looking through one of the dusty windows—like a face. But the translucent lead glass made it impossible to tell one way or the other.

I waited to see if it would reappear at one of the other two windows, but nothing happened. I stepped inside, Artemis and Captain following me.

"A hideout from World War II, I imagine," I said to Artemis. The decor certainly suggested that: faded baroque-style wallpaper mixed in with mid-century pieces. It would certainly appeal to a certain kind of tourist looking for an authentic experience.

"Or they tried downsizing the place to evade taxes."

I didn't think churches needed to evade taxes, but I supposed anything was possible in Italy.

I went to the desk first and found a backpack covered in dust like everything else in the room. I opened it and found a bottle of sunscreen, cotton summer hats crumpled into balls, water bottles, and a cartoon map of Venice, the tourist stops highlighted in bright colors. I frowned at them. The kinds of items tourists would use but not the kind that got left behind.

"Says the last family to stay here was the Smiths, a family of four from Massachusetts," Artemis said from the chesterfield, where he'd sat down to read the guest book, his bejeweled boots resting on the coffee table.

Considering that there were children's activities circled on the map and two of the sun hats were child-sized, that made sense.

Next I checked the bookshelf. More pamphlets: tours of the glass factories, city canals, kids' books.

"I don't think this place has been cleaned since the Smiths were here," I said.

Artemis shrugged. "Maybe they couldn't be bothered. Or maybe they got tired of catering to tourists."

"In Venice?" That was how most people paid the rent.

Artemis shrugged, running a finger over the coffee table, pulling it back covered in dust. "I've given up trying to figure out what you humans do and why. Maybe someone died? Like the person running this place."

"Or the guests," I said. I headed into the bedroom and opened the dresser, where I found four passports along with a purse. I flipped through the first one, skipping the photos—I didn't want their owners to be personalized. They were the passports of the Smiths, a nuclear family of four. June 10 of this year was the customs stamp. June—and this was November. I held them up. "These have been here for five months."

"Explains the sunscreen and hats, then, doesn't it?"

I made a face at Artemis's cheerful tone. "Get off the couch and look for something useful, will you?"

I picked a couple of books off the shelf and checked the covers. English—mysteries, a couple of adventure thrillers, and the odd romance novel mixed in with self-discovery new-age stuff. The kinds of books you pick up at the airport to read on vacation. Though from the spines most of them looked as though they'd been only half read, then discarded. Odd—usually a vacation rental library got more use. I know I'd gone through many a hostel bookshelf on short trips. It seemed odd that these would all be left half read, with dust catching on their spines and pages. Though maybe the kind of people who would rent an apartment in Venice had better things to do than read.

"Look at this," Artemis called from across the apartment. He'd found a piece of baroque wallpaper that had been pulled free and then taped back into place. Carefully he pulled at it, revealing a bronze-colored handle behind.

He took hold of it and, with obvious effort and a generous dusting of plaster, managed to turn it. The wall creaked and split down its seam, exposing a door that opened. I did my best to clear out the cloud of dust that emerged, waving my arm. When that failed, I used my sleeve to cover my nose and mouth.

When the dust settled, it revealed an unlit wooden alcove, large enough to house a gas lamp casing and a stairwell leading down. A hidden staircase in a hidden apartment.

"Looks like our host has a voyeuristic predisposition," Artemis said, peering over my shoulder. Somehow I didn't think the voyeurism was just for looking.

Artemis's nostrils flared. "And a vampiric one."

As the dust settled, I picked up the scent. It was reminiscent of lily of the valley, which I'd started to suspect I'd find, but it was wrong—rotten wrong, as in more than usual. And it was faint. Not enough to warrant my gas mask but enough to make me wary.

I frowned as I shone my flashlight around the alcove. With the missing vacationers, I'd been expecting as much, but the scent was throwing me off.

Captain seemed attracted by the strange scent as well, sniffing the stairs and walls, then snorting, as if not sure what he'd found. With the exception of the lamp fixture it was bare; a ragged hole cut out of the wall revealing a century or so of dusty timber and bricks, the parts that needed the most structural attention hastily patched up with mismatched building supplies.

Still, it was large and wide enough for a short adult to comfortably fit inside.

"Well?" Artemis asked me.

It took me a second to realize he was asking for my opinion. "Sometimes the best hiding spots are the obvious ones no one suspects," I said, and ducked through.

Artemis followed, swearing at the plaster that rained down on us, which was more than happy to settle on his jacket and the highlights of his hair. Mine too, for that matter; the difference was I didn't care.

As soon as Artemis was through, the hidden door slid back into place behind us.

"Oh, shit!" I pushed Artemis aside as I scrambled to block the door with my foot, but it was no use. I ran my hands over the back of the door but couldn't find a release.

I aimed the flashlight down the stairs. Well, there were no screams of terror or cackling laughter—yet.

I tested the first step, easing my weight to make certain it would hold. I made it four steps before I realized that Artemis and Captain weren't behind me.

I aimed the flashlight at the two of them, still hugging the top of the stairs. "Well? Are you coming or not?"

Captain didn't need a second prodding. He darted ahead of me, sniffing nose in the air.

"Have I mentioned that I hate fucking vampires?" Artemis said, as I felt his weight settle onto the steps.

My God. We had something in common.

The stairwell was short—only a flight of steps that wound its way down. At the bottom, I narrowly missed hitting my head against a wooden ceiling beam—would have if I hadn't checked. It's amazing how something as simple as good nutrition has altered our architecture over the course of a few centuries.

"You have a bad habit of finding staircases that lead nowhere good," Artemis said. "What's under here?"

"Hard to say. Before we hit the flooded parts? Maybe another floor—two, tops—but below that? There could easily be another flooded three stories built on Roman-era dwellings. And then there's disease. A bad case of the plague or cholera and the remains of an entire family, wiped out and forgotten." I shrugged and avoided another beam; it was easier now that I had my eye out for them.

"Buried through the ages."

The scent of still water got stronger, and I could hear the canal licking against the foundations. "Or in this case drowned. Unfortunately, salty swamp water isn't great for the preservation of books and parchment." Which was what I was hoping the Illuminati and Leonardo had left behind. I stopped my descent as my flashlight reflected off shallow water a few feet below. "Careful," I said as I eased my foot under and tested the first submerged step. "You never know what's rotted until you fall through." Despite my trepidation, the first step held, as did the second. A few steps later I felt a sturdier platform under my foot.

"Let me phrase that another way. What are we looking for?"

"Besides whoever has it in for tourists?" I asked, shining the flashlight around me. There were more stairs under the water, but that wasn't what I was interested in. I aimed my flashlight beam at the image carved into the door: Leonardo da Vinci's Vitruvian man. "In a word? Da Vinci's workshop."

Artemis let out a low whistle. "So, this is where Leonardo built his weapons against the supernatural?"

"Amongst other things," I said as I checked the door for traps and whether it could be opened without collapsing. "According to the IAA records and the Vatican investigators, this was a suspected hideout of his. Off the books, of course."

"Would have thought the Vatican was all for wiping out supernaturals," Artemis said.

"Often they were, but even they balked at using the occult."

"Weren't willing to burn their own immortal souls to save everyone else's?"

"Something like that." The door seemed stable enough and, more important, wasn't locked. I pushed it open and shone my flashlight around.

It was a small, damp workshop. The workroom had a low ceiling, held up with wood beams that had accumulated an impressive amount of rot over the decades. There was an old glass oil lamp sitting on a wooden desk—also waterlogged—and an accumulation of loose-leaf papers, well, everywhere: on the desk, pinned to the wall above the desk, shoved into the numerous bookshelves that cluttered the wall space. They all had the yellow tinge and curled edges that denoted neglect. And there were candles, a lot of candles, used and mismatched, the wax dripping off the holders and cooled into puddles on the floor and furniture. As I swept the low ceiling with my flashlight beam, I spotted incandescent bulbs suspended overhead.

Somehow the idea that someone had decided to run electricity through here didn't make me feel any more comfortable.

Captain let out a growl as he crept into the room, huffing near the table's seat, trying to parse the scents, his hackles raised.

"Doesn't look like anyone has been here in a while," Artemis said, too close to my ear for comfort.

"No shit!" I jumped back into Artemis as something mechanical rumbled and sputtered to life in the workshop. Captain bleated and abandoned the puddle he'd been sniffing at warily, fleeing for the safety of my feet.

It took me a second to identify the rumbling; a water pump had turned on in the room, a jerry-rigged electric number that quickly began to drain the puddles, depositing the water somewhere behind the walls.

Well, at least whoever was down here made a passing effort to keep the water at bay—not that it made me feel any better about the electricity.

"Hello? Anyone in there?" I said, running the flashlight beam around the workshop once again.

When there was no reply, I stepped inside. No electricity coursed through me. I spotted Captain creeping up to one of the many offending puddles the pump couldn't reach. I pulled him back. "I don't need a fried cat," I told him. With no idea where the electricity had been wired, I couldn't guarantee any of the floor was safe. Any and every puddle could be lethal. Captain bleated but otherwise avoided the puddles.

As the air circulated, I picked up the same lilylike scent I'd noted on the way down, stronger this time. Though I still had no idea what the other mingling scents were, I realized what was missing: it didn't have the narcotic-like effect. There was nothing, not even a buzz to rival a bottle of glue.

"Artemis, are you certain these are vampires?" I headed to the desk and carefully began to rifle through the discarded papers, lifting their edges with the sleeve of my shirt so as not to damage them any more than the water already had.

There were scrolls and more scrolls tucked into cubbies, lying on the desk, and pinned up onto the damp plaster, as if the person behind them gave little care to their state, despite the intricate work.

"Vampire—singular," Artemis said, a frown touching his face. "I only scented one—though you're right, there is something . . . off. 'Diseased' might be the closest thing."

"I didn't think supernaturals could get sick."

"It's rare, even for vampires, and usually traces back to a wasting curse of some sort—which I definitely don't pick up a trace of—magic, that is."

I wasn't sure what was worse: a supernatural who got his kicks fulfilling a deep-seated Venetian fantasy of knocking off tourists or one who was sloppy about . . . well . . . everything.

Regardless of the absence of a narcotic-like effect, I decided it was high time to put my gas mask on. There were things besides vampire pheromones lurking in waterlogged buildings that could do damage to your lungs.

"Vampires usually seek out drier places," I said.

Instead of replying to that, Artemis asked, "What the hell is wrong with your cat?"

It took me a second to locate Captain. He'd managed to wedge half his body into a pigeonhole cabinet that had been packed with scrolls. His hind legs kicked out as he tried to wedge himself farther in.

It wasn't unusual for him to chase his nose . . .

He gave a triumphant chirp and shimmied his way out. In his mouth was a scroll, which he deposited by my feet before sitting back on his haunches and wrapping his tail around them.

I picked it up. There were traces of green algae growing on the edges, and the corners were curled with humidity.

"Blueprints—for a pump of some sort." I frowned at the signature in the corner. No, that couldn't be right. I mean, these couldn't be more than a few decades old . . .

"What?"

I checked the paper. It was a reproduction of the kind of blueprint used back in the sixteenth century, but it was definitely recent. I didn't think any paper of any kind could last down here for ten years, let alone more than five hundred. "It's signed Leonardo da Vinci—but that can't be right. The paper on its own is only a decade old at most." Meaning we had one hell of an amateur forging operation going on—I mean, screwing up the paper . . .

Unless—but there was no way. I mean, something that juicy in the supernatural community would have to have gotten out by now, wouldn't it?

Artemis began rummaging through a number of boxes filled with more papers and scrolls left haphazardly in piles, some with more blue-prints, and some sprouting drawings—completed or not.

"I wondered what that smell was," he said. "It's been a long while. Chemicals for pressing paper—ah, here we go."

Lo and behold, underneath the last box, hidden under the pack rat–like collection, was an old paper press. "I remember these coming into fashion—expensive as hell to make paper this way." He glanced at me. "Strange, why not just buy paper?"

I frowned. Parts of it had been modernized—in patches, the modern metals and plastics gleaming under my flashlight—which made no sense. As Artemis had said, why not just buy paper? Even if our vampire was a recluse, it wasn't as though there weren't options. If he could organize an online B&B listing, he could use an online retailer . . .

"Fake or not, do you have any idea what these could be worth?" Artemis said, holding up one of the sketches.

I picked up a box full of discarded pump parts—salvageable, if not for the fact that they had been left to soak in a corner. Most of the metal was irrevocably rusted and warped out of shape, not worth selling even for the scrap. "I don't think our vampire is running with a full set of screws and gears," I replied.

I was briefly tempted to lift a few but I've never been one to peddle fakes. Even thieves have their low bars. "If I could spot it as a fake, so will an art expert." And I wasn't here for paintings or blueprints; I was looking for a link to the Tiger Thieves. I kept sorting through the items on the desk, wondering what the hell it was I was looking for exactly.

I noticed that Artemis had stopped searching through the boxes and shelves and had tilted his head to the side, his nostrils flared, as if he was appraising something. Even Captain stopped his rummaging to watch.

He didn't stand there for long. He went over to a pile of boxes on one of the shelves that neither of us had yet reached and began to pull them down. He narrowed in on a single box and brought it out after giving it a shake that sent the contents rattling against the wood. Then he opened it and held it out to me. "I think this may be what you're looking for," he said. "It smells like your amulet—faint but there."

Inside was a small wooden box that, unlike everything else in the room, hadn't rotted or warped away. It still retained its polished veneer and sported painted decorations. The hinges on the lid still worked.

I peered inside and found a collection of wooden and metal tubes, each lined with a series of numbers and letters on the outside—hieroglyphs, Latin, even some more ancient texts . . .

Hello, what did we have here?

I removed one of the wooden cylinders from the box, one whose letters had been covered with gold lines not unlike the ones on my Tiger Thief medallion: four heavy streaks of gold with smaller lines crisscrossing in an undetermined pattern and no alphabet I recognized.

"They reek of magic—supernatural," Artemis clarified, seeing my expression. I'd had enough run-ins with human-made magic that any mention of it usually sent my blood pressure soaring.

Not that supernatural magic was any better . . .

The problems with supernatural magic came when people tried to use it. Supernatural magic was never meant to be used by humans, only supernaturals. Think explosions, natural disasters, uncontrolled curses—and that was the bright side. Humans weren't meant to read or enact supernatural magic, yet that didn't seem to stop anyone from trying.

"God knows Leonardo da Vinci had a reputation for working with magic things he shouldn't have," Artemis said.

"You said he was a hunter? Of the supernatural?"

Artemis *tsk*ed. "Well, the Illuminati certainly were, but him? Who knows if he got his hands dirty? He was a genius, and his inventions were certainly used for those purposes—weapons, traps, devices of generic torture—though whether that was his original intent is debated."

"What else could his intent have been?" I asked as I rummaged through another box, this one filled with parts of half-built contraptions.

"Be careful with those, they reek of magic. And to answer your question, many things get repurposed from their original intentions. The weapons may have been designed to save people from the more nefarious of our kind—vampires, goblins, skin walkers, even the odd ghoul that decided it couldn't wait for the morgue to fill and decided to hasten things along." He nodded towards the desk, which still sported a pile of blueprints, one for a particularly nasty-looking pike sitting on top. "Take that, for example. For keeping goblins out of the canals, if I read the pictures right." He shrugged again. "Or perhaps he simply liked torturing supernaturals. I doubt it. The truly creatively gifted rarely go that route."

Another thought occurred to me. "How many of these do you think he actually made?"

"Hard to tell," Artemis said from the workbench he was investigating on the other side of the room. "I imagine he tried most of them. He went so far as to draw up the blueprints, seems like a lot of trouble to go to and not try them out." He glanced at the box I was holding. "See that club?"

At first glance I thought it was a simple wooden club—innocuous, not unlike a lot of other crude weapons—but as Artemis moved it under the gas-lamp light, I caught the glint of light reflecting off the etchings.

"Silver etched with lead," Artemis opined. "What you might call a brownie or pixie bat."

"Brownies?" Brownies were a rare subset of the fairy family—pixies, leprechauns, nixies, anything small with wings was pretty well known except for brownies, the veritable penguins of the fairy world . . . "They're harmless."

"A nuisance, yes, but not always benign. Their populations have shrunk and they tend to shy away from civilization, but back in Leonardo's day they were worse than a warren of rats under your bed and more aggressive; no one's larder was safe. When they got desperate, particularly in an island city like this, it wasn't unusual for them to suffocate the odd dowager or even an infant to free up space and food. Definitely not harmless."

I put the club back down. "What's this one?" I asked, picking up a silver metal ball.

Artemis peered at it, then shuffled through the blueprints. "Ah—I believe that's supposed to be a sunlight grenade of some sort."

Hunh. I discreetly slid it into my pocket. Could never have enough small, easily transported vampire deterrents . . .

Weapons. There were a lot of them, some of which Lady Siyu and Mr. Kurosawa might be interested in, but nothing reminiscent of the Tiger Thieves except the cylinder. No hints, no inklings . . .

"And what do we have here . . ." His voice trailed off as he stared at something under the pile of blueprints. "I, ah, think I found your tourists—or one of them," Artemis said, holding up a skeletal hand. I cringed; it was small—likely the woman's.

I spotted something silver on the wall, hidden behind the collections of pictures and blueprints. I pushed one of the papers aside. It was a mirror, an old one with bits of the silver chipped out. I stared at my reflection. I still looked gaunt, but in the dim light it was less noticeable than it had been in daylight. My hair was a mess, damp from the humidity.

I winced as the twinge of a headache hit me. I wanted to shut my eyes, but I couldn't look away from the mirror.

My face dissolved before my eyes as Rynn's came into view. He did not look happy. The pain in my head blossomed, and I pressed my forehead. Still, I couldn't tear my eyes off the mirror.

"*I'll warn you once, Alix. Stay out of my way.*" His lips didn't move, but his voice was clear and painful inside my head.

"Owl?" Artemis said.

Whatever spell the mirror had over me vanished. I shut my eyes tight and pressed my cool hands into my forehead. When I opened them, Artemis was glaring at me but any sense of Rynn had vanished. I glanced back at the mirror.

No sign of Rynn there either, only the chipped mirror and my reflection.

"What happened?" Artemis asked, still frowning.

I glanced up at the mirror one more time. Only my own reflection. I shook myself out of it. It was the proximity of Artemis and his resemblance to Rynn—plus the fact I was close to two months of running on empty.

"Nothing," I said. "Ah, just lack of sleep and probably low oxygen getting the best of me." Artemis didn't look like he believed me, so I added, "Really. Just my imagination playing tricks on me. I found a mirror. Scared myself." And really, what was more plausible? That my paranoid brain was inventing new and interesting ways to terrify me or that Rynn had found a way to haunt me?

Artemis shook his head. "I think I saw a vent in the stairwell. I want to make certain no one is waiting to ambush us, sick vampire or not. Stay here."

Fine with me, there were a number of blueprints I wanted to go through . . . now, what was this? Under one of the blueprints was a collection of papers with a close scrawl in Latin, clipped together with a modern paper clip.

At first I tried to cure the consumption myself with the supernatural element, but that has proved futile, not without a more powerful specimen, which I have little faith we will come across.

Tuberculosis. Not a lot of cures for that back then . . . I skimmed the pages, wondering if they'd been written by my sick vampire. I had to admit, I had no idea what happened if a terminally ill person was turned—did he or she get better? Stay sick? Or get worse? It was a good question.

A few poor fairies—a nymph, I think. Though their humors gave me relief from the symptoms it was temporary and unsustainable, since I had to drain both to create the elixir. I have one hope left, a vampiric gentleman who was apprehended last night by my brothers in the Illuminati. They still believe I am working on the device. I hate to deceive them, but if the consumption takes me before I finish, they will have no weapon. The lie is essential.

At least this one I thankfully won't feel guilt about experimentation. Not like the others.

Brothers in the Illuminati? Shit, this must be the accounts of Leonardo da Vinci—or one of his assistants.

I continued to flip. Sure enough, the author signed himself Leonardo da Vinci. Madman or the real thing, the experiments documented were real enough.

His quest for the elixir of youth had started off well, but as his condition deteriorated, so had his desperation until it read like an obsession. I don't think even he realized what had happened. The experiments got more reckless as did the type of supernaturals he was using; he was even mixing blood types, convinced that he'd eventually stumble upon the right mix. Completely and utterly obsessed . . . I reached the second-to-last page, where he described taking a vampire's blood along with that of another hapless pixie and nymph. I turned the page, a macabre branch of my curiosity wanting to know what had happened.

I frowned. There was no mention of the results, no more theories on pixies, nixies, types of metal needed to catalyze the reaction. Instead, the next few pages were covered with lines—patterns of them with nonsensical text scrawled underneath.

It wasn't a code or script I recognized. Supernatural, maybe? Leonardo had been crazy enough to play with their magic after all. "Hey, Artemis," I called out. "Come see if you can make anything out." I traced the lines with my finger. Even the gold ink used was similar.

Something crashed behind me, and I just about dropped the book. Captain stopped his mapping of the pigeonhole cabinet as well and reared his head.

"Artemis?" I called out, partially to see if it had been him and to call him if it hadn't. There was no reply—or any more movement.

But whether that was a good or a bad sign . . .

Captain jumped up on the table and bleated at me. Absently I patted his head as he nosed the pages of the journal, taking in their scent. "If you're not worried, I'm not worried," I told him. After all, what good was a vampire detection system if you didn't pay attention—

Shit! I grabbed at the arms that had sneaked around my neck.

"Ah, I see you've found my journal. I was wondering where that had gotten to," said a raspy older voice. I winced as warm breath laced with rotten lily of the valley and something else rotten—like flesh—descended over me.

New lesson, Owl, even the best detection systems fail . . .

"And you found Diana. I rather liked her and her family, wonderful conversationalists from the East Coast of America. I had hoped I'd be able to restrain myself, but alas, it wasn't to be.

"Now, normally I'd be polite and see if you wouldn't scream, but I'd rather not deal with your incubus friend at the moment, so . . ."

A canvas bag was slid over my head, and the rope noose tightened. A moment later I heard a muffled yelp as Captain was shoved into his own canvas bag. Then the chloroform hit.

Goddamn it. I hate it when I'm too unconscious to cause a scene.

6

FAILURE TO LAUNCH

Early evening: Just below the waterline of Venice.

I came to seated in a chair this time. The sloshing water woke me—and the cold sensation that engulfed my feet, which were submerged up to my ankles. Considering my boots and legs were soaked but the first chills of hypothermia hadn't set in, I guessed I'd been sitting here for ten to twenty minutes.

I checked my hands, but no restraints had been placed around them. In fact, I found I was completely free to move. The relief at not being tied up was short-lived—about as long as it took to realize that I couldn't see.

I remembered the canvas bag tossed hastily over my head and pulled tight—and the off scent of rotting lily of the valley. I blindly felt for the bag, and, finding the rough canvas, I felt for the string. I found an intricate knot and began to work my fingers into it, feeling to loosen it. I did a mental check: no grogginess, no problem with motor control. Whatever kind of vampire this da Vinci was—and there was no doubt in my mind that that's what he had to be—his pheromones were faulty, as was his regeneration if I read the scent of rotting flesh right. Somehow I didn't think a sick vampire was necessarily better than the healthy version—not when both tried to eat you and one wasn't packing a full set of painkillers. I also picked up traces of mildew and chemicals, reminiscent of oil paints.

Before I could parse out any more scents, the canvas bag was pulled off my head with a flourish.

"Let us try that again. You don't scream, and I won't use the chloroform on you and the Mau again, yes?"

Crouched in front of me, holding the bag in one hand, was possibly the strangest old man I'd ever seen. Long salt-and-pepper hair that hadn't been cut in years fell around his shoulders, and he had a beard to match. His clothing was in tatters and arranged in an odd array: a long canvas parka worn over rough jeans and tied with what looked like a combination of leather belts. A heavy wool shawl thrown over his shoulders added to the strangeness, giving his attire an old-fashioned effect despite the obviously modern pieces.

Old, unattractive, and with a lack of interest in fashion and grooming: all in all, it was the least likely looking vampire scenario I'd ever seen. Either through conscious selection or as a side effect of being turned, vampires were normally as fastidious as cats when it came to hygiene and grooming.

In fact, if it hadn't been for the lily of the valley smell, I'd have debated whether or not this was a vampire at all.

Vampires were the cockroaches of the supernatural world, but they were one of the only ones that started off as human. In contrast to the vampire legends, they didn't acquire super strength or powers of persuasion. What they did get was a secretable aromatic pheromone that had an opiate-like sedation effect on any nearby humans. It was a high that was as pleasant and addictive as heroin. Victims didn't always even know they were being preyed upon by vampires. They just kept going back for more until there was very little left of them but a living, breathing junkie whose only desire in life was to do the vampire's bidding. It wasn't a nice way to live, and they were used and discarded more often than not.

The point was that even the youngest vampire could incapacitate an adult human. A trace of pheromones alone should have me reduced to Owl-flavored Jell-O. Yet here I was. Cringing.

He smiled absently, showing me his slightly elongated incisors. They were a tartar-stained yellow. Again, not typical for a vampire.

I spotted the source of the chemical scents across the shallow room, set out on the easel below a half-finished piece of artwork, one that hadn't been in the workshop before. I got a glimpse of it: a macabre and beautiful work, featuring a family of four in various stages of decay.

"Ah—my last guests. Do you like it?"

I turned my attention back to my supposed Leonardo. "You know, I think you're really missing out on ironic comedy. You should really try to pass these off and watch the art experts sweat."

That earned me a laugh. "Thinking of escaping, are we? Don't lie, I saw you glance about my workshop. Not a bad survival strategy, running from predators, though I suggest you look up before you set your mind to it."

I did—still keeping the vampire in my sights.

Shit. Above me, suspended from pulleys, was a spiked metal ball large enough to take both me and the chair out, along with a decent chunk of the floor.

"If your weight shifts even a fraction, the spike is rigged to fall. It is quite deadly. I thought it would be a greater incentive to keep your half of the conversation civil."

"A little overkill, don't you think?" I asked but still shuffled my ass so it was square in the center of the chair. Even if he was bluffing, those pulleys and ropes didn't look stable.

"As I was saying earlier," Leonardo said, "I have a problem with eating people I like. As much as I try, my acquaintances never seem to last that long. It used to bother me, but now I find the best thing for my mind and soul is to accept the inevitable, enjoy the moment, and do my best to record their memory on canvas, yes?"

The fact that he was confessing to being an uncontrolled, impulsive serial killer who knocked off online vacation tourists because he couldn't help himself did not put me at ease, particularly the fact that he seemed to be asking me to admit it was okay. Over my dead body—scratch that, *not* over my dead body . . .

I noticed a canvas bag on the floor tucked underneath the table in a shallow puddle. It wriggled and huffed, then let out a forlorn mew. Even this close, though, Captain wasn't close to his normal vampire reaction. I did another mental check. No pheromone effects at all. I could smell the rotting lily of the valley, but even this close it did nothing.

Maybe da Vinci wasn't a vampire; maybe he just smelled like one . . . sort of.

I peered at his features, searching for the telltale signs of vampirism. Leonardo's deflated and wrinkled face smiled back at me, exposing his yellow fangs.

I swallowed. Just because he wasn't a normal vampire didn't mean he wasn't dangerous.

"Please understand that I don't want to hurt anyone, it's simply in my nature now, like a cat killing a mouse when there's a full bowl of food. But I do love conversations. I hoped we could have one," he added as he turned towards a desk to choose a new brush. I spotted the journal out in the open. Yeah, I was going to need that . . .

"Tell me, what is it you and the incubus are looking for?"

I hesitated. At the moment he wasn't trying to eat me. Once I gave him what he wanted? All bets were off.

Leonardo's upper lip curled as he *tsk*ed, the first sign I'd seen of displeasure. He turned his back on me, and I heard the sound of rustling papers.

At least there wasn't anything in reach that could lend itself to violence . . .

I heard the clink of metal out of my line of sight, heavier than a paint spatula or brush. He flashed me another yellowed, toothy smile and held up a set of pliers stained a brown that I didn't think was rust.

He held them up. "I find that fingernails are very effective. You will tell me what I wish to know, yes?"

When a crazed vampire threatens to torture you for information and has the stained tools to back it up, tell it whatever the hell it wants to know. Holding out is for martyrs and heroes.

I nodded and held up my hands. "No need for a manicure."

He smiled again and nodded as he shuffled towards me, wet slippers slopping against the floorboards. "After, yes?" he said, holding up the tools again. "After I take a fingernail or two, you won't be tempted to lie." He paused. "Or maybe I'll take all of them—for my collection."

I realized that the painting I'd been admiring of the American tourists was a collage made of delicately painted fingernails.

Leonardo closed in on me. I leaned back as far as I could without sliding off the chair. "I'm looking for the Tiger Thieves, all right?"

The pliers paused. "Ahh, I suspected as much," he said, and held up my amulet, the gold lines glinting in the lamplight. He narrowed in on me, grasping both my shoulders with his bony hands, the chair rocking back as his rancid breath washed over me. I glanced up at the spiked ball now rocking precariously overhead.

"Did they tell you to come after me, flush poor Leonardo out?"

Oh, Oricho was going to get an earful about not doing due diligence . . . "No! I just want to find them, that's all. I swear!"

His face took on a manic panic, and he began searching the room with his reddened eyes. "You're working for them, aren't you?" I flinched as neutered vampire spittle sprayed over my face. "Are they here? Is that why you're still here talking to me?"

"No. I'm still sitting here because you rigged a spiked cannonball over my head. Trust me, if it wasn't there, I'd be long gone."

"I don't believe you." He spat on the floor and searched the room again, his eyes turning an angry red. "I wouldn't put it past them—lurking, teasing me, laughing at me." He snorted. "You never know when the Tiger Thieves are watching, manipulating you—they're tricky that way." He turned back to his desk to rummage angrily once again. I saw where he placed my amulet—on the open page of the red journal.

A piece of canvas was jostled, uncovering a new piece he was working on: me and Captain, immortalized for the ages with terror-stricken faces.

"What a coincidence you came down here when you did. I'd given up on finding any more of these. You do know what it is, don't you?"

Best course of action? Play along with him until I figured out a better course of action.

I offered him a slow nod. "It's a Tiger Thief amulet. It's supposed to lead to the Tiger Thieves."

The madness left Leonardo and he nodded back at me with clear eyes. He held up his hand, and I realized he was holding a second amulet. "Not perhaps so much as a guide but as a puzzle to solve. The Tiger Thieves are a reclusive lot, but you are correct, these amulets are the key. I've been trying to find them for a very long time, hundreds of years now, I believe. I think they can help me with my"—he paused as if searching for a word—"predicament," he finally settled on.

That was one way to put it.

"An unfortunate one, a very long time ago, and one of many mistakes of which I've since lost count. All that blood . . ." he trailed off, apparently remembering something more pleasant.

Come on, Owl, think of a way to get out of here before you become dinner.

"The amulets," I tried, nodding at the two still clasped in his hand.

"Ah yes! The Tiger Thieves—where was I? They are not altruistic, as the stories make them out to be—or easy to find. Malcontents and rebels one and all—set on visiting their form of justice on the supernatural communities. I suppose you've heard that they're the righteous, the helpful?" His eyes reddened once again, the anger returning. "You'd be wrong. Otherwise they would have helped me a long time ago. History is written by the survivors, and there were not many back when they roamed the Silk Road. Now? In this modern era? They say nothing at all." He gave me a toothy smile before shuffling back to his desk. "Rather like me."

I was relieved that the rotting mix of scents retreated, giving my nose a reprieve.

"It's been a long time since I remembered the Tiger Thieves and their amulet," he said. "So I suppose I have you to thank for that. Did I mention I do like visitors? Blood really is quite the distraction, especially with global travel in this time. So many flavors and delicacies."

Okay, Owl, keep him off the topic of fresh blood . . . "What happened to my companion?"

"Ah, your incubus friend? I fear he is indisposed at the moment." Leonardo stood up and pulled back a brown-stained cloth. Underneath was Artemis, unconscious and prone. Leonardo crouched over him and with a heavy glass syringe removed a sample of the incubus's blood. Artemis didn't so much as wince. So much for the cavalry.

Keep Leonardo off the topic of blood . . . "I've never heard of anyone—supernatural or otherwise—able to reverse a turning," I said cautiously.

Leonardo clucked his tongue. "Ah, yes, but that would require a true turning, now, wouldn't it? And though I share some of their traits, even your cat has discovered that I'm not a vampire—not truly, at any rate."

Something I'd come across in his journal struck me, about the elixir components he'd experimented with—pixies, incubi, fairies—vampires . . .

"You did this to yourself, didn't you?" It also explained why Artemis had been confused by his scent. "And you think the Tiger Thieves can fix you?" I felt a spike of hope surface. If they could fix Leonardo, why not Rynn? Whatever the elves had done to the Electric Samurai armor couldn't be worse than what da Vinci had done to himself.

Leonardo hissed at me, flashing his canines and the reddened whites of his eyes. "Can? Certainly. But will they? Of course not. Why would they want to save Leonardo? Did this to myself—an eye for an eye, they like to think." He spat and it hit the water, sending out shallow ripples. "Warnings? They never warned me of this." His eyes flickered for a moment as his sneer turned into a grin. "Eye for an eye, they'll learn what Leonardo can do." He shook a cardboard box filled with objects not unlike the one Artemis had found.

My stomach turned as I saw another silver bat peek over the edge. A weapon against the supernatural.

"Revenge. It's one of the few things that keeps me from draining every human I encounter." He glanced at me. "Well, I suppose *delay* is a more accurate word." He glanced up at the ceiling. "Or perhaps *whet my appetite*," he said, picking up the canvas bag holding Captain.

Captain, as if sensing the shift in attention, growled and lashed out, his claws cutting through the canvas and grazing Leonardo's chest. Da Vinci, apparently aware of what a Mau could do, stumbled back.

He turned on me and let out a snarl, once again flashing his yellow fangs. "You put your Mau up to that, didn't you? And here I thought we were being civil."

Time to bargain before da Vinci's sanity could slip any further. "Look, we're both trying to find the Tiger Thieves. Wouldn't it make more sense to"—I was about to say "work together," but not even the most gullible would buy that—"share information?"

Da Vinci considered that and smiled. "I'll tell you what, give me the incubus and I'll tell you everything I know about the Tiger Thieves, hmmm?"

Wow. This was a conundrum. Throw Artemis under the bus in exchange for information on the Tiger Thieves, or try to save him. I mean, in general I'm against the idea of handing anyone over to vampires, but it was Artemis . . . Sometimes I really hate my conscience . . . not that it wasn't tempting, but considering his current state, I didn't think da Vinci was one to pay the fuck up on his deals.

"No offense, but leaving him here wouldn't be doing you any favors. Isn't the serum what got you into this mess in the first place?" Da Vinci's smile fell. I added, "And I'm not at all certain you'll hold up your end of the deal."

His smile returned. "Isn't that one of the spices of life? Uncertainty?

Consider it a hypothesis. Will I or will I not kill you? Or perhaps I've found another way to outwit you."

At first I thought the movement was my imagination—Artemis was still lying on the floor, his eyes closed. Then I saw his index finger twitch, followed by a tapping sound, barely audible over the water . . . it was a song, one of Artemis's from the late nineties, "I Have a Plan."

Because relying on Artemis's plans was such a fantastic idea.

I gave a quick, slight shake of my head when da Vinci turned back to his desk, hoping Artemis would see it.

"Now, where's that syringe?" da Vinci mumbled, back to the harmless-old-man routine. "It's a special one—I know I left it somewhere around here—ah!" He turned back to face me, a long glass syringe in his hand, much larger than the one he'd just used. "You know, in all of my elixir experiments, I never once tried spinal fluids—I think that's something to be explored, no?"

The tapping from Artemis increased in intensity, changing the rhythm while he kept his eyes shut. Another song, this one called "More Time."

I made a face.

"And of course I'll need to try the Mau blood."

What the—? I whipped my head up.

"And possibly some of the other fluids. It's hard to say what will work, but I'm hopeful your Mau's antivampiric properties will counteract the less savory side effects of the vampirism keeping me alive."

I glanced back at Artemis. One of his eyes was open. I mouthed "fine" at him. Buy the incubus more time from the psychotic vampire. I just hoped Artemis's plan involved getting all of us out. With my luck he'd be gone before I could scream.

I watched da Vinci as he worked, mumbling to himself—*dilutions, order, purification* all reached my ears—but it reeked of the ramblings of a man driven mad by desperation and obsession.

Desperation. Maybe that was my ticket.

I kept the journal and the pendants in my sights. "Look, why not try the Tiger Thieves again? It's had to have been what? Five hundred years?"

"Those glorified assassins?" da Vinci hissed. "The ones responsible for my decrepit predicament?"

I swallowed at the way da Vinci held the spinal syringe as if it were a knife, his thin hands turning white. The Tiger Thieves were definitely a sore spot. Kudos, Owl, you guessed right—though I doubted there was any kind of door prize.

I did not like the look of those fangs. "Well, you know, even the supernaturally inclined have to change management occasionally—I'd imagine after five hundred years it'd be worthwhile to try them again. I mean, who knows? They might be more willing to listen to you now—shit." I leaned back as da Vinci closed in on me, rattling the spiked ball hanging above my head. Artemis still hadn't done a damn thing.

"Supernatural?" da Vinci snorted. "The Tiger Thieves are poor imitations, the lot of them. Not worth the time of day compared to what I achieved. They're as much at odds with the real supernaturals as paltry humans such as yourself."

Not that I wasn't fixated on the swinging spiked ball suspended overhead, but even I couldn't help catching what he had said. Not supernatural or human? Now, that was interesting. I filed that tidbit away and nodded to the box he'd been rifling through. "All the better, then. I mean, I'd think they'd be interested in your devices now—like that one," I said as he lifted a small, smooth metallic orb that had been broken into two pieces out of the box.

Another huff from da Vinci. I could smell the mildew and algae that had taken up residence in his clothes over the years. The ones he'd probably stolen from his victims.

"This old thing?" he asked, holding up the orb. "It barely works. It was supposed to drain supernaturals of all their powers, but it does little more than wound them. Tried it on a vampire once. It died a wretched death, screaming in agony while it shriveled into a dusty corpse. One of my failures, that."

"You kidding? That sounds pretty fantastic to me. All right, you're right! It's one of your biggest failures, my mistake." I cringed as I smelled his acrid breath, devoid of the bacteria smell but rotting nonetheless—rotting while he lived. But the look on his face— I hazarded a glance at Artemis. I hoped to hell he'd made some progress . . . oh, you have got to be fucking kidding me.

Gone. He was gone. Completely fucking gone. He hadn't even bothered to loosen the tie on Captain's canvas bag prison.

Ungrateful, lousy, no-good—

"Any last words?" da Vinci whispered. His eyes had turned a weepy red. He licked his lips, running them over the yellow fangs. "I'm truly sorry about this, but I believe I have enough sketched here to remember you and your cat by."

I glanced back up at the metal spikes glinting above me. Da Vinci was oblivious as he loomed over me. I held my breath—not to keep out the vampire pheromones or whatever neutered version he produced—but to keep out the miasma of the lingering death that shrouded him.

I'd have to time it perfectly . . .

"That is the nature of my cursed existence. But you know what they say, genius always suffers for art."

His fangs were extended, the saliva gleaming as he gripped my hand and turned the wrist over, exposing my blue-green veins. "I'd like to say I'll only take a bite, but I'm afraid I won't be able to stop. It really has been lovely meeting you."

I glanced back up at the cannonball. Please let this work . . . "Wish I could say the same," I said. As soon as he bent to bite my wrist, I kicked back the chair with as much force as I could muster.

The world went in slow motion, and for a brief moment I watched the cannonball detach from the pulleys. My chair fell backwards, but caught in vampiric bloodlust da Vinci didn't—or couldn't—let go. His eyes went wide as realization struck him, but it was too late. The cannonball struck as the back of my chair crashed to the floor. I only heard the spikes crunch into his skull—and saw the aftermath as I scrambled up. Captain bleated in his bag, sensing that he'd missed a fight. I pushed myself up and went to untie him. "Trust me, this wasn't the vampire fight you wanted. Who knows whether your saliva would even have made a dent?"

Captain grumbled but settled for sniffing at the body. Da Vinci might have stumbled across an elixir of longevity, but it sure hadn't been one of immortality—as his very dead and mangled corpse told me.

Normally I'd celebrate a near-death escape. On the one hand, I'd gotten rid of a serial killer; on the other, he had been a victim—one of his own making but a victim nonetheless. I couldn't celebrate that.

"Well, that was quite the show. Not the way I would have done it—"

Artemis was leaning casually against the small door frame. My anger returned in spectacular form. "*Buy me time*? So what, you could save your own skin?"

If my tone bothered him, he showed no sign of it. "You got out. Both of us did, and without losing anything." He frowned as he glanced at da Vinci's corpse. "Well, except maybe for your dignity. Do you realize who you just killed? Possibly one of the greatest minds your species has ever spawned."

"He was a decrepit vampire."

He seemed to think about that as he crouched down by da Vinci's body. "Be that as it may, you've more than lived up to your reputation of destroying ancient sites. I mean, technically—"

"Technically I killed a serial killer vampire who was about to eat me."

Artemis didn't look convinced. He was the *last* person I needed to sway to my side. "Look, just wait there while I look through his things and, I don't know, entertain my cat."

Artemis said something under his breath but otherwise did as I asked—namely stayed back. While I rummaged through the desk, Artemis examined da Vinci's corpse.

"Not that I socialize with many vampires, but are they supposed to look this decrepit?"

I shook my head as I checked the journal to make certain it was the one with the references to the Tiger Thieves. It was. "No. Granted, the oldest vampire I've met is only three centuries. I've seen vampire flunkies look like that but it's more a consequence of pheromone addiction." The Tiger Thief pendants were both lying on the desk next to the wooden box da Vinci had been rummaging through, the one with the broken weapons. I picked up both of the necklaces and ran my fingers over the gold lines that decorated each before tucking them both inside my jacket. I paused, my eyes falling on the box.

I couldn't resist. I picked up the broken silver orb da Vinci had claimed could drain a supernatural of their power and rolled it over in my hand. It looked simple enough: a silver sphere split almost in half, the halves hanging on to each other by metal chains and copper threads, decorated with small pinpoint-precise holes and other markings I imagined had to be arcane.

Broken things could be fixed. I began to search the desk for blueprints that matched the orb.

"What is that?" Artemis asked from where he was now emptying da Vinci's pockets. I had a disturbing flashback to the peculiar looting style of World Quest, where the longer you looked for treasure on a victim the rougher things got—disturbingly so . . .

With a shiver I exiled that to the back of my mind. This was not World Quest, and Artemis didn't have da Vinci by the ankles to shake him out.

"Not sure," I said, which was partially true. "But I got the impression da Vinci thought the Tiger Thieves might be interested in it." Not entirely untrue. They *might* be interested in it. I certainly was.

Now, where the hell were the blueprints?

Even though I had my back to Artemis, I got the sinking suspicion he wanted to argue as I rifled through the piles of papers. He didn't get a chance.

Both of us came to a standstill at the sound of a crash upstairs, as if a door—or a wall—had been broken in.

I waited to hear footsteps or voices but none followed. "Maybe it was an act of God?" Lack of structural integrity, a beam that was destined to go and just happened to do so now?

Artemis shook his head. "That was intentional."

"Vampires or another monster?"

He shook his head once more. "The monsters don't make that much noise."

That narrowed it down to a whopping two possibilities. Either someone had stumbled into the old rooms—unlikely—or someone had come looking for us. "IAA," I said. It was my best guess, plus they were experts at bad timing . . .

The building shook once more, but it wasn't an earthquake or questionable structural integrity. It had been an explosion, I'd bet what was left of my thieving reputation on it. This time the murmur of voices reached us.

"Since when does the IAA use explosives?" Artemis asked.

I shook my head. "They don't." Which meant it was someone else. I knew one group after artifacts that had no issues throwing around small explosives. Mercenaries. And Rynn and his crew were the only ones with a reason to be following me.

Artemis came to the same conclusion. He checked the stairwell from the cover of the workshop. He darted back just as quickly, shutting the workshop door and throwing the lock. He grabbed my arm. "All right, change in plans. Can you keep the cat quiet?"

The question caught me off guard. "Except for vampires? Usually."

Apparently that was good enough. He pulled me towards one of da Vinci's closets and began throwing out enough contents that the two of us could fit inside.

Then he tried shoving me and Captain in. "Hiding in a closet? Are you out of your mind?"

"Trust me."

"No!"

Artemis glanced over his shoulder as footsteps hurried down the staircase. They'd reach the small platform in no time if they hadn't already, and then they'd be breaking down the door. Sure enough, the battering ram started pounding the door and shaking the room.

Artemis pursed his lips and shoved me and Captain inside before getting in himself and shutting the door.

"Wait a minute—" The rest of my sentence was muffled by Artemis's hand.

"I understand your reluctance to trust me, but believe me when I say I have no intention of running into my illustrious warlord cousin today."

I tried pulling his damned hand off my mouth. When that didn't work, I pinched him as hard as I could.

"If I take my hand off, will you keep your bloody voice to a whisper?"

I glared but nodded. Even if I wanted to find a different way out, I'd be hard pressed before they broke down the door. Besides, there might not be one.

Slowly he unmuffled me, searching my face for any sign that I might ignore his warning.

"What I was trying to say," I whispered, "is that the closet is the worst place to hide." The battering ram hit the door to the workshop again and fragments of plaster and wood rained down on us.

Artemis's upper lip curled. "No, it isn't," he hissed back.

The room shook once more, this time accompanied by a cracking sound. "Are you out of your mind? As soon as they see the body, this is the first place they'll check! If we were smart, we would have hid the body in here and looked for another way out!"

"They won't see us."

I would have said more, but at that moment the wooden door gave one last shriek and we heard boots pour in.

I froze in place, hands wrapped around Captain, and watched through the closet door cracks.

It wasn't just Rynn's mercenaries. In the lead, framed in the workshop entrance, was none other than Rynn. He was dressed in the same modern body armor he'd been wearing in Shangri-La, the Electric Samurai's modern guise. He looked like any other mercenary—only he wasn't. The Electric Samurai armor and the twisted spell the elves had cast had corrupted Rynn to the core. And for what? All because the elves had wanted to reclaim Rynn and force him into the mold of their perfect warrior. It had gone woefully wrong. To be honest, Rynn really didn't look that different. That was something the Electric Samurai was very good at, blending in with the times.

It was his expression that gave him away, just like it had in the mirror, the pale blue eyes so different from his normal blue-gray. It lent the rest of his face an icy expression, as if all the warmth had been sucked out. Behind Rynn I noted a handful of mercenaries, some of whom I recognized from Shangri-La, Zebras who'd fallen behind. They looked odd. Their faces were blank, devoid of any expression. They focused solely on Rynn, as if waiting to act on his slightest whim.

I held my breath as Rynn took another step closer and peered around the workshop before settling his attention on the closet. It was as if he could see me right through the cracks.

"Open the closet," Rynn said.

Artemis squeezed my shoulder in warning. "Keep quiet and perfectly still," he breathed into my ear as one of Rynn's mercenaries approached the door. The flashlight beam danced through the cracks. Cursory inspection done, he gripped the handle.

There was no way he'd miss us.

I shut my eyes and gripped Captain as the door opened and the flashlight beam fell on us—

"Nothing here," the mercenary said.

I opened my eyes. Two mercenaries stood outside the closet, staring at us, and I stared back in terror. But they didn't react, didn't attack. They didn't see us.

Rynn himself came over and peered into the closet. He didn't see us either, though he seemed less able to believe it. His nostrils flared as he sniffed the air and his eyes turned a lighter shade of blue. So much colder and more calculating since the last time I'd seen him in Shangri-La.

I thanked an assortment of gods that Captain decided to stay quiet as Rynn's cold eyes ran over us, once, then twice.

"Boss?"

Rynn looked away from me at the mercenary who had called him. "I found something," the man said in a monotone, mechanical-sounding voice.

When Rynn moved, I was able to see what the brainwashed mercenary had found: a ragged hole in the wall large enough for someone to crawl through. I guess da Vinci had created his own exits.

Rynn examined the hole, then stood up, once again running his eyes over the room. "They were here. I can smell the cat—and a faint trace of her." He nodded towards the canvas, the portrayal of terrified me and Captain. "And that proves it. Find them."

It looked as if they might all leave, but Rynn halted just shy of the door. His eyes narrowed, and he took a step back towards our hiding spot. I held my breath. He might not be able to see us, but if he decided to feel around . . .

Or to hell with it and just shoot.

But partway he stopped. If I hadn't known Rynn better, I'd have said he was second-guessing himself—which I'd never seen him do before. Maybe the Electric Samurai wasn't as well integrated as we'd thought. Maybe Rynn was still in there somewhere, fighting.

"Check the rest of the building. Don't let them slip through our grasp," he said, heading for the stairs. "All the floors and the water below. Owl isn't above a dip in putrid water."

The mercenaries fell into line with robot-like compliance, but not until the last one had left the workshop did I breathe again. It was Artemis who spoke first. "I don't know about you, but after that effort I don't have much left." His skin was covered with a thin layer of sweat, and he sounded winded.

I nodded. "My contribution? We run like hell."

"All for it. Which way, oh fearless leader?"

Good question. I inclined my head. As far as I could tell, the mercenaries and Rynn had split up after they'd left the workshop. "Think you can pull that trick again? If it were only one or two?"

"Not even if all I had to do was fool a pigeon. Do you realize what it took to hide us from my cousin?" He trailed off. "Do you hear that?"

"What? Mercenaries?"

"No. Running water—a lot of it."

I tilted my head to the side as I wrangled with Captain, who'd also decided now was the time to leave. Faintly I picked up the sound of running water, stronger than the dripping that was in the workshop—and there was the sound of something else as well, underneath the noise.

"It sounds like pumps—heavier than the ones he used in here," he whispered as one of the mercenaries passed by just outside the open door.

I'd wondered how da Vinci had gotten around the flooding—and now I knew what all those tubes had been for. He must have channeled the outflow from these rooms into a larger system, like a holding cistern for dumping into the canal.

"How much do you want to bet it leads just outside the city?" The currents there were stronger on account of the lagoon; it would be easier to hide a large outflow of water there than in one of the canals.

"I don't particularly care if it leads into a private swimming pool, so long as my cousin doesn't see us leaving."

That was something I could agree with.

We made our way to the workshop door. Through the crack we spotted two mercenaries almost immediately, standing above the flooded stairs as if guarding against something that might surface from the depths.

There was a jab to my shoulder. "I've decided to abandon my misogynistic ways. You go first," Artemis whispered.

I glared. "Not a supernatural, asshole. And of all the times you could have picked to become a feminist— Oh, for Christ's sake!"

Artemis shoved me into the stairwell. I scrambled for cover in the shadow of the door. Luckily the guards didn't look down. One benefit to dealing with mercenaries who'd been robbed of independent thought was that they weren't exactly quick on their feet. They were hanging out by the stairwell, staring off into space like a matching pair of living zombies.

"Now what?" I asked Artemis as he joined me.

In answer, he picked up a small stone off the floor and launched it up the stairwell. It hit the landing just above and like a pair of programmed NPCs, the two mercenaries ascended the stairs to see what had caused the noise.

Artemis nodded at the submerged stairs below us. "After you."

Try not to think about what's in there . . . I pinched my nose and quietly slid in.

Captain huddled by the edge of the water shivering with unpleasant anticipation, flicking the end of his tail. He remembered the last time he'd gone for a swim in my bathtub. There was an easy way and a hard way . . .

"The pumps should be no more than half a level down. You should be fine, as will your cat."

I pushed the wet hair out of my face. Yeah, well, I might realize that . . . Captain huffed his suspicions at me.

The hard way it was.

Footsteps were coming back down the stairs. Captain looked away from me, forgetting the threat of water. I grabbed him by the collar and pulled him in. I felt a pang of guilt at the look he shot me as he submerged and reappeared with a bedraggled head of fur. "Lesser evil than having Rynn or one of his brain-dead merry men use you as a pincushion," I whispered.

Artemis slid in and disappeared under the water. Not wanting to get lost in the depths, I took a deep breath and followed with Captain securely tucked under my jacket. Artemis had been right about one thing: the pump exit to the canal was nearby, an old cement storm sewer that had been forgotten and repurposed by da Vinci.

Everything went dark as the current created by the pump dragged me into the pipe. I counted to three before I spilled into colder water that was moving much faster. It dragged us farther under until the current stopped. I shot towards the surface.

Sun hit my face.

Through my tangled and drenched hair I took a quick look around. We were just on the outskirts of the floating islands. I searched the stone wall, but if anyone noticed us, they decided not to pay attention. More important, I didn't see any sign of Rynn or his mercenaries.

I winced as sharp claws dug into my shoulder and Captain climbed up out of my jacket to perch on my head, grumbling the entire way.

"Okay, yeah, I might have deserved that," I told him. My eyes stayed on the walkway, though, as I continued to search for signs of Rynn.

There was a flicker in a window overhead—slight and small, but it was there, just as it had been when we'd first entered da Vinci's lair. I found the source: another church, worn and boarded up, its stained glass dusty. I waited for the flicker to reappear as my heart beat hard. Not a flicker, not even a shadow to hint it had been real.

"Come on," Artemis said, swimming for the wall. "We need to get out of here before they smarten up and check the water. I know the way."

I followed him, once again placing my survival in his hands. That wasn't messed up at all.

I swam to the city wall. I shivered as I pulled myself and Captain out of the water—and not just from the cold. There was still no sign of Rynn or his mercenaries, but still, I couldn't shake the feeling that someone was watching me.

Before we disappeared into an alley, I took one last look over my shoulder to see if the reflection reappeared in the church window.

Despite my sinking feeling, there wasn't a soul I could see in the dusty glass.

7

THE DEVIL YOU KNOW

8:00 p.m., Venice: Back at the hotel,
heading to the bar to drown my sorrows.

"We're not staying here, and that's final!" Damn it, what the hell did I need to say to get it through Artemis's thick skull? I pushed the front door of our hotel open. I hit it harder than necessary, sending it rattling on its hinge. My efforts earned me a bored glance from the clerk. It was that kind of place, off the beaten tourist track. The only people downstairs were in the small bar off to the side of the lobby. Bonus, there was no sign of Rynn or his psychotic merry men inside either. I'd spent the walk back scrutinizing the shadows and rooftops, meaning I'd only had half my concentration and mental resources to argue with Artemis.

And the son of a bitch hadn't let up one bit.

I heard the door open and slam shut behind me once again.

"If your goal is to run blindly into my cousin's murderous arms, then by all means let's run." Artemis's voice chased me across the hotel's cracked floor as I made my way to the bar. The guests downstairs were well on their way to drinking themselves into vacation annihilation, and

I was late for a date with a couple shots of tequila and more than one bottle of Moretti . . .

I ignored him, my sights on the dusty bar doors mere steps ahead of me, behind which laid sweet inebriated salvation.

Artemis didn't take the hint. "Please, Rynn," he continued, pitching his voice high in what I could only assume was an imitation of me. "No need to search Venice for me. Just stalk all the city exits and wait for me to flee like I always do, like a panicked headless chicken."

My irritation flared. I was *nothing* like a headless chicken. "It's not running blindly," I said to him over my shoulder. "We're fleeing. *Intelligently*. There's a difference."

I don't know how he got ahead of me, but there he was blocking the bar doors. I suspected he was using his powers of dissuasion on me liberally.

"With no destination or plan, it's the same bloody thing! I need to recharge, and at the very least we both need to get out of our wet clothes. Look, will you just listen to me instead of giving me dirty looks?" He crossed his arms, still blocking me. "At least before you drink yourself into a stupor?"

I clenched my fists. "A *buzz*. And after almost being eaten by a mad vampire and stalked by my possessed boyfriend, I think I deserve a drink. And just who did Oricho put in charge? Me or the degenerate incubus?"

Artemis dropped his usual uncaring veneer to snarl at me. "You. Though why he'd put an alcoholic has-been thief in charge of *anything* is beyond me."

"Well, we all have our little life mysteries to solve." Sensing a standoff and wanting to make sure he was part of it, Captain let out a loud meow, directing it at Artemis. "Now get the hell out of my way."

Again Artemis stopped me. "All I'm suggesting is that we stay put—for the night at the very least—until we have a better idea where the trail to the Tiger Thieves leads."

"And give Rynn and his murderous band of merry men the evening to find us? Venice is small—there's only so many hotels."

Artemis ran a hand through his hair. "I'll make certain that doesn't happen. Blocking him from seeing us when he's staring right at me is one thing, but this—he won't be sure where to look. That I can manage."

I paused. The problem was that as much as every self-preserving bone in my body was itching to run, Artemis had a point. Running without a destination was risky—but so was letting Rynn find me. I was on edge, and despite my protestations to the contrary, inside I was panicking. Rynn had had no problem turning those mercenaries into his living zombie yes-men—what would he do to me if we crossed paths?

"It's the smarter choice—you know it, and I know it. They won't find us, and even if they do manage to stumble right into this hotel, I'll have enough warning to give us a head start, and we'll be no worse off than if you ran now. Besides," he added, nodding at my backpack. "You said you need da Vinci's journal."

The soggy wet journal—which needed to dry. And yes, it did hold the key to the Tiger Thieves. At least I thought it did.

I counted to three, to calm my own nerves. "How certain are you they won't find us?"

Artemis visibly relaxed and held up his hands. "On my dear mother's grave—and yes, she's dead. She was human and died well before Rome fell."

I rolled my eyes, but despite my itch to leave, I needed to wrap my head around what information I now had on the Tiger Thieves and what I still needed to find out. And I needed a location. I needed to breathe. Damn it. Once again I found myself in a spot where Artemis was more right than I was. "Only until morning. That's *it*—and we leave early."

Artemis crossed his heart. "As soon as the sun rises."

I turned around and headed for the elevator. "Where are you headed?" he called after me.

"To my room. As you said, I need a change of clothes." I was off my game with Artemis. I had never let Rynn steamroll me like this. Granted, he'd never really put me into a position where he could steamroll me;

he'd gone out of his way to let me make my own decisions—a sensitivity that was beyond Artemis's rapport with humans.

I reached the door to my room, adjacent to Artemis's, and headed inside. It was small and worn and looked over a back alleyway. No sooner had I dropped my soggy backpack onto the bed than I heard scratching at the window. It took a minute of fiddling with the latch, but I got it open. A bedraggled Captain meowed and, after getting a good sniff at the room, hopped in.

I hadn't had the heart to stick Captain in a soaking wet bag after our swim through the flooded building and the Venetian lagoon. As far as finding me in hotel rooms? It wasn't always easy to sneak a cat through a lobby; we'd done this routine before.

After he settled in on the heater to clean his fur and vocally register his complaints, I pulled out the journal and, along with a collection of towels, laid it on the desk. I then grabbed the hair dryer from the bathroom—a pink-tiled, shower-curtained number—and turned the first page of the journal, drying the pages as I read.

The answer to where next to look for the Tiger Thieves was in here somewhere. And to judge from the condition of the wet, wrinkled pages, it was going to take me most of the night to find it.

Three hours later, I sat back in my chair and rubbed my eyes. Captain had been stretched out behind my laptop, stealing its heat, while I had been going through da Vinci's red journal. I glanced to where my beer rested, half empty. The notes had been so depressing that I'd even let my beer get warm.

The journal was more of a lab book, a recounting of his various experiments and research into the supernatural, though it read more like a catalogue of misfortunes—a fantastic example of why desperation wasn't the motivator it was cracked up to be.

Da Vinci had been an accomplished painter as well as one of the greatest thinkers and inventors of our time. There's a saying that madness and genius go hand in hand, and he illustrated that beautifully.

And his tryst with the Illuminati seemed to be where the spiral downwards had all kicked off. The Illuminati were well known in archaeological circles for their dogged pursuit of the supernatural, but they hadn't started out that way. They'd started off manipulating politics through assassinations and spy networks. It was an esoteric branch of the Illuminati, one whose members really did believe in the supernatural, that had recruited da Vinci, and what started off as an ugly duckling rose to control the organization in a very short period of time. Some historians even think that very Illuminati branch eventually became the IAA.

The main difference between the Illuminati and the modern IAA was that whereas the IAA was concerned about keeping supernaturals and supernatural artifacts under wraps, da Vinci and his ilk's interests had been a bit more sinister. They'd wanted to understand the supernaturals intimately, particularly their magic and immortality.

Again, if the very sparse history of the matter were to be believed, the supernatural division of the Illuminati was more of a footnote—both obsessed with and terrified of its prey. Until, that is, da Vinci came along. He'd been a revolutionary figure to them. He'd reasoned that humans were afraid of supernaturals because we had nothing to counter their powers with. So he began building things that could—the brownie bat we'd found being one example, along with traps, cages, and anything else that could force the supernatural into a state where it could be controlled and studied.

Oh, how things had changed for the Illuminati—it's amazing the intoxicating effect immortality has on people. Power was transferred from the politically inclined to supernatural pursuits, and the organization's very own inquisition of a sort began. All through Europe tomes were written on the supernaturals: dissections, diet analyses, catalogues of powers—everything from basic biology to more macabre questions was addressed, such as whether a severed limb or a removed tooth would grow back.

And da Vinci's work had been the linchpin of all of that.

If not for him, we wouldn't know nearly as much about the supernatural and magic as we do today.

But that didn't make it nice—intentional on da Vinci's part or not.

I found myself focusing on the earlier entries, while he'd still been sane enough to write and still held hope of finding himself a cure. The more I read, the more I was inclined to believe I'd done da Vinci a favor.

I paused over the last sentence—the one pertaining to the device I'd taken, the one about da Vinci's dealings with the Tiger Thieves.

> *The Tiger Thieves are still reluctant to help me with my experiments; even though our goals for bringing the supernaturals in check are one and the same, they take issue with my methods. Science scares them, I imagine, though perhaps it is my mix of the scientific with the supernatural that turns them away. I wouldn't be surprised, not with their particular lineages. Nevertheless, I am certain they know more about creating an elixir of youth and immortality than they are revealing.*
>
> *I have high hopes my new device will change their minds. Though I am not done testing all the variables, my calculations and models lead me to believe that when finished, it will have the ability to drain the powers of any supernatural caught in its radius. Now, clearly there is the potential for abuse as well as productive use; however, I will know more when I can determine whether the effects are permanent or temporary. I have proposed to my associates in the Illuminati that we attempt the first tests on the more aggressive and less cooperative of the supernaturals—perhaps a cemetery ghoul or a goblin, or perhaps even a vampire if one can be found.*

I went cold. That was the device da Vinci had been talking about—that's what it did, stole the powers of supernaturals. But it hadn't sounded as though the Tiger Thieves had been interested.

I pulled out the silver ball. So small—and, to judge from the blueprints, so broken . . . I went back to the notebook, skimming the pages to find out if da Vinci had ever gotten it to work.

We ran the first set of experiments yesterday on a cemetery ghoul, baited to cross our path with a freshly dug grave and plague-ridden body, as they prefer diseased flesh over pure. Unfortunately, the experiment was a success—too much of a success, I am afraid. Rather than weakening the ghoul, the device entrapped it, reducing it to a pile of dust in moments. I suspect it is an issue with the strength of the settings, and though the Illuminati are pleased, I am reluctant to make more devices until I am certain about the strengths. I considered showing the device to the Tiger Thieves but am reluctant; I fear a ghoul reduced to dust will be a deterrent to their cooperation. My own health has been deteriorating as of late, and I am unwilling to risk alienating them more than I already have with my demands for help with the elixir. On a bright note, after the unfortunate incident with the ghoul, it appears that my latest elixir has given my health minor improvements. Less convalescing this morning. I am optimistic to look at the formula once again and see if there is room for improvement.

I flipped through the next few entries to see what had happened, but they were more about da Vinci's attempts with the elixir. One thing was for certain: he had been getting more desperate with each passing day.

Still, I couldn't get the device out of my head. What if he'd gotten it working? What if I could use it to bargain with the Tiger Thieves?

What if I could use it on Rynn?

A cold shiver followed the thought. On the one hand, if it could save him, I'd be willing to try just about anything—on the other, da Vinci hadn't said whether he'd managed to get the issue of killing the target fixed; nowhere in the rest of his journal was there another mention of the device, only his attempts with the elixir.

Fantastic.

I'd always considered da Vinci a voluntary participant in the Illuminati's pursuit of the supernatural and immortality, complicit in any pain or questionable tactics he'd inflicted on some of the more harmless supernaturals—but the journal raised doubts about that.

His intention to protect people from dangerous supernatural creatures with tools, not weapons, had been sincere, though his own struggle with immortality seems to have shaken his resolve on that. Eventually.

It was sad to see the change on the pages as da Vinci faced his own declining health. I turned to Captain, who was still curled up behind my laptop. "What do you think, Captain? Was da Vinci weak, or would anybody faced with the same challenges have made the same choices?" *Including me*, I added silently.

"He was naive."

Goddamn it! I turned, scaring Captain out of his spot. "Do you have to sneak up on me?"

Artemis shrugged, lounging against the door frame between our adjoining rooms. The invisibility act was starting to piss me off.

"And it won't work, you know."

"What won't work?"

"Whatever it is you're obsessing about. I'm not a mind reader."

"Then how do you know it won't work?"

"I don't, but you do—or your skeptical brain does. That you don't want to listen to your own common sense is your problem, not mine." He took a seat on the corduroy chair, and with the jingle of metal his boots were on the coffee table. "Well, what is the link? Between da Vinci and the Tiger Thieves. Show me what that infamous archaeological mind can do."

I was tempted to tell him to go to hell, that I'd been at it three hours, but I didn't think it would have the effect I wanted.

I shrugged. "Da Vinci was in business with them before he turned himself into that vampire thing. He claims he used to provide the Tiger Thieves with weapons, except after he turned himself into a monstrosity they stopped returning his phone calls. Not exactly what I'd call long-term friends."

"What about the device?" The way he said it was nonchalant, but I could have sworn there was tension behind the words. The glance I caught confirmed it.

Tread carefully, Owl . . .

"He said it didn't work." I held up the two halves of the sphere. "Just another broken piece of equipment." I shrugged, doing my best to return Artemis's detached affectation. "I grabbed it because he rambled on about it killing a vampire. You can never have too many vampire repellents in my book."

Artemis glanced up at me but didn't pursue the topic. Whether I'd satiated his curiosity or he was choosing his moments, I didn't know.

"So the thieves felt no responsibility for da Vinci's predicament?"

"I got the distinct impression that giving him the cold shoulder had more to do with the morality of his elixir—that and his ramblings that the Tiger Thieves were responsible." I opened da Vinci's red journal and flipped through it until I found the pages that detailed the elixir. "Nymph, vampire, even used troll and incubus blood."

"That's madness."

I inclined my head. "Or genius. It's not a horrible idea, like trying to inoculate yourself with a disease, only in this case the disease was death and he ended up with a round of symptoms he never bargained for."

"So he found the cure for mortality?"

I thought back to da Vinci and his corpse. "If you call that a cure from dying." I sure as hell didn't. "Oh, and he claims that the Tiger Thieves aren't human."

Silence descended between us. Finally I said, "Your turn—spill. What is it you know about the Tiger Thieves?"

Artemis glanced up and made a *tsk*ing noise. "What do I know? Well, for starters, the Tiger Thieves are not supernatural. They're of supernatural design; they even smell and taste a bit of magic but not supernatural."

"But if they're not human—" I started.

"Then they're something different than supernatural," Artemis said carefully.

"Well, regardless of what they are, this journal, the notes, the amulets. I still have no idea how they all fit together." I held open the book. What I wouldn't give for Nadya, even Carpe—though the pain that second thought brought made me wince.

Artemis sighed. "Here, give me the notes."

What did I have to lose? I passed him the notebook with the metallic lines that matched the amulets.

"It's as if he's trying to work through a decoding himself. They're familiar, but the way he's arranged them—" Artemis snapped his fingers. "I know what these are. Give me your necklace."

God, I hoped I wasn't making a mistake. Then again, if he really wanted it, he could probably steal it from me. I handed the two Tiger Thief pendants over.

Artemis placed them on the paper from da Vinci's collection that was decorated with similar gold markings, then held his wrist over them. He took a guitar pick from his pocket and made a small cut in the skin. "The Tiger Thieves were never supernatural, but they share our magic. They don't like us, but still, it takes a supernatural—willing or unwilling—to uncover some of their secrets."

A drop of blood fell from his wrist onto the first pendant, followed by the second. It spread onto the page, running over the smooth gold lines. I waited. It didn't take long. The blood sparked as the lines on the page started to expand, crawling over the gold lines as if filling in the blanks. Blood started to collect on the second pendant and run onto the page. Those rivulets added to a different set of blanks.

"See?" Artemis said.

The drawing was part of a larger picture, and the pendants were keys to filling it in. The question was, what kind of larger picture? Despite the fact that the lines were more filled in, I still had no better sense of what the hell I was looking at. "What is it? A code, a picture?"

Artemis offered me a sly smile. "A map. See these lines that run parallel to the page—and these that run vertical?"

Faintly crisscrossed amongst the less constrained parts of the design was a series of more structured vertical and horizontal lines. "They're not evenly enough spaced to designate latitude and longitude—not in a conventional sense," I said dubiously.

"You're thinking like someone from the twenty-first century—GPS coordinates, distances, and map positions. The trick isn't getting a location, it's getting the route. Once you're on the path? Well, the Thieves find you, not the other way around. It's always worked like that." He pointed to a pair of narrowly spaced lines. "This means easy terrain, most likely a desert—followed by rougher terrain," he said, pointing to the next set.

I frowned at the next vertical line—though it ran parallel to the side of the page, it wavered, going from thin to bold.

"Water, most likely—large, considering the next two lines are the same. A sea—maybe the Red or Mediterranean. Hard to say, though, without a starting point."

Five hundred years ago, I imagine, it wouldn't have been much of a conundrum; people didn't have the global mobility they have now, not even the supernaturals. I took the book back from Artemis and began flipping through the rest of the large pages.

"What are you looking for?" he asked.

"Leonardo da Vinci was one of the greatest minds the world has ever known. If anyone could figure out the starting point, it would be him." I couldn't help but sigh, though, as I turned over the workbook pages. It was going to take me a while to start making heads or tails of this. And right now I needed to clear my head.

I shoved the book at Artemis. "Here, see if you can make anything of the location."

"Where are you going?"

"To get some fresh air." I headed to the balcony overlooking the alley and stepped outside. Captain followed me, scenting the air for prey—of the vampire or rodent variety. For a moment I stared at the buildings and the skyline, wondering what the hell I was going to do. A map was one thing, but a bunch of lines on a page? Riddles and more riddles. The more clues I uncovered, the further away the Tiger Thieves seemed. Da Vinci had driven himself irrevocably mad chasing after the Tiger Thieves. I was starting to think I was heading down the same path.

Captain's bleat brought me out of my rabbit hole of thoughts. He had hopped onto the rail and was staring at the rooftops of the adjacent buildings—a church, I supposed from the cross, though that might have been just a decoration. I narrowed my eyes at a glint of metal I thought I saw, reflected in the lamp and moonlight. Someone was on its roof.

With my luck it'd be one of Rynn's mercenaries.

Captain bleated. I grabbed him, crouched down behind the balcony, and waited.

Nothing happened. There was no more reflection, and I didn't see any more signs of a spy.

Captain continued to search the air with his nose but didn't make any more sound. I kept my sight on the roof. Someone—or something—had been there . . .

"What happened?"

I swore and just about peed myself. Artemis had sneaked up behind me and was standing on the balcony.

I glanced back at the roof. There was nothing there. I shook my head. "No idea." And whatever or whoever I'd seen was gone now.

He stepped to the edge and scanned the rooftops, but if he saw anything, he didn't say, only stepped inside after me, locked the door, and closed the drapes.

"Keep the lights off and these closed, at least until morning," he said.

"What was it?"

He gave me a last glance over his shoulder and shrugged. "As far as supernaturals go? Your guess is as good as mine; they put themselves downwind. I don't imagine they'll give you any trouble though, otherwise you'd be dead already." He turned to head back to his room.

If he didn't know who was out there, I'd—well—not drink for a week. Okay, maybe a day, possibly two. "Artemis, if you know who was just out there—"

He stopped, his hand on the door handle. "There's a thought that's been crossing my mind, a problem, one I'm certain you haven't even begun to contemplate."

Reflexively my hands clenched by my sides. I had a good idea of what was coming as I saw his eyes drift towards my desk, where the pendants and the device laid. "What's that?"

"That despite the incredibly remote chances, you need to consider the consequences of succeeding."

The face I made must have shown my confusion, because he added, "Let's say that against all odds you get that device to work or you manage to get the Tiger Thieves to help you and Rynn comes out alive."

Engaging was a bad idea. Artemis was manipulative. I swore silently in my head. I couldn't help myself. "Everyone gets out alive and lives happily ever after?"

He offered me a sad smile, with none of his usual cruelty or sarcasm. "Ah—human fairy tales. Always thought they were quaint. My point is this: fairy tales always leave out the aftermath, such as whether you'll be able to live with what you'll have to do to succeed—no, on second thought, I think you'll have no problem living with what you need to do, provided you get Rynn out of that suit—you and I really aren't cut from that different a cloth in that regard. Rynn, on the other hand—" He *tsked*. "My cousin can forgive a lot. He's better than the rest of us that way, but don't kid yourself, Hiboux. You save him, and you just might lose him forever. Think about that—and sweet dreams."

With that he slammed the door between our rooms shut.

It took me to the count of three to unclench my fists as I stared at the door. Then I headed back to my computer, where Captain was waiting for me. Artemis was manipulating me. The problem with a good manipulator is that he excels at believability.

I did wonder about how sure Artemis had sounded—and what he knew about Rynn's past that I didn't.

The Tiger Thieves pendants were out on the room desk, alongside da

Vinci's broken silver ball, all so deceptively harmless. Dangerous? Maybe, but I'd rather have two birds in the hand than one. I just hoped I hadn't ended up with two very dead ends of different carcasses.

Captain mewed from behind my laptop, and I patted him. "Don't worry, I'm not sympathizing with the devil. I'm just wondering what the story is." He started to purr.

I checked my email. Silence from everyone—Nadya, Oricho, Lady Siyu—though silence from Lady Siyu might be a blessing in disguise.

My stomach started to grumble, reminding me that I'd had nothing to eat. Beer might have calories and coffee caffeine, but I was close to running on empty.

I picked up the phone and called room service, ordering pizza off the evening menu—when in Italy . . . I even added beer to the mix.

I sat back down to continue researching the Illuminati. About fifteen minutes later there was a tentative knock at my door.

Room service was prompter than I expected. I got up to answer, Captain close on my heels. "The food's not for you," I told him. Still he sat back on his haunches like a begging prairie dog, waiting in anticipation. I shook my head. Captain and his nose for food, which I could now smell under the door.

Regardless, I checked through the peephole. There was a silver tray on a cart and a young man wearing a bored expression pushing the cart. I opened the door just as Captain bleated.

Two men who'd been hiding on the other side of the door, both of slight build and wearing hoodies, pushed their way past the confused and dazed waiter. I picked up the faint scent of forest leaves and grass.

Shit. Elves.

No way, no how. I slammed the door, but the elves wedged the cart into the door.

Nothing good ever came of supernaturals bearing room service.

Having lost the door, I backed up, Captain with me, growling at the two elves all the way. "Look, guys, can we have a civilized talk about this?"

No answer. As I reached the desk, I grabbed my beer bottle and tried to hit the closest elf over the head with it. He dodged. "Artemis?" I called.

No answer. Probably headed down to the bar. Of all the times I could really use Artemis barging in . . . I turned my attention back on the elves confronting my growling, hissing cat.

"Seriously, I'm not in the mood for this espionage shit," I said as the two of them closed in. The closest to me, wearing a blue hoodie, carried a rough brown cloth in his hand: a burlap sack.

"Can I at least take my beer?" I yelled. The sack was thrown over my head.

8

ROOM SERVICE

8:00 p.m., Venice: About fifteen minutes away
from the hotel, by my best guess.

Hands secured behind my back, I was shoved into a hard chair. Then the bag was removed from my head with a flourish. I blinked after the darkness of the bag and street. Low light courtesy of candles greeted me, so low I didn't even have to wait for my eyes to adjust to it. I got a vague impression of the building I was in: high rafters, wood ceilings, stained glass. A church. A better-maintained one than the dive da Vinci had been squatting in; the floors and pews were polished and although the church was small, it was well maintained, with no dust to be seen.

I'm an atheist, but even I had to admit the place evoked a hearthlike warmth. There was even a scent reminiscent of green things, forests and trees.

There was a ring of roughly two dozen candles surrounding me, closing me in. Outside the circle I could make out four individuals, their hoodies pulled down over their faces, obscuring what the shadows couldn't on their own. The four of them were dressed in neutral colors—brown, gray, green, blue, all muted and unremarkable—and nothing looked new. Even odds there were one or two more elves hidden in the church—if I were them, that's what I would do, conceal my numbers.

I swallowed. "What am I doing here?" I asked when none of them offered me an explanation.

I thought a few glances were exchanged between the hooded figures, but it was difficult to tell with the way they used the mix of flickering candles and resulting shadows to conceal themselves.

I counted a slow five without a peep from my captors. I cleared my throat. "Not that I don't respect the cold silent treatment, but this isn't getting us anywhere."

The tallest of the group, who was wearing a dark gray hoodie and ripped blue jeans, stepped into the circle of candles and pulled down his hood.

If I'd had any question about my captors being elves, they were put to rest. Like Carpe, the one standing in front of me had long brown hair that was tied in the back, and his body was slim—not emaciated but more like lithe. His skin was the kind of pale you got from avoiding the sun or heavily investing in high-SPF sunscreen, not the sickly version I'd also seen on elves. I thought he might have been one of the two who had accosted me at my hotel room.

They were not exactly like Carpe, but the similarities were undeniable—except for the eyes. Whereas Carpe's were a soft, dark brown, this elf's eyes were a pale, ghostly ice blue.

Oh yes, and there was the ever-telling glimpse of elongated ears peeking out from underneath his hair that put any remaining lineage questions to rest. Pointed and unmistakably elven.

He regarded me with his head inclined to the side like an inquisitive bird's, reminding me of another elf with evil red eyes I'd rather forget. There was no obvious emotion on his face—nothing to give away what their intentions might be. That made me more uncomfortable.

He watched me for a long-drawn-out minute, the pale blue eyes burrowing into me, making my skin crawl with nervous energy.

"Where is he?" the elf in the gray hoodie asked. His English was unaccented but had the same undertone of arrogance Carpe was famous for in my books. But *he*? Shit, the elves must still be looking for Rynn, despite the spectacular disaster that had occurred in Shangri-La, where their plans to make Rynn their living enslaved warrior had failed spectacularly. Fantastic—their entire species was suicidal.

"Rynn? I have no idea where he and his circus of mercenaries are. They were in Venice a few hours ago, but that's about as useful as saying Waldo's somewhere in that picture— Ow!" One of them hissed behind me, and my chair was jostled. I spilled onto the floor, landing hard on my knees. That was going to leave a mark. "What the hell was that for?" I demanded, glaring at the blue-hoodied elf directly behind me. So much for nonviolence, another of Carpe's rose-colored descriptions of his kind.

The elf crouched down until he was at eye level with me. There was still no malice or any other emotion on his face. "We have no interest in Rynn," he said.

My face must have shown just how bewildered I was because he added, "Where is the one you call Carpe Diem? The last time he left us it was to work with you, no?"

Carpe? "He— I . . ." I started, then trailed off. The elf watched me, waiting for my answer, his face intent. I hazarded a glance at the others. The ones I could see were also watching me with just as much intentness.

They looked less like supernaturals and more as though they'd raided a Salvation Army surplus store or a backpacker hostel's lost and found. Two of the elves held thin rapierlike weapons that glinted in the candlelight.

Friends of Carpe? Possibly, but that didn't rule out their being foes. Though even my paranoid mind had to admit, it was hard imagining these four as kneecap-breaking debt collectors.

Gray's brown eyebrows knit together.

Well, I could be certain they didn't appreciate stalling.

"Look, no offense, but you really expect me to tell you where the elf is after kidnapping me?" I tried to keep a wary eye on all four of them, glimpsing bits of their faces as they exchanged looks amongst themselves.

The fact was that I knew very little about elves; all of it could be summed up between what Rynn had told me and close personal contact with a grand total of two of their kind, Carpe and Nicodemous. Nicodemous had been an ancient megalomaniac set on taking the supernatural world over by enslavement, excessive force, and on the whole dubious means—and Carpe? Well, let's just say Carpe might not be evil, but his intentions were occasionally suspect and he had a bad habit of choosing the wrong side.

I had no idea how these four would react. The last I'd seen of Carpe was his drawn face as he had pushed me through the Shangri-La portal in some kind of self-sacrificing—oh hell, I don't know what he'd been thinking . . .

"She's right," a woman said this time. I craned my neck around, careful not to make any sudden movements or otherwise spook the elves as I tried to pinpoint where the female's voice had come from.

The elf in the green sweatshirt and Salvation Army runners and jeans stepped beside Gray Hoodie and lowered her own hood, revealing a shaved blond head covered in tattoos, a collection of swirls and patterns that I suspected held magic.

"We can't treat her like an enemy and expect her to divulge what she knows," she said. To me she added, "It was not a unanimous decision to abduct you. Some of us wanted to ask you to a meeting."

There was a whispered hiss from behind me. It was the red elf, one of the two holding a rapier.

"We also agreed that the incubus made that impossible—and dangerous," Gray said. "All we want to know is where our friend is."

That was the other odd thing about this. Carpe had disappeared three months before. Why were they just looking for him now?

Something dawned on me as they waited patiently. Son of a bitch. "Carpe didn't tell you where he was going, did he?"

The four of them gave me blank stares.

"Carpe keeps many of his plans and activities to himself," the green woman said. "We had hoped you would—or could—illuminate our missing friend's circumstances."

Goddamn it, Carpe . . . I thought about lying, I really did. That might have been easier for everyone. Send the elves back to whatever grove they lived in and, if Carpe ever resurfaced, make sure to punch him for it.

But looking at them, I couldn't do it. They didn't seem like the sort who were planning on killing anyone, let alone Carpe. If anything, as I stared into their faces, I thought they looked desperate. The kind of desperation you'd have if you were looking for a missing friend.

Besides, they hadn't hit me yet. That went light-years towards earning my cooperation on the supernatural front.

I sighed. "Okay, but you're not going to like it," I warned them. I began to fill them in on the sordid series of events that had led to Carpe's disappearance: the elves, Nicodemous, the Electric Samurai, and the eventual trashing of Shangri-La.

I had to give them credit, they didn't interrupt me once. They listened in silence until I was finished. "I got the impression he wasn't volunteering out of the goodness of his heart. The elf Nicodemous sent him to keep an eye on his investment," I finished.

"Why did Carpe not leave when you did?" the woman asked.

I shook my head. "Trust me, I've asked myself that enough times." I held up my hands. I'd come up with everything from thinking he had another exit to he had decided for once to be altruistic or show me some kind of lesson. Or he'd just wanted to get under my skin. I wouldn't have put it past him.

More whispered exchanges flew amongst them. "Marta has a sense for lies, and she says you tell the truth," the gray-hoodied elf said.

There was a low hiss that interrupted him. "She's hiding something," one of the elves standing behind me said—Red again. "Talking in circles. Remember, Carpe said not to trust her."

I grimaced. Not to trust me? Why, that no-good asshole . . .

I strained to turn my head so he had to look at me and caught a glimpse of a sneer under the red hood. "Let me guess—first-time kidnapper?" I asked, arching an eyebrow.

There was another exchange of glances, more flurried this time, and a flustered look from him. If it weren't for the uncertainty the candles created, I would have sworn I saw him blush. Regardless, he took a step towards me with the sword's pointy business end aimed at me.

I raised my hands. "Whoa, it's okay. No accusations here! I just wanted to point out that most of the time when I've been in these situations, the people on your side start with violence, not questions. Don't get me wrong, I'm not complaining. It's a refreshing change."

The four of them were staring at me now. I pushed on, "Since we've already veered drastically from the traditional kidnapper/kidnappee roles here, why not try something new? How about you tell me why it is you want to find Carpe? It'd go a long way towards me figuring out where we all stand—think of it as a trust-building exercise."

More whispering, louder and more frantic than before. Arguing?

"Why should we trust you?"

The one wearing the ratty blue hoodie spoke—another male, and this one spoke English with less familiarity. The youngest of the group?

Regardless, it was a good question. "You can't," I said, going for honesty. "That's one of the tricks about us humans: you're never entirely clear or certain when we're going to lie and why. But Carpe trusted me." That was a white lie: he hadn't, which was how we had ended up in this predicament.

More glances and softer whispers. I sighed. This was getting us nowhere. "Look, the point I'm trying to make is that one of us has to start the trusting game—"

"You are wrong. Your assumption is that Carpe is dead—he is alive," the woman said.

The other elves fell silent. The revelation hit me like bricks smashing through a window. It took me a moment to recover. "Ah—how—" I stammered.

"—do we know?" She arched a blond eyebrow. "He sent us a message a few days ago, asking us to find you."

My heart pounded as I wrapped my head around that. "What—was the message he asked you to give me?"

The gray-hoodied elf spoke next, shaking his head. "There was no message, no indication where he was, no explanation of what happened. Only the single command to find you."

The blond, tattooed elf offered me a sad smile. "We were hoping you would be able to shed light on Carpe's actions—or what had happened. Whether you believe us or not, we are"—she paused as if looking for the right words—"the closest thing he has to family. We'll leave it at that."

If Carpe had wanted to get my attention, this was certainly a good way to do it. But that also begged the question, what the hell was he trying to tell me? It was like being thrown a riddle without actually understanding it.

I noticed that the elven woman was still watching me. I sighed and gave her a chagrined smile. "Not a lot of clues to go on."

She smiled. "Carpe has a bad habit of that."

With that, the four elves made to leave, resheathing their weapons and fading into the shadows. Whether it was them or coincidence, the candles dimmed.

"That's it?"

None of them answered. It was as if I had ceased to exist as one by one they vanished. I find out Carpe's alive, and the elves decide to do a disappearing act before I can question them—

"Seriously? Directions would be useful here—you realize that Venice is crawling with vampires and mercenaries."

The green-hoodied woman was the only one left. "Nothing will befall you on the way back," she said. "But I suggest you do not leave again without the incubus."

Do not leave the hotel again—it was good to know that the fault was with my choice to come down here with them . . .

"Who are you? If I find Carpe, how do I get ahold of you?"

The female elf paused at the edge of the shadows. "We will find you," she said, then paused, hesitation in her step. "If I may offer you a piece of advice?"

I nodded, hoping it was cryptic directions back to my hotel.

"We sense you will have two paths, the one more easily traveled and the one that is more difficult. We suggest you choose wisely."

With that last piece of cryptic advice, she vanished.

The candles went out. All of them. At once. Leaving me in an abandoned church. By myself. Where I couldn't fucking see to let myself out the door.

I sighed. That was supernaturals for you. They kidnap you, stare at you like the specimen you are, then, once their curiosity is sated, leave you where they didn't find you.

I pushed myself up, favoring my knees. I banged them into the pews twice, growling a number of curses that were definitely not church appropriate, then found the door and stepped out into the mild, sound-filled evening air. No sign anywhere of the elves.

They were a little weird and misguided, and I couldn't help worrying what would happen to them if they came into contact with other humans wearing those outfits and carrying swords . . .

I shook my head. Old Polish proverb: not my circus, not my monkeys. At some point I'd have to stop piling other people's messes onto my plate.

The very least they could have done was leave me with some damn directions. I glanced up at the roofs, searching for a familiar landmark. That proved useless. I focused on the voices instead, guessing that the majority of them would be heading towards the bridge and the piazza.

Goddamn it, I had a long walk back to the hotel. Here's hoping I wouldn't stumble across any wayward vampires.

I set a fast pace in the crowd, wondering what it was the elven woman had meant with her warning. One thing was certain: if Carpe really was alive, he'd be getting a big piece of my fucking mind.

9

MALI

9:00 a.m.: A small airport in Timbuktu, Mali . . . I still smell.

I splashed tepid water from the rusty tap over my face. It was lukewarm, tinged brown, and did little to alleviate the sweat due to lack of sleep stemming from the night before. Damned elves . . .

I'd omitted telling Artemis about my unsolicited rendezvous. I wasn't certain I could make heads or tails of it yet, and I didn't see the point of confusing things. As I'd said, not my circus . . . I supposed he counted as a monkey I was at least partially responsible for.

Even though the water and the climate were warm, I felt cold descend over me, starting a brand-new round of sleep- and shower-deprived sweat. The one saving grace was that Artemis had been able to make everyone else on the plane ignore us. I hoped he would be able to keep up the trend.

I dried my face with my long-sleeved shirt and tied it around my waist before heading back out into the dusty provincial airport, the only air access to the once bustling Silk Road trade center of Timbuktu. My, how a few centuries could make the mighty fall. Made me wonder what the big US and European cities such as London, New York, and Paris would look like in a thousand years. You laugh, but I doubt the ancient Malinese ever thought that Timbuktu would fall.

Despite its small size and location in the middle of nowhere, the airport was not deserted. A number of foreign backpacker types were milling around, UN aid workers who'd flown out of Mali's capital, Bamako, to Timbuktu. I wasn't sure exactly how Artemis had gotten us on board and which of his powers he'd exerted, and I decided this was the one time I didn't care. If he hadn't gotten us on the flight, our options would have been a four-day trip up the Niger or risking a trek in a four-by-four. Considering how unstable the region had become over the past few years between religious fanatics and minor warlords, the UN flight had been the fastest and safest option.

I made an attempt to pull back my hair before heading back out of the washroom to find Artemis. A number of the UN volunteers were still milling around. Artemis must have been getting tired because one of them spotted me, frowning, as if trying to place my face.

Showtime . . .

I forced a wide smile onto my face and waved at her. Whether she recognized me or not, the friendliness did its job well enough to assuage her curiosity. A lesson I learned a long time ago is that it's amazing what pretending you belong does to the reactions of others.

Now, where the hell was Artemis?

I found him on one of the benches, reading another gossip rag. He seemed to have an endless supply; every time I found him, there was a new one.

"Research?" I asked, sagging onto the bench beside him.

He shot me a dirty look. "Wallowing in my misery. I can't believe you made us fly economy. And pull your hood back up. My powers are not infinite, and Oricho told you to lie low."

I obliged. Oricho had been right about one thing: the fact that Rynn was on my trail was not good: especially if it was the armor trying to stamp me out. Rynn might resist for a while, but, as both Artemis and Oricho had pointed out, he couldn't do so indefinitely.

I smiled once again as another aid worker waved at me. I'd sat near her on the plane and she'd been wearing way too much perfume. Still I smiled.

"A few more like that, and one might begin to think you're becoming a people person."

"Just tell me you found our hotel," I said.

"And a ride. Worry less about our accommodation and more about the temple."

The temple was where we figured, from the da Vinci notes, the next Tiger Thief clue should be—and hopefully with better instructions this time.

"Come on," he said, shouldering his own bag and discarding the magazine in an ashtray, something long since banished from most airports around the world—except at the ends of the earth, apparently. "We should stay with the crowd."

"You sound scared."

I said it lightly, but Artemis leveled one of his rare serious looks at me. "Mali is one of those places where the supernaturals scare even me."

I picked up my own duffel and Captain's carrier and headed after Artemis to where the rest of the aid workers were hanging around. I noticed that my phone had a few messages on it—I'd had it off for the majority of the day, so no surprise there.

I checked and found messages from both Nadya and Oricho. The one from Nadya mentioned that she hadn't found out anything relevant regarding the Tiger Thieves but was hopeful she'd uncover something useful in the Russian archives. Oricho's was a little more ominous.

I waved my phone at Artemis. "Oricho says there hasn't been much movement in Tokyo with the Come-Out-of-the-Closet crowd, but he's got a line on Rynn. Apparently he's already in Morocco."

Artemis snorted. "Everyone in the supernatural community has a line on Rynn at the moment. He's fucking terrifying. Your boyfriend is making quite a name for himself, usually prefaced by 'Run for your lives.'"

I didn't add anything. What was there to say? To be honest, the fewer details I knew about Rynn's escapades, the better. Every minute he was left in that suit running an army . . . there was only so much guilt the Corona could suppress.

There was one thing, though, that Oricho had mentioned in his email that had me worried. "He says Rynn can use his powers of persuasion on supernaturals."

That got Artemis's attention, and he shot me a sideways glance over the trashy magazine he was leafing through. I wondered where the hell he found them all.

He seemed to consider it. "Makes sense; the more powerful he gets, the further his talents reach. I don't envy the elves the political fallout."

"I figured the 'Run for your lives' trumped any infighting at this point."

Artemis smiled. "Ah—that's where you're wrong. Just what exactly were the elves planning on doing with a warrior who could exert his power over the rest of us? Hmmm? One they and they alone controlled?"

Nothing good . . . I might have said as much, but I was distracted by a commotion up ahead by the main doors. Some of the UN workers were arguing with a local, and considering the piles of suitcases and the bus parked outside, I figured it was an attempt by the driver to renegotiate the transportation price.

I looked but didn't see anyone paying particular attention—or really any attention—to me and Artemis. Everyone was focused on yelling at the driver. I realized Artemis was still speaking to me.

"The takeaway point is that your boyfriend is redefining our version of the bogeyman—which you seem rather oblivious to."

For a moment I thought the man behind the coffee and food kiosk might be watching us, but his eyes passed over us as he served the next customer.

To Artemis I said, "Well, maybe it's about time you guys got a taste of your own medicine."

He arched his eyebrows. "Now, that's interesting. Tell me, do you always throw rocks when someone lobs a spitball your way?"

"I prefer Molotov cocktails—and sometimes the means are justified." I wished I'd given more than I'd taken from the IAA, and by the time I'd realized it, it had been too late. Hindsight is 20/20.

A half smile spread across Artemis's mouth. "People who say that have almost never actually seen the means they're talking about." He nodded to where the UN relief workers were gathering their things and heading out of the building. "Come on, it looks like our ride has finally finished haggling." Artemis grabbed his small bag and started for the crowd of UN relief workers now gathered around the back of the transport, what was in fact an old school bus.

"Just what the hell is that supposed to mean?" I said, chasing after him. We got into line behind a couple of medical students I recognized from the plane. They'd been sitting in front of us and discussing their various plans. They'd struck me as adrenaline junkies, more interested in the challenges of practicing medicine without support or equipment and potentially under gunfire than anything else. My impression had been that they figured patching up gunshot wounds in the inner city had prepared them to do medicine in a war zone—and their jovial manner as they climbed onto the bus didn't change that view. They would soon find out that it hadn't—prepared them, that is.

"It means that it's very easy to say that the means are justified in a given situation when you have neither experienced nor witnessed said means," Artemis said. "I have. Trust me, they're almost never worth it—or never enough to justify using them. Take the Electric Samurai. The elves still claimed that the end justified the risks, though most of them are terrified and in hiding now. Apparently Warlord Rynn has taken issue and offense with their entertaining the idea of controlling him. Ironic, isn't it?"

Yeah, just peachy . . . I pushed past Artemis and hopped onto the bus first. I was completely ignored as I took a seat near the back, conversations going on around me as if I weren't there. I would be just a minor blip on their memory that might or might not resurface twenty years from now. There was a sense of relief about not being the object of people's attention, even if just for a brief interlude.

Artemis slid in beside me, also not eliciting a single look as he dropped his bag into the aisle. The next person simply stepped over it, as if there was nothing strange about leaving a bag in the aisle. I glared at Artemis, but it had more to do with the fact that I admired that he didn't need to care about what everyone around him thought.

"The first thing you need to understand about the situation with Rynn and the rest of the supernaturals is that it is a complete fucking mess. Yes, my cousin is currently running an army, but we have no idea whose. Originally we all thought it was the elves pulling the strings from behind one of their twisted curtains, but without Nicodemous running the show, they've all gone cowering back to their catacombs and trees. Which means that no one is running Rynn's army except Rynn and the armor, which is truly fucking terrifying since no one knows what he wants. No demands, no ultimatums, no grabs for territories. Everyone is on edge, and, knowing Rynn, I'd say it's on purpose."

The bus sputtered and coughed before lurching into gear and pulling away from the dusty airport. "He must want something," I pressed.

"Yes. A fight. With anyone." Artemis glanced at me before turning back to his trashy magazine. "Not exactly what I had in mind when I said I wanted a good seat to watch Rome burn. Not when I'm in the firestorm's path. And mark my words, there's only so much more Lady Siyu and Mr. Kurosawa will be able to cover up. The whole thing is likely to spill into the real world soon if Rynn can't be stopped—and though I'm all for chaos—"

I undid Captain's compartment so he could stick his head out, which he did, testing the air for supernaturals. "Well, that's what the IAA is for. They'll have a chance to earn their keep hiding Rynn's antics."

"They're staying out of it—too many supernaturals fighting—and you said the elves were manipulating the ranks. The stunt you pulled in Shangri-La likely scared them off."

Great, fantastic. A supernatural war on three fronts, and the IAA was still finding a way to blame things on me. At least some things never changed.

"What do you think he's after? In Morocco."

Artemis shrugged. "My guess? There are a lot of powerful artifacts hidden in Morocco. The Moroccans spent enough time invading northern Africa during the Middle Ages."

That they had, including Mali and Timbuktu.

"There are a handful of scrolls that went missing around then," Artemis mentioned. "A few weapons, all supernatural. Mr. Kurosawa's list even has a few of those listed—oh, don't glare, I was bored, and you left your laptop open. My point is that there are things in Morocco that would put Rynn ahead in the arms race."

I sat back. One could hope. If all Rynn wanted with Morocco was weapons, I'd be breathing a sigh of relief.

"Or," Artemis mused, "he may have decided that was the best way to pick a fight. Everyone else is clamoring after any supernatural weapons left lying around, why not him? He's bound to run into more than a few of our kind trying to clear the playing field." He looked at me. "And then again, maybe he decided he'd hit Morocco on his way to take care of you. Sends an interesting message."

There went my relief—down in a trailer park bonfire of tires. "Which is?"

"That Rynn isn't worried one bit about stopping you." His eyes narrowed as he regarded me. "Are you certain there isn't anything else you'd like to tell me?"

Yeah, Artemis, I'm pretty sure Rynn's figured out a way to get into my head and scramble things around. No way was I divulging that, not unless it happened again. Artemis had said it in Peru: I was fast becoming a liability; I didn't need to help myself onto the tire bonfire.

"By the way, don't you need to at least make a passing attempt to find artifacts?" Artemis asked. "So as not to give Lady Siyu any more excuses to render your hide than she already has?"

I gritted my teeth. "We'll go after what I say we go after, and when."

Artemis didn't bother disagreeing. Instead he said, "Or maybe she'll just feed you to the vampires."

I saw Timbuktu looming ahead on the road, a sleepy town with huts in the outskirt sands along with a few permanent concrete-based buildings. It wasn't what I had expected from an ancient metropolis, certainly not the end of the Silk Road.

"Oh, how the mighty can fall."

I shot Artemis a dirty look before turning back to Timbuktu. I sure as hell bet the original inhabitants had never considered that the city would end up like this one day.

As we entered the city center, I spotted our hotel—at least I assumed it was the city center, as the majority of merchants and businesses seemed to be concentrated around the small square.

The bus pulled off to the side of the road in front of what I guessed had to be a government building. With an unhealthy bang the driver released the door and the UN relief workers and Doctors Without Borders volunteers began to file off. It was a surreal experience as not a single one of them looked at us. They simply got out of our way, knowing we were there but unable to pay us any attention. Granted, it was due to Artemis's powers, but I couldn't say I hated it. There was something appealing about having not a damn person see you. We passed the people waiting to collect their larger pieces of luggage and headed for the white adobe–style hotel across the road.

For a place that existed at the run-down end of the world unnervingly close to a war zone, the three- or four-story hotel was well built. There was a red, yellow, and green colored rooster painted on a placard that hung over the entranceway, the colors of the Malian national flag, and two short flagpoles bearing the three-striped Malian flag of the same colors flanked the wide entrance. I say entrance because there was no door proper, only a metal gate that I imagined was closed for security during the evening and a series of thin curtains that alternated to let us pass unfettered but blocked a view of the hotel lobby by passersby. Unlike the other buildings that flanked the square, the hotel also had potted plants inside and out.

It was a veritable oasis. Only the government building across from us was as well put together.

The lobby was small but matched the outside. The interior decor was inviting; brightly colored textiles in dark pinks, whites, and reds had been used to upholster the soft parts of the furniture and drape the windows and walls. Wood furniture polished to a shiny gloss had been used, and there were even some tile murals in matching colors. It reminded me of Morocco—it wasn't opulent, but it was also a far cry from run-down. A comfortable Goldilocks just-right. I was pleasantly surprised as I joined Artemis by the counter. The reception was clean and well maintained, and the hotel owner had even seen fit to install an air conditioner and fans.

There was a single young man behind the counter, who smiled at us both as Artemis checked us in, but the way his eyes glazed over as he looked at us, I got the impression that Artemis wasn't letting him see a lot of memorable details. We took our keys and headed for a generous staircase as there was no elevator, or not one we could see—not surprising since there were only three or four floors.

Or I headed for the staircase. Artemis saluted me and, duffel bag still over his shoulder, headed for a set of curtains that, from the noise drifting our way, I imagined separated the bar and restaurant from the rest of the hotel.

"I'm off to drown my sorrows at the bar," he said.

The melancholy way he said it . . . I made a face. We would have a retrieval as soon as the sun set, only a few hours from now. I knew incubi didn't get drunk like humans did, but with the mood he was advertising . . . "The world isn't burning yet," I said.

He pivoted and held up one of the many gossip rags he'd accumulated over the past few days at hotels and airports, brandishing it like a stick he'd like to throw. "Mine is. I'm not bloody well mentioned anywhere, not even the gossip I leaked about my rehab stint and resulting bender in Europe."

He said something else under his breath that I didn't catch as he headed for the bar, but I was fairly certain I'd heard "Hollywood casting tar pit" and "degenerate reporters" more than once.

"Well, Captain?" I said. "What do you say? Kibble and nap, or follow Artemis and try to keep him out of trouble?"

He mewed from inside his carrier, long and drawn out. I decided it was an affirmative on the kibble and nap. Also, I still had prep to do before we hit the temple tonight, and considering how close Rynn was, I didn't want to take any chances.

I started to climb the wide white steps.

She was on her way down, face buried in a handful of papers, reading glasses askew on her nose and threatening to fall off. Middle-aged, brown hair peppered with white that she hadn't bothered to dye away. I recognized her from the bus, so she had to be with the volunteers. A doctor or nurse maybe, or an academic. She wasn't dressed conservatively enough to be a bureaucrat. I guessed she was someone who worked behind the scenes to keep things moving. Unremarkable—except for the overwhelming quantity of perfume she was wearing. My God, it was all I could do not to cover my nose right there. Something mixed with roses . . . a lot of roses and maybe patchouli? It just about made the air unbreathable.

I drew in air through my mouth. Still the rose-drenched perfume penetrated my defenses. Captain sneezed once, twice, three times from his carrier.

The woman's eyes brightened as she glanced up, and she offered me a warm smile. "Hello, there," she said with the mannerism and enthusiasm of a cheerful grandmother. I doubled down on my nurse guess. It also occurred to me that Artemis wasn't shielding me from view anymore if she was stopping to talk to me on the stairs.

She peered at me, her brows knitting together like friendly gray caterpillars. "I recognize you from the bus," she continued. "I'm Sandra, I'm one of the relief effort coordinators. Are you one of our new volunteers? I don't recognize you from orientation."

Interesting. However Artemis blocks us from view, it isn't permanent. They eventually remember. I filed that tidbit away as very important.

I did my best not to show just how much her perfume made it difficult to breathe. "Ah, no—here to see the ruins—anthropology," I offered. It was safer than archaeology, and I knew enough from my own studies and my father's long career in the field to fake it. "I'm working on cultures of ancient metropolitans." It amazed me how easily the bullshit flowed off my tongue.

She smiled, her eyes crinkling at the corners. You'd never have known we were in a war zone by her demeanor, more like that of someone on a Mediterranean vacation.

"I'm off to see the city. Make sure you don't miss the sightseeing tour this evening—I imagine it will appeal to you."

"Sightseeing? At night?"

She nodded enthusiastically. "Best time to see the night sky, plus it's not nearly as hot. Plus I rather like the idea of seeing the old ruins at night—brings the ghost stories to life."

I tried not to grimace as she laughed. Yeah, right. Until you stumbled into real ghosts, that is. I smiled and nodded affably, and she continued downstairs. She headed past the front desk and into the street, stopping to fix a bright blue hat over her salt-and-pepper bob. If she'd noticed the concerned look from the young man at the front desk, she didn't show it. I shook my head as she headed out of the hotel onto the street. Hopefully she wouldn't get herself mugged or wander into an impromptu war-zone gunfight . . . Captain made a curious mew. "No accounting for tastes, Captain," I said, and continued on my way up to the third floor. I found my room easily enough and was once again pleasantly surprised by the room decor, in keeping with the white, red, and pink patterned theme used in the lobby.

I let Captain out first to scope the room, and once he gave the OK, I stepped inside and set up my laptop before I even considered hopping into the shower. I opened the files I'd collected on Timbuktu and the temple.

As I said, wasting any of the hours I had would be, well, a waste.

—ɱ—

I pulled up an old map of West Africa showing Timbuktu during the Middle Ages, when it had still been one of the most important trade cities on the Silk Road, the gateway between Europe and the infamous salt mines of the Sahara Desert.

Timbuktu had been part of the Malian Empire during its heyday in the Middle Ages—that is, until the neighboring nations invaded. After a hundred years of warring, Morocco ended up with it, having decided it was a nice addition to its own empire. Timbuktu became the capital of the Moroccan Empire, which promptly managed to run it into the ground. By the time da Vinci was alive, Timbuktu was little more than a dusty, run-down Silk Road legend, a remnant of a fallen empire and a lost city at the end of the world. A good example of how the mighty can fall.

I covered my eyes to rest them, and when I opened them again it was the Tiger Thieves medallions that they rested on.

I made myself look away from the medallions, even with their gold lines flickering under the lights. I'd learned the hard way that things that called to me were usually not my friends, no matter what they promised . . .

Captain stretched and yawned from his spot behind my computer. I focused back on the screen and the details of the temple, trying to notice anything I might have missed, however slight.

I found my thoughts drifting towards da Vinci's silver ball, a device that could incapacitate supernaturals, strip the magic right off of them. At least that was more or less what da Vinci had said.

Broken or not, what I'd be able to do with that kind of magic . . .

I forced my eyes back on the screen. I wasn't that reckless or desperate. Yet.

I placed da Vinci's device back in my bag well out of sight and zippered it shut. Oricho and I had a plan, which was finding the Tiger Thieves and convincing them to help us wrangle Rynn. I did not need to go chasing down every magic rabbit hole I found.

"Then why does it leave such a bad taste in my mouth, Captain?"

He lifted his head, yawned, and mewed.

I sighed. If this was being responsible . . . I checked my email. There was only a quick message from Oricho saying he'd received my message that I was in Timbuktu and wishing me luck. Nothing with regard to the situation in Tokyo. That worried me, but there was little I could do.

There were three other emails, though, one from Nadya and the second from none other than Lady Siyu. Nadya's was brief, a quick update on Tokyo with a handful more details than Oricho had offered. It boiled down to things getting weird—supernaturals misbehaving and strange happenings reported in the news.

I swore. Making the news at all meant that despite Oricho's and the IAA's best efforts, things were unraveling.

I sighed. Well, I'd see how bad it got, then I'd start to worry.

The one from Lady Siyu was short and to the point, berating me for the lack of any progress and skipping the Vatican. She wanted to know what item I was fetching for Mr. Kurosawa in North Africa and what I had found in Venice. I swore. I'd need to come up with something to explain the travel, and soon; otherwise they'd start wondering exactly what the hell I was doing running all over the planet.

There was also an email from the World Quest duo saying that they had no fucking clue how and why World Quest was still online but that I could go to hell and stop emailing them.

Fucking fantastic . . . assholes . . .

I sent a sharply worded message back, telling Frank he owed it to Carpe if not me to look. It'd at least get the two of them thinking.

The next stop on the Tiger Thieves' trail, according to da Vinci and the map Artemis had uncovered, was the Temple of Shifting Faces—Shifting Gods was more like it. The temple had been reused and co-opted by various gods over the years, many of them long forgotten with the fall of the Silk Road. Supposedly, according to the texts that existed, this one hadn't been named for a god but for the way the temple walls changed colors in the shifting sunlight. If I had to guess, I imagined that they'd used polished sandstone or some reflective stone layered over the top of the structural stones, like a veneer. You wouldn't think that to look at it now; it was little more than a handful of pitted, worn sandstone pillars peeking out of the sand.

Still, despite my research, the one thing I really wanted to know eluded me: why, out of all the temples in ancient Timbuktu, had the Tiger Thieves picked this one in which to leave their bread crumb?

I hated going into a job with only half the information.

I glanced at the time on my screen: 6:30 p.m., half an hour away from sunset and therefore time to head to the temple remains. Artemis had insisted on nightfall because he'd be able to hide us easier in the dark from any supernaturals that might be lurking around.

Considering we were on the edge of a war zone and the Sahara, I'd have been surprised if there hadn't been something sneaking about. I hoped Artemis was sober . . .

I stood up to get ready and got a whiff of myself. Despite the air-conditioning and fans, I was in desperate need of a shower. I headed for the small bathroom and turned the water on.

I caught sight of my face in the mirror above the sink. I was still gaunt and needed to gain back a couple of pounds and catch up on sleep, but the reflection that stared back at me was markedly better than it had been in Las Vegas. I was on the mend, despite what both Artemis and Rynn had hinted at about my being damaged goods. I was not hell bent on destroying myself.

My eyelids felt heavy as I tried to focus on my reflection. That made me frown. I hadn't been about to fall asleep moments before; if anything, that should have happened while I'd been sitting at my laptop, not while standing up and about to take a shower.

My head slumped forward like a rag doll's, my eyes weighted shut. "Alix?"

I lifted my head and forced my eyes back open as Artemis's voice reached me. "Where the hell are you? We're supposed to be leaving now."

I blinked again, trying to force my eyes to stay open. His voice was distant but clear.

I shook my head to clear the sleep fog that had settled over me and stared at my dark circles. The water was still pelting in the shower. I hadn't even made it in. I must have been more tired than I realized. I don't fall asleep like that—not standing on my feet and sober.

I turned off the hot water and pulled my jeans, T-shirt, and jacket back on. Body odor would have to wait.

There were three bangs on my hotel door. I swore under my breath. "Coming—sorry, didn't mean to run late." Damn it, I was apologizing to him. My head was most definitely not screwed on right today.

Clothes on, I opened the bathroom door and almost stepped on Captain.

Instead of bleating his displeasure, he stretched, arched his back, and curled around my feet. I frowned at him. Odd, he didn't normally behave this affectionately—not with me, at any rate.

He leapt up onto the sink and pressed his front paws up against the fogged glass, leaving small footprints in their wake. He gave me a baleful mew.

I frowned. That was definitely new. Captain didn't bother being polite—not even with me.

He jumped down from the vanity. There was definitely something under the fog . . . I wiped the paw prints away with the sleeve of my flannel shirt and peered at the glass.

There was something wrong with the reflection of the bathroom. I took note of my surroundings: familiar white tiles and tempered soft lighting. When and how the hell had I gotten back to Vegas?

My knees wavered, and my stomach lurched. I grasped the counter to stop myself from face-planting on the floor.

Damn it, what the hell was going on? It wasn't as though I'd eaten anything. My thoughts drifted as my eyes fell on the reflection in the mirror. Rynn's face stared back at me this time. His eyes were as cold as they'd been in Shangri-La, but more calculating. I squinted as words began to unravel in what was left of the fog. *"I warned you. Time to pay the piper, Alix."*

With that he was gone—Rynn, the words, the fog . . .

I stumbled out of the bathroom and spotted my laptop on the desk. I'd been doing something important on it.

I frowned and sat down. The window was open to my World Quest game screen. There was a reason I hadn't been playing recently. Why was that?

Something flashed at the bottom of the screen. A message window. Carpe. Something pinged at my memory; there was something strange about that . . .

I opened the message box. *Careful, Byzantine—you may have bitten off more than you can chew.*

Before I could decode the message, I started as something banged at the door.

I swung it open. No one was there. I checked down the hall both ways, but still no one and nothing appeared.

I closed and locked the door and headed back to my desk. The World Quest screen was gone. I tried to pull up my message window with Carpe, but it was no use. I gripped my head as my mind reeled with pain.

Captain meowed from his lookout on top of the bookshelf, his tail flicking at me. He hissed, ears back, fangs extended. A cold shiver made its way up my spine. There was only one reason Captain would hiss like that.

I startled again as a glass broke. It had come from the small kitchenette. I headed to the sink, but couldn't find any broken glass. Instead, there was a drink on the counter. Tequila on rocks—not ice—with a lime already in it. I picked it up and sniffed. Top shelf—sipping tequila—and the rim had been salted.

I placed it back on the counter oh so carefully. Only one person I knew poured tequila like that.

I spun again only to see none other than Rynn sitting at my computer. He was dressed casually in jeans and a long-sleeved black-and-gold T-shirt and bike boots. I could even smell his sandalwood cologne. There was no sign of the Electric Samurai armor that the elves had bound to him, corrupting both him and it in the process.

I reached for the counter to steady myself, my throat dry at the sight of him. It had to be my mind playing tricks on me . . . For the briefest of moments I even let myself wonder if I'd dreamt the whole thing: the Electric Samurai, Shangri-La . . .

"It *is* your mind playing tricks on you," Rynn said, his face taking on a cruel smile that had no right being on his face. His eyes flared blue. I looked away—at the tequila on the counter, the clock, the fridge's LED—anything to avoid his eyes.

"Alix? *Look* at me."

Unable to resist the command, I faced him. Whereas before his eyes had been either a brilliant gray or blue, now they were a pale glacial shade. If I just kept watching, forgetting whatever it was that was nagging at the back of my thoughts . . .

It was the cold ice reaching into my thoughts that stopped me. I'd seen a lot of things in those eyes over the past year—disappointment, compassion, caring, frustration, exasperation—the last usually directed at me—but cold, calculated indifference hadn't ever made that list.

That undid whatever the hell supernatural bullshit Rynn was trying to put over on me. I threw off the grogginess and the living room lost some of its defined edges, as if my buying into the fantasy had been part of the kindling fueling the believability. Now it was only a blurry haze of something half remembered—whether in my or Rynn's thoughts.

"A bit of both," Rynn offered. Unlike this place, his voice was clear, cutting, underlined with a cruelty I'd convinced myself I'd imagined in Shangri-La. He regarded me. "To be honest, I think you would have enjoyed things much better if you'd bought in a little longer."

I swallowed. This wasn't really Rynn. Not anymore—or not right now. "You know me, Rynn. I hate cheap impressions." I suppressed a shiver.

His eyes narrowed. "Hardly cheap, arranging this."

I forced a smile. "I was talking about you."

The temperature in my strange dream dropped to positively icy as Rynn's eyes bored into me.

What was it they said happened if you died in a dream? That had to be a myth, right?

Watching Rynn observe me, I wasn't so certain . . .

The room wavered, and the glass vanished from my hand. I glanced at Rynn; the jeans and T-shirt had vanished as well, replaced with the armor in all its black, modern glory.

I took a step back, and the room shuddered as though a violent wave passed through it.

I wondered . . . I stumbled into a chair, knocking it over, as I continued to back up and put more space between me and Rynn. "I think I'll keep my own grip on reality, if it's all the same to you." I nodded at the apartment. "So what is this? A figment of my imagination?"

He smiled—not cruelly, there'd have to be more emotion for that. In anticipation, like a cat stalking a mouse. "In part. It's real enough. As real as I want it to be."

If that was true, I really could have used that glass of chilled tequila about now.

Well, where alcohol fails me, sheer bravado often serves as a cheap replacement. It's just as much trouble, there's just not nearly the hangover or buzz. I remembered that I kept a set of knives near the sink. I changed direction as I continued to put distance between me and Rynn.

"So, up to anything new?" I nodded at his outfit. "Besides the new wardrobe? Can't say it's an improvement, though it does suit the new eye color. Let me guess, contacts?" My back bumped into the drawer, and I reached behind me as carefully as possible.

Amusement danced across Rynn's features, and another chill coursed through me, this one freezing me in place. Well, there went my knife plan. It was all I could do not to cut and run—not even Alexander and Lady Siyu looked at me with that kind of calculating malcontent, and the two of them really wanted me dead.

As if reading my thoughts, Rynn said, "I haven't decided whether I want to see you dead, Alix. Though I'll be the first to admit that I can't quite seem to determine why I used to care so much whether you survived. That's what's become so perplexing about this." He glanced away from me, and the cold gripping me in place lessened. I keeled forwards.

"You're an anomaly. An interesting one." He torqued his head to the side. "Tell me, were you going to let yourself waste away in that dungeon?"

Son of a bitch. All this time Rynn had been playing me. He'd been able to walk into my thoughts whenever he wanted to.

"Dreams, not thoughts. You need to be asleep—and it won't work with just anyone. Only those I had a connection to . . ." He trailed off, and I thought I saw conflict cross his features, but only a flicker. "Before," he finally said.

I chastised myself for not taking Rynn's threat more seriously. How powerful would an incubus have to be to actually start wandering into people's thoughts?

Dangerously so, was the answer.

And here I was. A human, defenseless except for the small fact that Rynn seemed more interested in toying with me.

Yet how much did he actually know? Walking through my dreams was one thing, but I caught the edges wavering again every time he used his powers in other ways. Time to test the theory . . .

"What do you want?" I asked.

He arched his eyebrows. "For starters, I want to finish wresting power from the supernaturals who think they're in charge."

"For whom? To what end?"

"For myself." The perplexed frown was back as he renewed his icy evaluation of me. "And you're stalling. I remember your tricks. It won't work, whatever it is you're trying to achieve."

He couldn't read my mind. He could break in and walk around my house but not open the closets and drawers . . . or something like that. Another waver. Rynn was losing control of the dream. If I could just keep him talking . . .

"*Alix*," he said, more forcefully, the cold smile fading into a tight line.

I'd used up whatever patience Warlord Rynn had for me. "I know you've got something underhanded going on in that rattled head of yours—I can feel it."

I shrugged. "I'm just a human, Rynn—one of a few billion. I wander around, steal stuff for Mr. Kurosawa. I haven't really thought that much about you at all."

The tight line of Rynn's mouth turned downwards as he regarded me, and my limbs chilled. Another waver, stronger this time, like waves crashing violently. "I will warn you this one last time. Whatever it is you are up to, whatever plans you have cooked up in your mad head, *stop.*"

I clenched my teeth against the cold, my mind set on riding it out. The armor hadn't made Rynn omnipotent.

He got off the counter and walked towards me, slowly, like a predator—more snake than cat . . .

He grabbed my neck too fast for me to block and bared his teeth. "I don't have the time to chase after you. Stay out of my way."

"Or what?" I managed between gulps of breath.

His grip tightened. "You don't think I won't kill you?"

I smirked at him, hoping to hell my second hunch in this strange, weird dream was right. "I don't think you *can.*" I put as much arrogance behind it as I could muster with my throat trapped.

The icy grip tightened, and I saw the fury in his eyes.

If there was one thing I knew about Rynn and his powers, he had a bitch of a time dealing with them when he was angry. It was why he'd always kept so much control over his temper and berated me so much when I went off the program or grid.

The parts of Rynn that the armor had warped and twisted didn't know that or didn't care. Meaning he might still be somewhere in there—still fighting.

The dream construct truly started to waver. The room shook, and it startled Rynn. For a moment his eyes shifted back to the ones I remembered, the bright blue ones in a face that was much paler and more wan than it should have been. They fixed on me, and the cold veneer vanished as panic set in. "You need to hurry," he said in a thin voice. It was all he said before the ice-cold eyes were back.

This time they were furious.

"That was very, very stupid," Rynn whispered to me. "And you are going to pay dearly for it." He shook his head at me. "And here I planned to be merciful. Keep your secrets, Alix Hiboux. You can die in here with them."

The hand released me, as did the cold, and I crashed to the still wavering floor.

I laid there on the floor, the short carpet fibers soft between my fingers. I'd get up as soon as my head stopped spinning.

Wait a minute, my head wasn't spinning, the floor was shaking.

Shit.

I forced myself up. It wasn't just the floor, the entire room was shaking, wavering. And Rynn was gone.

My head cleared. I was back in Mali in a hotel washroom; the carbon copy of my rooms in Vegas was a dream. And now that Rynn was gone, it was collapsing.

I closed my eyes and willed myself to wake up. I opened my eyes. The room only wavered more. Damn it.

Maybe if I could get out of my room, whatever magic or supernatural manipulation was forming the room would break. It was worth a try. I stumbled to the door over the shaking floor. It took me three tries to get the lock turned; then I threw open the door and froze.

The hall outside my door was filled with bodies, the usual mix of tourists that regularly populated the hotel, but with one difference. Underneath the bright floral vacation shirts, dresses, and strappy heels was putrid decaying flesh. A set of white dentures snapped at my fingers as I slammed the door shut. Zombies—Rynn had filled my hall with undead weekend gamblers.

I needed another way out. I ran to the window, unlocked it, then broke the safety latch. I started to crawl through and stopped when I saw the roiling cloud and fog below. What the hell could Rynn have conjured outside the window? Oh, for fuck's sake—

I rolled back from the ledge about as gracefully as a walrus and crashed to the carpet as an oily tentacle slapped at the glass. That's what I got for letting Rynn watch anime: tentacle monsters.

One of the many suction cups attached to the sill while another tentacle reached in and grasped the latch. Red orbs flickered like eyes trying to see inside.

I shut the drapes and turned frantically around my apartment, wondering what the hell to do now.

There was a banging at my front door followed by splintering wood. I turned in time to see an arm reach through. To my horror, it went for the door handle.

No fair, Rynn. Zombies aren't supposed to be able to open doors.

I started to pile furniture in front of the door. First my desk chair, then the desk—I put my back into knocking over the armoire. It crashed in front of the door with a cacophony of shattering glasses and dishes. Still, arms made their way through.

"Mroew!"

I cringed at Captain's wail.

Captain was standing in the kitchen hovering over his bowl, his tail flicking.

Even in my dreams my cat thinks with his stomach . . . "Not now, Captain, I'm trying to get out of Rynn's zombie apocalypse."

He hopped up onto the table and let out another loud, obnoxious mew.

"Off the table!" I told him. I was fast running out of furniture and needed it to add to the barricade.

Captain wriggled towards me, straining his neck as he did when he wanted a pat.

"I'm not petting you! Shit!" I gripped the edge of the table as the floor shook once again. There was another crash, and the plaster beside the window cracked. I turned to Captain, who was still on the table. "Rynn is trying to kill me. Now off the— Ow! Son of a bitch!"

I looked down at my hand where Captain was latched on. "Let go, you crazy cat!"

Instead of letting go, he growled and ground his teeth in deeper.

I swore and tried to shake him loose. Note to self: don't trust friends' monster-filled dreams . . .

Wait a minute. I frowned at my hand, which had turned a dark shade of purple. Damn it. I felt my mouth, where what I feared most protruded from my gums: pointed, slightly elongated incisors. Just like a vampire's.

Son of a bitch, Rynn, that's a low blow.

"That was your greatest fear, no? Becoming one of us sordid cockroaches?" came the heavily accented English. French, attached to a voice I wouldn't be able to forget if I lived a thousand years. Alexander; Euro trash vampire extraordinaire.

Of course he'd make an appearance in my nightmare. I stumbled, but it wasn't just because of the room shaking. There was a groggy fog descending over me. I tried to shake it off and saw the first few drops of sweat hit the table. Alexander gave me a vicious smile and nodded at my hand, still gripped between Captain's jaws. "I hear those are quite lethal for our kind, the Mau bite."

"Tough luck, loser."

It was another voice I recognized. Bindi's. She was standing in the bedroom, stretched out and blocking the doorway.

Not only were the zombies and tentacle monsters just about through, but there were vampires boxing me in. The grogginess overtook me, and at the next rumble through the construct I collapsed to the floor.

My breath was coming in short bursts now, and I didn't think the air was getting to me.

I recalled something about dying in dreams—God, I hoped that was an urban legend. The grogginess turned to sleepiness, and my eyelids descended over my field of vision, now too heavy to keep open. The first of the zombified tourists broke past the barricade, their running shoes passing across my field of vision. I felt a suction-cupped tentacle brush my face, and it brought to mind sandpaper.

The first of the zombies, a woman with hair extensions trailing down behind her, crouched beside me. She clicked her teeth at another zombie who tore at her floral halter dress, trying to dislodge her in a zombie battle for first dibs.

Now, if only the sandpaperlike tentacle would stop fellating my face . . . I was thinking that death by zombies was the lesser of the evils.

I wondered how the hell Artemis was going to explain this one to Oricho.

I gasped as the first zombie bit into my shoulder—

And opened my eyes. My heart raced inside my chest. I was on the floor of the Mali hotel bathroom, my face pressed into the floor, a streak of drool running down the side of my mouth.

Captain chirped in my ear. The rough sandpaper had been his tongue. I pushed myself onto all fours, Captain dancing away out of my range.

I'd woken up. Either Rynn and the Electric Samurai had become much more subtle over the last minute, or I was safe and back in Timbuktu. I decided not to start looking for zebras and to accept that I wasn't dead. Though my hand was killing me. It took me a second to see why.

My hand was wet and sticky with blood—my blood. Two suspiciously Captain-sized puncture wounds stared back at me from the soft bit between my thumb and forefinger.

I glared at him, holding up my still bleeding hand. "Son of a bitch, you bit me!" I said. He took a break from licking his paws to lift his head and mew.

I didn't know whether to be mad at Captain for attacking me or reward him for figuring out he needed to wake me up.

As if sensing my conundrum, he mewed again and exited the bathroom. I heard the distinct ring of him upending his food dish, putting in his two cents' worth.

Well, with that taken care of . . . I pushed myself to standing. "I'm starting to think bad things happen when I fall asleep sober," I told him. I'm sure if my head hadn't still been pounding, I could have come up with something much more clever.

Man, oh man, zombies and tentacle monsters . . . it was like a bad video game. Rynn had never understood why some tropes had to be separated.

Captain poked his head back in.

"You're not off the hook completely," I told him. "You knew it would hurt." Having a two-way conversation with my cat—the picture of sanity.

The door between my room and Artemis's crashed open. Artemis's eyes were bright green and angry as he took in the room and finally me slumped by my desk. Probably pissed off that I'd interrupted his beauty sleep. The only thing I could muster any energy for was an apathetic wave of my hand. Great, the gang was all here. Oh, goodie.

Artemis's eyes narrowed, and he looked about to yell at me. Then he took in the room and got a good look at me. The expression he wore turned from anger to—if not quite concern, then something akin to curiosity. "I think you need to tell me whatever it is you're hiding," he said, after a long five seconds had clicked by on the room clock.

I thought about arguing, refusing him, but the more I ran that idea over in my head while he stood a few short feet away in the door frame . . . I realized that trying to hide Rynn and what he could do at this point was fast turning me into a liability.

I pulled my pajama robe tighter and capitulated. "Grab yourself a beer from the fridge," I said. My computer was still open, lying on its side on the floor. Captain had probably knocked it over during our scuffle. The screen was still flickering. There was a better than fifty-fifty chance it was still working.

Artemis disappeared back into his room, leaving the door open. He returned a moment later and headed for my fridge. "Here," he said gruffly.

I looked up to find a beer shoved in my face. I took it, drew a long pull—I deserved it after the fiasco with Rynn—and jostled the mouse pad. After a long moment, the screen came back to life. Greater than fifty.

There was another tap on my shoulder. It was Artemis, holding out a bottle of antiseptic and gauze. I took them with a nod of thanks. I figured he'd have better ways to try to stick a knife in my back than by offering me medical supplies.

I concentrated on fixing my hand, procrastinating until the blood from Captain's bite was stanched.

I sighed and took another swig of the beer. "Okay, so Rynn might have a few new tricks," I said, then told Artemis—slowly and succinctly as I drank my beer—everything that had happened, from the hint of Rynn watching me at da Vinci's lair to the monster mash dream.

To his credit, he waited until I was finished.

"How long? How long has he been able to travel into your dreams?"

"A day or two at least, maybe more. For all I know, he was keeping tabs on me in the Albino."

Artemis's upper lip curled, and his nose flared. "Why didn't you come to me sooner?" he demanded, the anger rolling off him now.

I didn't answer. He already knew what I would say. I might have agreed to forgive him, but that didn't mean I would trust him as far as I could throw him.

He shook his head. "And you suspected he was trailing you." He swore and grabbed my carrier, tossing it at rather than to me. "This changes *everything*. He'll be onto us in no time, especially if he has an inkling of where we are. Take your bag, we're heading to the temple now and leaving Mali as soon as we have what we came for."

I began to gather my things—laptop, notebooks, handbag—but despite my protestations to Artemis, I was still woozy from Rynn's show. I headed into the bathroom. Water on my face, hot or cold, it didn't matter; that was what I needed to wake me up . . .

I froze as my eyes focused on the foggy stained glass. It was cracked, condensation caught in the new creases.

It wasn't the cracks that bothered me, though—it was the message they spelled out, in jagged, harsh letters: *No more warnings, Alix.*

Shit. Rynn's work.

I gripped the counter as my heart pounded through my ears and waited until my heartbeat slowed to something resembling normal. Captain, going against his nature, was silent while I tried to push the panic back down. It didn't listen very well.

If Rynn could warp glass without being in the room, what else could he do?

I took a deep breath.

"Hiboux?" Artemis called from the hall. "Hurry your ass up before everything hits the fan!"

Ignoring Artemis, I tried to wipe away the message and, when that didn't work, threw a towel over it.

I clutched my jacket tighter around me and grabbed my supplies plus the amulets before following after Artemis's hurried footsteps, Captain on my heels.

Here was hoping we didn't all get killed.

10

THE ROAD TO TIMBUKTU

8:00 p.m.: Sitting in a jeep on the edge of the Sahara.

"Well, at least it's something new for him."

I glared at Artemis. It wasn't what he said but his cheerful, devil-may-care conversational tone. I'd let him drive the jeep since he'd been the one to find it. We'd been on the road leading to the ruins on the outskirts of Timbuktu for an hour—the Temple of Shifting Faces had been a ways from the city even when it had been a metropolis.

As I kept my eyes on Artemis, I had the sinking suspicion he'd used some of his powers of persuasion to convince me to let him drive . . .

"I mean, Rynn's been in such a rut over the past few centuries. I'm rather amazed at the change, corrupted armor or not."

He had definitely used his powers. There is no way in hell I'd have let him drive otherwise. "Do you ever stop with the morbid sarcasm?"

Keeping his eyes on the road, he arched an eyebrow. "Do you?"

I didn't dignify that with an answer. Instead, I leaned against the door as far away from him as I could get.

"Careful. I wouldn't trust that lock. I don't nearly have Rynn's healing ability. I'm much better at hiding in the shadows. No, despite its macabre nature, I have to admit I'm impressed with my little cousin's current quest for murderous self-improvement."

The murderous self-improvement wasn't what got my attention. "*Younger* cousin?"

Artemis raised his eyebrow at me again. "*Little* cousin. I'd helped lead armies before Rynn was born. I suppose he never told you how he looked up to me in his younger days? Hmmm? No?" He *tsk*ed. "I'd be hurt if I didn't expect his indifference so much."

"Contempt, not indifference. The distinction is subtle." I scanned the desert hills in the last bit of setting sun, searching for remnants of Timbuktu. Artemis had grilled me about Rynn's visit; I'd answered as best as I could, but that hadn't stemmed conversation on the topic. On his side anyway.

"Things are about to become very dangerous," he mused, drawing my attention off the darkening sky and sand.

"What do you mean?"

"What I mean is that your boyfriend is getting stronger—" He paused as we went over a bump, the jeep rattling and earning an un-settled mew from Captain. "More to the point, he's taken an interest in your activities, enough to test the extent of his new powers—recklessly, in my opinion."

"Struck me as pretty damn efficient." I'd jumped real high.

"Rynn is a lot of things, but he was never reckless. Which means the armor, the suit—whatever the hell the elves bound to him—is finally making some real headway."

I kept silent. I'd already realized that, and it was tearing me up. It was something we agreed on: Rynn was losing.

I was grateful for the cold desert night air that numbed my face. "Is there anything else you need to tell me?" I asked him, my voice dry and more than a little defeated-sounding. "I thought you guys couldn't do that—warp minds and read thoughts."

Artemis inclined his head to the side, keeping his eyes on the road. "Some incubi, very powerful ones, can do what he did: enter the human subconscious and manipulate it beyond the usual tricks pulling your emotions." I knew he was hedging his answer. "Emotions lead to thoughts: desires, wants, needs, passions. There's much less division between the two than you humans seem to think. It's a glimpse of just how powerful the suit could make him."

I don't know why I offered it; chalk it up to boredom. "Inside—the dream, whatever it was—for a second he seemed to break away. He said I didn't have much time left and to hurry."

Artemis's mouth drew into a tight line. "Might have been him. Might have been the suit learning our tricks. Nothing like kindling hope to get humans going—usually in the wrong direction. Either way, so long as he's still in there, you serve as a distraction."

I waited, watching him. After a moment he inclined his head. "But the wavering of your dream, the construct—it does suggest that either Rynn doesn't know the limits of his power or the suit is still teasing control away from him."

"So there's still a chance? That we can get him out?" That was us. We humans couldn't resist hope. Not even me. There was silence while I held my breath.

"Yes," Artemis finally said, and silence stretched between us. Artemis was the one who broke it. "Did Rynn ever tell you what I did? Before."

I shook my head. Besides Artemis's career as a sordid rock star, Rynn had told me very little about his cousin—and himself, if I was being honest. Though I had no idea why that was bothering me now. It wasn't as though I was an open book, even if my emotions were.

Artemis pursed his lips. "Rynn's talents might have predisposed him to more martial pursuits, but me? People like to talk to me—supernaturals and humans alike—I'm harmless, after all. An entertaining drunk." He glanced at me. "Being able to fight is only one-half of the equation. If you don't know who your enemies are, you never really know whose battles you're fighting."

"You were a spy."

"*Am* a spy—and you'd be smart not to forget it." Another hesitation. "I mention it because there is another way to read what Rynn said to you in the dream. That the suit has full control over Rynn and is baiting you—just enough to give you pause."

He took his eyes off the dirt road and held mine for a brief moment before I glanced away.

He was right, and it didn't matter. If there was a chance of getting Rynn out, I needed to try—and fast.

Ten minutes later of silence interrupted only by the jeep's engine and the odd bang as we dipped into a pothole, we reached the location the GPS had guided us to. Though the light was fading fast below the horizon of dull gold sand, I could make out the first sandstone pillars peeking out over sand dunes in the distance as we crested over a hill. They were the only parts of the old Timbuktu temples that hadn't been claimed by the sands.

The sun had set by the time Artemis pulled the jeep to a stop in front of the temple, only the stars and a crescent moon for light.

I hopped out and opened my cat's carrier. "Time to get to work, Captain." He mewed as he crept out, nose held high in the air. Once he deemed the place relatively safe from predators and vampires, he stuck his nose to the sand in search of prey, preferably of the small and fuzzy variety.

"Chances are you'll have to settle for the scaly and six-legged varieties," I told him. He ignored me and began to dig.

I grabbed my tool bag out of the back of the jeep, then surveyed the four massive pillars peeking out of the sands. Now . . . where to begin?

I heard Artemis get out of the jeep behind me. "Where the hell is it?" he asked.

"See those four pillars?" I said, and started to hike towards them through the loose sand. "That's the top." I heard Artemis swear.

I had really been hoping there would be an access shaft in the temple ceiling, preferably not too far under the surface of the sand. With Rynn on my tail and the possibility that Mr. Kurosawa's opponents were watching me, organizing a dig team hadn't struck me as the wisest or safest course of action. I'd be winging it—and hoping that the temple hadn't already been looted.

Mali hadn't been the picture of stability over the past few years—or decades—which meant that doing archaeology and preserving historical sites hadn't been on anyone's radar, here or elsewhere in the country. It's all well and good for the world's archaeological community to claim a site is protected; it's another to enforce that protection, especially when there are hostile militias, bullets, and grenades flying. Not even the IAA was willing to throw talent away by making its graduate students dig in land mine–infested dirt.

Which meant that just about all of the archaeological sites in Mali had been reclaimed by either the jungle or the sands . . . or blown up . . . or pulled down . . .

"You knew it was like this?" Artemis demanded, the buckles and hardware on his boots jingling as he chased me. "And you couldn't have told me before?"

There were four pillars. If the renditions of the temple hadn't been lost to ancient scribe telephone, there was a good bet I'd find an entrance near the northernmost post. "Well, it was on a need-to-know basis," I told him. All the old diagrams had indicated that under the four pillars there should be closed compartments, built to be safe from sandstorms and hopefully the assault of time as well. If the inside hadn't collapsed under the weight of the sand, and if I could get us in, we still had another problem, which had more to do with the temple's isolation on the outskirts of Timbuktu. "And that's the least of your worries," I told him.

"If I'm not supposed to worry about the place being half buried in sand, please tell me what I should be worried about." Artemis kicked the sand, sending it flying to drive home his point.

"That places on the outskirts of half-abandoned towns tend to be inhabited—by supernaturals I'd rather not get to know or people I'd *really* rather not get to know."

Now, which way the hell was north? I stood in the center of the four pillars and began to turn, staring at the constellations above me. Wow, were there ever a lot of stars up there; they made it harder to find north, not easier. I mean, usually the only ones you could even make out were the Big Dipper and Orion's belt, maybe Cassiopeia if you were away from the glare of city lights.

"Smell anything?"

Artemis shook his head. "Not a damn thing. Goblins, maybe. They like these deserted haunts. Makes them feel civilized in a way caves never do."

I scanned the area. Goblins were a possibility. Goblin tribes were relatively common on the African continent. They were always nasty and difficult, and rarely could you barter with them. There were a lot of vampires in North Africa as well—and mummies and medusas and ghosts. I racked my brain to come up with anything else that might have decided to take up residence in a Malian temple on the edge of the desert. Genies? Trolls? They were rarer, but trolls were attracted to well-traveled routes. Highway underpasses and canals were some of their favorites, but they wouldn't stick their big noses up at an ancient trade route, even if it was all but abandoned . . .

Ah! There was north. I made my way to the northernmost pillar and began to clear the sand away from its base.

I didn't need to clear everything away; I only needed to reach the base. "A place at the edge of the world, buried in the sand—that was what da Vinci said," I reminded Artemis.

Luckily for me, the temple had been built tall, and the pillars had partially protected it from being buried completely. After fifteen minutes of digging, I reached stone. A few minutes later Captain was the one who located the air shaft opening—it was tight, but if I sucked in and squirmed . . .

"Do you hear that?"

I glanced over at Artemis, who was leaning against a pillar, ripping pages out of a gossip rag he'd produced from somewhere.

I tilted my head and listened. Sure enough, I picked out the rumble of an engine, punctuated by backfire.

Artemis flattened himself to the sand and began crawling towards one of the shallow dunes. I followed his lead. Headlights flooded the site as a school bus—the same one, I wagered, we'd taken from the airport—came to a stop beside one of the other ruined buildings. Its headlights missed our jeep.

What was it doing out here?

My question was answered as the door of the bus opened and people streamed out, flashlights in hand. They were far enough away that I couldn't make out their faces, but it had to be the same UN workers and doctors we'd headed into town with.

"What the hell do you suppose they're doing here?" Artemis asked.

I shook my head as I watched them begin to fan out, waving their flashlight beams like deranged airport runway workers. "I ran into one of them in the hotel. She said they were going on a night city tour."

"An awful long way from the city."

And nothing to see except terrified nocturnal wildlife. A few laughs and excited shouts and yelps carried our way, along with comments on the stars . . . regardless of the strange nature of the so-called city tour, their good mood had carried all the way out here.

I decided I didn't have time to figure out why they were out in the desert—not now. I grabbed my bag and started to shimmy back towards the air shaft. "Watch them," I whispered to Artemis. "And see if you can keep us hidden from them."

"Just get the pendants, and get the hell out. I don't like the smell of the desert anymore," he whispered after me.

A shiver coursed through me. I chalked it up to the descending night and tied off my rope to a rock outside the shaft.

"Ready to take a short walk down a deep, dark dungeon?" I asked Captain, holding my backpack open. He chirped and dived in. I zipped him up, shouldered him onto my back, then checked the rope one last time. For good measure I shone the flashlight through the narrow shaft, searching for anything arachnid and poisonous in nature that might have gotten in there.

Deep breath, Owl. I counted to three and, flashlight clenched in my teeth, shimmied through the hole and began to rappel down.

As I descended, I flicked my flashlight beam around the shaft. It was well constructed, a vent covered in graffiti, ancient versions of "Mike was here," "Lorna loves Jack," and "Security in this place sucks." We aren't the first civilization to love damaging goods or to revel in a sardonic sense of humor.

It also meant that others had climbed this shaft successfully.

Ground loomed below me, patches of stone peeking through the sand that had settled. I cleared the shaft and ran my light along the chamber I was now in. For a priests' temple, it wasn't particularly ornate. A few cracks ran through frescoes that had been painted and carved into the walls for decoration, but the place looked as though it had been built for function, not as a monument.

The floors as well, at least the parts I could see through the sand, showed the same conservatism. They were the kinds of floors that had been meant to be used every day—by the priests and patrons of the Temple of the Shifting Faces.

I dropped the last three feet to the floor, Captain grumbling in my backpack at the hard landing. Reckless? Nope—it made no sense to booby-trap a floor people used daily. A loyal penitent or priest might set it off by accident.

I'd dropped into a small antechamber with rounded corners that tapered in at the ceiling, forming a dome with the shaft in the center. Each wall held a recessed statue, four in total: a young woman, a child, a young man, an elderly person. Both the child and the elderly person were androgynous enough that I couldn't tell whether they were meant to be male or female; ancient gods still watching over their chamber.

This would have been a reception room, where the priests had met people of moderate means. The poor would have been met outside or not at all, and the rich would have had a much more opulent chamber, I wagered, with furniture. Wouldn't want the big spenders to be uncomfortable while they petitioned their gods to cleave their enemies' heads off.

Now, if I were a Tiger Thieves pendant, where would I be?

I turned a slow circle as I surveyed the antechamber for a hint.

I found what I was looking for on the domed ceiling.

Above me were murals, four in total, one for each face of the room. They depicted animals: a lion, a camel, an elephant, and—a tiger.

I don't look a gift horse in the mouth. Especially when the gift horse is a clue that falls straight into my lap.

Underneath each of the statues was a doorway. The tiger was above the woman, which I passed under as I entered a hallway that ended in a door that had long since rotted away. I brushed my hands against the stone markings on the wall. They were not as detailed as the murals or statues, quick pictures of sticklike men carved into the edges. Decorations, maybe? Or a warning.

I shone my flashlight beam through the pieces of dried wood and metal. Beyond was another room, smaller than the last and with a lower ceiling but with the same smooth corners and domed shape. As I looked around the room, I noticed more of the stick people, depicted this time in a variety of scenes: dancing, trading, barbecuing, traveling by caravan. What were they trying to say?

I sensed more riddles about exactly who the temple was supposed to be supplicating . . . more than I would have liked, anyway.

"What do you think, Captain?"

All he did was sniff against the mesh of the bag then mew softly. Well, if Captain didn't think there were monsters and I couldn't find any traps . . . I stepped inside.

Regardless of how certain I was that no disasters would befall us, still I let out a breath when only the sound of my feet echoed around the small chamber.

On one side of the chamber was a stone altar. I made my way quickly to it. There was no bowl, no artifacts, just the smooth polished surface—and a set of pictorial instructions of a man sticking his hands into the wall. Sure enough, above the altar were two holes carved into the stone.

I consulted the images again. "Okay, stick your hands in and what? Say the magic words, and loot appears?"

Maybe it was lever based.

I shone my flashlight inside. The stone chambers were large enough to accommodate a large man's fists. Their walls were smooth, but darkness blocked out the end, or maybe the holes just went on that far. I didn't see any levers—maybe there had been ropes or wood that had decayed or broken? Regardless, I wouldn't know until I stuck my hand in.

Which was about the last thing I was going to do—not until I found the lever system . . .

I searched the walls with my flashlight and found more of the same at eye level—murals of stick people sticking their hands into the holes, people dancing in joyous circles around them, raising their hands to the heavens under beams of sunlight, others enjoying a banquet. It was like Disneyland subconsciously advertising the mouse toys. "*Stick your hands in the holes! It's awesome! Good things happen!*"

Yeah, and when you have to shout out praises that much . . . especially considering that not a damn one of the drawings hinted at what qualified as "awesome."

I angled my flashlight up to get a better look around. It reflected off something metallic.

It was an old dish lying on a recessed shelf. One that had probably been used to collect blood from sacrificial animals as the smooth metal would have been easy to clean afterwards. Hmmm . . . I ran my sleeve over the dusty metal. It still retained its polish, so much so that I could see my face in a blurred, vague, imperfect reflection.

I'm not one for movie tricks, but this one was worth a shot.

I leaned the plate against the stone altar and angled it up. Then I played with the flashlight beam until it hit the metallic dish at the right angle.

The temple antechamber filled with a soft light; I wouldn't want to light my place with it, but it worked for the task at hand. More images lined the walls all the way to the ceiling, also extolling the praises of sticking your hands in the holes, but with no more explanation. Then I spotted it: the image of a tiger, stripes and all, at the head of one of the banquet tables.

Bingo. Now all I had to do was figure out a way to get it without finding out what wonders the altar held.

Something in the metal dish caught my attention. I stared at my reflection. There was something strange about it—something blue.

I shook my head—or tried to, but the muscles resisted.

Just stare into the dish, everything will be okay.

The image began to clear. It wasn't me who stared back but Rynn. The scent of sandalwood flooded the room.

Pain exploded in my hand, sharp and piercing. The sandalwood-scented grip on my brain faded, and pain replaced it. I cried out and wrenched my gaze off the dish. Captain held on to my hand, blood running down his mouth where he'd bit me. As soon as he saw I was watching, he bleated and let go.

More pain flooded my hand. "Mother of God! What the hell was that?" I held my hand, wrapping it in my sleeve, trying to stem the blood flow.

Rynn was getting more powerful.

Captain jostled in the bag, chirping at me. "You said it, buddy," I told him. No more mirrors if I could help it—and it was high time to get what I had come for and go. Maybe I could pry the altar top off? If I hit it hard enough with a hammer, it would break.

I crouched down to retrieve a hammer from my bag. A cascade of rocks echoing from farther back in the temple stopped me.

Shit. I aimed my flashlight beam towards the entrance of the chamber but didn't see anyone or anything. Animals if I was lucky, goblins if I wasn't. I stared at the two holes placed conspicuously above the altar.

There it was again, the sound of pebbles ricocheting against stone. This time Captain rustled in his bag and chirped.

My alternatives were rapidly disappearing. I swore again, let Captain out of my backpack, and stuck my flashlight back between my teeth. I readied my hands above the altar, once again reading the instructions. I wasn't leaving without the pendant. I so hoped this wasn't the ancients' version of trolling . . .

I closed my eyes and shoved both my hands in. Nothing happened. No knives, no roars. All I felt was smooth sides. Well, that was anticlimactic. Wait. Both hands found the grooves at the same time. My fingers fit inside them easily. Something moved; stone scraped against stone as hidden gears moved. I pressed down harder and found more grooves.

Slowly but surely the top of the altar began to slide open.

"*Stick your hands in, and we'll give you loot.*" Damn, I could use more treasure troves like this.

Underneath, nestled in a simple stone box, was the next Tiger Thief amulet, its gold lines glinting under my flashlight beam.

Bingo.

Time to grab the loot and go. Shit.

I tried to pull my hands out, but the wall held them in place. Whereas the holes had been large enough to easily slip my hands through before, the space had tightened, closing in around them. I heard the faint grind of gears and felt stone turning, tightening even more.

Shit. I tried to free myself again, this time bracing my leg against the wall for leverage. More gears churned, and the cold stone blocks clamped down on my wrists like a vise. What I had thought was a smooth stone cylinder was made up of hundreds of small mobile pieces controlled by gears. And they showed no sign of stopping.

I renewed my efforts as the stone pinched painfully against the bones in my wrists.

Then I saw the picture that had been painted underneath the altar's lid, the colors still fresh, protected from the elements. Lying underneath the pendant was the final picture of the instructions: a man with two stumps where his hands had been, holding his arms up to the sky, a box of treasure at his feet.

Asshole trolls of the ancient world . . .

I reached with my leg and tried to knock the pendant out of the open altar with the toe of my boot. It only reached the edge, not enough to touch the pendant inside. The stone was shrinking around my fingers too, holding them hostage. And it didn't stop at snug. I yelped as the grinding of the ancient gears continued and pieces of stone dug into my hand.

Behind me my cat growled.

"Captain! Time to earn your kibble!" I shouted. There had to be a release, otherwise the priests wouldn't have been able to reset the trap. My eyes fell on the altar. How much did I want to bet that shutting the altar would stop the trap? "The pendant!" I shouted at my cat.

He stared at me as if I wasn't about to have my hands ripped off. Then he turned and sniffed down the hall.

Now was not the time for a training relapse. "The pendant!" I shouted at him over the ancient gears. I tapped the altar with my foot as best as I could.

This time Captain trotted over. I nodded at the altar. He hopped up and sniffed at the box before looking at me and meowing. Considering all the objects my cat had ever knocked off a table, why the hell couldn't he do it with the necklace?

I winced as the stones crimped my palms, causing them to spasm. Captain just stared at me. I needed more time. I took my flashlight and shoved it into the right-hand hole with my mouth, jamming it in as far as it would go. The pressure on my hands eased as I heard the metal flashlight wrench. Now for the other side. With effort I removed a pen from my pocket with my teeth and tried that. Again the pressure lessened.

"Captain, I am begging you: play with the necklace so I can shut the altar." Much longer and I wouldn't be doing anything with my hands, let alone getting us out.

Captain mewed and batted gingerly at the pendant. The flashlight snapped.

Like hell did I plan on giving the temple a new sacrifice . . . "It's a shiny thing with a string, how the hell can you not want to play with it?"

Captain looked at me.

I winced as the stone dislocated the thumb of my left hand. "Captain, so help me, if you don't knock that pendant off the altar, neither of us is getting out of here."

Captain let out a loud meow and knocked the pendant off the altar. It clinked as it hit the stone floor, bouncing twice before coming to a stop. He jumped down and chased it.

I kicked the lid down with my boot, sighing as the stone pins retreated and slumping to the ground. My hands were a spasming mess, but nothing had been broken.

Doubled over on the altar steps, cradling my hands on my knees, I stared at my cat. He was licking his paws, the pendant between them.

I shook my head. Of all the pets out there . . .

I fumbled the pendant into my jacket pocket and reclaimed what was left of my cracked flashlight where it had fallen on the floor. It flickered on and off like a geriatric strobe light as I balanced it under my chin.

"What do you say we get the hell out of here?" I asked Captain.

It wasn't a mew I heard, though. It was a scrape against stone, like feet being dragged. And this time it was closer. I shone the flickering flashlight down the hall. The scraping stopped, and in the entrance stood a woman I recognized. Though I couldn't see well in the light, I wouldn't miss the blue hat and bag anywhere. It was the UN relief worker, Sandra, the one I'd met in the hotel.

I tried to angle my broken flashlight towards her, with minimal luck. She did the honors, shining her own flashlight up at her face, giving it a ghoulish cast.

Her heavy floral perfume filled the antechamber.

"Well, hello there! Fancy meeting you down here!" she said. The shadows from the flashlights did not compliment her face.

"How did you get down here?" I asked.

She ignored the question, a strange gleam in her eye as she nodded at the open altar. "It wants blood. The pendant. We've been keeping it here a long time. Not many people get out of our trap."

Our trap? Out of instinct I backed up towards the altar since she was blocking the door. She looked normal. I didn't get a supernatural vibe off her.

Captain let out a hiss, and Sandra stopped closing in. Definitely not human.

It was then I picked up the faint trace of urea underneath her heavy floral perfume. I knew that scent. She hadn't been worried about body odor, she'd been covering the scent of urea, the telltale mark of a skin walker.

Sweat began to accumulate along my forehead.

If vampires were the cockroaches of the supernatural world, skin walkers were the locusts, a supernatural species of predator that preyed on humans and stole their memories and skin, wearing them like a new suit. Skin walkers mimicked their hosts seamlessly, using them to navigate the human world and picking off family and friends as the need for new skins arrived, like pantry preserves.

I'd had a run-in with a skin walker at the Japanese Circus. It was how I'd found out that Rynn wasn't human. It hadn't been a pleasant encounter; it had almost killed me. With supernatural reflexes, great strength, and a violent cruel streak, their reputation as dangerous killers wasn't overblown.

"You get as old as me, and you forget some of the players over the centuries," Sandra continued. "But not them, not the Tiger Thieves." She shivered involuntarily, then regarded me closely. "Though I must say I also haven't had anyone stroll into my house for a few centuries. It's what I'd call a pleasant surprise."

Her home? It hit me: the Temple of Shifting Faces, the stick figures etched into the walls . . .

This was a skin walker temple.

She clicked her tongue and smiled, her lips parting enough that I could see the serrated skin walker's teeth, which were too small for her face and slightly pointed. I hadn't noticed that the last time I'd run into one. I backed up until I reached the wall. Skin walkers weren't exactly sympathetic with their food. The distance between us was rapidly growing shorter.

"Ah . . ." I started. When all else fails, best to keep the monster talking.

"Sandra, or that's what the clothes tag said." She winked at me, the expression ill fitting her face. "Or *label* might be more appropriate. What would you say? Friendly middle-aged white American, size medium?"

I abandoned the idea of running. I wouldn't make it three steps.

Often hired as assassins by the supernatural community to deal with human problems, they'd become even more popular over the last twenty years with the advent of international travel. If skin walkers had a weakness, it was that they needed water to survive.

Which prompted the question, what the hell was one doing out here in the desert?

"Airplanes, trains, and automobiles, dearie," the skin walker wearing Sandra's skin said, guessing or preempting my question. "It's really made this world such a wonderful place to travel. You know, I hadn't planned on chasing you when we ran into each other in the hotel." She *tsk*ed, reminding me of a kindergarten teacher. "We've had much too much trouble dealing with *him*. He's taken quite the interest in you. We all stay out of his way—rumors abound. But then I saw that you were coming out here with the other incubus in the jeep, and my curiosity begged to know what you were doing out here. This one used to watch a lot of soaps; try as we may, we can never block out their thoughts entirely."

I swallowed. "What do you want to know?"

"Oh, that won't be necessary. I'd rather just read your thoughts. Harder for you to lie and misdirect." She closed the distance between us with inhuman speed, until her face was inches from mine. This close the smell of her perfume mixed with the scent of skin walker urea, producing a foul mix. I tried to push myself away, but it was no use.

"And I've decided I need a new suit. Granted, the tag ought to read

'Comes with IAA and dragon liability,' but every now and again I figure I can splurge on throwaway fashion."

I swallowed hard, searching for something, anything, to stall her with until I could think myself out of this disaster. My terrified mind glommed on to the sole thing that had jumped out like a beacon while she'd been talking.

"Wait, you said you were afraid of him—Rynn. Why? What rumors?"

"Ah, you didn't know? The other useless incubus didn't tell you? Should I tell you, then? Why not?" she mused. "What harm could it do? You'll be dead momentarily." She let me go, and I scrambled away, searching the room for something, anything, to use against her while she spoke. "Tell you what, if you surrender like a good little girl and give me your memories, I'll tell you. I so prefer it when my prey doesn't fight. Ruins the outfit." She winked and began stalking me as a cat does a mouse.

I saw the white and brown fur overhead.

Captain had managed to find his way into a shaft above us. He twitched his tail and shuffled his hindquarters, eyes on the skin walker.

God, I hoped I wasn't giving my cat too much credit. I changed the direction I was retreating in, slowly backing up until I was underneath where he was waiting, keeping her attention on me.

Back up . . . just about there . . . "No deal," I said.

Captain meowed, and a heavy object struck the skin walker on the top of her head with a crack. Her eyes rolled up into her head, and she toppled to the ground.

An antique hammer, still gripped by a grave robber's skeletal hand, laid beside her.

Thank God for trespassers and vandals . . .

I stared at the skin walker's motionless body, wondering if I should run or attempt to restrain her first.

I was still rooted in place, deciding, when the floor shook. "Oh, you've got to be fucking kidding me . . ." It was the temple. What the hell had I done to jostle the foundations? No dynamite, no massive collapses . . . maybe the gears and mechanized stone pieces behind the altar; they probably hadn't been triggered in hundreds of years.

"Come on, Captain!" I yelled, and bolted back towards the entrance. I skidded to a stop in front of my rope. The temple floor shook for a third time, strong enough to almost knock me over.

I motioned for Captain to climb onto my backpack. I felt the weight as he gripped tight.

I grabbed the rope and climbed faster than I ever had, hand over hand, adrenaline helping me ignore my lungs' protests. There was the top—I heaved myself over the edge and gasped for breath, my legs dangling. I pulled myself up and began retrieving the rope.

"Wait!"

I just about dropped the rope back in.

"I wish to bargain with you, human," Sandra called out over the rumbling temple noise.

Bargain with a skin walker? I've got some magic beans to go with that . . . But curiosity got the better of me. I crept back to the edge of the shaft and glanced down.

There she stood, blood streaming down her face from where the hammer had bludgeoned her.

It dawned on me that I had the only rope leading out. She must have used mine to climb down and not considered taking a backup. That was skin walker arrogance for you.

Sandra might be a skin walker, but she wasn't stupid. "I know something about the soldier that you don't!" she shouted up at me.

The soldier? She must mean Rynn. I snorted and began retrieving the rope, winding it around my arms.

"About his plans!" she continued. "Do you know why the supernaturals are so frightened of him? No, I can tell from your face and your scent that you do not."

I turned to go but paused. She'd hinted in the temple that she knew something about Rynn. If she knew something, anything, that could help me . . . "What do you want?" I shouted down.

"Leave the rope, and I will tell you."

Yeah, right. Tell my dead body, maybe—after she skinned me alive . . . "Tell me, and if it's any good, maybe we can deal," I called back down as the temple shook again.

"Miscreant human!" The temple shook again, raining dust around her.

"Wrong answer!" I'd have to abandon this roof soon; it wouldn't be safe much longer, not if the structure below was failing.

She licked blood off her lips, betraying her desperation. "He's started taking us," she called back. "Yes, that's right, he can manipulate us now as easily as the humans he's acquired, warping and twisting us until we're just as dark and damaged as the elves made him and the armor."

So that was what she'd been cagey about earlier when she'd hinted that the supernaturals' fear of Rynn was more than just from his random violence and his reign of chaos . . .

It also meant he was getting more powerful. "How? How is he doing it?"

Sandra smiled and shook her bloody head, knowing she had me now. "Not until you agree to throw me the rope."

There was another shake of the building beneath us. On the one hand, I really didn't want to let a skin walker out—I had no illusions she'd be happy letting me get the better of her and just stroll away; on the other, if she knew how Rynn was manipulating supernaturals—

As if she were reading my thoughts—or maybe was just desperate— she added, "I'll sweeten our deal. I swear I'll let you and the incubus leave, *with* the Tiger Thieves amulet."

I paused. I wasn't going to get a much better deal than that, not from a skin walker. And wasn't the amulet what I had come here for?

I readied to throw the rope down just as screams erupted behind me.

"Throw me the rope!"

I ignored her and abandoned the shaft for the nearest pillar. Below was mayhem—the UN workers and medical student volunteers were screaming and running for the bus, flashlight beams moving above them like minnows in the black night sky.

I stood there dumbstruck for a moment as a smaller group of UN workers chased them. The screams rose as one of the running people was tackled to the sands.

I ran back to the shaft. "What's going on?" I yelled down.

She smiled at me. "Jumped the gun, did they? Poor dears out there are a little desperate. They've been down on their luck as of late. Plenty of bodies to steal, but it's like having a black-tie event to attend and all you have is jeans and a T-shirt. A Malian passport isn't exactly a ticket to an international flight right now, and considering how infrequent tourists have become with all the violence—" She *tsk*ed. "We don't like being fenced in. Me? I'm in the mail-order business."

I just stared at her, dumbstruck. She'd lured all those people out here and sold them to the other skin walkers as convenient tickets out of Mali, like used clothing.

"Now. My *rope*, and perhaps I will tell you how to stop him. I know the armor, I know the Thieves, this was my temple." Her fists clenched by her sides. "Throw it down, and I can help you make it all go away. I swear! You know what happens to supernaturals who break their word, especially when it's sworn on holy land."

The ground shook again, and this time I heard stone collapsing inside. Deals with supernaturals were hard to break—almost impossible for them. Doing so usually involved nasty curses. It was why they were so reluctant to make them without a litany of clauses.

If she was willing to swear, it meant she could help me.

I was tempted, sorely so, but looking at her, the woman whose memories and skin she was wearing . . . just how many people had she killed over her lifetime? Would she continue to kill?

"Here's your rope," I called down. But before I dropped it down the shaft, I cut the rope into four pieces. She shrieked, something sharp, piercing, inhuman, but her screams melded with all the others' as I slid down the sand. A massive crack sounded through the desert, followed by the ground shaking and a cloud of sand being thrown into the air.

Well, there was another temple I could add to my list.

I skidded to a stop by the jeep and opened the door. "Got it, now get it started! Oh, shit!" Where the hell was Artemis?

I searched the area around the jeep for him, but there was no sign of him. However, three flashlight beams were hurtling my way. Between the flailing lights I made out three young UN workers being chased by an older man who wasn't moving as a human should. It was the two doctors who'd sat behind us, comparing working in gang-infested projects with training for a war zone.

"Find somewhere to hide!" I shouted.

I spotted more groups of fleeing people running like headless chickens every which way, herded and chased by the skin walkers who had hidden amongst them, luring them here.

Bodies fell. It was a massacre.

I ducked behind the jeep as one of the UN workers/skin walkers looked my way, having discarded all pretense of humanity in his now jerky, quick movements.

I needed to hide, and inside a jeep was not the best option. Where the hell was Artemis? My eyes searched the dunes for him but didn't get a glimpse.

My phone rang. Shit. I scrambled to get it out of my jacket. Luckily, the chaos and screams hid the sound. It was Oricho. I swore again but answered it. Oricho wasn't the kind of supernatural you ignored. "Ah, yeah, Oricho—not a great time. We've stumbled into a skin walker problem."

"I have heard reports that you are in Mali," came Oricho's smooth and not-a-damn-bit-concerned voice.

Of course, right now, in the middle of a skin walker massacre, he'd bring it up . . . "Yeah, look, like I said— Damn it!" I ducked back down behind the jeep, making myself as small as possible behind the wheel as a flashlight beam passed my way. Thank God they didn't have the olfactory talents of other supernaturals.

I heard the rumbling of the bus and more screams as a few of the UN workers and doctors made a break for it. The skin walkers sniffing around the jeep bolted towards the fresh sounds of mayhem.

I brought the phone back to my ear. "Short answer: yes, I'm in Mali, currently an unwilling participant in a skin walker massacre. I'll call you back and fill you in on the details *if* and *when* I survive," I said, and switched off the phone.

"Pssst!" I heard the sharp whisper coming from an overturned diesel barrel discarded in the sand with a rusted hole in its side. I caught sight of Artemis's ornate boot.

I waited until the skin walker, who was now sniffing my way, looked back towards the three he'd been chasing. I baseball slid in beside Artemis. Captain followed, not quite sure what to make of the turn of events.

"Can you hide us?"

He arched an eyebrow. "Me? Certainly, but they're looking for blood." He nodded at the skin walker sniffing towards our jeep. "Look, he's already scented you."

"You're the supernatural. What's your escape plan? Shit." I ducked back down as a retreating aid worker, a young woman, skidded to a stop by our jeep. She was jumped by two skin walkers—a mild-mannered–looking gentleman and the bus driver—they must have gotten him earlier in the evening. Their limbs bent into shapes they shouldn't have been able to as they pinned their victim, every move betraying the thin-limbed yellow creatures that resided underneath.

I winced and looked away at the echoing snap of the woman's neck breaking like a twig. A bright red backpack with a white aid cross landed inches from my feet.

"There have to be half a dozen of them at least. That makes an entire troop," Artemis said, pointing to three more skin walkers who appeared from behind the now-empty school bus.

A bus full of passport-carrying professionals—the coveted accoutrement for globe-trotting skin walkers everywhere.

I watched the two medical students who'd managed to escape the first wave of attack abandon their sand dune and slide under the school bus—the cover of the bus being too much of a temptation, especially since the skin walkers had already gutted it of people. They were the last—all the people they'd counted as friends now reduced to a handful of memories and uric acid–soaked hides in a matter of minutes.

Three skin walkers without human skins were headed towards them, their jaundice-colored yellow bodies deceptively frail and thin as they lurched across the sand.

A sinking feeling formed in my stomach. It wasn't as though I'd spoken to them or they'd even seen me on the bus, but I knew who they were.

"It's like the damned Pied Piper all over again," Artemis offered. "You know why the Pied Piper traveled with droves of children? Because they were the preferred food for trolls and he wanted to make sure he had enough to pay his way through the gates."

He was right, though this time it was much too close for me to see the gallows humor. "There has to be something we can do—you're a damned supernatural!"

"I'm an incubus—and not even Rynn could do anything against an entire troop on their home turf. He always waited to deal with them one at a time. Look, it's too late."

Like jackals rather than the humans they were wearing, the two in the lead narrowed in on the bus. They stayed still.

Come on, come on—stay still, moving will get you killed . . .

Two more skin walkers appeared without their skins, their lean yellow bodies moving more like a desert insect's than anything close to human—or even mammalian. That is, except their human eyes, which were all their own, in varying colors—completely human—and their almost human teeth.

One of the skin walkers, having caught the familiar scent, began to sniff around the wheel. The other quickly joined him. I couldn't see the two med students, but that didn't keep me from smelling the sweat dripping from them, an olfactory advertisement pinpointing their location.

They were out of sight, though. If they just stayed where they were . . .

When I was a little girl and traveling with my anthropologist father, every time we were in a new place, I convinced myself that there were monsters hiding under my bed. I would lie perfectly still, hoping they wouldn't see me, and I remember just how hard it had been not to run screaming from my room.

When the skin walkers, absent human skins, dropped on all fours near the bus wheel, those two didn't stand a chance.

They bolted for the road.

"Not the road, you idiots!" Artemis whispered beside me. Before I could think, I started for them, not knowing exactly what I would do.

Artemis stopped me. "There are too many."

He was right. And I hated him all the more for it.

I had to look away as the skin walkers picked them off. I'd seen horrible things, been beaten to a pulp by vampires, been chased by mummies, zombies, dead pirates; it wasn't the same thing as seeing a defenseless person rendered before my very eyes.

Artemis didn't give me much time to process the images I'd just seen. "Come on, into the jeep." He abandoned his hiding spot and headed for it.

"I thought you said we'd be sitting ducks," I said, turning my anger at the skin walkers on him.

"It's better to be moving ducks while there are still sitting ducks left."

"You can't be serious!"

He spun on me. "Deadly." At my expression he made a face. "The underdog is only a hero in fairy tales; here, they're martyrs. Keep your head down." He pulled me after him and shoved me into the passenger side before hopping in himself. "I'm hoping they stay distracted while they feed."

He turned the key. Nothing happened. Not even a sputter. He frowned and began hitting the fuel gauge. "Oh, you've got to be fucking kidding me!" He took out a lighter to see the dashboard. "The assholes siphoned the gas!"

"I thought you were supposed to watch them!"

"I was—and they were all over there, ergo, so was I."

A guttural laugh cut him off. On his side of the jeep with the door open was a bare skin walker, smelling of urea, his yellow skin looking even more sickly under the minimal moonlight.

Artemis froze, but only for a moment. He kicked at the skin walker as it tried to pull him out of the jeep.

I glanced back at the others. It was only a matter of time before we attracted attention.

I don't know why Captain chose that moment to leap onto the hood of the jeep, but then again I'm never entirely certain why he decides to do anything. Whatever had inspired him, he laid back his ears, raised his hackles, and bared his teeth with a hiss that could only come out of a vampire-hunting cat.

It wasn't that Captain was a danger to the skin walker—far from it—but when a twenty-pound cat leaps onto a car hood with its ears back and fangs out, well, he was startling enough to make a Naga jump. Not that it would do us much good . . .

Artemis still had his lighter out.

I grabbed it and struck it three times until the flint lit the flame. A skin walker hide is incredibly dry, preserved with chemical excretions that mimic the effects of tannins and formaldehyde solvents. It was one of the reasons they were so dependent on water sources. And also very flammable.

I threw the lighter at the bare skin walker while it was still recovering from Captain. The result was both spectacular and instantaneous. Its skin lit up like dry parchment, engulfed in a bright yellow flame. It screeched, slapping at the flames engulfing its body before dropping and rolling in the sand—not that that did much good.

"Run! Run now!" yelled Artemis, and jumped out of the jeep.

I followed, grabbing Captain off the hood of the jeep, leaving the screeching skin walker burning in the sand.

I ran, doing my damnedest to keep up with Artemis as we put

distance between ourselves and the skin walkers. There was nothing more I could do; the people from the buses were already dead, and even if I could get near the other skin walkers with the lighter, some of them were already wearing skins. I wouldn't be saving anyone. I'd be martyring myself, and that never did anyone any good.

That's what I kept telling myself over and over as we ran, until eventually Artemis slowed to a walk. Sometimes I even believed it. Mostly, though, it was one word that coursed through my monologue, and it was in Rynn's voice.

Coward.

I gripped the third pendant close. I suppose some things burn themselves on your conscience, much like the skin walker writhing in the sand.

11

PLANES, TRAINS, AND AUDIBLE SCREAMS

A while later, in the wee hours of the morning:
Somewhere north of Timbuktu.

I hate trains. Metal binlike cages. The IAA had tried to toss me in one a couple years ago. "Just tell me we won't be sharing a car with livestock," I said. Livestock and cargo holds brought uncomfortable memories of Carpe to mind. I stopped to shake out my shoe. I had sand just about everywhere it could get now, even though we'd kept to a packed road made where the sand had given way to bedrock.

Artemis inclined his head. "If a train's cargo hold bothers you that much, you could always hike back and see if the skin walkers will give you a ride in their school bus."

The silence we'd enjoyed after escaping from the skin walkers hadn't lasted past two hours. I suspected that the last twenty minutes of peace had been due only to Artemis having winded himself. Innate supernatural fitness apparently had its limits.

I was also winded—and bored. I started to whistle the tune that had stuck itself into my ear.

Up ahead, Artemis stopped. "Oh, for the love of all that is holy, will you please stop whistling that infernal song?"

I pulled my shoe off and dumped the contents. Sand spilled out.

"I can't help an earworm."

"You can help sharing it! Why don't you take a cue from the cat? At least he stays quiet."

I felt Captain stir and lift his head at that. He let out a sleepy mew from his carrier. He'd opted to use me as his packhorse.

"You hate my cat."

Artemis huffed, and I settled back into my whistling. *Istanbul was Constantinople* . . . it was keeping my mind off the massacre, and if the only fallout was annoying Artemis . . . Besides, I dared anyone to try not thinking of that song when planning to catch a train towards Istanbul.

Artemis didn't bother me again. I figured he knew how tentative my rein on panic was.

Up ahead I could see lights and what looked like a small adobe building, sticking out of the sand in the middle of nowhere. "Is that it up ahead?"

"What gave it away? The middle of nowhere or the people milling around?"

I sighed. If it had been up to me, we would not be traveling by train.

More silence as we trudged towards the lights—well, except for me humming . . .

"It wasn't your fault—the skin walkers." Artemis looked at me over his shoulder. "The running was what killed them. The skin walkers were cats playing with new toys by that point."

"Why the hell didn't you try to warn them, then?"

"Because it wouldn't have done any good. If they hadn't run, *maybe* the skin walkers wouldn't have noticed them, but if we're being completely honest here, they were probably all dead as soon as they boarded a plane to Mali.

"Needless to say, it doesn't bode well when the skin walkers are scared of what Rynn might do."

I didn't reply. Neither did Captain, who usually couldn't resist adding his two cents' worth to a conversation.

"There has to be more to this than chasing after the Tiger Thieves," Artemis said, changing topics as we trudged towards the station. I could make out the people waiting now, shadows moving into and out of the lights.

Artemis shook his head. "I keep running this over in my head. Rynn—he must be after something. Was there anything the two of you were searching for?"

Shit. I reached for da Vinci's silver device in my pocket, keeping my emotions calm—or trying to. It felt cold in my palm. "Ah, no—why do you think that?" I asked.

He shrugged. "The Tiger Thieves are more legend than reality now—they existed, and enough people are left who have had run-ins with them and lived to tell the tale—but their capabilities and whether they still exist are unknowns."

"Unless he knows something you don't," I said.

Artemis snorted. "If I don't know, Rynn doesn't know."

"Then he's worried that they can do something or that I can convince them to intervene." Artemis frowned at me. "It just doesn't seem that complicated. It's an unknown. He's worried; ergo, take me out."

"Hmmm. Not his style. He chases known threats, not ghosts of threats. The Tiger Thieves are ghosts, and you aren't a threat. There has to be something more."

If he hadn't been so close to the truth, I would have been inclined to agree. The safest bet was to keep my mouth shut, which I did. Artemis was still frowning at me.

He didn't look away. "What?" he asked.

Shit. "What?" I parroted back.

His frown deepened. "What are you so perplexed about?"

I shrugged, gripping the silver ball tighter. "Nothing. Just still bothered by the skin walkers, that's all," I said, and picked up my pace.

He didn't buy it. "No, you're not. You didn't like seeing people killed by a pack of skin walkers, but on a sliding scale you're dealing unnervingly well."

Silence from me. I could see the lampposts in the distance. I was not going to tell Artemis about the silver orb in my jacket . . .

"Did I insult you? Saying you weren't a threat?"

Everyone underestimated me; of course I found it insulting. I was also used to it. I thought about lying and answering yes, but I figured he'd pick up on that. "Look, let's just—I don't know—get on the train. I'm tired, and I need to think about the next location." We'd used the third pendant to see where it directed us next. The map had said Istanbul, but it hadn't been very specific about the location. Water and caves.

Artemis didn't let up. "I've already figured it out."

"What?" I ran to catch up with him, grabbing his jacket. "Why didn't you tell me?"

He shrugged me off. "You hum your idiotic song, I forget to mention crucial information. Be happy I decided to tell you at all."

"You know, if it wasn't for the fact that you haven't stabbed me in the back yet, I'd think you'd joined in to sabotage me," I said, moving past him.

That got a reaction. "Hold on one fucking minute," Artemis said.

I spun. "What?" Captain added a belligerent meow over my shoulder. Artemis hesitated but only for a moment. "I gave my word I would help rescue my cousin, which, despite what you believe, I have no intention of not doing. But you?" He *tsk*ed. "You I'm not so sure about anymore."

He turned his hand over. In it was something small and silver. The device.

Shit. I patted my jacket pocket to see if it was a trick. It was gone. Goddamn it, I hadn't even felt him take it.

He gave me a vicious half smile. "Not much of a thief, are you? Now, for the last time, nicely. What the hell is this, and why does Rynn want it enough to chase you around the globe?"

I glared at Artemis. "It's one of da Vinci's inventions, and what it does is none of your—" I snatched it back.

"Oh, for fuck's sake. You realize he was a madman? You can't seriously be thinking that using one of his derelict devices is the answer. If you do, you're a lot more reckless than I thought."

I did not need a lecture from Artemis, of all people, on how to save my boyfriend. "Am I still banking on the Tiger Thieves? Yes, but I'd be an idiot if I didn't consider other options. You said it yourself: they're a legend!" It was another option, simple as that. Maybe not the wisest one, but I wasn't about to leave it in the depths of Venice, not if there was a remote chance it might end up being a desperately needed Hail Mary. I didn't give up that easily.

"You don't get to cast me as the bad guy," I said. Artemis had the track record for being the villain, *not* me.

And despite Artemis's hand clenched around my wrist, I still had da Vinci's device.

I was the one in control.

Artemis let go and took a step back. "Just what is it you want, Alix? Because that"—he nodded at the silver orb—"is not the way to help my cousin. So I'll ask you once again, what the hell is it you're really looking for?"

I met his green gaze, keeping my thoughts and emotions as well hidden as I could. "What the hell are *you* doing here?"

"Me? I made a deal with Oricho."

"*Exactly*. You're the hired help." I turned and picked up my pace. We were well within hearing range of the station now, yet no one even glimpsed our way. "And stop using your goddamned powers!"

"With *pleasure*."

A young man sitting on the ground looked up from a mug and started at the sight of me. Another followed. Amongst the local Malian passengers I was attracting a great deal of silent attention; everyone in the station was staring at me as I sat down on the cement bench. Okay, maybe I'd been a bit quick to tell Artemis to lose the powers.

"Just the hired help," he said, repeating my words, as he brushed by me.

He had no right to be upset. Not after everything he'd done.

I took a seat on a bench beside a woman who looked me up and down until she caught me staring at her as well. She glanced away.

"Just remember, I might not like my cousin and the stick up his ass, but that doesn't mean I want him dead," Artemis said, sitting down beside me and offering me one of two tin cups. "Water—drinkable at that. The height of hospitality during some periods of time."

I considered refusing it, but I was too damn thirsty. I took a sip and gave the rest of mine to Captain.

"You really want to stoop to the level of a mad vampire sickened by his own disease?" Artemis asked.

"Something like that." I huddled in my jacket tighter. One by one the passengers seemed to stop seeing me, their eyes glazing over whenever they were looking directly at me. I decided it wasn't the bridge I was going to stake my war on.

I held the silver ball in my pocket. It might have been my imagination, but it felt as if it were coating my fingers with a slick taint. I shoved it deeper into my pocket and removed my hand into the chill evening. It mollified the sensation, but only a bit.

"Contrary to what you think, I'm not willing to compromise people so easily," Artemis said.

I laughed. "Yes, you are. You had no problem doing it in LA."

He fell silent.

Me? I stared in the direction everyone else was as they waited for the incoming train, listening to my cat lap his water.

A piece of reflective metal glinted on the station wall, and I quickly looked away.

I sat like that for twenty minutes, until Captain hit my hand with the top of his head, chirping to get my attention.

I thought I glimpsed something in the reflection of the tin cup's water, an eye that was too blue to be mine. I could have sworn it winked at me before disappearing. I gave the cup and water to Captain.

I elbowed Artemis. "Did you see that?"

He frowned and picked up the cup. "He sure as hell couldn't do that before," he said.

The wind picked up, and there was a scent in the air that grated on my nerves. I winced as a high-pitched screech echoed across the sand. Silence descended around the train station. The screech pierced the night a moment later—louder and closer.

"Oh, I have a bad feeling about that," I said. It smelled *off*. Captain couldn't shake the feeling that something was wrong with the air either. He picked his nose up from the metal cup and sneezed three times before letting out a low inquisitive growl at the tracks.

I checked my phone. No reception. I held it up for Artemis to see. We were in the middle of nowhere by a wood shack in the middle of a desert. There were no witnesses besides a few local passengers.

"When does the train arrive?"

Artemis's eyes were searching around the station and the sand dunes now. "It comes when it comes."

"The schedule—"

"There is no schedule, bur from the number of people, I'd say no more than an hour."

I let out my breath slowly, watching it condense in a cloud before me.

The station's halogen lights flickered. A young man beside us jumped. I wasn't the only paranoid one here—or the only one that had heard the screech.

"A hyena?"

"There are no hyenas out here, and even if there were, they don't sound like that," Artemis replied.

I frowned as I heard the rumble in the distance. I glanced down the tracks along with everyone else and saw a blur of white lights. They seemed awfully close considering how much farther away the train sounded.

I stood to get a better look, and so did Artemis, looking whiter than he had a moment before.

The scent of the air even changed. It carried a dry rot, not unlike death. I had the urge to run and hide. Every bone in my body—I stopped myself.

The distant sound of the train was overshadowed by a hollow whistle around us, as if the night air itself were shrieking at us in warning.

"Try and get reception again," Artemis said.

His expression was enough to stop me asking any questions. I pulled out my phone. Nothing, not even a browser. I shook my head. "It's flickering in and out."

"It's blocking it," Artemis said, and jumped to his feet, fast. "This chill—it's too cold for this time of evening. Hopefully just a ghost."

I'd had run-ins with ghosts before in Mr. Kurosawa's casino. The powerful ones could interfere with electronics, lights, noises, even smells—but something about the way Artemis was standing, his face still white, told me that wasn't what he was worried about.

He nodded down the tracks. "We'll see soon enough."

Others were noticing the whistling wind now over the sound of the oncoming train. A few people got up and stepped away from the tracks and station, away from the light and towards the dunes. Others stayed in their seats but looked uncomfortably undecided.

The light was getting closer and brighter, though the sound of the train wasn't nearly close enough. The wind picked up, stirring sand and clothes around the entire station.

Ghosts had their bags of tricks, but this was on a scale I hadn't seen before.

A gust of icy wind stole a woman's scarf, flicking the tails in her face before drawing it into the sand.

Something crunched beneath my feet, and I glanced down at the ground. A thin layer of frost covered it, creeping up the toes of my boots.

Artemis swore beside me.

"What?"

The passengers milling around the train station looked uncomfortably down the tracks. Cold descended icy, to the bone, and biting. The ones with wraps and light jackets clutched them tighter to ward off the cold. There was another strong gust of the wind that pushed through us, and then the light, which had been getting closer, flashed and sputtered out.

The whispers that had buzzed through the group halted. There was a sense of foreboding in the air now, despair and something else—fear. An unnatural fear, descending on my skin like a clammy sweat.

The man sitting beside me had lost his hat in the gust. It was a nice one, a fedora. It danced across the sand and over a dune, just out of reach. He hesitated to chase it, but it was within sight, a few paces away. He fought against the wind to reach it as it danced beyond him, then again, leading him farther and farther away until he was just over the dune.

Over the wind we heard a bloodcurdling scream. I and everyone else covered their ears. Captain howled.

A moment later the man stumbled back to the station, clutching his hat to his chest. His face was stretched in an expression of horror—and it glittered.

He tripped over the edge of the concrete platform and reached for me. He was frozen, his face covered in pale ice crystals.

Before I could get out of the way, he grasped my wrist.

"He wants what you have," he said, though it was a woman's voice that spoke. "Give it to him, and maybe you'll live," and with that, the man collapsed, dead.

Four bright white lights appeared above the dunes.

"Shit," Artemis said. "It's worse than I thought." He started to back away from the station and the tracks, in the opposite direction from the lights. "Everyone run! Hide in the sands," he shouted as loudly as I'd ever heard him before he took his own advice. A woman screamed.

"What the hell is it?" The ice cold prickled at my neck again.

He shook his head as he hastened his retreat; everyone was running now. "It's not ghosts!" he shouted over the wind that had renewed its assault over the station. "It's wisps! Pick up the pace if you want to live, Hiboux."

Will-o'-the-wisps? Shit, that was bad.

I grabbed Captain and picked up my pace. Artemis was already ten feet ahead. Behind me was pandemonium as everyone scattered.

"Ghosts I could hide us from, even bargain with after they'd had their fill of scaring the passengers," Artemis said in short breaths as I drew up beside him.

He pushed me into the sand as one of the glowing white orbs flashed along the sand dune beside us. "Bury yourself," he said, and began doing the same. "If we're lucky, they won't pick up on the heat."

Will-o'-the-wisps, or fairy lights, were ghostlike creatures; the difference was that wisps never played with their prey. Grad students in the northern bogs were warned never to stray from well-marked trails, and stories abounded of stray flashlights and lanterns amongst the trees, the odd call for help that sounded like a cross between a woman and a bird. Every few years someone ignored the warnings, and a grad student wouldn't make it back to camp with the rest. He or she would be found the next morning, lying in a bed of moss, freezing cold and very dead. Wisps consumed the warmth and breath of their victims until there was nothing left but a cold, dead husk.

But wisps were a cold-climate creature, native to the bogs and forests of northern Europe and Russia. What the hell were they doing in the African desert? "I've never heard of them screeching like that," Artemis said. Or attacking their prey in a group like that. Wisps were dangerous as all hell, but they were lie-in-wait predators, not the kind that ambushed you.

Artemis inclined his head. "That would be new." He finished burying himself. I scrambled to do the same.

White linenlike strands churned within the globes of light. There didn't seem to be anything solid to them, just light and sheer strands.

"Remember what I said about Rynn being a talented enforcer? Well, he always knew how to intimidate his prey. Do you know what he used to do when someone got away?"

I shook my head.

"It didn't happen often, but if you got away the first time you could be guaranteed he'd send an even worse monster."

The wisps shrieked again.

"They're more like wild animals than soldiers. They'll attack anything that's warm and breathes, and, unlike ghosts, they're impossible to control. They don't think about anything except feeding and will inflict pain and misery on any supernatural or human they come across."

There was shouting now. Some of the people who'd run into the sand dunes began screaming, and there was a flash of silver in what was left of the evening light. I winced at the bloodcurdling screams. Then silence descended again.

A glowing light hovered over where I'd buried myself in the sand. It zipped past, then stopped and returned, circling over where the three of us were buried.

It concentrated on the area where Captain and I were buried, the icy cold dripping off it and chilling the sands. There was no body that I could discern, only wisps of muslinlike tendrils that descended to lick the sand, more delicate and less well defined than those of a jellyfish. I held my breath as it hovered near my face.

Oh man, I hoped Captain would keep quiet.

The seconds dragged on like minutes as I watched the wisp inspect the sands over and around me.

A train whistle sounded, nearer than it had been. It pulled the wisp's attention away from me, and with a screech it signaled to its three friends. They responded with the same piercing shriek, nothing like the soothing female voices that supposedly lured travelers into their traps.

Other people had heard the train whistle too and couldn't resist. I heard their shouts as they ran for the tracks. The wisps couldn't resist either. There was a buzz of activity before they bolted after the more obvious prey.

I had to see what had happened, how close the train was. I counted to five and slowly sat up.

The four wisps were closer to the tracks. I could make out the things' silvery silhouettes, their flickering tendrils like swirls of white smoke. Two of them caught up to and pounced on a man, their high-pitched shrieks sending the remaining two into a frenzy. The screams of the man were bone chilling as he succumbed.

I was out of my mind staying buried in the sand; the train was coming. The need to run, or at the very least do *something*, took over. I cleared away the sand—I had to run far and fast now. Captain let out a high-pitched, terrified mew beside me. He was on board too.

A firm grip on my shoulder forced me back into the sand before I could bolt.

Artemis.

"Let me g—" A warm hand covered my mouth to keep me from screaming. It was the warmth that brought me back to my senses, penetrating through the icy cold that had gripped me and every other living thing near the train and the wisps.

"It's the wisps," he said. "Powerful old ones can scare their prey into running." He shook his head as he whispered, "I've never seen it on this scale before. Something is very wrong."

The people who had waited it out near the station were in full panic. A few ran back into the small station; a few crawled under it.

"Not into the station, spread yourselves thin—there are only four." He cursed under his breath as three of them were caught by one wisp's tendrils. "Why is it your species never bothers to think when they're scared?"

But my attention was on something much more disconcerting: the train that was pulling into the station had stopped slowing down, even as the waiting passengers waved at it, the station night staff shining their flashlights.

One desperate man stepped onto the tracks, waving two flashlights in a cross. The train sounded its horn once. That was all the warning it gave.

Son of a— I closed my eyes as the train crushed him, then came to a grinding halt a hundred fifty feet later.

In a morbid twist of fate, the train's colliding with the man had resulted in his body jamming the track. There was a commotion on the cab as the engineers scrambled—arguing, I imagined, about who should get down.

The passengers near the station lost no time climbing onto the train, their movement attracting the renewed attention of the four wisps, who had been feeding on their last prey.

Other passengers who had been hiding in the desert either decided that they weren't going to get another opportunity to escape or noticed that others were running and figured all they had to do was reach the train first.

I concurred. I started for the train.

"Wait," Artemis said, grabbing the strap on Captain's carrier. I hit the sand hard on my stomach. "And watch."

I did.

One of the engineers managed to shove the other one off, then threw him a rake or hoe. He scrambled to pull the body out, acting like a maniac.

Others had caught up to the train, and a flurry of madness ensued as they clambered onto the cars, grabbing whatever they could, even kicking at one another to keep their spot. One man grabbed a woman and threw her back into the sand along with a small boy, then took her space. No one tried to stop him.

The woman and boy managed to climb up on another car, disappearing inside just as the wisps arrived, their screeches sounding across the sand dunes.

"They're fed now," Artemis said. "They'll be more powerful—and hungrier. They'll never be satiated now. Now—run!" he commanded as the wisps clambered over a man they'd knocked off the train. The engineer hacked at the tracks with his rake.

I grabbed Captain and bolted after Artemis. Down the dune I ran.

I glimpsed a face I recognized from the station, a woman with a white shawl and a worn carpetbag. The carpetbag was long gone, but the shawl still twisted in the sand. She saw us run and must have decided that the odds of three surviving were better than one. Out of the corner of my eye I saw her scramble up from where she had fallen and run after us.

A wisp crested a dune in front of us. The woman's white shawl waving in the night sky, reflecting what little light there was—well, it was irresistible.

Artemis knocked me down in the sand. I fell hard on my stomach, and Captain skidded to a stop beside me.

"Are you out of your mind? The train is right there!" And if the commotion on top of the cab was any indication, it was about to get going.

"Just wait," Artemis growled.

The wisp that had come to investigate bellowed high and sharp as it bore down on the woman. She screamed, and I could have sworn she picked up her pace.

Bad luck, wrong place, wrong time—if she'd been ten feet in front or to the right of us . . .

"She's right there. Can't you hide her?"

Artemis's hand clamped down over my mouth. "Keep quiet," he hissed in my ear. "Wisps may not hold a conversation, but they react to sound like bloodhounds to a scent. I can barely hide you and me, and once she's done with her, she'll probably be able to sense past my defenses."

"You're one of them! Isn't there something you can do to stop her?"

"*I'm not Rynn.*" There was uncharacteristic venom in his words. "I'm sorry," he added in a softer tone. "It's us or her. I wish it wasn't so, but there's very little I can do except hide us."

The woman was close now, still trying her damnedest to escape from the wisp. In a moment she would pass by, close enough for me to trip her.

"I know what you're thinking—*don't,*" Artemis pleaded. "If you do, I won't be able to hide you from the wisps. She'll kill you, the woman, and everyone else here, and what for? To prove you're not an asshole? All it will be is a waste—and you'll never know if Rynn lives or dies in that armor because *you* will be dead."

I balled my hands into fists as the woman scrambled up the sand dune, close enough for me to touch her.

And then she was past my reach, heading towards the tracks and the furiously working mechanic.

The woman cast a glance over her shoulder at the oncoming wisp. It cost her; she fell on her knees. For a moment I thought she had seen me. Her eyes widened, and she reached her hand out towards me, beseeching me for help. Then the wisp was on her, a flutter of translucent white strips that wrapped around her neck like a noose. A layer of white frost crawled up her face, eventually covering her eyes.

I couldn't help. I couldn't do a damn thing about it. Worse, I hadn't even tried. And I felt sick about it.

I was thankful I couldn't see any of the other people who were screaming.

"Now!" Artemis said, and we set off at a run for the tracks, ahead of where the train was. A few other stragglers ran to where the train was stopped.

I saw what Artemis had been hinting at: the engineer had finally managed to free the mangled body. The train crept forward, the wheels crushing past the remaining debris—and the closest person still had a hundred meters of sand left. We had a hundred fifty, so we aimed ahead. The change in the four wisps at the renewed movement was instantaneous: they slid across the sands, glowing bright white. There were maybe four of us in total who had waited until the last minute. She descended on the first one she reached, a young Malian man. He tumbled head over heels, caught up in the translucent nets of white vapor. There was a quick scream that died in a gasp.

A glance over my shoulder showed that he'd been frozen into a tangled, unnatural heap of limbs. The wisps rose back into the air and burned more brightly, as if they had found something they were looking for—and that was me.

Shit. "Run faster!" I yelled at Artemis as two of them screeched and bolted across the sand for us. I forced my own legs to pick up the pace.

We reached the tracks as the train started to pull forward, picking up speed with each meter. The wisps were close on our trail, icy cold creeping across the sands until frost slid down the tracks. Artemis pulled alongside the tracks and kept running. I could hear the train behind us.

"Jump when I do!" he shouted.

That was the plan? Fantastic, another thing I never ever wanted to have to do in life scratched off the list.

The train pulled alongside, and quickly the engine car passed.

"Now!" he shouted, and threw himself at a ladder before pulling himself into an open car's belly.

I meant to jump, I really did. I saw a shoe—and then the severed leg it was still attached to.

Fuck me, jump.

The train sped up.

Shit.

Artemis saw that I was still running alongside the train and swore. "Grab my hand, then," he said, leaning on the bottom of the car and holding his hand out. "Jump on the count of three. One, two—"

I watched as another person tried to jump and fell as the wisps descended on him.

Oh, hell . . .

"It's either jump now or become an icicle."

I felt the ice trickle along my back as Captain howled. Out of time. I gripped Artemis's wrist and leapt.

"*Oomph!*" The wind was knocked out of me as my midsection hit metal, my body half in, half out.

Artemis reached for me with the other hand and pulled me and Captain in, away from the wisps licking at my heels. I collapsed against the metal side of the empty car, breathing hard, and Artemis slammed the door.

Four shrieks pierced the night. My adrenaline spiked as I peered through the crack in the car door. The only thing I saw was the white glow of the wisps fading in the night as the train picked up speed.

We'd escaped. For now. It didn't seem the consolation it should have been. All I could think about was the white shawl fluttering across the sand.

"We'll need to get off in Dakar," Artemis said, his eyes closed, "and fly to Turkey. Rynn and his mercenaries won't expect that. They'll still send someone out to look, but they won't waste resources there. They won't expect us to veer off the Silk Road, not with the ancient armor running the show. Then again, maybe he'll damn it all and throw all his forces into Istanbul. Just sit and wait for us to deliver our lamblike selves to the slaughter."

I shook my head, pulling myself out of my own shock, though I'm not sure how exactly my brain had been able to function. "They don't have the map," I said, my voice small. So much death in such a short time . . .

"Istanbul will be on their list. The Silk Road didn't have that many other stops."

I sat back and closed my eyes. Try as I might, I couldn't get that white shawl out of my head. "Rynn sent the wisps."

Artemis glanced at me. "Wisps are too unpredictable, too wild, unthinking. He never liked chaos on the battlefield. He's not thinking like himself." I shook my head, still processing not one but two supernatural massacres I'd seen in twenty-four hours. "Why? Why send something you can't control?"

Artemis shrugged. "Who knows? Perhaps he thought the wisp might be pushed to retrieve you without killing you, perhaps he decided just to outright kill you, maybe he was curious whether the wisp would kill you or leave you marginally alive. Or maybe he was curious to see if the wisps would kill your cat. Who knows what chaos he thought to flush out?" He shook his head. "There was something wrong with them. Wisps don't behave like that. They lure their prey, they don't attack." His look went from pensive to suspicious as he regarded me from across the car. He turned it on me.

My heart rate spiked, and there was nothing I could do to stop it.

"First the skin walker singles you out, now the wisps," he said. "What the hell are you not telling me about that device?"

"Nothing," I said, and oddly enough it wasn't a lie—I *didn't* know what was so special about it. I wished I damn well did.

He snorted. I expected more of an argument as his eyes drifted to the pocket where I kept the silver ball. "Fine, don't tell me, Hiboux, keep your secrets. But don't blame me when they get you killed." He folded his jacket behind his head and settled uncomfortably against the cargo hold. "Our next stop is Istanbul, and she doesn't mess around."

"The city isn't sentient," I said.

He opened a sleepy eye. "Of course not, but the Medusa of the cistern is. According to your Tiger Thieves and their map, that's our next stop. Let's hope she's feeling agreeable to parting with her piece—and that it's only her we need to deal with."

I tried to copy him and get some sleep—for that matter, so did Captain.

I felt for the silver ball in my pocket and gripped it tight in my hand. Rynn was afraid, and I still had no idea why. It certainly wasn't for something that could nuke a couple of vampires—which prompted the question, what else could it do?

I went back to staring through the cracks in the train car, watching for lights on the sand.

"You might as well get some sleep. The wisps will have lost interest by now. They have their fill to gorge on now." I couldn't read Artemis's voice any better than I usually could, so well schooled was his indifference.

Either too tired or too numb, I didn't argue. My silence only seemed to agitate him.

"You keep saying you don't care what happens in our little war provided you save your wayward boyfriend. Well, this? The skin walkers, the wisps—this is exactly what will happen to your kind if the other side wins."

I turned back to face him. "Don't you dare try to guilt me."

"Me?" He arched an eyebrow, making his face look more sinister. "Never. I'm just pointing out the choices you're consciously making." He settled in. "Sleep well, Hiboux. Or try—because I have no idea what's waiting for us in Istanbul."

I laid my head back, the silver ball cold and clammy in my pocket. If there had been any doubt before in my mind that the device could do something besides incinerate vampires . . . all those people, dead.

I clenched it until the grooves bit into my hand. If it saved Rynn before he could hurt more people than he already had, then it was worth the risk. I had to believe that; otherwise I really was no better than any other thief out there.

And once I got Rynn out? Then I'd destroy it—or hide it down a bottomless pit.

At least that's what I swore to myself. Temptation was a powerful thing.

I pulled my jacket tighter as Captain curled into a ball on my stomach and drifted off into a restless sleep.

12

THE ISTANBUL OF CONSTANTINOPLE

Tuesday, 7:00 a.m., three days later: Istanbul, yet another hotel lobby.

I sipped my coffee and ate another of the baked delicacies the server had brought out. The coffee was different from what I was used to—thicker and sweeter than American or European espresso, and there was a hint of cardamom in it. Different but, I had to admit, a pleasant change. I could count the pleasant changes over the past few months on one hand.

We'd reached Istanbul late this morning. After spending a full day on the train, tired of both each other's company and the complete lack of food and showers, we'd disembarked in Dakar and hopped on a flight to Istanbul. I'd checked my email at the airport during a spot of cell phone reception. It was maybe not the wisest course of action considering that a cell phone could be hacked and monitored, but being cooped up in a cargo container was a bit like being back in the Peruvian jail cell. Locking me in with my own thoughts and misgivings was never a good idea. I'd needed a distraction.

Granted, the communications I'd received hadn't made things much better.

Oricho had warned me to avoid altercations with any more supernaturals; however, he'd offered no suggestions on how to do that exactly. And considering I had supernaturals chasing me down trying to kill me . . .

He'd also warned me to avoid pissing off Mr. Kurosawa and Lady Siyu. That was not nearly as easy a task. He had a point, though, as illuminated by Lady Siyu's message. Hers had been short and to the point:

I assume since you are in North Africa you have a weapon to show for it. Mr. Kurosawa eagerly awaits your report.

I'd momentarily entertained the idea of a stopover in Marrakech to raid the museum, but there'd been no time. I'd stave off her emails in the meantime. Maybe I'd find something for her and Mr. Kurosawa in Istanbul—maybe a nice golem, a genie trap—those were always useful. There might even be an enchanted sword or two lying around the city's underground network of cisterns.

The next location the Tiger Thieves map had pointed to was in Istanbul, the Basilica Cistern, to be precise. Istanbul was full of underground cisterns hidden all over the city; the inhabitants never knew when they'd dig under in their basement and fall into one. The Basilica Cistern, however, was the largest. Built in the sixth century by roughly seven thousand slaves during the reign of the Byzantine emperor Justinian, it was an ancient water storage and filtration system that had supplied the ancient palace with water. It had been named for the basilica, a public building that had once sat on top of it. You could walk through it now, have coffee, sometimes even see a concert.

Oh yeah, and see the giant carved Roman-era Medusa heads at the bases of the pillars. Some historians claimed that they had been brought in as convenient building supplies during construction from another temple or building that had fallen out of use. Others claimed that they had been protection against bad luck. Both were somewhat true, but they missed out on the most important reason for the Medusa heads: they were the rental price the Medusa living in the cavern set.

As far as the IAA was concerned, there was still a Medusa living in the cistern. As to whether or not it was the same one, who could say?

The problem with Medusas was that they were a bit of a wild card. Like cats, Medusas tended to be solitary creatures, only occasionally co-habitating with mates or offspring—all female, so the legends always got it wrong, calling them sisters. They weren't—once a Medusa reached a certain age, she became territorial and chased out her young or killed them—again, a bit like cats.

So chances were that there was only one there—more detail than that couldn't be found in that short a period of time. Possibly it was even the same one who had originally bargained with the Byzantines for the place back in the sixth century. I sighed and closed the window on the cistern. Well, I wouldn't get anything more than unfounded theories until I was there. Let's just hope Artemis could talk her into seeing us—and letting us take the fourth Tiger Thief pendant out.

I sipped my cardamom-flavored coffee again and readied to shut my computer off. I found my cursor hovering over the World Quest icon.

It was a long shot that Carpe would rear his head in World Quest. Chances were good that the elves were very wrong about Carpe. Every way I'd thought about it, I didn't see Carpe leaving Shangri-La alive; maybe we all just looked for threads of hope where there were none. If Carpe was really alive and sending messages, why the hell hadn't he shown his face? Anywhere?

The only plausible reasons I could come up with kept getting more and more convoluted.

It was idiocy to hope I'd find anything—still, what the hell. I clicked on the World Quest icon and logged on.

I frowned as the log-in screen flared into existence. Frank and Neil had redesigned it with a Himalayan vibe—an ode to their internment in Shangri-La, I supposed. That wasn't what had my attention, though; it was the flashing orange marker under my in-game mail tab—not the messaging window I used to talk with Carpe but where we sent each other in-game items.

It was from the dynamic designer duo, Neil and Frank, or, as I liked to call them, Michigan and Texas. Like all their communications with me, it was short and to the point: *Call us.*

I checked the hotel café to make certain no one was nearby, put my headphones on, and opened a new message window.

Texas answered on the fourth ring. "Before you start in, try sitting down and shutting up," he began.

Glad to see we knew each other well enough to skip the pleasant-ries . . . oh, wait a minute. Still, I did as he asked.

There was a big breath on the other end. "All right, we looked into your elven friend's account," Michigan said. "As far as I can tell, there's no sign of him logging in, but, there's been some weird stuff going on behind the hood."

"Define weird stuff," I said, wondering how it related to Carpe.

"Ah—someone accessed his account using a back door. They didn't take much—a few magic items, clothing, food, a scroll of resurrection—"

"We figured it was you," Texas told me.

There was Texas, always thinking the best of me . . .

"But the signature is too subtle," Michigan jumped in. "No offense, but you don't exactly do subtle. A master programmer did this."

Which Carpe was: a master hacker who'd gone by the name of Sojourn.

"It doesn't make any sense. If it's Carpe, why not contact me or log in to his account?" I said it more to myself than to them, but talking out loud helped me think.

"You ever think maybe, just maybe, your friend had enough of you? Let's face it, Hiboux, you're a walking fucking archaeological disaster," Texas said.

"Okay, I will admit that my activities have led to some damage, but none of it was intentional or my fault. You especially can't pin Shangri-La on me; that was the IAA, the elves, and the mercenaries."

"It doesn't matter whose fault it is!" Texas was shouting now. So was

I, for that matter. "Wherever you go, mayhem, destruction, and legions of supernatural shit follow—in that order!"

"You know where you can go, Texas? You can go blow your—"

"Okay, enough!" Neil let out a long-suffering sigh. "Will you two just quit it? For my sake if no one else's? Frank, just because Alix correlates with supernatural and archaeological disasters doesn't mean she's the cause of it, and Alix?"

"Yeah?" I said with more than a little trepidation.

"Just being honest here, but you're kind of the train wreck of the archaeological world."

I gritted my teeth. "So I've been told."

Neil sighed. "Okay, now that that's out of the way, check your inbox. I sent the email address they use to log in."

I checked. Sure enough, it was there, a generic call sign with a string of numbers and letters.

"It's a long shot, but it could be him," Neil began, but Frank cut him off. "And now you've got his number—lose ours."

With that the line went dead.

Short, far from sweet, but to the point.

I typed the email address into a new email. My cursor paused over the Send button. Nothing but a rabbit hole, and I didn't need another one to jump down, not right now.

But it was the kind of sign I couldn't just let go. As I'd said many a time before, what the hell?

I made up an in-game invitation, nothing too out of the ordinary, an invite to a map quest I'd had lying around—somewhere in the Nordic fjords. I hesitated over the Send button. But I couldn't not try. Even a minuscule chance was still a chance. I hit Send.

I shut my computer and sat back to savor my coffee, eyes closed. I really thought Neil and Texas were warming up to me. Texas had insulted and threatened me only once, maybe twice . . .

I sat up with a start as a shadow fell over me—one heavy enough that I saw the change in light through my eyelids.

A red-haired man with inhumanly white teeth smiled down at me. Tall and attractive enough in a sporty, LA-bike-messenger kind of way, his red hair was his most memorable feature.

Hermes.

"Oh, for the love of God—not you too?"

His smile widened as he plopped the chair on the other side of the table and sat across from me.

"You kidding? Wouldn't miss it for the world."

A moment later the server brought over a second cup of Turkish coffee and placed it in front of him along with a plate of baked treats the same as mine.

I still wasn't entirely certain what Hermes was. His moniker, that of the patron god of messengers and thieves, was appropriate, as he managed to be a bit of both, though I doubted very much that he was an actual god—the inspiration for one maybe, but a deity he was not. As supernatural creatures went, however, he was up there with the Red Dragon, Mr. Kurosawa, maybe even higher up in the food chain.

He also seemed to be in favor of monsters staying in the deep, dark closet . . . though exactly why I hadn't quite figured out. Powerful he might be; altruistic he was not.

He held out his hands. "What can I say? You're a popular girl. So," he said, settling into his chair and grabbing one of the cookie snacks, "still plan on staying out of our little war?"

"Yes." I said the word, I heard it come out. Hell, I even believed it.

He grabbed another of the cookies and made a show of washing it down with coffee. "See, here's the thing: you say that, but deep down I don't think you have what it takes to be that much of a coldhearted bitch."

I met his green eyes. "Why don't you try me?" I don't know what my goal was—to goad him? irritate him? piss him off?

His eyes crinkled at the corners. "Here's the thing, Hiboux, that right there is what's making my bet that much better. Because *I* think you've already decided exactly what you're going to do, you just haven't admitted it to anyone, not even yourself.

"For example, let's discuss your most recent activities and plan to get that delectable incubus of yours out of hock." He held up a hand and began counting off on his fingers: "Bold, stupid—which I kind of expect from you—but bold and definitely on the reckless side." He leaned in towards me.

"So I've been told," I said through clenched teeth. "Let me guess, this is your attempt to dissuade me?"

He sipped his coffee. His face might be pleasant and affable, but his eyes conveyed something much more chaotic. "Now, granted, most of the other parties involved in this little bet figure you're after the Tiger Thieves, which, for the record, will just as soon kill you as help you, but Rynn?" He *tsk*ed. "Got to hand it to him—as corrupted as that armor's made him, he still thinks outside the box."

He took another sip of coffee. "No one ever considers the nuclear option in these political skirmishes, but him?" He paused to take another bite of a cookie. "Though whether that's because Rynn's intimately familiar with your personal brand of bullshit or whether he's just as crazy as you now is anyone's guess."

"I don't want to hurt anyone." ·

He arched a red eyebrow, more serious than mocking. "Yet here we are with you once again at the center, except you don't have a *clue* what you stumbled on."

Hermes's brand of half truths and innuendo had outworn its welcome—not that I'd ever really welcomed it. "Hermes," I said, "feel free to take this the wrong way, but unless you have something useful or can help—" I rose and made to go.

"Keep your seat, Hiboux. I didn't come here to talk you out of or into anything." He made a face. "Well, maybe a little, but just hear me out."

I sat back down, suspicious of his intentions. "What if saving your boyfriend means that every monster that's itching for its big moment on prime time gets its wish? You really expect me to believe that you're fine with the monsters coming out of the closet?"

I wasn't in a patient mood to begin with, and Hermes had run it thin.

"Can you honestly tell me that anything will really change? Seriously," I added as his eyes widened. "I mean, isn't it a bit like voting? Doesn't matter which party is in place, the policies don't really change. Monsters will still kill people. They do now anyway," I said, thinking back to the skin walkers shopping for new passports.

Hermes rolled his eyes. "Okay, you are not that jaded."

I shrugged. Mr. Kurosawa's little war had honestly been the furthest thing from my mind the last twenty-four hours, but if I were being completely honest . . . "Oh, a few things will change. Vampire dating shows, a new CNN segment with experts from the IAA who couldn't tell a supernatural anomaly from a bagel, Artemis hosting a talk show, probably on the trials and tribulations of being one of them in a human world—but besides a few surreal novelties, can you honestly sit there and tell me anything will really change? Monsters will still eat humans, and we won't be able to do anything about it. That fact will probably still get shoved under the carpet, and no one will be the wiser."

Hermes polished off his coffee. "Okay—first, that is a defeatist attitude and I've never known you to be a defeatist, and second, I'd so pay to watch Artemis host a talk show. All joking and your bad attitude aside, Rynn knows exactly what that little silver device of yours can do, even if you don't, and he's already coming after you. If you plan on going the nuclear route, you gotta move fast."

"Why do you keep calling it the nuclear route?"

"Because it is. Trust me, as soon as that cat is out of the bag, they'll all forget their war and set their sights on you. Unless, that is, you don't have it. If you missed it, that was a hint."

"You think I should give you the device?" I snorted. "Why should I trust you?"

"Think about it, Hiboux. You won't want to have that device anywhere near you when you're done with it, and you can quote me on that."

He passed me a white card. Tentatively I turned it over. On the back was a seven-digit number prefaced with a US area code in gold embossed ink.

"It's not a get-out-of-jail-free card, but when you decide to take me up on the offer, use it. Keep it up, Hiboux, I love me some chaos." Hermes stood, ate his last cookie, and headed for the door.

"Any other pieces of unsolicited advice?"

He glanced at me over his shoulder. "Yeah. I thought I told you not to ditch the guy."

It was all I could do not to throw my empty coffee mug at him as he headed for the lobby.

Fantastic. More supernaturals in the mix to worry about . . . just what I needed.

I began packing up my computer—the lobby had lost its charm, and besides, if what Hermes said about Rynn going to the ends of the earth to hunt me down was true, I needed to find Artemis and get to the cistern.

A woman cleared her throat. I looked up to find the server. "Ah, excuse me, miss, but your friend, he said you would pay. For his?"

Of course he had stuck me with the bill—the self-professed king of thieves . . . *asshole* was more like it.

I added more liras to the pile and went to find Artemis at the cistern.

I leaned against a wall across from the cistern, drinking a soda and eating a sandwich. I'd donned a brown baseball cap—Rynn knew my red one too well. I watched the entrance to the cistern in between checking my phone. Just another tourist enjoying Istanbul—nothing to see here. I'd been watching the court by the cistern on and off for an hour now, from various positions so as not to arouse any suspicion. The Turkish government took security around its monuments seriously and was touchy on the subject of surveillance. I hadn't had much choice; Artemis was late.

I gritted my teeth. Just when I'd begun to expect more from him . . .

Captain stirred in my backpack. An hour and I hadn't seen anything suspicious—or anyone who betrayed mercenary training.

Captain mewed. "Well, let's see how Nadya is doing," I told him. I'd hesitated to call her since leaving Venice, but I'd expected an update by now. It was hard not to be worried.

She picked up on the second ring.

"Alix, it's getting worse—much worse," she said, after we exchanged pleasantries.

"Shit." Not that there was anything I could do about it, even if I were there—not when the problem was supernaturals running amok. "What's happening?"

"People are dying. Not in droves, but some of the Tokyo monsters and demons are getting bold. Oricho can do only so much—though, thankfully, they're so set in their ways that they aren't doing anything outright blatant."

"How so?"

"You know the salaryman deaths?"

Salarymen were businessmen who worked themselves to death; it was something that happened in Japan due to cultural traditions around work. It was sad in a tragic sort of way, but also wasn't exactly out of the normal.

"Let's just say, Alix, that the rate has gone up—significantly, the news reporters are calling it an epidemic. According to Oricho, a handful of demons are behind it."

They weren't actually demons, but that was the designation that the Japanese had given to the various species of supernaturals that called the Japanese islands and Korean peninsula home—ones that had an affinity for thematic nature shows and a lot of magic. None of them had ever disputed the demon moniker, and so it had stuck.

"No one has connected the dots yet," Nadya continued. "But it's only a matter of time before something can't be explained away easily with Photoshop—and then?"

"And then people will do what they always do, Nadya: they'll take whatever excuse you give them, however improbable, as long as it doesn't involve monsters."

"I hope you're right, but I'm not so sure. The major websites and news organizations are being scrubbed clean, but everywhere else on the Internet is full of monster sightings."

The Internet drew dirty laundry to its ugly, awful, fluorescent haze like a strobe light did moths on acid. There was no reason the supernaturals' bullshit would be any different. "I'll try to get there soon," I told her.

"One more thing, Alix, I found something about the da Vinci device."

"You're kidding me," I said. I didn't hide my surprise.

"Don't thank me just yet. It was a footnote in a Russian thesis on da Vinci's devices in general. There's an entire chapter on his supernatural and magic endeavors. It might not be anything." I heard the click of computer keys. "All right, this is the passage:

> For all da Vinci's ingenuity, his supernatural artifacts employed esoteric activation methods. Rather than using traditional methods, they employed numerical and pictographic codes and riddles. Users were more likely to cause the devices to backfire without the precise instructions. Whether that was purposeful to prevent misuse or sheer accident is unknown, though either is possible."

Nadya was right—it was generic. And I hadn't seen a code attached to the devices. In fact, I hadn't seen codes attached to any of the discarded devices. There had certainly been pictures over the device . . . wait a minute.

I pulled the notebook out of my jacket and began flipping through the pages until I found the ones full of symbols—what I'd originally thought amounted to the designs of a madman, but they should have predated da Vinci's descent into elixir-filled madness.

I scanned the pages. Some of them matched the ones that decorated the orb. From the looks of the labels, different configurations of hand-drawn symbols were clustered under names for various monsters: Nosferatu, Romanian for *vampire*; lycanthrope; espiritos; even incubus was listed, with another series of the diagrams underneath. Just like codes.

I looked around the park before pulling the sphere out of my pocket. I wasn't stupid enough to try fitting the configurations in now; who knew what might happen, but it couldn't hurt to see what configurations the orb had been fit into. Half of the mobile images looked jammed, but they'd been jammed in the order for vampires.

Well, it fit with what he'd said in his notebooks about dissolving vampires . . .

I noticed two men on the other side of the road. There was nothing obvious about the way they were dressed—jackets, caps, like a lot of other tourists in Istanbul—it was the way they held themselves and walked: alert, straight, as if they were ready for a fight. "Nadya, I'm going to have to call you back later." I slipped the orb back into my pocket and angled my head down so underneath the cap it looked as if I was staring at my phone.

If I hadn't been certain they were Rynn's mercenaries, the way they glanced around, their stares vacant as they scanned the crowd—

"Fancy seeing you here."

I just about jumped. Artemis was leaning against the wall beside me. "Don't worry, they can't see us."

Sure enough, the mercenaries' eyes passed right over us. They didn't interact, speak to each other, look at each other.

"Definitely Rynn's mercenaries," Artemis said, confirming my suspicions.

"What's wrong with them?"

Artemis stared at them with concentration, for once looking perturbed. "Can't say," he said after a moment. "I can't even get a reading off them. I slid right off their minds—it's as if they aren't feeling anything."

"How is that possible?"

He shook his head. "It isn't."

That wasn't necessarily ominous . . . I realized that Artemis could hide himself from me as well as from anyone else. For all I knew, he'd been listening in on my conversation with Nadya . . . "How long have you been hanging out here?"

"Long enough" was all he said. "She'll meet us now—and she's open to a trade. I figure she hasn't gotten wind of any of your recent shenanigans—which is all the more reason for us to go now. Your call, O fearless leader."

I supposed it was my call. I let out a breath as I watched the two mercenaries round the corner and disappear out of sight. What I would have liked was a week to suss out the entire cistern and find a couple of exits. But, I wasn't going to get what I wanted, and if I waited any longer I might piss off the Medusa.

"It's now or never."

We crossed the street and entered at the front of the line. No one noticed us, not even as Artemis pushed aside a guard so we could pass the other tourists heading down. I caught my own reflection in a mirror above the stairs that led into the stone cavern, the one that allowed the ticket sales personnel and guards to see who was in the crowd. I saw my blond braid sticking out the back of my cap and my cargo jacket. I still looked the worse for wear, but that wasn't what got me. It was the blond head right behind me, his blue eyes staring into the mirror, looking right at me. I gasped and turned, my heart racing despite my best efforts. There was no one there except a couple from a Chinese tour group. I searched the crowd, but none of them looked remotely like Rynn.

I stole another quick glance back up at the mirror. Rynn was gone. Either I was completely losing it, or Rynn was busy learning new tricks . . .

Artemis was staring at me.

"Got the sun in my eye," I lied. "Let's just get the necklace." I picked up my pace as we descended the steps, weaving around the other people as if we really weren't there.

I shouldered Captain and took one last long look at the crowd above us. "Let's hope a Medusa is all that's waiting for us down here, eh, Captain?"

The light dimmed as we entered the cistern. Despite the fact that we were in an underground cavern, the smell was of fresh, not stagnant, water. The sound of water dripping from the cavern ceiling punctuated the din of voices as we descended. Lights placed under the water projected ripples onto the ceiling, giving the entire cavern an appearance of being underwater. Wooden walkways wound through the massive natural aquifer, filled with people snapping pictures of the ancient civil engineering and architectural handiwork of the Romans.

And then there were the carved pillars, the warning of the Medusa heads, and the column carved to look like a tree—whether the practice work of an apprentice or a full-scale artistic plan cut short because the artist died, who knew?

We maneuvered around the coffee shop line and the metal wire tables and chairs set around the beginning and end. One thing was certain: with all the people down here, I had a hard time believing a Medusa could blend in, let alone hide.

"Medusa was the name of one Gorgon," Artemis told me as he led the way through the people gathered along the boardwalk looking for fish in the water. "It's not a species name. You'd be smart to remember that."

"How exactly do we meet her?"

"Oh—that." He looked around at the packed cistern and curled his upper lip, making a face. "Yes, they are a bit of a problem. The Gorgon won't like trespassers; she has enough fountain statues as it is. I suppose we'll need a distraction."

Before I could stop him, Artemis took his silver lighter from his pocket and lit a cigarette, which earned more than a few disgusted looks from people who couldn't see us but could smell the smoke. He took two drags off the cigarette and then held the lighter's flame underneath a smoke detector directly over us.

I swore and pressed myself against the wall as the fire alarm sounded, echoing off both the water and walls, the distortion making it sound all that more ominous.

The effect was immediate. People began to flood out, none of them seeing us even as they stumbled and pushed past us. Captain let out a warning mew, but none of them noticed. Soon the place was empty except for a skeleton staff who spread out to track down what had set off the system.

"See? Not a problem." Whistling, he ran his hand against the wall until he found what he was looking for. Stone ground against stone as a section of the wall slid open, exposing another walkway—this one lit with lanterns.

Artemis leapt onto the new boardwalk and held his hand out for me. I ignored it and hopped over all on my own, thanks very much. Artemis shrugged and led the way. The stone door slid shut behind us.

The walkway and new cavern were similar to the other, but as opposed to a sterile tourist attraction, it was clear that this was someone's home. There were vine and lantern decorations that showed someone's personal touch; even the boardwalk was detailed. The wood was more expensive than what had been used in the tourist section and was stained a slick, shiny dark grain, gleaming more like prized teak furniture than something you would tread on. Even the tread pads were more expensive looking and obviously much less used. I was thinking that the place looked more like a fairy-tale home—like something a fairy up on modern style magazines might live in; there was an enviable Zen-like quality to everything.

At least until I almost stumbled into the first statue . . .

It was floodlit with a submersible LED that bled blue into the water, reaching out as if it were ready to pull you in. The statue wasn't the shiny gray of polished granite but the dark matte black color of cooled lava. He—I assumed it was a he because of the clothes, despite the fact that the details of his face had been mostly smoothed away by the cistern's water over the centuries—had what was left of his features twisted into a permanent grimace. His hands were clasping a spear that had been rammed through the Roman armor. I shivered. It didn't look as though it had been a nice way to die. I realized that it was only the first of a forest of statues; throughout the Zen-worthy hidden cistern there were hundreds

of them. Some, like the Roman, were highlighted on their own like cher-
ished pieces of art, while others were clustered—cowering, readying for
battle—collections of vignettes capturing the moments before they had
died. Most had seen better days, the water having worn away their features, while others had stumbled in during the last hundred years, their
features still crisp and clear. All shared one characteristic: their faces
were terrified.

They were displayed like art, but that's not what they were, not entirely.

"Territorial markers," Artemis offered. "To warn off any other Gorgons or other supernaturals who might think of taking up shop here."

"You'd be amazed how well it works." The voice wasn't Artemis's nor
that of any other male. It was decidedly female.

I swore and spun around. Behind me was a woman—and not a
human one, not by any stretch.

Unlike the depictions of Gorgons around the cistern, all of which
sported thick snake tendrils in lieu of hair, this one's hair was not quite
that. It was hair, a mix of dreadlocked and braided strands that were an
inky, shiny black. Instead of lying flat, though, they'd been given a life of
their own, the ends twisted, knotted, and sculpted into snake heads—
and they snapped. Magic, most likely.

There were no snakelike qualities to her body beyond the shape of
her hair. Her legs, neck, and what I could see of her chest were covered
in iridescent scales that highlighted her olive skin under the soft lights.
She was more fish than reptile.

Older legends claim that Medusa was one of three Gorgon sisters
born to the marine deities Phorcys and Ceto. In those stories, the Gorgons are monsters through and through, with wings, snake hair, and
horrid faces—so horrid looking are they, in fact, that they turn mortals
into stone. More modern interpretations paint Medusa as a beautiful
Greek woman who flees from Poseidon to Athena's temple, beseeching
her for protection. She's raped, and Athena, disgusted by her weakness,
curses her so no man will ever touch her again. Apparently Athena was

not the goddess you asked for favors before she had her morning cup of coffee . . .

Like most legends and myths, it had been warped over the millennia to serve whatever lesson they wanted taught. They were also both mostly a load of shit—except for the part about their starting off as monsters. That was true enough.

Gorgons looked like beautiful human women, but they weren't. They were Gorgons. And they turned people into stone statues to mark their territories against predators and other Gorgons who might want to move in. Like Captain marked plants, people, and furniture with the scent glands in his head and paws and good old-fashioned cat pee to tell other cats what was his. Except that instead of using olfactory cues, theirs were visual—very visual and explicit, like the one we were standing beside, the Roman soldier clutching a spear sticking out of his abdomen, his face permanently fixed in an expression of shock and terror.

It was one hell of a warning . . . definitely not what the beautiful face before us would suggest.

"Artemis," she said. The sleek tendrils of her hair churned in on themselves, the magic that coursed through the Gorgon animating them. Her voice had a thick, seductive quality to it; "womanly" might be the best descriptor.

"Naomi," Artemis said. He was avoiding looking her directly in the face. I followed his lead and averted my gaze. Looking a Gorgon in the face wasn't an automatic stone sentence, but they turned it on and off at will, and if Artemis wasn't on that kind of buddy-trust level with her, I definitely wasn't.

"Lovely to see you," he continued.

She snorted. "Wish I could say the same."

"I'm not here for a social call or to cause trouble," he said, holding up his hands. "We're here to barter, then leave. You have my word."

She snorted again. A nearby statue held a shield, its surface reflecting a blurry image of the natural cavern. In it I thought I saw the Gorgon arch an eyebrow.

"Barter? Is that what you're calling it now? Things have changed greatly if the peddling of your wares is now called bartering."

I glared at Artemis. The impression I'd gotten from him was that he and the Gorgon were on friendly terms.

Artemis didn't lose a step. "You know what we're here for, Naomi."

"Ah, yes. You want me to let you search through my home for some artifact." I heard something clink and hazarded a glance at her hand, careful, so careful, not to look her in the face.

Dangling from her fingers was a small stone pendant.

Shit.

"I'd forgotten about this old thing," she said. "I found it on the Gorgon who was here before me, too many years ago to remember things clearly—someone came here asking me for this many years ago as well. Might have been a Roman, might have been a Turk—might have even been one of them." She nodded at the statues that filled the cavern.

I averted my eyes back down at the water as she turned her gaze on me.

"I was curious when you called," she said, still addressing Artemis. "I assumed the thieves had reared their ugly heads and were back to killing our kind. Then I began making my own calls." She smiled. It wasn't friendly. "You'd be amazed at what I found."

Her voice was still even, but there was a tension in the air now that hadn't been there a moment before.

I noticed the water near the statue churn. There was a small splash, then a second one, then a third. Okay, there was no way that was natural. Shit, was that a fin? I turned to get a better look, keeping my eyes rooted on the water.

"So tell me, Artemis, why should I give you this?" She leaned over the boardwalk railing, her skin as reflective as the polished wood. All pretense of pleasantries was gone from her face.

"Who did you speak to, Naomi?" Artemis asked, a warning in his own voice now.

She might have responded, but I was fixated on another splash beside me, then another. There was a fin in the water—no, make that two, three, four—

Oh, that was not good. "*Artemis*," I said. He looked down at the water and spun back on the Gorgon. "Naomi," he chided her, "I thought we were friends."

She laughed at that. "I'm afraid I had an offer I couldn't refuse."

"If it's money—"

She made a clicking sound, and the tendrils of her hair reared, animated and hissing once again. The water underneath us was churning, stirred up by whatever the hell was in it. One of the statues crashed to the submersed floor, cracking under the water. I got my first good glimpse of a long, sinewy tail preceded by the back of a bone-white female body.

Yup, bad was going to worse. I backed the hell away from the edge of the walkway, putting myself and Captain square in the center.

Artemis spun on Naomi. "Call your mermaids off," he said.

She *tsk*ed, placing the necklace around her neck, the pendant dangling against her scales. "How about you explain to me why your cousin Rynn and his merry band of mercenaries are clamoring to get to you and the girl. And don't lie, Artemis. You did that last time before you took that delectable creature away from me." She pointed to an empty pedestal. "She was to have her own spot. I still haven't found a replacement." She smiled at him. "Whatever happened to her? She must be dead by now. Just think, if you hadn't stolen her from me you could still visit."

Fantastic, Artemis had saved someone from her. Of all the times for him to have altruistic tendencies. Shit!

The mermaids reared up against the railing, forcing both Artemis and me back.

I froze. I'd never seen a mermaid before. I'd read about them, seen drawings of them, but never seen one in person. From the back they might resemble a human woman with a fish tail, but belly side up was a different matter. Rows of needle-pointed teeth ran behind their lips, and milky, vapid eyes stared up at me. Their mouths moved, but no words came out.

Artemis pushed me along the walkway until I shook myself out of my torpor and ran. "You didn't say anything about mermaids!"

"Mermaids and Gorgons are distant relatives. It was always a possibility they'd be down here."

We dodged another mermaid, who threw herself out of the water at us. "Gorgons live most of their lives on land, preferring swamps and caverns to open water. Mermaids live most of their lives in the Mediterranean. They're more interested in finding food and hoarding anything shiny than holding a conversation. Why do you think there were so many shipwrecks?"

I dropped to my knees as one launched overhead, her pale, glassy fish eyes set in a bloated corpselike face seeking me. She screeched as she hit my shoulder, sending me sliding for the cistern's water. The legends about their being beautiful women were certainly off. Survivors' prejudice, I figured. Those who got a good look at a mermaid's face rarely lived to tell the tale.

That did not bode well for me.

"Naomi," Artemis warned, all trace of civility gone. "We had an agreement. All I'm interested in is that pendant."

"I'm not that naive."

"Tell him I left before you could catch me. He knows me well enough to know that's plausible." He was pleading with her now, trying to avoid a fight.

For a moment, watching Naomi as I stayed out of range of the mermaids, I really thought she might go for it.

"If only it was you he was interested in." She pointed at me and let out a high-pitched screech that echoed throughout the cavern.

The mermaids returned the call, their shrieks warped by the water. Artemis swore.

Captain, deciding he didn't like anything that smelled supernatural and lived in water, spat and hissed.

One of the mermaids' tails crashed into the boardwalk in front of me, while another hit the railing behind me. The statue of the Roman toppled, shattering with a loud crack.

"Run!" Artemis shouted.

He didn't have to tell me twice.

I grabbed Captain and scrambled down the walkway after Artemis. A steel grip closed around my ankle, tripping me and making me drop Captain. He slid a foot away before shaking himself and attacking the clawed, corpselike white hand, which was now dragging me towards the water.

My legs went over the edge, and I gripped the post as though my life depended on it. Captain growled, and the mermaids shrieked and splashed back at him.

Artemis realized that I wasn't behind him and skidded to a stop before doubling back towards me, but the mermaids cut him off.

I looked down into a face full of teeth and began to kick. "Let—go—of—me!" I shouted, punctuating each word with a kick.

The mermaid's algae-stained nails slipped as Artemis reached me and began to pull me up. He pulled me after him, towards the exit, but it was too late. The mermaids churned the water, cutting off our retreat.

"Any bright ideas?" I asked.

"Not unless you happen to be carrying a boatful of ancient soldiers around in your backpack to appease them with."

The churning made the underwater LEDs appear to flicker like strobe lights, highlighting the many swimming forms closing in. My foot caught on one of the boards as we backed away from them, and luckily Artemis caught me before I could fall. It wouldn't have happened if not for the damn lights, and they were everywhere.

That gave me an idea.

Naomi was bearing down on us. Between her and the mermaids, I would have to act fast.

I looked around, searching the walls for wires. They had to be here somewhere—there! I saw them, black waterproof tubes running down the length of the cavern walls and spreading out to the sunken LEDs. Now, how to reach them? The walls were all too far away from the boardwalk—there! Behind a statue of a Greek woman, her clothes long since reduced to silk covered with water slime.

"Stay here," I said to Artemis and Captain.

One, two—on three I jumped. I hit the statue and had the wind knocked out of me, but I held. I kicked at a mermaid hand and a set of snapping teeth set in an uneven face, then climbed. The woman's features had long since worn away; the porous, lavalike rock was nowhere near as sturdy as it looked. Captain let out a moan. I looked over my shoulder and saw him standing on the railing, switching his tail as if readying to jump, but the water below stopped him from following. He renewed his assault on the mermaid tails that flicked towards him and Artemis. I scrambled up the statue until I was standing on her shoulders, the old silk turned to soft mush in my hands, and bits of the black rock crumbled as I tried to reach the wire.

Try not to think what you're breaking, I thought as the statue's fingers broke off. I wedged my foot in the crook of her arm. The statue wobbled on its pedestal as I reached for the wire.

Whether the mermaids understood what I was trying to do or simply realized that I'd escaped the boardwalk I'll never know, but the water churned around me as I reached for the insulated black wire.

"Alix, watch it!" Artemis shouted.

I glanced over my shoulder in time to see the Medusa push him into the arms of waiting mermaids, who pulled him into the water. She turned her green eyes on me.

Shit. I closed my eyes and turned away before her magic could wash over me. God, I hoped it didn't work on cats.

I doubled my efforts to reach the wire, balancing on my toes as I stretched my arm towards it.

My fingers closed around the wire, and I pulled. For a long moment it held, bolted to the cavern wall, but then it gave, the fixtures popping out one by one. Now, where the hell was my knife?

I searched my jacket with my free hand until I found my pocketknife. I set the blade against the wire and sawed madly at the insulation.

It gave, and the LED lights flickered out. The cavern was illuminated only by the lantern lights now, the water a dark, churning pit. A mermaid knocked against the statue, sending it rocking on its foundation. The ends of the wire slipped from my hands and almost fell into the water.

"Artemis? I'd get the hell out of the water—like now!" I shouted.

I couldn't see him, but I heard him curse at me. Then I heard splashing and shrieks and footsteps. He must have made for the boardwalk.

The statue rocked again, and I yanked my foot out of the way before a mermaid could snatch it. More mermaids were swarming around me, if the splashing and jostling of the statue were any indication.

I glanced down at the water but couldn't make out the now dark forms. The statue rocked again, and I hoped that enough of them were there. I dropped the severed wire ends into the water.

The effect was immediate and spectacular. There were no sparks or flashes like you see on TV or in the movies. But there was noise, a lot of it: the heightened shrieks of the mermaids and the intensified splashing. Then I smelled burnt flesh—not like a fish's, more like smoked bacon. The violent splashing lasted only a minute, and then only the scent of smoke remained as silence descended. The lights above reflected off the glasslike water, disturbed only by the long bodies floating on the surface.

The Gorgon screamed.

Okay, Owl, don't ruin the plan by falling into the electrocuting water. I leapt off the statue and for a moment feared I might hit the water before crash-landing on the boardwalk.

I stood and turned towards the doorway, in sight but very far away.

Naomi was standing in the way. And she had Artemis, the tendrils of her hair wrapped around his neck, arms, and waist, the snake-shaped heads of her hair snapping at his face.

I froze. Captain crouched by my feet.

"Why?" Artemis managed, his voice strained.

Naomi's hair struck his face as she snarled, "Because *he* wants her. It was either capture her or serve him."

The skin walker's words came back to me: "He can manipulate us now as easily as the humans he's acquired, warping and twisting us until we're just as dark and damaged as the elves made him and the armor."

"You've heard the stories about the thralls," Naomi continued. "They're all true. He's gathered enough mindless followers—draining them of self-will, turning and twisting them until they're little more than weapons and cannon fodder." She spat into the water, and I didn't miss her glance down at the floating mermaid corpses.

Despite the circumstances, I felt bad for them.

I shook my head. I did *not* have to feel bad about the mermaids' trying to eat me.

"He's taken quite an interest in you," the skin walker had said. "And you're too naive to know the danger you're in. Better that I take your skin and end your suffering now. Kinder than letting you run and hide."

"He's on his way if not here already," Naomi said. "It was either me or you, Artemis, and I think you know who I'd rather see skinned alive." The snakes flailed around her head.

Artemis grunted. He was going limp now, fighting her less.

And there was nothing I could do to help.

"Consider this payment for *her*—"

Naomi didn't finish the sentence. Instead, the snakes holding Artemis loosened and began to flail. Her beautiful mouth formed a shocked *O* as a black pool formed on her chest, just above the spot where a human heart might have been. There was a blade sticking out of her chest, the handle in Artemis's hand.

I hadn't seen it; neither had Naomi.

Jesus. I took a big step back.

The tendrils of her hair fluttered once, twice, before settling around her face as the life drained out of it. She slid to the boardwalk, and Artemis crouched down beside her.

If he was perturbed, he didn't show it. "Live long enough as a spy, and you learn it's better to stick someone in the back with a knife before they can do it to you." He wiped the knife off before it disappeared somewhere into his jacket.

I stood where I was, glued in place as I tried to wrap my head around what I'd just seen. I couldn't help it; she might have been a monster, but now she was dead. And it hadn't happened in a fight.

Artemis removed the pendant from around her neck and tossed it at me.

I caught it—barely. "I thought you didn't get into fights with other supernaturals," I said.

He smiled at me, cold and vicious. "And sticking a knife into someone's back isn't fighting—nor is it a talent. Getting close enough to do it is."

I shook my head. "You just killed her."

"And you killed a school of mermaids with a power cord."

"Yeah, but—" I was going to say that it had been different—but had it? A moment ago I'd figured it was black and white, but now? I wasn't so certain. Like everything else in my life, things were settling into an uncomfortable scale of gray.

Artemis either didn't care about or notice my state of duress as he continued to roll the Gorgon, searching for items. It made all those times I'd roughly searched bodies in World Quest seem a lot sicker than they'd been. "Once we're out of here, we'll have a thorough discussion about what the hell it is you dragged out of da Vinci's lair. And don't tell me it's a broken antivampire weapon."

"But that's just it! That's what da Vinci called it. I don't know what else it's supposed to do."

"Then you aren't looking hard enough!" he shouted. He pushed the door open and headed into the abandoned tourist side of the cistern. The wires I had submerged must have short-circuited more than just the water-submerged lights; the entire cistern was bathed in a red glow.

Artemis gave me a sour look. "There is no way my cousin is terrorizing half the supernatural community trying to chase you out of hiding because of the Tiger Thieves. It has something to do with that thing you keep clutching like a junkie holding the last eight ball on the planet."

I let go of the silver ball in my pocket. "According to her, it's the entire supernatural community. And I'm far from a junkie."

Artemis snorted. "A pit full of vipers with treasure in it, and you'd dive in." He looked as if he was about to say something more when his eyes went wide. I turned around slowly.

Shit.

Behind the coffee tables and chairs scattered in people's rush to leave stood Rynn. The armor looked more like a jacket and bike leathers than it had the last time I'd seen it. More casual, blending into its surroundings.

Rynn didn't look like he was here to say hello. More important, he was blocking the exit.

13

RABBITS AND THORNBUSHES

Noon, beneath the cistern.

"What have you been up to, Artemis?" Rynn asked, the corner of his lip turning up into a sneer. His footsteps clicked on the boardwalk as he made his way towards us, the red emergency lights lending a disturbing cast to his face.

"Haven't the faintest idea what you're going on about."

I had to give Artemis credit for suicidal tendencies.

"Hand over Owl now and walk away," Rynn said. He stopped a few feet away, well out of arm's reach, though somehow I was certain that he could stop us if need be.

I searched his face, but whether it was a trick of the light or himself, I couldn't see any of his usual warmth—only the icy chill I remembered from my dreams. Artemis continued as if we were catching up over coffee.

"Interesting proposition, Rynn. Tell me, what do I get out of all this cooperation?"

Rynn lowered his head, looking ever more the predator. "No one ever need be the wiser that you involved yourself in this debacle. You can go back to whatever debauchery you crawled out of."

Artemis made a clicking sound, mocking Rynn with the feigned consideration. "As lovely as that sounds, *no*."

A twitch rippled over Rynn's face. He dropped any semblance of geniality, his mouth twisting into a vicious snarl. "You're not usually this stupid—or reckless, Artemis. What do you have up your sleeve?"

"Simple. I never underestimate just how much I piss everyone off— Shit!" Artemis ducked, narrowly missing a knife that embedded itself into the wood railing.

Rynn turned his icy gaze on me. "Alix, hand it over," he said.

I backed up, more to buy myself time than in the hope of getting away. I hadn't even seen Rynn throw the knife.

But like hell was I about to hand anything over.

I searched his face for something familiar, but there wasn't a trace of the Rynn I recognized in the cold, icy eyes that were looking at me now.

"Well, Alix? Is this the part where I let you live or rip your throat open for pursuing a fool's errand?"

I swallowed. "Fancy seeing you here, Rynn," I said. "And can't a girl just be out for a stroll looking for some run-of-the-mill ancient artifacts? Istanbul's full of them."

"Option B it is." Rynn produced another knife.

"If that device does anything, now would be the time to tell me," Artemis whispered from where he was still crouched.

I inclined my head as Rynn strode towards us. "Why don't you make us disappear?"

"Because it doesn't work when he's standing right there in front of us!"

Of course not. I kept my footing even as I backed away from Rynn. Never run from a predator; that was something he had told me.

His lip curled. "I know you're terrified of me, Alix. I can smell it."

Terrified was maybe a strong word for it— Shit.

Rynn threw another knife, and it embedded itself into the boardwalk right by my feet.

Apparently he meant business. "Run," I said, and turned to do just that. Maybe we could lose him in the cistern—or buy ourselves time.

My shoes clapped against the wooden slats, echoing across the water and off the cavern walls. Rynn bellowed behind us. I expected a knife. Instead, there was an ear-rattling explosion. A bullet struck the railing beside me.

Great, now there were guns. We skidded to a stop as the gun barked again and the bullet struck inches away from our feet.

There was a branch in the suspended boardwalk. "Split up," Artemis said, and shoved me towards the left arm of the boardwalk.

"That's a horrible idea—goddamn it!"

Artemis was already running.

With no other choices and Rynn closing in, I bolted for the wire coffee tables that less than an hour ago had been filled with people. A handful of chairs had even been overturned in people's rush to leave. I darted around one of the café tables, putting the wire and metal between us—not that it would do much, but he'd still have to push it aside.

I turned, hoping Rynn would have chased Artemis. No luck; he was heading my way. Well, no point in putting off the inevitable . . . maybe I could throw him off. "Finders keepers, Rynn!" I shouted, holding up the silver device. "Back off, or I'll do what I do best—break it!"

His mouth twisted in the red light, and he lifted the gun, aiming at me. "You and I both know that you'll do what you always do—it's only a matter of time."

I searched behind Rynn for Artemis, hoping he might have looped around. No such luck . . . *Coward.*

"And what would that be, exactly?" I asked as Rynn drew closer. He hadn't fired yet, but even in my most hopeful state of mind I couldn't see him missing me at this range.

Still no sign of Artemis . . .

I searched for a trace of Rynn in the supernatural bearing down on me, but I saw only the Electric Samurai.

"Simply that you might feign putting up a fight, Alix, but you always buckle under a bigger bully, which in this case is *me*." He fired at me, the bullet striking the metal table. I cringed, despite my resolve not to let him intimidate me—or at least not to let him see it.

"Hand it over, and for once you can avoid the pain you invite others to visit on you."

I won't lie, it hurt—partly because there was an undeniable grain of truth in it. Rynn knew he'd hit pay dirt. My emotions were ebbing off me.

"You know it's only a matter of time before you fold, Alix. And trust me, if you continue to make me chase you, I'll make it hurt."

It already hurt. But if there was one thing I had learned over the past year, there was a hell of a lot more to me than being an underdog. It had been Rynn who'd showed me that.

I glimpsed something out of the corner of my eye, a slight flicker in a dark cavern corner so faint I had to chance taking my eyes off Rynn to get a second look. Artemis. I wasn't exactly certain what he was planning, but somehow he'd managed to get himself behind Rynn. And he let me see it. Meaning that he was going to toss some kind of ball into my court.

His words came back to me: "So long as he's still in there, you serve as a distraction." "You're forgetting the most important part about me, Rynn."

His upper lip twitched in amusement. "And what might that be?"

Here's hoping Artemis had read it right. "That I manage to piss all of you supernaturals off." I shoved a table and chairs at him before bolting for the exit.

"Alix, get back here!" Rynn roared, following up with more bullets. They struck the table and boardwalk but missed me. The real Rynn still had to be in there; otherwise the Electric Samurai would just hit me and get it over with.

I might not be the most athletic woman who ever crawled through a tomb, but what I lacked in athleticism and grace, I made up for in raw, clumsy agility. I leapt onto the next metal table, sliding over the surface and knocking what was left of someone's coffee and lunch onto the floor. I hit the ground running.

More bullets struck around me, and I heard Rynn knocking the over-turned tables and chairs out of the way in pursuit.

I had no illusions about my chances of outrunning him. I was lucky to have gotten even this far. I kept my eyes peeled for any sign of Artemis—nothing, not even a glimpse of him in the shadows.

If you were going to do something spectacular, Artemis, now is the time— *Oomph!*

I hit the boardwalk face-first, Captain protesting from his perch on my backpack. I scrambled to get back up and couldn't due to the thick rope weighted with heavy ball bearings wrapped around my ankles. A bola. He'd tripped me with a fucking bola? Oh, for Christ's sake . . .

Rynn was bearing down on me, pushing the tables out of his way, looking decidedly pissed off. "Since when the hell do you use bolas?"

I tried to untangle myself but to no avail. I couldn't let Rynn get ahold of da Vinci's device. I searched for a hiding spot but couldn't find one that didn't scream "obvious."

Captain chirped, dancing back and forth as if he weren't quite certain whether to sit and beg Rynn for a pat or attack him.

Desperate times . . . I grabbed Captain's collar and looped it through one of the broken segments of the silver orb, hoping it wouldn't break into two. I then took hold of his head so he had to look at me. "Hide," I said, and pointed towards the coffee shop.

I highly doubt he had any idea what I was getting at; he's a cat, after all. But he's a resourceful cat. Whether it was my tone of voice, the fact that he was now in possession of one of my "treasures," or that he really didn't like the smell of Rynn, Captain decided now was as good a time as any to play. Your guess is as good as mine; the inner workings of my cat's mind are a mystery. Whatever the reason, he let out an excited chirp and bolted for the coffee stand, his hind legs furiously scrambling to get his dark brown and white bulk underneath.

Rynn reached me, crouching down beside me, his eyes still that ter-rifying icy blue. He gave me a sickening smile. "I use a lot more tricks than you remember." He searched the inside pocket of my jacket roughly and when he didn't find what he was looking for, went on to the rest of my pockets, then my bag. Captain had the good sense to stay hidden.

I caught the glint of the knife in his hand—the kind I imagined people used to gut large animals. "The device, Alix." He held out his other hand. "I won't ask again."

I shrugged. "Sorry, Rynn. Must have dropped it—or maybe someone picked my pocket." Fear and the urge to submit coursed through me as I stared into his icy-blue eyes. Just hand it over. Really, what was the point of keeping it? I wasn't even supposed to be here, I was supposed to be collecting supernatural weapons for Mr. Kurosawa and Lady Siyu. Why bother with any of it? Just let the supernaturals beat the shit out of one another. With any luck, they'll all kill one another and leave us humans alone.

Those were the thoughts fueled by the emotions that coursed through me as I stared into Rynn's eyes.

Only problem: emotions were a poor substitute for the real thing. Nowhere near the subtlety that Rynn used, it was like having them forced on my thoughts with a sledgehammer—or an ice pick. The tactic was obvious, executed with brute force and a lack of imagination.

The armor might have Rynn's memories, but it didn't have his finesse.

I have never taken kindly to supernaturals telling me what to do.

"Looks like you'll just have to gut me then," I said through clenched teeth.

Confusion, then anger, flickered across Rynn's features. The armor might have control over him, but all it could manage was a poor imitation of him—a powerful and dangerous imitation, but an imitation.

Nevertheless, it hadn't counted on my saying no and wasn't quite certain how to deal with it. It might have control of Rynn, but it didn't have enough to kill me outright. Maybe that was the answer? The armor had a temper. That's what had happened the last time, wasn't it? When Rynn had broken through.

Whoever would have thought my talent for pissing off supernaturals to homicidal extremes would come in handy?

"Didn't expect that, did you?" I asked, addressing the armor. "You know, for all the control you're supposed to have over my boyfriend, you're really not managing much more than a cheap impression."

His lip curled into an angry sneer, looking less like Rynn. "Oh, trust me, Alixandra, I have everything—every intimate thought, every fear. What do you think I feed off of?" The voice was Rynn's but hollowed out as the armor spoke directly to me.

At least we were done with the facade. He reached out, gripped my throat, and squeezed it—not enough to knock me out but enough to stop me talking. "And more important, I know exactly how much pain killing you right here and now would cause." The hand tightened. "I'd planned on drawing things out—instant gratification is very overrated, and you're a bargaining chip. But just this once I could make an exception." The knife pressed up against my chest, and I winced as it bit into my skin, but I still didn't break eye contact. Please, Captain, no heroics— just stay hidden.

"I'm not the one wearing my boyfriend's skin like a really bad knock-off."

"Silence," the armor hissed in its hollow voice.

"Like Guggi-level bad."

I might have come up with more, but Rynn's face twisted in rage and he began to squeeze. For a moment I wondered if I'd overshot my own card—my vision began to fade at the edges.

The hand gripping me shook—then loosened.

Rynn was staring at me, his eyes back to their normal shade of blue-gray. The knife at my ribs diminished its pressure. "Alix?"

It was Rynn's voice—*his*—I was certain.

"That was very, very stupid," he strained to say. "You can't keep baiting the armor like this—I'm barely holding on as it is."

Sure enough, the knife shook in his hand as the armor struggled to regain control.

"Fight it!"

Rynn shook his head. "There's only so much I can do. Its lapses in temper are fewer and farther between now. It's learning. Every day, every hour, it works its way further into my mind. You need to stop."

"Like hell—"

"It wants da Vinci's device," Rynn said, cutting me off. "It won't tell me why, but it also won't risk hurting you; otherwise it might lose control of me. But that will buy you only so much time. You might not have enough."

"Tell me what the hell you want me to do, then."

For a moment I thought I saw Rynn slip under the pale, icy eyes, but he managed to hold on. "I want you to stop trying to save me and start trying to figure out how to kill me."

"Are you out of your mind?" Like hell. Not even on the table.

"For everyone's sakes—otherwise it may be too late." He winced and doubled over.

"Rynn!" I shouted.

Artemis was standing behind him with a chair in hand that he discarded on the floor. "I wasn't even certain that would work."

I worked the bola off my ankles and I whirled on Artemis, my hands clenched. "It was him! He'd broken through."

Artemis ignored me and grabbed Rynn's gun. He threw it into the water, then rifled through his jacket and found a series of syringes, the kind the Zebras were fond of carrying around to use against supernaturals. "What do you suppose these do?" he asked, holding two of them up, one red and one green. "Well, only one way to find out." He jabbed them into Rynn's shoulder, one after the other.

Rynn seized as the chemicals coursed through him, his face turning red as he gasped for air.

I stopped Artemis before he could add any more. "Enough! It was him!"

Artemis's lip curled as he dragged me up off the boardwalk and started towards the exit. "I'm well aware of that," he said, glaring at me. "I heard him just as clearly as you did."

"We're *not* going to try to find a way to kill him."

He shook his head. "Not that. The part about the armor taking over."

I started back for Rynn, but Artemis stopped me. "You're not thinking," he said.

"I'm thinking he's still in there and we're leaving him." He was unconscious; if we could keep him unconscious somehow—

"Or the armor is manipulating the situation, only letting you think it's him. Of course you can't go back there. Instead of rushing in like you always do, try stopping and thinking."

I clenched my fists. It had been Rynn. I knew it, Artemis knew it . . .

And so did the armor. As much as I wanted to tell Artemis to go to hell, he had a point.

"What if we got him back to the Japanese Circus? Mr. Kurosawa has to have something that would hold him."

He stopped and turned to me once again. "And do you truly want to gamble that he won't simply try to kill him? It would be easier, let alone safer, for everyone. What if the armor escapes? Better yet, what if it temporarily releases Rynn, then stabs everyone in the back while we aren't looking? Mr. Kurosawa and the Naga aren't going to risk that, not when there is a much simpler solution." His expression was impassive; there was no charity or sympathy in it.

And he was right. I don't know who I hated more for that, me or Artemis.

There was a groan behind us. Rynn—

"Shit, the drugs weren't nearly as effective as I'd hoped," Artemis said.

"Any more tricks?"

Artemis shrugged. "Run?"

I swore and bolted for the stairs, which were still empty. The emergency vehicles were likely held up in midday traffic, and no one had yet cleared the cistern and shut off the alarm. IAA interference, I imagined, wanting to prevent supernatural fallout. Small favors. Captain bleated as he caught up.

The three of us emerged into the daylight. I stopped short of running out into the street. Which way, left or right? I started right, but Artemis stopped me.

"Look around you," he whispered.

Sure enough, down the street were two of Rynn's mercenaries, watching the cistern entrance. There had to be more nearby.

"I'll take care of the mercenaries," Artemis said, and took off to the left. The two mercenaries saw him and chased after him.

Goddamn it, what the hell was I supposed to do? I decided to run. I headed right, down the road, and ducked into the first alley I saw.

I took two more corners before I slowed to catch my breath, my legs screaming, and not just from the effort. I doubled over to catch my breath. Five more seconds, that was all I needed . . .

Jesus, that had been a colossal fuckup. I wasn't even certain Artemis had the amulet.

I forced myself to stand. Should I head back to the hotel or hole up somewhere?

Captain let out a long-drawn-out, hostile hiss. I heard a noise behind a stack of cardboard boxes and turned in time to see a body shuffle out from behind a stack of crates, one that dressed in designer shoes and a dark suit. The disheveled appearance and rumpled suit made me do a double take.

It was Charles, from Alexander's Paris boys.

I collected Captain as best I could and covered my nose with my sleeve. Through the cloth I smelled the rotting lily of the valley. I hoped it would at least dull the narcoticlike effect.

Charles's face was covered in a slick layer of sweat, and I could see his arms shaking in the suit, which hung more loosely on his thin frame than I remembered. He took another step towards me, apparently unaware of my cat, which was hissing up a storm in my arms.

"Charles," I said, "don't tell me Alexander's roped you into this." Oh man, Alexander was going to get an earful for this. You'd have thought we were on good enough terms now to merit a "Heads up, your evil ex-boyfriend now has a handful of my vampires at his beck and call."

In fact, there was no recognition in his eyes. The cruelty and smugness I associated with vampires was gone. He looked more like an empty shell of one—sunken eyes and all.

"Charles? It's me, Owl. We're supposed to have a truce, remember?"

There was no response—no "Go to hell," "Damn your infernal cat," or any of their other usual insults. There was something . . . off. His eyes had the same blank stare as the mercenaries'. He shuffled, a defeated zombielike walk, and his eyes were bloodshot.

I realized I'd seen that same bloodshot look before. It had been in Marie, a vampire—one I'd known before she'd become a vampire, who had made herself highly powerful and crazy feeding off other vampires, an expansion of a vampire's already homicidal tendencies.

Oh man, if Rynn was making Charles feed on other vampires, that was very bad—and not just for me.

Still no sign of Artemis . . .

"Hey, Charles? This would be a good time to apologize for the whole Balinese oven thing." I danced out of the way as his arm shot out, making a grab for me. "In my defense, you *were* trying to kill me, and we did let you go."

No answer. Instead, he lunged at me with preternatural speed, almost grazing me. Captain lashed out and landed a hit along his hand. Angry purple welts appeared where his claws had gouged skin.

That gave me an idea.

I loosened my grip on Captain's collar as I fumbled for my UV flashlight. God, I hoped his training stuck. I'd get only one real shot . . .

"Hey, Charles, did Alexander ever tell you guys what happened to Marie?"

No answer; only a glimpse of canines as he readied to strike again. Despite his zombielike state, he was wary of Captain's claws. Meaning he wasn't looking for the flashlight.

I switched it on and waved it over his face, then his arms and hands—anywhere I could see skin. Smoke rose, and Charles screamed as he retreated away from the burning light.

"Guess Rynn glossed over that bit too." Captain howled disapproval as I kept a firm grip around his ample middle and turned to bolt out of the alley.

Four more men dressed in rumpled suits stood in the alley, blocking my way. The rotting lily of the valley mixing with the scent of Charles's charred skin left no doubt as to what they were.

And then there were five.

And where the hell was Artemis?

I tried to aim my flashlight, but the vampires were too fast. One grabbed me, while the other three grabbed Captain. Charles licked his wounds in a dark corner on the ground. I kicked the one holding me, twice, but it was like kicking a cement pylon; he didn't budge. His lips peeled back, showing his teeth, the canines only slightly more pointed than human ones, his breath smelling like rotting meat.

Charles got up and started towards me. I searched for something, anything, that I could use to stall or repel them.

Around Captain's neck the silver orb hung, the designs already set for vampires. I delivered a kick to the vampire directly behind me. The surprise of it more than any strength I exerted forced him to step back. I lunged for my cat and managed to grab hold of his collar while the vampires absorbed this new turn of events. One thing I'd noticed about Rynn's thralls was that they were not the fastest thinkers. Before the vampire could wrangle me, I had the orb off Captain's collar. The vampire got hold of me and pulled me back just as I rammed the last off-kilter symbol into place.

Nothing happened.

Shit.

Maybe it needed blood. I nicked my finger on the edge and let the blood pool over the metallic surface.

Still nothing.

It should have worked. I'd added blood and lined up the configuration for vampire—I knew that almost everything with a magical design needed blood of some sort.

Maybe I just wasn't using the right blood. My eyes fell on the scratches that Captain had dug into Charles's hands and wrists, which were bleeding a steady trail of vampire blood from the purple welts.

"Charles, catch!" I tossed him the silver device.

As soon as it touched his hand, it flared with brilliant white light.

The vampires holding me and Captain were hit the most spectacularly. They froze, their faces a mix of shock and confusion. Then they turned paper white and crumbled into two messy piles of white ash and dirty suits. That close to the device, they hadn't stood a chance. The other two remaining vampires besides Charles had a chance to scream; they hadn't turned to ash like the first two but were sporting third- and fourth-degree burns on their faces and bodies. Smoke rose off them as their skin blackened, their hands and faces charring to crisp black before my eyes. Then they collapsed into unmoving piles of charred remains. The only one left was Charles, who had been holding the device. He regarded the device and the piles of dead vampires. His eyes, which had been a vapid mix of violent reds, cleared. He dropped the silver ball in shock and wiped his hands on his suit. Then he pulled them away with a click of disgust, as if just realizing the bedraggled state of his clothing.

Now, that was very interesting. Not only did the device need vampire blood, it didn't kill the one holding it. I'd have to let Nadya know about that one.

The confusion written over his face was short-lived. As soon as his eyes found me, standing with one hand raised, the other arm holding the furious Captain, his expression twisted into one of hate.

"*You*," he said.

"Me? What the hell is that supposed to mean?"

"You're the reason behind this—this—disaster!" Charles said, gesturing at the vampire corpses and piles of ash.

"Whoa! I told you not to touch it, didn't I?"

He *tsk*ed and his face twisted into a more familiar vampire disdain. "The Electric Samurai only came after us because of Alexander's cooperation with you."

"Oh, you got to be— Cooperation? Agreeing not to kill me wasn't cooperation. Again, not my fault. You have your elves to blame for that one. I tried to stop them."

"And apparently you failed miserably, just like you do in all your endeavors."

Had to go for the low blow . . . I should have let Captain at him more. "Says the vampire who five minutes ago was a mindless thrall! I didn't get the impression that Alexander switched sides this often."

Charles flashed his fangs at me and snarled as Captain lashed, while I turned the UV flashlight on him and tried to wrench the device away from him. Charles wouldn't let go.

"You can't ward off my Mau forever. Eventually he's going to get through."

"And you'll be so indisposed from vampire pheromones you'll barely be able to hold the infernal flashlight!"

He was right—not as though I was going to admit it. It did mean I needed to get out of this predicament fast. I kicked at his knee hard, hoping he'd lunge and give me a chance to wrench the device free—or at the very least that it would put him off balance enough to give Captain an opening. Charles saw it coming.

"Three wars in my lifetime, and you think a slip of a girl like you can get the upper hand?"

That was something I forgot more often than I should have when dealing with vampires; they might look young, but enough of them were old enough to have seen the French Revolution. He managed to catch my wrist and pull me in to him.

He was angry. All red-eyed and vamped out, I expected him to lunge at me with his fangs, hit me, give me some show of the violence vampires were famous for. He didn't, though. Instead he gritted his teeth and said, "Call off your cat."

Definitely not what I was expecting . . . "Why? So you can eat me?"

He *tsk*ed. "*No*. So I can deliver a message for you to pass on to Alexander." He was angry enough that spittle rained over my face as he spoke.

I wrenched my hand free and wiped madly at my face.

"Tell Alexander to stop looking for us," he told me. "It will do no good, the possessed incubus is too powerful. Better they all stay back and survive. There is no defeating him—not for supernaturals, let alone a human. If you have half an ounce of sense, you will run and not turn back."

We both heard the shouts and commotion near the alley, coming closer. Time to go.

Charles covered his wound, still visibly in pain, and stuck it into his ruined suit, and headed towards the commotion, resigned.

I grabbed my cat, ran the other way, and didn't slow down until I was out of that alley and through the next two. Then I doubled over to catch my breath.

"There you are."

I swore and jumped at Artemis's voice. I don't know if it was coming down from the adrenaline high or the mix of vampire pheromones— probably both—but I was sluggish on my feet. I barely caught myself on the wall.

"Where the hell have you been?" I demanded.

Artemis frowned at me as he watched me gasp for breath and double over once more. "Leading Rynn and his mercenaries away. What's your excuse?"

"Oh, you know—" I started, but the mix of pheromones and my own exhaustion overwhelmed me. I almost collapsed. If not for Artemis's catching me, I would have. Of all the humiliating ways to end this disaster . . .

"Trust me, there are a hundred other women I'd rather be carry- ing than you or that infernal cat, but there's nothing to be done for it. We need to leave now, regardless of the vampire pheromones coursing through you." His voice was softer and more soothing than it usually was, though the chances were good that was the effect of the phero- mones. They made vampires look and sound more appealing; why the hell not Artemis?

"He won't be able to do any more damage this evening," Artemis continued.

"You saw that vampire?"

He nodded—or I think he did.

"What is Rynn doing to them?"

"In a word? Causing chaos."

I recognized a few of the buildings above, as well as the bridge. We weren't on the way back to the hotel. "Where are we going?"

"I'm getting us out of Istanbul—to the next step on the Tiger Thieves trail." Artemis dangled something in front of my face: a dark stone pendant with gold lines running across it. "With this," he said.

So that's what he had been doing. Somehow I wasn't surprised to see the pendant dangling in front of me. Rynn had never done that well with thieves; there was no reason to think he'd do any better with spies . . .

Who knew? This time being the bad guy had paid off. At least, that's what ran through my head as the gold-inscribed pendants hastened me off to unconsciousness.

"You're going to do the incubus healing thing after I pass out, right?" I coughed as the nausea took over.

Artemis *tsk*ed. "Sorry, not really my skill set."

Well, shit . . .

14

THE QUEEN OF SHIVA

*Day? Not sure. Time? Sun's up. My newest lesson
in being careful what you wish for . . .*

Ohhh, a hangover would have been better.

I pushed myself up. To say I was uncomfortable would have been an understatement. Hard floor, loud noises, moving vehicle.

I sat up. The nausea and all my bruises were still there. I was in a jeep. The top was down, and warm air—almost tropical—brushed my face.

I was in the back of a jeep on a dirt road in a humid climate. Thick tropical forest lined both sides of the road. Continental Asia—maybe Africa—the Congo?

Son of a— I jumped as a bug landed on the seat beside me, knocked off as the jeep hit an overgrown branch, the thin, elongated limbs looking alien.

Stick bugs. South Asian stick bugs—southern India, to judge by the temperature, but where exactly . . .

Captain meowed as I sat up. He was perched on the front-seat headrest, flicking his tail at me.

"You'd jump too if you got woken up by a stick bug," I told him, and began taking stock of myself, starting with who the hell was driving the jeep and how the hell I'd gone from Istanbul to Asia.

"You're awake," Artemis said.

"That's up for debate," I told him. Well, at least I knew who was driving now. "Here, try this," he said, and tossed me a plastic grocery bag over the seat. I opened it: bottle of water, orange juice, both cold. I took the orange juice.

The jeep lurched into a pothole just as I was chugging it.

I winced. Ouch—everything hurt. Oh man, of all the things I did not feel like fucking dealing with right now . . . I held the orange juice bottle to my forehead, absorbing what relief I could.

I didn't even have the booze to justify the hangover. "God, I hate vampires."

"Be thankful the vampire was there. Otherwise it's very possible my cousin would have caught up to you and killed you."

"You want to trade headaches? Be my guest." I winced at the sound of my voice echoing around my head. There was no way my brain was running on all pistons. "Where the hell are we?"

"Finish your breakfast," he said, and nodded ahead at the dirt road. "All in due time."

Yeah, like I was going to sit back and enjoy the ride through the mystery South Asian jungle. I pushed myself up and crawled about as gracefully into the front seat as a large walrus would, my head protesting the whole way. Artemis had a GPS device on the dashboard. I grabbed it before he could stop me, earning me an annoyed look.

"You ever wonder why my cousin is so effective with supernaturals? He's *patient*. He waits until his prey *panics*, then flushes them out." He grabbed the GPS device from me and put it back onto the dashboard. "Which is exactly what he's trying to do: flush us out, see where we run to, then chase us down. It's an old tactic of his; at least my cousin's unoriginality can be depended on. Falls right back into his old patterns, despite the armor."

"I'm not panicking. I want to know where the hell I've woken up."

"We're headed for the next stop on the map," Artemis offered.

I rolled that around my vampire-addled head. "Ah, when—"

"I found the point on the map while you were sleeping. It wasn't hard. I took the map da Vinci had started in his journal and used the amulet. All I needed was my own blood after all."

I spotted the journal on the front seat and snatched it up, flipping to the map. Sure enough, the map had been extended on the page. This time the gold lines crossed over ruffled terrain, which became shallower and flanked by dense dashes reminiscent of foliage the closer it reached the end of the page, ending in a gold *X*.

"An ocean, followed by a river and jungle," Artemis said as I ran my fingers over the lines.

It was a substantial ocean if the map was any indication. Where would I have been going to find a river and jungle in the ancient world?

"The Tiger Thieves are in Muziris," I said to Artemis. "We're in India."

He inclined his head, not taking his eyes off the dirt road. "Give the girl a prize. She knows her ancient trading ports."

Or in this case, ancient lost cities. Muziris was one of the lost cities of the ancient Silk Road. Located somewhere along the Malabar Coast in southwestern India, for more than a thousand years it had been a major trading port between southern India and Persia, Greece, Egypt, and Rome. Unfortunately, its exact location was unknown. Many historians assumed it was hidden somewhere in the jungle along the Periyar River on account of the hoards of ancient coins that littered the coast and the river's shores—ancient trade stashes. But a massive flood had destroyed the area in the 1300s, wiping the entire port city off the map. It must have been one hell of a shock to the traders coming from Europe to off-load their goods. One year, there would have been a metropolis on the banks of the river. A few years later? Gone, only the mud banks remaining.

People had been searching for the ancient city for a few hundred years. My best guess was that the original was buried under mud—unless the Tiger Thieves had dug it up or moved it.

An ancient lost city and the Tiger Thieves—somehow I wasn't surprised that the two went hand in hand. I took stock of our surroundings. The jungle on either side was thick, and there were no cities to be seen in the distance. If the Tiger Thieves were out here, they were well hidden.

"How long until we reach it?" I asked. "Muziris?"

"Not long," Artemis replied. There was a pause as the jeep rumbled along, the jungle encroaching on the road more and more the farther we went. "So. It worked," Artemis finally said after we'd rounded the bend and gotten our first view—or my first view, anyway—of the river.

I felt the hairs along the back of my neck bristle. "In a sense." Not exactly the way da Vinci had hinted at or described, though. Maybe he'd already gone mad by the time he made the damn thing.

Artemis snorted. "I'm sorry to see that it did."

I frowned and cleared another stick bug off the jeep. "Sorry I wasn't eaten by a pack of ravenous mad vampires."

"I meant for Rynn."

Shit. I tapped down my jacket pocket.

"Oh, it's still there. I haven't stolen anything from you. I meant that powerful magical items like that carry more costs than they are worth. The benefits never outweigh the price. I thought the Electric Samurai would have taught you that."

There was too much bitterness in his voice for him to be talking about anything except firsthand experience. An unwelcome image of the dead Gorgon lying on the boardwalk pushed its way into the forefront of my thoughts.

The jeep jolted violently and came to a shuddering stop.

My headache revolted, and I swore. "What the hell was that?" I asked when I'd recovered from the shaking.

"Pothole." Artemis hopped out and checked the wheels. "Bad one. Will you find a stick? Something thick enough to get the wheel out?"

I hopped out on shaky legs and searched the nearby underbrush for a stick the right size. I found a watered log that on further inspection hadn't reached crumbling stage—yet. I maneuvered myself around a low-lying branch and pushed the leaves out of my way, only to yelp at the stick bug that had made the branches its home.

"You know, it's much more frightened of you, the giant loud thing stomping through the forest that might eat it," Artemis called out.

"I'm not going to eat the bug." I pulled the small log out of the mud and returned it to Artemis, who wedged it under the wheel.

"No, but from its perspective and life experiences, it's a reasonable assumption."

At my expression he added, "Fine, then it's terrified that your cat is about to eat it—and rightly so."

I swore and turned in time to see Captain batting at the unfortunate bug, which was scrambling to escape into the branches. My cat was mesmerized by its leaflike movements. I grabbed him as he snapped at the bug. "Knock it off," I said. "The last thing I need is you puking by poisonous bug."

Captain let out a mew, letting me know just how much he disagreed with that statement.

I set him down on the ground before shooing him away. There were fewer bugs there.

"Better hope he doesn't find one of the leeches."

"Leeches live in water," I said.

"Not here they don't—land leeches." With a grunt Artemis wedged the small log under the wheel and, putting his back into it, eased the jeep's wheel out of the hole.

Of course. The Tiger Thieves had chosen a humid, tropical jungle for their hideout. There had to be land leeches . . .

I think it was probably my imagination, but I could have sworn I saw something black and slick in the low-lying brush leaves. I peered into the green foliage, but on second look there was nothing there.

"What was it the Gorgon was talking about?" I asked Artemis. "When she said 'last time'?"

Artemis lifted an eyebrow. "Something that happened a long time ago." He shot a furtive glance at the forest around us. I realized that he'd been doing that since I'd woken up. My spidey sense went on edge. Captain seemed to notice it too as he sniffed the air.

What the hell did Artemis have up his sleeve? "I'd like to hear about it," I told him, not leaving room for argument.

Artemis started the jeep's engine back up. "And I don't want to discuss it."

I slid my hand back into my pocket and closed my fingers around the device. "You mistook that for a request. I assure you it wasn't."

Artemis shut the jeep back off. His eyes were cruel as he fixed them back on me.

Oh man, I hoped this wasn't where he tried to stab me in the back . . . "Why are we stopping?"

Artemis turned his cruel eyes on me. "How certain are you that my cousin is still in there?"

I went cold. "He's trapped—"

"He's being *controlled*," Artemis interrupted me. "He almost killed you that time, didn't he?" He snorted. "Don't bother answering that. You already have."

An odd, icy chill formed in my chest, and I clenched the device tighter in my fist. "You want me to admit I was wrong?"

Artemis shook his head. "I wanted to point out that there are other ways to torture someone than beating her up. Offering hope is one of the most effective."

I couldn't stop the anger welling up inside me. "He's *in* there."

Artemis shook his head. "And you just made my point for me." He set his eyes back on the road. "Just think how much more it will hurt if you find yourself wrong, if the Tiger Thieves can't or won't help you. How much more tempted will you be to use that, just like you were with the vampires. Your weakness is your desperation."

The cold pit grew. The problem with hope is that it's a double-edged sword. It can either make you crumble or drive you to do great things—especially for those you care about.

Rynn was still in there. I was certain of it.

"I'm not the one you need to be afraid of," Artemis continued. "I'm trying to help you!"

That hit a nerve. "Bullshit. The only thing you're doing is waiting to stab me in the back, just like you did in LA!"

"Oh, for—" For a moment I didn't think he was going to say anything more, then, "Not that it matters now, but I was doing exactly what my illustrious cousin requested I do."

I was floored. "There is no way—"

"Didn't tell you, did he? Not exactly the way he suggested that things unfurl, mind you, but now that he's incapacitated I don't see any harm. I was spying. For him and Mr. Kurosawa."

I clenched the device even tighter. There was no way . . . "You're lying," I said, my voice low.

Artemis flashed me a sardonic grin and clapped. "They didn't tell you, did they? I was told to find out exactly how deep some of the supernaturals were into overthrowing the status quo—Nicodemous in particular. Rynn was quite upset about the whole wraith thing. Not that I had much of a choice; it was that or get nothing. Though, in retrospect, I think Rynn was more furious that I didn't find out more about the plans that had been set in motion. Ow!" Artemis doubled over as I slugged him in the gut.

"Take it back," I said. Okay, part of me was disappointed that I'd resorted to violence that quickly. Then again, my threshold barrier to violence had greatly diminished over the last year.

"What are you, five?"

I clenched my fists by my sides and vowed not to hit him again—or at least try not to.

"Don't you throw your temper tantrum at me. I'm not the one who said to do whatever it takes to find out what the other side is doing. You have my cousin and Mr. Kurosawa to thank for that, and if you're looking for someone to level blame at, try my cousin; it was his idea." Artemis gave me a look of pure hate. "He's more than happy to banish me from his sight until he needs a spy; then he has no problem calling me up. You should think about that: what kind of person sneers in disgust at a spy or thief for what he does but has no problem using him to do dirty work when need be? How does someone like that keep his conscience clean, do you imagine?"

"Now who's manipulating whom?"

Artemis smiled. "I imagine he has no problem letting others whore themselves out to do the things he finds distasteful until he can no longer stand to look at them—funny, since from what I remember, someone told me it was you who had been calling him a whore. Funny how the tables get— Shit!" Artemis ducked as I launched the water bottle at his head. I was only slightly disappointed in myself. It was plastic.

As opposed to getting angry, though, Artemis only smiled. "Funny thing, you wouldn't be this angry if I didn't have a point."

If there's one thing I have learned over the past few months, it's when to remove myself from a conversation entirely. I tried to leave. Artemis stepped in front of me, blocking my way. "Get out of my way," I told him.

"Gladly."

I stormed past him, not entirely certain where I was going to go. I hopped into the jeep and turned the key. The engine sputtered.

I caught the glint of metal in Artemis's hand as he held it up. "What is so damn important about this?" he said.

Son of a bitch, he'd picked my pocket. I clenched my fists. "You saw what it does. It pulverizes vampires."

Artemis shook his head and made a *tsk*ing sound. "See, there's where you're good—better than Rynn gives you credit for. You aren't lying, you're just holding back—and not feeling a damn bit guilty about it. That's what fooled me before." He tossed da Vinci's device into the air and caught it. "What is it?"

I clenched my teeth. "I told you."

"Fine. Since we won't be running into any more vampires out here—" He wound up his arm as if he were about to launch a baseball.

"No!" I lunged over the jeep door at him, but he danced out of my reach.

"Spill, or I throw this device into the jungle and leave you here stranded. Trust me, you'll never see it or me again—and good luck ever finding the Tiger Thieves without me."

I believed him. Even if I managed to retrieve the silver device and make it to the Tiger Thieves' lair, I would be in no condition to barter with them. "I'm telling the truth, I don't know—" I started.

Artemis made another warning *tsk* and wound up his arm.

"But the skin walker knew what it was. She was convinced it does more." I gestured at the journal still on the seat. "Unfortunately, da Vinci was so mad by the time he started testing the device, he barely managed to keep the instructions coherent—or on the same page—or in the same goddamned language— Shit!"

Artemis's hand shot around my throat like a snake. He looked more furious than I'd ever seen him; all his sympathy—feigned or sincere— was gone. "You idiot!"

"It works," I managed. "You saw what it did to the vampires."

Artemis shook his head. "You may be fine playing games, Alix, but Rynn is not, and for that matter, neither am I."

"I think it can strip a supernatural's power, okay?"

My feet hit the ground hard as Artemis stepped back and let me go. I don't know who was more shocked that I'd told him, me or him. He actually looked shell-shocked.

"Are you out of your mind?" he demanded, spitting the words through his teeth.

I rubbed my neck. "You saw what it did to those vampires. It's a very powerful weapon. I'd be crazy not to keep it."

He stopped me. "You—you think this is about building an armory? It's not just a weapon, Alix, it's chaos—all packaged up in that tiny silver ball."

This time I managed to wrench the orb back—or he let me. "Stripping a few of you of your powers is hardly chaos—"

"No, it's genocide! Use that thing stuck between your ears that passes for a brain, and think. If a human has this, he can level the playing field, but if a supernatural has it?" His upper lip curled. "It would have power over the rest of us, it could make us do whatever it wanted. And the last person on this planet who needs that kind of power is my cousin." He swore. "I wondered why the hell he'd taken up this chase. It's not like him."

"He doesn't know exactly what it is." Neither did I, for that matter, not from da Vinci's notes.

Artemis snorted. "Thank God for small favors. Otherwise half the supernatural community would have your head on a pike."

"*And* I'm not even certain it will work. As far as I can tell, it's broken. Da Vinci figured the same thing."

"The fact that any of da Vinci's devices work is the problem, not the solution."

"I was hoping the Tiger Thieves might be able to shed some illumination, since they're the ones who used to deal with supernatural and magical mayhem."

"Out of the fucking question!"

"Why not? If they can't defeat Rynn, maybe this can."

"Give me that," he said, and made a grab for it, a determined look on his face I hadn't seen before. I swore, but managed to dance out of the way and around the jeep. "What the hell do you think you're doing?"

"What I should have done when you first found it."

I feinted left but Artemis was on to me. He cut me off and managed to get ahold of me. We struggled as he tried to pry the device out of my hands. "I'm getting it out of your corruptible, thieving hands before you do something catastrophic. *Nothing* good ever came out of da Vinci's devices. They work, and that's half the problem. Do you have any idea how much blood is on his hands? Ow!"

I bit him hard on the hand. It worked; he let go.

"Why, you little—" The mark on his hand was already fading, but his anger wasn't.

"So what happens if the Tiger Thieves can't do anything for Rynn?" I asked him. "That's it? Leave Rynn in the suit and watch Rome burn—again?"

I saw more raw anger in Artemis's face than I'd ever seen. He balled his fists up at his sides and took a step towards me. "That was never—" He stopped as Captain jumped out to stand between him and me and let out a challenge. Artemis stopped—and recovered himself.

"This isn't sitting back and letting Rome burn. That could wipe out multiple species in a matter of months if placed in the wrong hands. It'd be genocide! You want to save Rynn and the world from his and the armor's antics? Fine, just don't complain when everything starts to burn and he blames you—yes, that's right, you." He snorted and threw up his hands. "Who am I kidding? You'll be dead long before that—the next skin walker who crosses your path, or whatever else Rynn sends next. Good luck, Hiboux, you're going to need it."

He grabbed his bag out of the jeep.

"What about helping Oricho? What about your deal with him?"

He shouldered his backpack and held up his hands. "Keys are in the ignition. At the end of this road you'll find traces of a ruined city. I'm sure a Tiger Thief will find you wandering around. Just be yourself; you'll probably ruin something."

"Artemis!" I shouted as he started down the poorly marked trail.

"I've now gotten you to the Tiger Thieves' doorstep. I'm done with this; I stop short of genocide. Pray my cousin doesn't find you first."

I didn't know if he was bluffing. Maybe he was ready to abandon me; maybe he was just blowing off steam. Maybe it was all manipulation.

I didn't get a chance to find out. A few feet away from the jeep, Artemis stopped dead in his tracks.

"Are you coming or going?" I started, and stopped as Artemis raised both his hands slowly and gestured for me to do the same. Then I saw them. "You didn't think we'd seriously be able to sneak into a secret society?" he asked through a forced grin aimed at our audience.

I spotted more of them now—in amongst the foliage and trees, dressed not in military uniforms or camouflage but in clothing that blended into the green-and-brown background nonetheless. And they were far from smiling. They also had guns—pointed at us.

Fantastic. This was going into the "how not to wake up from a hang-over" handbook.

I spotted Captain crouching in the jeep. I shook my head at him—his brown-and-white fur would camouflage him only in a snowy forest, if there.

He wriggled his hind end before crouching down under a blanket—hopefully not in anticipation of his idea of a preemptive attack.

"Why the hell do they look so hostile?" I whispered.

Artemis inclined his head. "You get a lot of bandits through here. Better to be trigger-happy than dead."

Yet most of the guns were aimed at Artemis. "Seems to be more than that."

His upper lip twitched, ever so slightly. "We may have a bit of a history I failed to mention."

Goddamn it! I lifted my hands over the back of my head as one of them motioned for me to do so, then go stand beside Artemis. "You knew the Tiger Thieves were here, didn't you?" I whispered.

Artemis looked uncomfortable again, switching his attention between me and our audience, who were adjusting their guns and exchanging glances amongst themselves. "This was one of a few spots where they might have hidden themselves. I wasn't certain until you found the map."

Oh, for the love of— Artemis hadn't been screwing me over, he'd just been lying about how he was doing it. "And you're just thinking of telling me all this now?"

"Well, the time just never seemed right."

I started to back up, more to put distance between myself and Artemis than to retreat, but a knife embedded itself into the ground before my feet point-first, halting any ideas I might have entertained of escaping in the jeep.

A tall woman stepped forwards from underneath the dark green foliage. She wore a canvas army-surplus jacket over an off-white tank top—both worn but not threadbare—a pair of blue jeans, and a pair of black rubber boots that came up to her knees and had been designed for the rainy monsoon weather endemic to the region. She wouldn't have looked out of place on a major city campus—blended into the background. Oddly enough, she didn't really look out of place here either, except for the sword in her hand. Her hair was thick and black, loose around her neck, which was decorated with a thick gold choker, gemstones set into the metal in an ornate pattern. She could have easily been mistaken for a modern young Indian woman with international tastes as opposed to a member of an ancient group of assassins schooled in the supernatural—except for the bottomless black pits that masqueraded as her eyes, advertising, or maybe warning, that the bearer was darker and more dangerous than her face and appearance suggested.

"Alix," Artemis said, his tone careful, "let me introduce Shiva, resident queen of the Tiger Thieves. Shiva, may I present Alix Hiboux."

She gave Artemis a momentary appraisal, then turned a black liquid stare back on me. "The thief known as Owl," she said.

"Pleasure to make your acquaintance," I started, but as others moved in, some wearing masks, some not looking entirely human at all, I got the impression it was anything but.

"Why the hell do they look so pissed off?" I whispered.

"Don't say I didn't warn you," Artemis replied as one of the Tiger Thieves grabbed his hands, wrenching them behind his back before securing them with rope.

Oh shit. "There's been a misunderstanding," I said. "I'm not here to steal anything, I'm here for your help." I raised my hands and backed up as two of the masked figures came towards me—right into a large, broad chest.

"I don't think they care, Alix," Artemis called from where he was kneeling on the ground.

Yeah, no kidding . . . I spotted a burlap hood in one of the men's hands and a glass vial held by the other. Oh no . . . I raised both my hands. "You really don't need to knock me out. I've had my fill of it, and there is a small chance I'll just drop dead—oh, for fuck's sake—"

While one held up the burlap bag, the other held out his hand and blew. A spray of bright-pink dust blew in my face. Then they did the same to Artemis. I blinked, once, twice, three times, then sneezed. My eyes crossed and wouldn't uncross. Oh hell, no, not again.

I didn't get a chance to finish that thought as a sweet-smelling bag was dropped over my head, lowering me into a drowsy darkness.

Why the hell does no one ever listen to me?

15

POT, MEET FRYING PAN

Thursday, maybe evening. And my head still hurts.

My eyes opened to three flickering orange flames suspended over me. I watched the wax pill and drip down the candles for a while, until my vision cleared and the three of them melded into one.

Rock wall, cold dirt floor, a pail off to the side, and a metal grid door. I closed my eyes again. Fucking fantastic. Another prison. Definitely not the way I'd hoped to find Muziris.

Oh man—this was what? Prison for the second time in two weeks? That had to be some kind of lottery win . . .

"Congratulations. The Tiger Thieves decided not to kill you on sight," Artemis said.

Here we go, Owl: one, two, three—using the wall I pushed myself up. No nausea, but ooooh, did it ever bite. My eyes crossed but thankfully didn't double up. I was getting old hat at mitigating death-defying headaches.

I tested turning my head until I saw him in the corner across from me, his head lowered, his arms wrapped around his legs. His leather pants, expensive boots, and shoes had taken on more dust and made him indistinguishable as a rock star and almost unrecognizable as him-self. "Do I get a medal?" I asked.

"I'd keep the jokes. Just because you're alive doesn't mean they have anything pleasant in store for us, let alone are willing to cooperate."

As though I hadn't heard that from the supernaturals before. Noth-ing smarted, there were no new bruised ribs, no shackles . . .

"Why do I get the distinct impression Shiva has a bone to pick with you?"

"A lot of people have a bone to pick with me. It's a very long and detailed list."

That wasn't an answer.

"Really," Artemis continued, "the chance you'll be dead in the very near future is about the only thing I'm willing to bet on at the moment."

I tested my legs. Both worked, and there was no mysterious pain in them either. "They can get in line." There were no restraints, but the bars of the door were flat and gridded in a tight pattern. Hard to maneuver your arms around—and even if I had been able to, the lock was on the other side as well, and even if I could reach it, I didn't have anything to pick it with.

"Or I suppose Rynn could get here before they make up their minds. Just burn the place down around us, stride in, and take whatever the hell he desires."

"A little less pessimism," I told him. "And can you please explain to my compounded headache why you failed to mention that the Tiger Thieves were your long-lost buddies?"

I could just make out the twitch of his lips in the candlelight. "It's a little more complicated than that," he said.

Isn't it always? "Enlighten me." When there was no answer forth-coming, I tried a different approach. "Well, they're not human." Thinking back to the woman's dark eyes and the presence she'd had looming over us, there was no way she was run-of-the-mill anything.

Artemis inclined his head. "No," he admitted. "But they're not en-tirely supernatural either."

I stopped my examination of the bars and peered at him. "How does that work?"

Artemis's face was unreadable in the dim light. "Partially." I could hear him hedging his answer. "They're what you would call half-breeds."

"Half-breeds?"

His green eyes flickered in the candlelight. "Offspring of supernaturals and humans or different breeds of supernaturals. The ones that never inherit a full set of either parent's powers. It happens more frequently than the supernatural community would have you believe."

I frowned. "But you said—"

"Incubi and succubae can breed with humans, but that doesn't always lead to a full-blooded incubus or succubus offspring; every now and again you get a half-breed. Oh, they inherit something—a long life span, powers of some sort, some physical characteristics—but never enough to make them one of us. The Tiger Thieves are their society—a middle ground, if you will. Outside the influence of supernaturals or humans. I'd heard they'd taken over this city centuries ago. Apparently the reports were right, though they've kept to themselves—more than they used to."

From the tone I gathered that that was a point of contention. "How come no one has ever heard of a half-breed? I mean, there have got to be . . ." I trailed off as it hit me. "Grendel in *Beowulf.*"

Artemis's smile was chagrined. "Very good. It's the humans' version of the fable, but it's close enough. There was a dragon, and she did have many sons with the Nordic chiefs, more out of boredom, I suspect, than anything else. The most famous of them were abominations." He inclined his head again. "Shiva's not quite that bad, but she's close."

The Tiger Thieves had policed supernaturals and humans alike along the Silk Road—at least that was what the stories said. "They've got to have some kind of power in order to have given all of you the finger."

"And believe me, they revel in it," he said, almost under his breath. "Stories like *Beowulf* tend to miss the part where they take issue with their parents."

Well, maybe the Tiger Thieves and I had more common ground than I would have thought. "Where did they take my cat?"

Artemis just snorted.

I opened my mouth to ask again, but the sound of feet scraping against stone stopped me. A lantern approached us, carried by a human-like hand. The pair of eyes that reflected the dim light like a cat's, though, were far from human. The guard came up to the cell and held the lantern against the grate to get a better look at us, his eyes lingering on me with an impartial stare.

Artemis jostled me. "I'd stand up if I were you," he said, and promptly took his own advice.

I followed his lead, groaning as I pushed myself from seated to standing. They might not have beat me up, but they hadn't exactly been gentle when they were sticking me in here—then again, maybe they weren't used to handling fragile humans.

The guard exhaled sharply, and Artemis stepped back, hands up and behind his head. The guard hissed again in what I figured was an order for me to do the same. Not wanting to start an argument with his large fists, I did.

The jail cell swung open. "Right on schedule," Artemis said. Hands still behind his head, he stepped out. I did the same. The guard motioned for both of us to walk in front of him, then followed close behind.

"Normandy," Artemis said, after we were away from the cell.

The man behind us only grunted. Artemis wasn't dissuaded.

"I thought you'd have tired of this outfit by now. You always struck me as having more sense than Shiva."

"You know them?"

Artemis jabbed me in the arm. "Come on, you can't seriously tell me you're happy locked up in here?"

Still no answer. "Just think of all the opportunities passing you by. Why, with your battle cries and penchant for overly dramatic fights, you'd be a shoo-in for the fiasco the humans call professional wrestling. Lots of spandex, shiny costumes—no bloody Viking battles, but still—"

Normandy growled, "If you don't shut up, Shiva has said I can take your tongue."

Artemis laughed, loud and sounding just a little mad. "Yes, I suppose she would say something like that."

Whether he was crazy enough to keep challenging Shiva's guard didn't get answered as we reached the end of the tunnel.

There were lights, rows and rows of them, both lanterns and candles lining the cavern wall. It looked as if every free nook and cranny had been filled, the white wax dripping down and forming eerie wax stalactites, the oil flames staining other places black with soot. The cavern itself had been shaped into a dome, images and pictorial scenes carved into the rock, none of which I was able to get a good look at.

People, easily a hundred or so of them, stood in the domed cavern, encircling a platform as if it were a coliseum and they were attending a play.

Or a trial, my wandering mind offered. I shoved that idea back down. The people were packed into the entrance so thickly that I couldn't see through them to the center of the cavern.

One by one they turned, watching us. I swallowed. "Ah, hi there—" I started. I almost bit my tongue as the guard, Normandy, shoved me in the back, sending me forwards into the crowd. They stepped aside, forming a path to the center, where none other than Shiva sat on a thronelike slab of rock. This time she was dressed in clothes that more befitted a warlord: head-to-toe black leather, visible weapons, and gold jewelry adorning her body and hair. Her face was bare, though, except for a jeweled eye painted on her forehead. If it hadn't been for the fact that I knew she wasn't entirely human, I'd have thought she was too young to be the leader of the Tiger Thieves.

In case I hadn't gotten the message the first time, a shove in the small of my back served as a reminder. I stumbled forwards. "Walk, head up, even pace. They're very concerned about appearances—particularly ones of guilt," Artemis whispered.

I walked down the path with an even pace until I was standing before

Shiva. Her eyes were just as black and dark as I remembered them, her thick hair plaited with gold into a braid that rested on one shoulder. There was nothing forgiving or understanding in those eyes but nothing overtly cruel either, which surprised me. Being tossed into enough cages and backed into enough tight spots over the years, that's what I'd come to expect.

She didn't exactly look a picture of kindness, though, as she turned her dark stare first on me, then on Artemis. I distinctly noted a hardening in the look she gave him and a twitch of her mouth, not far from bared teeth. I searched the crowd, but there was still no sign of my cat. That made me more nervous than anything else.

"What are you doing here?" Shiva demanded.

I had to give Artemis credit: if he was scared of her, he didn't betray himself, not one bit. "I've escorted the lady here to negotiate with you," he said.

Shiva's mouth turned down in the start of a frown, and her eyes narrowed at him. Then she turned them on me. "Is this true?"

I swallowed. That was not the direction I'd expected this to go in. I glanced at the Tiger Thieves, staring down at me. All of them seemed to hold me in their sights, waiting with bated breath for my answer.

"Ah—yes," I said, surprised at how small my voice sounded.

A murmur spread through the crowd. I turned to Artemis. "What the hell did I just say?" I whispered.

"The Tiger Thieves have rules. They have to hear what you want to negotiate before they can execute us for trespassing."

"Execute us for trespassing?" I asked, earning a shove from behind from Normandy. "When the hell did that get put on the table?" I whispered.

Artemis frowned at me. "You wanted to reach the Tiger Thieves no matter what, yes? Well, trespassing, then begging for them to cooperate and not kill us, was the only way I could think of."

Thank you so much for enlightening me . . . "What about the damn amulets? I thought they were an invitation."

"No, not really."

Shiva hit the stone floor with a stick and silence descended over the cavern. "We've heard the request to negotiate and will hear the penitent's plea," she said, her low voice echoing around the room.

All eyes turned on me.

Great, just fantastic, the talking had been left to me. I swallowed. Well, let's hope things didn't go as they usually did with supernaturals. Maybe the Tiger Thieves had a different, more accommodating disposition . . .

"Ah—yeah." Inside I winced at the way the words sounded: hesitant, lacking confidence. I cleared my voice and pushed on, "I'm here to ask for the Tiger Thieves' help freeing someone from a cursed suit of armor."

Another murmur traveled through the crowd.

I looked at Shiva. "The Electric Samurai," I said. "Maybe you've heard of him? He's a danger—" I trailed off at the look Shiva gave me. The neutral expression was gone, replaced by something else: contempt.

I spun around. I was getting that look from all corners. "What? What the hell did I say?"

Shiva smiled as one might at a child. "We're well aware of the armor and the victim. We've even heard of you, Alixandra Hiboux." She leaned forward. "The Electric Samurai is your boyfriend, no?"

I glanced at Artemis. He shook his head ever so slightly. I turned back to Shiva. "No—I mean, yes, but not since the elves stuck him in the armor. And what the hell does that have to do with anything?"

Shiva arched a dark eyebrow at me. "Tell me, do you enjoy being a perpetual victim of the supernatural?"

Victim? "Okay, not a victim here—"

"The vampires? The elves? The dragon? Forgive me, but you epitomize a victim. The only thing I see in front of me is someone who needs to be saved from herself."

This was a tangent I hadn't expected. "That's a little harsh and kind of unrelated, don't you think?"

Shiva snorted. "Not from where I'm standing. And make no doubt about it, Hiboux, be careful with what you say next, because I am in charge. Be happy I don't revel in victimizing humans like the men you've surrounded yourself with. It's not your fault."

It wasn't my *fault*? For a second I was speechless. I'd dealt with a lot of misogynistic assholes throughout my career—real misogynists, the ones who knew their female students were doing the work better than their male cohorts but favored the guys with publications, good digs, and all the credit anyway. They were assholes first and foremost and would have probably been assholes even if they'd been feminists . . . I wasn't arguing the existence of misogyny. But this was the first time I'd been labeled as some kind of systemic victim of it. Oddly, that made me feel more of a victim than anything else, especially because of the way she was looking at me, with a mix of pity and patience.

Damn it, she felt *sorry* for me. And feeling sorry for someone only breeds contempt. Especially when the person you feel sorry for asks for something.

Shiva wasn't done, though. "Argumentative, unpleasant, devoid of mediation skills—oh, we've heard of you. I really can't blame you; you are possibly the easiest target I've come across. You should consider working on that. It might help you avoid as much trouble as you attract."

"You're really taking things out of context here— Shit." I glared at Artemis, who'd just jabbed me with his elbow. Be careful what you say. "Look, just—forget about me for a minute. Rynn is a threat to everyone, humans, supernaturals, everyone."

This time she lowered her head, reminding me of Captain before he's about to charge a toy. "So you'd like us to defeat him for you? Rescue him? Or rescue you?"

"I'm not asking you to defeat him for me, I'm asking for your assistance. Hell, I'll even take information at this point." I turned so I was facing the guards. "You used to defeat supernaturals on the Silk Road, no? Tell me how you did it. How do I nullify the Electric Samurai's power? That's all I'm asking for."

There was another murmur in the crowd, and I felt the tension palpable in the air. Everyone seemed tense except Shiva, whose eyes narrowed at me.

Shit, what had I said? Where had the misstep been?

She didn't leave, though, or tell them to throw us back into the cell. She waited for the murmurs to cease. "All you need is for us to stop him?" she asked.

In for a quarter, in for a pound . . . I nodded.

"You know there is a price for any assistance the Tiger Thieves offer?"

"Anything—*oomph!*" Artemis kicked me. I kicked him right back. He was in no position to be dictating the way this negotiation went, not after he'd landed us in a cell.

"Look, tell me what the cost is. If it's within my power to pay, I'll do it."

"Your request is granted."

I knew I'd stepped deeper into things from the way Shiva smiled at me but looked at Artemis. Artemis swearing beside me also indicated that something had gone wrong. But I hadn't seen any other way out.

"Shiva, stop playing games with her. If you plan to punish me, get it over with," Artemis said.

"Hold him," Shiva said. Armed Tiger Thieves emerged from the shadows and grabbed hold of Artemis, restraining him.

Then two of the Tiger Thieves grabbed me. It wasn't friendly. "Wait—I thought we had a deal?"

Shiva looked at me, her face unreadable. "Oh, we do."

Rough hands steered me towards a pedestal in the center of the cavern. A human-sized birdcage was lowering from the ceiling.

Oh, that was not what I'd been hoping for . . .

I dug in my feet, but it did me no good. I hit the inside of the metal cage face-first and heard the door clang shut behind me. "This does not look like an agreement!" I shouted.

"Ah, yes, well, the price for our assistance is your life."

"Shiva, you're being unreasonable," Artemis said, warning in his voice, though how the hell he figured he could do anything . . . If he did have something up his sleeve, he needed to do it now.

"Considering she broke one of our sacred rules, it seems very reasonable to request her life. Especially since I've granted her request. You can't deny the fairness in that—Father."

Father? What the hell?

"Oh, for— What sacred rule? She's barely been here five minutes."

Shiva stood, looking more imposing than she had yet as she yelled at Artemis, "Imprisoning one of our sacred creatures is punishable by death!"

"Sacred creature? What sacred creature? I leave for a few hundred years, and look at you all, acting more like a bunch of superstitious half-wits—" Shiva started to yell over Artemis, and the two derailed into a shouting match. Something about barely holding on to power, but I didn't care about that. Not with "sacred creatures" being thrown around.

I fought against my restraints. "Hey—Queen of Shiva, what the hell did you do with my cat?"

"Your cat? The Mau is not a possession, it is a sacred creature. It is blasphemy to restrain them."

Well, Captain and blasphemous certainly went hand in hand—oh, shit!

I yelled as the stone floor gave way.

Below me wasn't a pit of lava or flames but darkness. I heard a pebble strike water, followed by churning—something like a fish. I caught a glimpse of something in the dark water that looked like an elongated fin, followed by matted hair.

Oh no . . . there was no electricity to be seen.

One of the Tiger Thieves hit a gong, and the floor of my cage fell out like a trap door.

Shit. I threw my bound hands at the door and, miracle of miracles, caught them on a twisted piece of metal as a bloated white face broke the water, its pincerlike teeth clicking as it reached for me, then disappeared back under the black surface.

A buzz of excitement coursed through the crowd, followed by

shouts. The bastards were probably betting on when the mermaid would eat me—assholes.

"Artemis!" I shouted.

"Your mother would be ashamed!" Artemis shouted at Shiva.

"Consider it a test; if she survives a dip in mermaid-infested water, then the Tiger Thieves favor her and we should all be so blessed."

My feet dangled inches from the surface. I pulled them up just in time to avoid the mermaid as she reached for me with spindly arms, screeching as her fingers brushed my boot. More shouting coursed through the crowd.

"Fantastic. Why don't *you* go take a dip and see how the gods favor *you*?"

Oh, for— I kicked the mermaid in the face as it launched for me again, but a second one was ready. She sunk her teeth straight through the leather. I screamed and kicked the boot off before they punctured the skin.

I wouldn't last much longer playing keep-away. Eventually one of them would get ahold of me.

I realized that a silence had settled over the crowd, and I searched around frantically for the new monster they must have thrown at me.

I didn't see a monster, though, but a ball of white-and-coffee–colored fur racing through the crowd. As opposed to stopping him, the Tiger Thieves scrambled out of his way as he raced towards me. He reached the pit and didn't stop. Instead, he let out a yowl and launched himself at the cage.

The drum picked up in the crowd once again, though this time it was with underlying fear rather than excitement.

Captain's claws caught on the metal. Hanging there above the water, he meowed at me.

"Fantastic idea, I'd love to get off the cage too—now grow opposable thumbs, untie me, and open the cage door!"

A mermaid launched at me again, followed by its friend. "Get off the damn cage!" I shouted at my cat. He just meowed at me.

I should have gotten a raccoon for a pet. I started to swing; maybe I could get us over solid ground, preferably before a mermaid ate my cat. Somehow I didn't think the mermaids knew Captain was a sacred Mau—or cared.

A crowd had pressed in around the pit; Shiva herself pushed her way through. "Throwing your life in with this one's is beneath you!"

This time, Captain turned and hissed at her. Another murmur ran through the crowd, and more Tiger Thieves were looking at her now— expectantly, critically, even.

Captain chirped.

There was an answering chirp and then another. Heads started to poke out of the stonework. Cats. A dozen or so at first, then more and more until there were at least a hundred cat eyes glaring down at us from nooks and crannies everywhere. It was like an army of Captains, all looking down at me.

Shiva looked furious. "This does not concern any of you!" she said, raising her voice.

Captain gave a louder, more insistent chirp.

The other cats answered with the same piercing chirps.

Captain, please say you're making friends for once in your furry life . . .

Another murmur washed through the crowd, more rebellious and filled with the tension that had been in the room before while Shiva fumed at me and Captain.

It was Normandy who spoke. "The Maus have spoken, Shiva. Let her out."

Shiva looked as though she would have liked nothing more than to disagree and leave me where I was.

The cage began to rise, and the next thing I knew, hands were depositing me on the ground near Artemis. Captain followed, and no one dared stop him. With one last glare Shiva turned her back on me.

I scrambled to my feet. "Shiva," I called out. "You're still going to help me, right?"

She kept walking.

Like hell—I tried to follow, but Normandy stopped me. He and another guard grabbed me and Artemis and steered us back down the tunnel we'd come through before, though more gently this time.

"Shiva does not like to be outmaneuvered. Especially by her father," Normandy said.

Goddamn it. I glared at Artemis. He had the good sense to look away.

We reached our cell, and Normandy held the door open.

"Welcome to Muziris," he said, and slammed the door shut behind us. "Your extended stay promises to be very eventful."

I didn't think that was a good thing.

16

EAT, LOVE, AND PRAY A TROLL DOESN'T STEP ON YOU

Friday. Just another early morning
in the deserted jungles of the Malabar Coast.

I came to smelling dried fish and kitty kibble. Captain meowed, then licked my face, his rough tongue scratchy. "Okay, I'm up," I said, and pushed his face away from mine. *Note to Owl: If we ever get out of here, we need some serious upgrade to our self-defense. I'm sick and tired of everyone knocking me out when it's convenient for them.*

After checking myself and letting Captain check me, I looked for Artemis and saw him in the corner, still unconscious.

"Artemis?" I whispered. No movement, not even a stir. Whatever the Tiger Thieves had used on me had apparently been more potent on him. I started surveying our cell, checking through the bars to see which, if any, of the Tiger Thieves was guarding us.

"Ask," Artemis said, not bothering to open his eyes. "About my daughter. Determining the reasons behind people's emotions is not my forte, but the curiosity dripping off you is just plain obvious."

It surprised me enough that he would ask that before my brain could catch me, so I asked, "Why does she hate you?"

Artemis inclined his head. "Over a bargain we made a long time ago in very uncertain and violent times. She's never forgiven me for it." He glanced up at me. "I wasn't able to save her mother."

I couldn't think of the right thing to say to that, so I didn't say anything.

Artemis continued, "I never claimed to be a good parent. You humans obsess over it now, in my opinion, but even half-breeds tended to die off at surprising rates before this last century—colds, famines, new and interesting virus and bacteria strains waltzing into town. Whether you were a good parent or not boiled down to whether you could get your children to live past their tenth birthday, not whether they liked you or you spent quality time with them. Shiva isn't unique in hating me. Most half-breeds end up hating their parents—the supernatural side, that is."

No one was in the hall guarding us. I could try to escape, but I didn't favor the chances that I'd be able to sneak by supernaturally inclined assassins. "Why?" I could understand an aversion to Artemis. He was an ass, and I had no doubt that a lot of supernatural parents were jerks, but all of them?

"Mmmm—less to do with the parent, more to do with the outcome." He glanced over his shoulder at me again. "All of the drawbacks and only a spattering of the perks, and that's if you're one of the lucky ones, like Shiva."

"All the drawbacks?"

"Think of it this way, Alix: imagine you've inherited a supernatural lineage; other supernaturals can smell it on you, but you don't have nearly enough power to defend yourself against them and you're much, much, easier to kill. You're a walking target and usually weak—and there are supernaturals who derive pleasure out of exploiting their halfling cousins."

"Couldn't their parents protect them—I mean, if they wanted to?"

"They certainly do; we're not complete monsters. But tell me, how long until you'd tire of depending on a parent to keep you safe? Ten years, twenty years? Shiva lasted fifty before the resentment turned to hate, another ten to leave me."

"So she's old?"

Artemis inclined his head. "Yes, very, one of the longest-lived half supernaturals I've come across. It's both her gift and her curse. I rather think she finds it more of a curse. She hates me for that as well, I suppose."

Son of a bitch. It finally clicked why Artemis had insisted on coming along, on helping me. "You used me to find her," I said.

"More or less. I couldn't come on my own, she wouldn't speak to me, and I wasn't entirely certain she was here—or where they'd moved the city to—so I suppose I did use you a little. But don't act like that's a surprise, you've expected it all along."

Yes, but not for that . . . I shook my head at him. "Do you have any idea how fucked up that sounds?"

Artemis shrugged. I let the silence stretch while I stared into the torch-lit hall.

"I was telling you the truth. I was spying on the other side when I hurt you," Artemis mused. "And I would probably do it again if the need arose. That's why I'm such a good liar. I usually mean every word of it."

That I could believe. "Did Rynn know?" I found myself asking.

The corners of Artemis's mouth turned up in a terse smile. "Who do you think came up with the idea?"

My momentary sympathy evaporated. "You're a real asshole, you know that?"

He laughed, and his smile widened. "And you're more like me than you realize. Oh, you pretend not to be like me, but when push comes to shove, I think you'll be more than happy to bend your morals to get things done. I'm certain of it. In fact, I think you already have."

I clenched my fists. I wanted to give him a piece of my mind, but his head rolled forwards once again.

I shook his shoulder, trying to rouse him, but it was no use. He slumped forwards, his eyes closed and his head down, out cold. Captain alerted me with a bleat to something outside the cell, and I turned to see Shiva watching me from the other side of the bars, like a predator emerging from the darkness.

She bared her teeth at me. "I think you are lying," she said, the candlelight flickering off her face.

No guards flanked her, and Normandy was nowhere to be seen. I glanced at Artemis, but if he'd awakened, he gave no sign of it. "What did you do to him?" I asked, nodding at his unconscious body.

"What you came here for," Shiva said. "We have ways of dealing with the supernatural. And that is not an answer to my question."

"Lying about what?"

"When you said you would pay any price to save the incubus trapped in the armor." She played with the knife, drawing it along her hands, just shy of cutting the skin. She caught me watching it and held it up to the light, arching an eyebrow. "Well?"

I gripped the bars of the cage in my hands. "Death is a stupid price to ask." I shrugged. "The Dragon has me steal for him; Artemis used me to help me find you since he couldn't do it himself." I shook my head at her. "You're no fool. You just want to see if I'm a coward."

She smiled at that but didn't argue. Or open the cage. Captain squeezed through the cage bars and bleated at her feet. She didn't take her eyes off me but crouched down to pat his head. "Shame I don't know if I can trust you."

"Artemis does." I realized my mistake as soon as the words left my mouth.

"I suggest you stop baiting her, Shiva," came Artemis's voice. "Despite first impressions, she isn't one to suffer fools lightly. Tell us what it is you want so we can stop the charade."

Shiva leaned against the grate. I wasn't certain if Artemis had helped or hindered.

"I will agree to help you stop the Electric Samurai," she said carefully. "But you need to help me."

I leaned against the grate as well. "I already made an agree—"

"What is it you need?" Artemis asked. He sounded almost bored.

Shiva bared her teeth, pulling her lips back. "From you? I need nothing."

"Fantastic. Then let us out and give us the powder. We'll be on our merry way, and you need never deal with us again."

It was subtle, I barely caught it myself, a slight twitch at the corner of Shiva's mouth.

Artemis arched an eyebrow. "Unless you can't?"

Shiva didn't answer. "Don't tell me that that's what this is all about, Shiva. That you can't help us." A slow, unfriendly smile spread across Artemis's face. "Things not so pleasant in paradise? I thought the Thieves had rules, ethics, morals, unlike the rest of us heathens."

Shiva grasped the bars. "You know it is not so simple!"

"Yes, it is. Tell them to let us out of this cage, give us the powder so we can stop my cousin from dragging all of us into the godforsaken spotlight, and we'll be on our merry way."

I decided it might be worthwhile to draw her attention away from Artemis. "Seriously, he's telling the truth. That's all we want."

There was a moment of hesitation on Shiva's face, as if she were deciding whether to divulge whatever it was that had her unnerved. "A hundred, two hundred years ago I could have helped you, but now it is not so simple. We've become isolated, and some of us have forgotten why we used to police the Silk Road—and why we stopped."

"You've let your power slip," Artemis said. "Funny how ruling a group of altruistic assassins gets you stabbed in the back—an oxymoron if I've ever heard one. I wonder who it was who warned you about that?"

Her eyes hardened. "At least I can admit my mistakes."

"Grow up, Shiva, or hurry up and ask me who it is you wish me to gut for you."

She let out a breath. "Again, it is not so simple." Her eyes drifted to me.

I glanced from Artemis to Shiva and back again. "Oh no, I'm staying out of this feud."

Artemis stood and meandered over to the bars, leaning towards his daughter. No matter how hard I tried to see it, I couldn't find a family resemblance between the two.

"She means she has so little grip on the others that having me assassinate her rival outright would chip away at what little of her influence and power is left. She's a shadow of her former self." To Shiva he said, "You really are leader of the Tiger Thieves in name only. Your mother would be very disappointed, I think."

Shiva bared her teeth and gripped the bars. "Come out here and say that to my face."

"No, because you'll lose and then I'll have to spend the next hundred years feeling bad about killing you."

Jesus, and I thought my relationship with my own father was strained at the best of times. "Will you two knock it off?" I turned to Shiva. "Okay, what the hell is it you need us to do, since I'm apparently the only one who doesn't seem to know what's going on?"

"She needs me to kill a rival in open combat," Artemis said. "It's the only way she knows to solidify her power." He sneered. "You never showed much artistic inclination. Free advice? Stop before it gets to cold-blooded murder."

"It's a troll," Shiva said. "And I need you to kill him—in open combat."

I snorted. "Oh, is that all?"

"Who is it, Shiva? Bramah? Darshan? I'd be surprised if they hadn't made a play for power by now."

"Gajaanan," she replied.

Artemis turned to me. "The Elephant Face. You can imagine whose side of the family he inherited his features from." To Shiva he said, "If he's biting at your heels for power, then it's worse than I imagined. He's no leader, only a follower. How much power over them have you lost, Shiva?"

She didn't answer him, her mouth drawn in a tight, terse line.

"I knew it—I knew you were in over your head." To me he added,

"Alix, Gajaanan is one of the stronger half trolls; he might not be a leader, but he can scent weakness. He's a giant; he stands ten feet tall and is all muscle. What little intelligence he has he uses to find new and interesting ways to squish things—preferably living."

And he was giving Shiva problems. Ones that couldn't be handled with a knife to the back. I asked the question that was the drunken pink elephant in the room: "You guys are supposed to be the semisupernaturals. Why haven't you done it yet?"

Shiva pursed her lips. "The half troll may not have inherited his life span from the trolls, but he makes up for it in size and strength."

Shit, that didn't bode well.

"And he has a fixation with stepping on things. Living things."

Why the hell couldn't anything ever go smoothly? "And if I defeat him?"

"Then I will consider our arrangement complete."

I thought about it as long and hard as I could spare from my side of the cell. At the end of the day, that was the crux of the problem. I could do nothing from this side about anything, Rynn included.

I opened my mouth to agree.

"Fine. Piece of cake," Artemis said, pronouncing each word.

I turned to him, but he was fixated on Shiva.

"Easy?" she said. "You think dealing with rival factions and half trolls is a simple task?"

"I'm used to cleaning up your messes, Shiva."

I did not like the way she was glaring at him, her jaw tight. Neither did I like the way he glared right back. Some fights you just don't want to get caught in the middle of. "Artemis—" I began.

Shiva beat me to it. "Then let's make this interesting, Father. If the two of you are unable to remove the troll, you'll be leaving your Mau with us. New blood for the pack."

Oh no, I was putting a stop to this now. "Not a damn chance," I said.

"Fine."

I spun on Artemis. He was making this worse; I had been planning to agree. What the hell was he goading her for? "What the hell do you think—"

I didn't get a chance to give him—or Shiva—a piece of my mind.

"We are in agreement," Shiva said. She whistled, and Normandy stepped out of the shadows and opened the cell.

They didn't grab Artemis, though, they grabbed me. "What? No! I don't do the fighting!"

"You said you would do anything to save your boyfriend, yes?" Shiva asked.

"And if we don't?" Artemis asked.

Shiva narrowed her dark eyes. "Then I really have no choice. If you refuse to fight him in the arena, I drop you right back in with the mermaids, only this time it will be both of you."

"It won't get you power," Artemis said.

Shiva's eyes clouded over. "No, but I'll take the semblance of power, if only for a little while longer."

Normandy dragged me out of the cell. I shook him off. I would walk. At the curious looks Shiva and Normandy gave me, I said, "I figure out a way to defeat your troll, and you help me?"

"I give you my word." Shiva lowered her eyes and regarded me. "And have no doubt about it: I can't fix the Electric Samurai, but, if persuaded, I can help you stop him. And stopping supernaturals is nine-tenths of the way to defeating them."

I swallowed. Rocks and hard places . . . "I suppose you'd better introduce me to this troll."

———※———

I spotted two pillars, worn down and degraded in the dirt on either side of the hall. Sunlight bit through the foliage, and though vines had overgrown the entrance, chipping away at and obscuring the writing and symbols, I could still make out what I was being led towards: an outdoor arena.

"Down there they await," Normandy said.

Through the stone pillar gate I could see a large, gray-tinged man. From this distance he looked normal sized. He was not.

Jesus Christ, what the hell had I been thinking agreeing to this? Combat with a half troll? Trolls didn't move; that's why they were trolls. Full-blooded trolls didn't budge from their bridges, and there was no reason to think a half troll would be any more inclined to move from whatever spot it had chosen. Second, and more important, I didn't fight!

"You know, I often threaten to sell people a bridge," I said, and pushed a strand of hair damp from the humidity and heat out of my face. "This just made things, I don't know, surreal? Or maybe *meta* is the word I'm looking for." Normandy's large mouth turned down at the corners, confusion on his face. If Carpe had been around, he'd have gotten it.

We reached the tennis court–sized arena outside. It was not so much in the Greek or Roman style but a modified version adapted to the uneven terrain. The high stone bleachers were overgrown with vines, reclaimed by the jungle, but today the vines had been trampled, filled by Tiger Thieves. In the sunlight I had a better look at the Tiger Thieves and the various ways they deviated from human. I also got a much better look at the half troll.

Shiva hadn't overstated his height—he was easily ten feet tall, and as if his height weren't enough to make him stand out in a crowd, there was also his grayish skin, much like the hide of his namesake elephant. His face was also more troll-like than human, his eyes smaller and partially hidden by ridges of gray skin and bone on his forehead, made even more apparent by his bald head. His nose was bulbous and trunklike, covering much of his mouth. His hands were massive clubs of thickened skin, good for pounding things into a pulp. And then there were his feet; rather than human-looking feet and toes, his massive legs ended in elephantlike feet, all the better for pounding you with, my dear.

He saw me watching him and smiled, then stamped his feet in a slow tempo. The ground shook.

Oh boy . . .

Artemis glanced at me. They'd given us back some of our supplies but no weapons to speak of. Either of us. "I don't suppose you can fashion a weapon out of thin air?"

Beside me, Artemis was a mess, from the tips of his unwashed high-lighted hair to his dusty designer boots. He shook his head. "No."

"Fantastic." *Just remember, Owl*, I told myself, *every minute you wait is another minute that the armor sinks its tainted claws into Rynn.* Another minute it had to wipe out whatever was left of him in there. Another minute it could make him kill, maim, and enslave both people and su-pernaturals at his whim.

"Any suggestions?"

Artemis shrugged. "Don't let him hit you. And whatever you do, stay away from his feet?"

I could have told him that . . . "You know, this would be a really good time for you to make us disappear— Shit!" I swore as Normandy shoved me past the stone gate. I stumbled into the arena.

Shiva, who was sitting in a stone throne above the nosebleed bleachers, stood, and the crowd noise lowered to a murmur as all eyes fixed on me, including the troll's. Shiva looked at me. "Let the combat begin."

The crowd cheered, and the half troll grinned at me, showing block-sized teeth as he drove his fist into the ground.

Oh hell, what had I gotten myself into? Saving Rynn was one thing, but I couldn't do it if I was smooshed on an arena floor. Nuts to this. I turned back to find a portcullis lowered and Artemis decidedly on the other side.

I grabbed the gate.

"Get in there and fight! Shiva must have something up her sleeve, or she wouldn't have arranged this spectacle. She wants to remove a rival, not send a goat to slaughter," he whispered.

I rattled the gate—no use, it didn't budge. The crowd was laughing now as the troll roared. "Move! You're making us look bad."

"I'm not entirely convinced that her goal isn't to feed me to the half troll!"

"Well, it'd be more guile than she's ever shown before. A parent can only hope."

"You're an awful parent."

"I'm well aware of that—now move!"

I glanced over my shoulder. The troll was running towards me with a wide, galloping gait. Shit. I let go of the gate and dived out of the way. Artemis dodged just in time as the troll's clubbed fist came down. Its fist crunched into the metal, rendering and twisting the bars out of shape.

I did the only smart thing I could: I ran until I reached the other end of the arena.

Maybe I'd get lucky and the half troll would be clumsy . . .

My hopes were crushed as I watched him pivot and with a roar chase after me. Despite his massive feet, he moved with the grace and agility of an athlete, swinging his fists as though he were wielding mallets.

I was fucked.

"Hey, don't I get a weapon?" I shouted at Shiva.

"That wasn't in the agreement," she called down. It was followed by a snicker from the peanut gallery.

I swore as the half troll moved on me. I dodged his fists once again and then dived as he tried to step on me. I knew better than anyone watching that I couldn't keep this up forever.

We made a fast lap of the small arena until I was once again at the gate. Maybe the lock had been broken . . . I gripped the gate and tried to pull it open while the Tiger Thieves guarding the door looked on incredulously. I'm certain I looked ridiculous. I didn't care. Laughter rose from the crowd and Normandy tried to detach me, pushing me back with the rounded end of a spear. With a none-too-gentle push he dislodged me and sent me stumbling into the arena once again—into the chest of the half troll.

I'd like to say I dodged, that I made a noble attempt to stay on my feet. Instead, I crashed into his gray, hidelike chest like a campus drunk reeling face-first into the ground after a run-in with a wayward beer bong. I hit him so hard I knocked the wind out of myself.

His mawlike hand gripped the back of my jacket as he laughed, low and rumbling, and I got a good look into his flat, gray eyes, laughing at me. Then he threw me. My back hit the stone wall of the arena before my ass hit the ground. Oh, that was going to hurt later on.

"I expected more from the great Owl. At least for some nimbleness on your feet," Shiva called down to a course of snickers.

Come on, Owl, get up. "Open the gate and call the show off, then," I called up to her as I used the wall to get myself back to standing. Okay, my head was wobbly, but nothing was broken—yet.

"Seriously, Shiva, you need to stop this. I'm not a fighter."

"You'd better learn quickly, then. Gajaanan has not had a good fight in many months. His last opponent let his head be crushed in the first minute. Very disappointing," she called back.

I was starting to think that the plan really was just to get me killed to spite Artemis. There were more snickers as I turned and ran right around the arena, Gajaanan roaring and the ground shaking as he chased after me. I needed time to think. Supernatural monsters, half or otherwise, were not my forte; they had always been Nadya's domain.

"At least give me a last phone call!" I pleaded.

I winced as I saw the half troll raise his fist above me and closed my eyes. Nothing happened. I opened them again. Shiva was holding up her hand, the troll's fist inches from my face. "I agree to your phone call," Shiva said. "You may tell your loved ones you are about to die. See? I am not so cruel." She whistled and made a gesture before one of her hangers-on handed her my phone. With a flick of her delicate wrist, she threw it down to me.

I dialed Nadya as the crowd watched me. *Come on, pick up, pick up . . .*

"Owl?"

"Hey, Nadya! Look, I'm in a bit of trouble." I turned away from Gajaanan. "Know anything about stopping trolls?"

There wasn't the slightest pause. "Don't try. Owl, just what have you gotten yourself into?"

"You really don't want to know. The good news is that I found the

Tiger Thieves. The bad news is that Artemis kind of threw me under the bus, though oddly enough it wasn't intentional." I shook my head. Off topic . . . "The point is that they're willing to bargain. I just have to kill a troll—well, a half troll."

There was a lot of swearing in Russian on the other end.

"The only weakness I know of is that they are supposed to have trouble following more than one moving target, though usually it's not a problem as they kill you with the first blow."

"So what the hell does that mean?"

"It means run! And Alix—" I frowned as static garbled the line. Shit. "Nadya? Nadya?" I smacked the phone against my leg. Nothing—fucking fantastic. "Hey!" I shouted as the half troll snatched my phone. "That's mine!"

"Time's up," Shiva called down. I heard the crunch as the half troll crushed my phone. I ducked out of the way as he threw the remnants at my head.

Then there was only the massive half troll looming over me, grinning with his blocky, graying teeth, his nose reminiscent of a small elephant trunk; to be honest, it reminded me more of an elephant seal's trunk. Oh shit—

I dodged as the half troll struck again. Okay, it would be hard for him to track more than one target, but where the hell would I get another one? Shame Shiva couldn't have thrown Artemis in here along with me.

I heard a crack as something hard hit the ground, and then I flew forward. I skidded and ate sand. The half troll was in a crouch behind me as if having landed, and I was on my ass on the ground—again. He recovered faster from the leap this time and in seconds was stalking me. His right mallet of a fist struck the ground in front of me. I managed to slide my legs open just in time to save my kneecaps, then rolled out of the way as he followed with his left fist, then tried to stomp on me with his right foot. I used the lull between the strikes that it took him to regain balance and ran.

Right mallet fist, left mallet fist . . . right foot.

Jesus Christ, how had I not seen that before? Just like the many video game bosses I'd done battle with over the years, he had a pattern—an obvious one.

Right, left, right foot . . .

World Quest couldn't have designed a more picture-perfect, predictable bad guy if it had tried.

What I needed now was something to exploit it with.

I bolted for two guards standing near the edge of the arena's bleachers. "Gimme that!" I demanded, and wrenched the nearest guard's spear away from him. Whether he was surprised or simply wanted to see what I'd do with it, he let it go.

Not having time to rethink my course of action, I turned and planted my feet in the sand. The half troll stomped the ground with his left fist, then the right fist, then charged.

I turned the spear handle, my hands clammy against the wood. God, I hoped this would work like it did in video games . . .

Gajaanan struck—right swing, left swing—shit, left foot! I stumbled back, avoiding the foot as it struck where my feet had been a moment before. I fell back on my ass, but not before I raised the spear and jabbed it at the open spot. And I hit him—I actually hit him, uncoordinated, unathletic Alix . . .

The spear tip bounced off the half troll's hide. I stared at the ineffectual tip, the unmarked gray skin, then up at the half troll's face. He laughed, a rumbling, inhuman sound.

Then he batted the spear aside and wound up his fist to the Tiger Thieves' jeers.

I readied to dodge once again, but the troll wasn't aiming to beat my head into a pulp. As I dodged, his left arm caught me and pushed me into the wall.

I was pinned like a bug on a board.

"I don't suppose we could talk this through? Come to an arrangement where I don't die?" I managed to gasp out, struggling against the immovable arm.

He laughed, as did nearby Tiger Thieves—and then he squeezed.

I gasped as the air in my chest was compressed out. I tried to inhale, but my lungs couldn't expand. I couldn't breathe. I pounded my fists against the half troll's stony hide while my vision faded, my lungs screaming for oxygen I couldn't draw in. Through the panic overtaking me I was vaguely aware of the crowd's increasingly loud cheers and jeers.

Gajaanan wound back his other fist.

I closed my eyes and hoped to hell dying didn't hurt.

But the fist didn't come down on my face, and the tone of the crowd changed from anticipation to surprise, and confusion.

I opened my eyes. Gajaanan still had me pinned like a butterfly, but he wasn't looking at me anymore; he was staring over his shoulder at something beyond the bleachers—so was everyone else, for that matter. But what it was, I hadn't the faintest idea, as the blood roaring in my head drowned out all other sound.

Whatever it was that had the Tiger Thieves' attention, the half troll's grip loosened. I gasped, sucking in sweet oxygen. The blood started circulating in my head again, and it was then I picked up what had the Tiger Thieves' and half troll's attention.

A chirp—then another chirp and another. I spotted the cream-and-coffee–colored coat skimming the top of the bleachers, nimbly navigating the stone wall, and then I picked out the other coats—a mix of gray to brown spotted fur, a mass of them, making their way through the Tiger Thieves.

Captain was in the lead, and when he lighted on the stone above me Gajaanan let go and took a step back.

The rest of the Maus took up residence around the perimeter of the arena, chirping to one another and letting out the odd hiss when someone tried to stand up.

Shiva stood up to a chorus of hissing, her face twisted in fury. "Get that Mau out of the arena!"

Despite my predicament I snorted as I rubbed my chest, trying to return the circulation. "You get my Mau out of the fight!" Half of me was curious just how far she'd get.

I wondered how Captain had gotten all the other damn cats to follow his lead; they'd struck me as pretty docile where the Tiger Thieves were concerned. He did look the worse for wear; he had a few more scratches and welts than had been there before . . . I watched as one of the other Maus, a large tomcat, came up to Captain and mewed. Captain whirled on the cat and batted him in the face, sending him scurrying back.

Oh, dear God, my cat had taken over the Tiger Thieves' Maus and somehow beaten them into submission. I did not think that boded well for the future of the obedience Shiva had bragged about.

"Fight!" someone in the crowd screamed.

Captain ignored Shiva and the crowd and leapt in front of me, hissing at the half troll. Gajaanan didn't seem to know what to do with himself or the angry Mau with the nontraditional coloring hissing and growling at his massive feet. I had to hand it to superstition—he didn't even lift his feet in warning.

That's how we found ourselves at a very strange standstill. It's got to suck when your pseudoreligious icons don't play ball with your plans.

"She's making a mockery of our ways!" someone shouted, though I didn't catch who. There was a murmur of agreement.

I lifted my hands as angry faces turned their attention back to me. "Whoa! Hey, I did not go and break your damned cats!"

"You are a harbinger of destruction!" came one voice, followed by "You are bad luck!"

The cats began to growl and turn on the crowd, Captain leading the mutiny.

Oh, for Christ— How the hell was I supposed to make this not a disaster?

While the cats growled and hissed and the Tiger Thieves tried to figure out why their sacred animals weren't sticking with the program, I looked around for something—a weapon, a sign, anything that I could use to stop a fight.

A glint caught my attention, but whether it was the glint of metal or a trick of magic that caught my attention, I'd never know. Regardless of what drew me to it, the fact didn't change that it was Rynn's reflection I saw, staring right at me, smiling while everyone else around argued about how best to kill me without angering the Maus.

I heard his voice clearly in my head as I stared into those eyes, a whiter blue than they had been before. *"Have you ever heard the saying about giving someone enough rope to hang themselves with?"* he asked, his voice clear in my head, and him so close it seemed as if I could have reached out to touch him.

Oh shit. I tried to block him out and force him back.

"It's time for me to pull in the rope."

Somewhere behind me I heard a scream, followed by another, while I tried to force Rynn out. And then he was gone. I looked around me, but there was no sign of him, either in the arena or in the half troll's eyes.

I was scanning the crowds, searching for where the screams had come from, when something large and wet-sounding landed at my feet.

It was a body, a heavily rendered one, tinged with the scent of rotting lily of the valley.

Just about then, the arguing in the stone bleachers turned to screams.

17

MURDER ON THE MALABAR COAST

The Lost City of Muziris, aka the Tiger Thieves stronghold. Time? Who cares? Corrupted supernatural-eating vampires.

I covered my nose with the sleeve of my jacket, ignoring the scent of three days' worth of sweat. It was better than—well—

The body had fallen from above the high walls surrounding the arena, its head striking the stone floor with a sickening crack. I got a better look at it than I wanted to. An arm and a leg had been severed, but the head still remained. It rolled to the side as commotion spread through the crowd, a mop of dark hair falling over and partially covering the beaten and blood-soaked face. The features had been smashed to the point of unrecognizability, but the iridescent scales that flecked the skin were unmistakable: Normandy.

Shit, he had not struck me as being a pushover.

Shiva stepped back, her eyes wide as she stared at the face. "Normandy was one of my best. He left five minutes ago to find a perimeter patrol that failed to check in." She shook her head, as if not believing what she was looking at. It looked as if something had bitten straight through the scales covering his neck—and hadn't been dainty about it.

The scent of rotting lily of the valley got stronger. Captain hissed and began to dance in a slow circle, trying to locate his prey.

"They're above us," Artemis said.

Artemis, Shiva, and I all looked up. Sure enough, suspended above us, clinging to the wall, were three humanlike forms. Their suits hung off them in tatters, and even from this distance their long hair looked greasy and unkempt. Very much like Charles's had been.

It was their eyes that really gave them away, though, bloodshot red as they found me. Their mouths were stained with blood. Better yet, it was fresh.

"What's that?" Shiva asked, taking a step back from Normandy's lifeless body.

"Exactly what I was trying to warn you about," I said, following her lead. I held Captain tight. "Your second cousin, Rynn"—I glanced at Artemis—"or uncle might be more appropriate, considering the age gap."

"What's wrong with them?" Shiva asked as two of the vampires crept down the wall towards us, moving with an eerie, jerky gait. Captain growled a warning. It did no good. I watched two more drop down and corner a pair of fleeing Tiger Thieves.

"That's what happens when vampires eat each other."

Shiva swore. Three above, two across, and four more emerged from under the gate—nine vampires at least, and from the looks of it, they'd all taken the long stroll to the cannibalistic side.

Well, at least I knew their weakness: UV light. I reached for my UV flashlight, forgetting that I didn't have it or any of my other equipment. I backed up until I hit the wall. *Come on, Owl, think fast . . .*

I backed away from the vampire that was stalking me. I thought I recognized the three as Alexander's. Then again, the red eyes, disheveled hair, and manic expressions could have thrown me off. One of the vampires dropped to the ground, followed by the other two. They stalked towards us, looking feral.

"Please tell me your pink powder works on the vampires too," I said.

I noted that the exit to the stone compound was about a hundred fifty feet away. If we ran.

Shiva shot me a sharp look. "Why the hell would we need that?" She placed her index and middle fingers between her lips and whistled, high and sharp. It echoed off the stone, and every cat that had previously been surrounding the Tiger Thieves perked up. Their noses shot into the air and curious probes and growls began. Captain had also perked up beside me, his ears twitching forward, sniffing the air with a renewed interest, fast homing in on Normandy's body.

"It's the vampires who should be worried about us," Shiva said.

As much as I knew that Captain and the other Maus could handle vampires, this was different. I mean, there were only a few dozen Maus surrounding the Tiger Thieves.

I heard growls before the scrape of small claws on the stone and wood lattices above me. I looked up. All over the walkways and stone ledges there were cats, hundreds of them, all crouched and growling at the vampires, a few of them wriggling their haunches in anticipation.

Man, oh man, these vampires were in for a very rude and painful awakening.

The vampires didn't know what hit them. It was Maus—a few dozen of them, chirping and bleating as they swarmed the three vampires.

From the way they howled and tore into them, covering them with a carpet of spotted fur, they were out for blood. And not delicate about it one bit. Captain growled and lunged. I might have let him at them—I mean, it couldn't have hurt—and it would have made him so happy.

I stopped him, though, because of what I saw coming through the damaged portcullis, the one Normandy had been standing behind.

More vampires. Every last one of them one of Rynn's twisted, warped creations. And the Maus were already completely occupied with their vampire-killing operation.

I needed to get them off, at least a handful of them. "Hey!" Shiva stopped me. In the mayhem she'd ascended her throne and looked like an intimidating warrior once more, not a figurehead ruler.

She shook her head at me. "They'll need time to finish the first job.

I don't want to draw them too thin—if they were normal vampires, that would be one thing, but these?" She shook her head once more. I watched as one of the vampires succumbed under a carpet of angry spotted Maus, his exposed hand a mess of purple and black bruises, while another vampire, still standing, pulled a Mau off himself and threw it across the court. It rolled, shook itself off, and charged back into the fray.

Shiva was right, normal vampires wouldn't stand a chance, but these? Even with their bruised and poisoned flesh they were still standing, as if they couldn't stop or feel pain. Knowing how vampires usually reacted to Captain, it had to be Rynn's doing.

I searched the battle scene for Captain, but despite his red collar and cream-and-coffee pattern, I couldn't pick him out against the sea of bronze and dark gray spotted coats. He'd been swallowed by the sea of fur.

The new vampires stalked towards the cats.

"We'd better run," I said, and did just that, back under the portcullis and into the fortress. If I could lure the vampires away from the cats, it would give the Maus enough time to finish round one. If the other cats were anything like Captain, they'd race like bats out of hell to find round two. The important thing was to buy them time . . .

There were two things vampires hated—sunlight and Maus—and I was all out of UV flashlights. I hoped that Rynn had made them hate something else. "Hey!" I shouted as loud as I could and waved my hands over my head. The vampires only had eyes for the Maus.

"What the hell idiot idea are you trying now?" Artemis demanded, trying to block me.

I pushed him out of the way. "Executing something resembling a plan." I needed something to throw. I searched the ground for a rock and found a loose broken tile. I picked it up and hefted it over my shoulder. "Hey! I'm talking to you!" I launched it. For once my aim rang true and I hit one of the vampires, a blond man still dressed in the tatters of his designer suit, one that now sported numerous tears and dirt. "Over here, asshole!"

That got his attention. His lips curled into a snarl, and Artemis swore as the vampires turned their attention away from the cats and towards me.

"Run," I said, and the three of us did just that. For once I didn't look back over my shoulder as we hit the fortress steps. Shiva went to close the portcullis. "Leave it!" I shouted.

"Are you out of your mind?"

"You said the cats needed time, so let's give it to them." I'd spent how long running away from vampires? Fifteen minutes in a maze of a fortress wasn't beyond my means. I careened into a wall and redirected left. It might have been my imagination, but I swore I could hear the clacking noises of beaten-up dress shoes behind me.

"I have an idea. Where do you keep the cats?" I asked Shiva.

"The cattery is down the left corridor, but you do not want to go there. The smell is overpowering."

"That's exactly what I'm counting on," I gasped, and took a sharp left. Artemis and Shiva followed, though Artemis cursed me in the same breath.

My legs protested loudly as the smell of stale ammonia alerted me that we had to be near. The tunnel spilled into a cavern, not as high as some in Muziris but large enough to echo our footsteps, broadcasting our location to anyone who might be in pursuit. The ceiling was filled with nooks and crannies that cats would find a veritable paradise. And then there was the offshoot cavern that sand was spilling out of.

Bingo: jumbo-sized cat litter box. I'd initially thought to lead the vampires into it, but with the smell as powerful as it was, I didn't think we'd have to.

I heard the vampire growls echoing towards us. "Can you hide us?" I asked Artemis.

He nodded, and a moment later, when the vampires rushed in, skidding to an unnaturally abrupt stop, I watched as they searched the cavern with their eyes and then did what I knew they would do: turned up their noses, lifted their upper lips, and sniffed, breathing in deeply.

Two of the six immediately collapsed in a pile on the floor—which only served to make things worse, their hands turning bright red as the traces of Mau saliva and dander raised angry welts on them. Two others tried to halt the coughing fits that threatened to overcome them, their faces turning a bright red, then purple with the effort—and probably from the toxic first deep breath. They exploded in coughs, doubling over, then sunk to their knees as well, their skin smoking.

And then there were two. They were more resilient than the first two; their skin was welting red, but if I had to guess, they hadn't taken in that first noxious deep breath. Artemis tapped me on the shoulder. Our respite wouldn't last much longer. We crept past the vampires back to the exit, and when Shiva and Artemis broke into a run, I followed, keeping fast on their heels.

I let the breath I'd been holding out as Shiva slammed a door behind us, putting at least one hurdle between the remaining vampires and us.

"I've read every text there is on vampires, I've bred Maus for four centuries, and I've never seen a vampire like that," Shiva gasped.

"It's a new trick," I said between labored breaths. "And guess who they learned it from? If you don't like it, tell me how to defeat him!"

We hit a door, one that had been locked. Shiva swore as she tried the padlock. Then Artemis stepped in and struck it, once, then twice. Nothing happened.

"Tell me!"

Shiva hesitated. I really think she would have told me except for the footsteps in the hall behind us.

Two vampires, their mouths covered with the ruined sleeves of their jackets, loomed in the entrance. Their faces were red, and the delicate tissue around their eyes, mouth, and nose was raw. It lent their faces an even more menacing appearance.

Oh, they could not be happy about that . . . "Ah, guys, sorry about the cat urine—" I began, backing up as Artemis hit the padlock harder. "Let's think about this, though—two of you against three of us? And you don't exactly look in the best shape for a fight, what do you say we just call it in— Ah, shit!"

Like madmen, the vampires roared and lunged for us.

It was Artemis who took the lead. "Split up," he said, and grabbed Shiva by the arm.

Shiva and I began to argue, but the vampires were almost across the small room and Artemis had shoved me in the opposite direction from the way he was running.

I didn't have much of a choice. I ran and started to wish I'd left the portcullis open. I really hoped the rest of the Maus didn't try to hold on to their dead vampire prey as Captain always wanted to. *Please let that be the one habit Captain doesn't give them . . .*

I refused to look behind me as I bolted down the hall. I could have sworn the scent of lily of the valley was getting stronger and the heavy breathing and footsteps closer. I hit a wall and randomly chose the hall to the right, hoping the vampire would be slower on his feet. I didn't have much time left before the rotting lily of the valley would turn me into a puddle of lactic acid–filled muscles.

When I hit the wall, my legs wanted nothing more than to give in. I made them keep going. If I lived through this, I was going to give Shiva one hell of a piece of my mind about rethinking coming up with one of those colored chakra powders for vampires . . .

I hit another wall. Which way, left or right?

The vampires turned the corner. Shit—of course both of them had followed me, one of them couldn't have gone after Artemis and Shiva. Goddamn my luck.

Left had a decline so I chose it, almost tripping over my own feet.

And found myself face-to-face with a dead end.

The vampire behind me snickered.

It was the vampire I'd hit with the stone, the one in the damaged Italian suit with the straggly blond hair. I ducked, but the blood-drunk vampire was faster and stronger than I was. He managed to grasp my jacket collar. He pulled me in close, growling at me. I turned my face away and strained back, trying to avoid the toxic saliva and sweat laced with pheromones.

I closed my eyes. This was going to be bad.

But nothing happened.

Slowly I opened my eyes, first one, then the other. The vampire was gone. In his place was none other than Rynn.

Shit. I backed up against the dead-end wall, not certain whether he was an apparition or the real thing. Then the air in front of me frosted.

I swallowed. "Rynn. So this is where we're at now? Throwing vampires at each other?" My mind searched frantically for a way out of this predicament.

He smiled at that. "Well, it's a little cheap. Then again, so are you."

The Electric Samurai might have Rynn's mind, but it certainly didn't have his originality.

I thought about running, but, faster than I could act, he closed the space between us.

"I'm going to let the vampires eat you, Alix," he said, a smile playing on his lips as he pinned me to the cold stone wall. I smelled his breath—the trace of amber and sandalwood was still there, but tinged with something burnt. I closed my eyes, waiting for the violence that resided under the Electric Samurai's skin to explode. But it didn't.

Instead, a gloved finger stroked the skin just under my chin. I opened one eye. Rynn was staring not at my face but at my neck with something akin to a vampire's hunger.

"How did you manage to rope my illustrious cousin into all this?"

I didn't answer, sensing that any answer I gave him wouldn't make things better.

"I'm full of mixed feelings about killing you, Alix. You hold a strange fascination for me, one I remember even if I now don't quite understand it." His eyes roamed up from my neck until they met my eyes.

"How about you call off your vampires and I'll take my cat home."

Rynn *tsk*ed. "I wish it were that simple, Alix. I can't let your interference go unpunished." He stopped stroking my neck and leaned in until his lips almost pressed against mine. Unlike any time before, though, there wasn't anything resembling affection—or even lust. The only thing that emanated off him right now was pure, unabashed malice. And every last cold bit of it was aimed at me. He was still smiling, but it was a twisted caricature pasted onto his face. He reached inside my jacket pocket, the one in which I kept the silver orb hidden. I swore and twisted away, but it was too late.

He tossed it up in the air, taunting me. "One of da Vinci's weapons. How does it work?"

"Haven't a clue," I spat out. "Seriously, I don't know. I'm not sure da Vinci did either, though he was pretty mad by the end, so for all I know it's a magic paperweight."

Rynn's smile was full of malice. "Let's see whether you were telling the truth when you said becoming a vampire was a fate worse than death." He let me go and took a step back.

The blond vampire emerged from the shadows behind him.

Shit. I tried to back up, but there was nowhere to do so. I considered running, trying to outmaneuver him, but that would have left the device in his hands. That I couldn't do. So, Owl, what the hell else do you have?

"Alix?" Shiva's voice rang out loud and clear down the corridor—and not that far away.

Shit.

Artemis and Shiva skidded to a stop a few feet away from me, sizing up both the vampire and Rynn. "Oh hell, what is he doing here?" I heard Artemis say.

All of us, Rynn included, stared at one another in suspense, waiting to hit the other side of the imminent hurricane.

It was Shiva who lost no time: she blew a mix of colored powders into Rynn's and the vampire's faces. It did nothing to me but the effect on Rynn and the vampire was instantaneous; Rynn only shuddered, but the vampire? It—he—devolved into a fit of hacking coughs as the rims of his mouth and nose turned red.

I lost no time either. My strength sapped by the vampire, I delivered a kick to the only place I knew I could still hurt him: the vampire jewels. Between the hacking coughs he let out an involuntary squeal and let me go. I dived for Rynn, not aiming for anywhere in particular except his jacket. I yelped as his armor seared the skin on my palms and coils of smoke arose, quickly filling the tunnel.

It didn't matter. I didn't care. I forced my hand into Rynn's pockets until I found the device. I then fell more than ran towards Artemis and Shiva, who had the good sense to catch me.

The vampire on the ground and Rynn were both incapacitated. Rynn's face was turning an angry red I'd seen on the Electric Samurai before. He shouted after us, "You can't win, Alix. Not this time—not against me."

I was getting tired of hearing that. We ran. I hazarded a glance behind us, but Rynn was gone, the vampire now hurling on the ground.

I crossed my fingers and hoped he stayed that way.

"The exit is just up this way," Shiva said, winded despite her supernatural gifts.

I was too tired myself to ask anything except, "How did you get rid of the other vampire?"

Artemis skidded to a stop up ahead, so abruptly that I careened into his back. "Oh, hell," I said as I got a look at what had halted him.

"Easy. We didn't," answered Shiva.

I covered my mouth with my sleeve—not that it would do any good against vampire pheromones. "So blow some more colored powder at it," I said.

She shot me an irritated sideways glance. "It was Mau cat litter—and I'm out of it."

Shit. A roar from back towards the dead end told me that the other vampire was recovering. I turned my attention to the vampire directly in front of us. *Rock, meet hard place . . .*

As I was trying to decide what to do, I picked up a low, deafening murmur echoing through the fortress, like hundreds of pattering soft padded feet.

Bloodcurdling screams echoed behind us—the other vampire.

Whether the blood lust had worn off or the vampire had some sense of self preservation left, he finally stopped stalking us and turned to see with his bloodshot eyes what the commotion was all about.

That's when the first cat dropped.

It was none other than Captain, in the lead of an army of Maus. And they smelled vampires. For a moment the entire fortress seemed to go quiet as the Maus encircled the vampire. Apparently Rynn's control fell just shy of imminent death. The vampire backed up as the Maus spread themselves out.

I think, at the very end, he might have gulped and contemplated his fate and what steps and missteps had brought him here.

Captain let out one of his menacing growls as he stalked the vampire.

Or else the vampire was just terrified by the sight of a very, very angry Mau.

I winced and looked away as Captain and the others pounced.

—⋘—

When we emerged from the fortress, there was one vampire left alive. The Tiger Thieves had decided to keep one alive, though he was heavily guarded by both the Maus and the Tiger Thieves' weapons. He was raving, angry, vicious—one of the worst off I'd seen of Rynn's new brood, dressed in a tattered suit, a sole designer shoe left on his foot— Son of a bitch!

I got a good look at his face as one of the Tiger Thieves wrestled him back to the ground. Sure enough, it was Alexander. Well, now I knew why I hadn't heard from him after sending my message about Charles.

I spotted my pack, held by one of the Tiger Thieves. "Gimme that," I said, snatching it back, and pulled out my UV flashlight. Normally Alexander is the last vampire on the planet I feel sorry for; he's always arrogant, pompous, trying to kill me. But the way he sunk into himself as my flashlight beam passed over him, I couldn't help but feel sorry for him.

"He's mad," Shiva said.

Yeah, just like Charles had been . . . I felt for the device, now back in my pocket, and pulled it out. As before, I pressed the device into the right configuration. "Hold him, will you?" Okay, how had this worked last time? Device, check. Half-mad vampire, check. Now all I needed was blood—but whose? Alexander's or mine? And would it work without other vampires around to drain? There was only one way to find out.

"I'd really step back," I told the others. Then carefully, ever so carefully, I motioned for the Tiger Thieves to open Alexander's bloody hand. "On the count of three," I told them. One, two, three—I dropped the device into his hand and dived out of the way, the two Tiger Thieves doing the same. Alexander flashed his fangs and stumbled after us in his feral gait. Then da Vinci's device burst in an explosion of white light.

When the bright spots finally subsided, I lifted my head. It took me a second to take in the scene before me.

The vampire carcasses that had been strewn over the ground had disintegrated, just as the live ones had before, leaving small piles of ash in their wake. In the middle was Alexander, and just like Charles, the red eyes and feral look were gone, the arrogance and judgmental personality I'd grown used to left in their wake.

Captain crept forwards but I stopped him, picking him up under my arm as I strode over and crouched down to Alexander's eye level. I needed answers. And there was only one thing I really wanted to know. "Where the hell is Rynn?" I asked him.

Alexander glared at me before spitting on the dirt floor. There was blood mixed in, and though I got only a brief glimpse, my mood lifted when I saw that one of his canines had been broken off in the fight. "We had what you'd call a disagreement."

"In plain English," I said.

Alexander clicked his tongue, not taking his hateful eyes off me. "He took my vampires," he said, spitting out the last words.

Yeah, well, unfortunately my bleeding heart was all bled out. Alexander and I had had a tentative truce, and I did owe him one favor. He didn't want to see the supernatural spill over into the real world any more than I did, so on that page we were square, but that was where our tentative truce began and ended. He'd shelled out more than his fair share of pain and retribution, in the process making my life a living hell for a good year. If Alexander were reincarnated as a high school girl, we'd be arch-frenemies. "Wow, tough times, eh, Alexander?"

Alexander sneered, "I imagine you and your cat are enjoying seeing me reduced to—this." He held up his arms and made a noise of disgust.

I realized that only half of Alexander's mood was attributable to his predicament. The other half was the wounding his pride was taking at having me and the Tiger Thieves see him this way.

"You're welcome for unthralling you," I said instead of the multitude of snide comments that came to mind.

Alexander made a rude gesture. I didn't care. "Where is he hiding?"

"Where is who hiding?" Alexander asked, feigning innocence.

"Cut the bullshit, I'm in no mood for it. Tell me where he's hiding, and maybe, just maybe, you'll get your vampires back."

"Like this?" Alexander glared at me from under lowered brows, a hint of fang showing from under his curled lip as he gestured towards the piles of ash.

I shook my head. I suspected that some of Alexander's vampires had been amongst the thralls—not a hell of a lot I could have done about it. "Look, I feel for you, Dandy Fangs, but you know as well as I do that that was Rynn's fault, not mine."

"You incinerated them!" Alexander screamed, his face twisting in fury as he let the ashes of one of the vampires run through his fingers.

I inclined my head. "Actually, technically *you* incinerated them."

Alexander swore—loudly.

"And Rynn's the one pulling all the puppet strings, not me."

At that Alexander smiled. "Little bird, you have no idea."

I frowned. "What the hell is that supposed to mean?"

"It means you should not be worried about where Rynn and his band of merry mercenaries, as you call them, are hiding but where they intend to go. Where I was supposed to go with my vampires if things had gone according to plan."

"Where?" Captain let out an accompanying meow, adding his two cents' worth to the discussion with the vampire—the one he'd rather be eating.

Alexander smiled. "Ah, not so fast, little bird—a trade of goodwill, if you would," he said, flicking his eyes towards the Tiger Thieves.

Alexander wanted a safe way out. I couldn't blame him; I wouldn't trust his frenemy status to get him out of hock with the Tiger Thieves either.

"What do you want?"

"For you to guarantee the safety of my remaining vampires under his thrall."

"Shiva, you use bait to train your cats?"

The request surprised her but only momentarily. One corner of her mouth twitched up. "Frequently."

I turned my back on Alexander and started back for the fortress.

"Alix—Hiboux!" he shouted.

I waved over my shoulder. "See you, Alexander," I shouted to another round of curses, this time in French. I waited. I could sympathize with him, but there was no way I could promise to save his friends or subjects or whatever he called them. They were vampires, meaning that they would try to eat me. Promising something I couldn't deliver would be stupid, even for me.

Despite how upset Alexander might be, deep down I think he knew I wouldn't agree to his first demands. Drama queen? Sure, but he was a businessman as well.

"Guarantee my safe passage!" the vampire shouted after me, sounding more panicked, though I suspected that was due to the Maus that were growling at him as they advanced.

I stopped and glanced at Shiva. It was subtle, but she shrugged. I turned back to Alexander. He was done bartering. "If you ever wished to stop a supernatural war from spilling into the human world, you have two days left," he said through clenched teeth. "Because that is when the Onorio is meeting with the malcontents to discuss a truce. In Tokyo."

"That is a trap if ever I heard one," said Artemis, who had been silent up until this point.

Yeah, no kidding. Looks like I would be going to Tokyo. At least if it was a trap, I knew Rynn would be a show. "Let him go," I said, nodding to Alexander.

Surprise shone in the vampire's calculating eyes. "You would spare me?"

"In a few days," I continued.

Alexander swore and spat. "Why, you—"

"Sorry, Alexander, but, like you said, Rynn has your vampires. I can't trust you to crawl back unless you can't. Let him out in a few days," I called after the Tiger Thieves as they led him away. "And I mean it!" I hoped I could trust the Tiger Thieves not to rough him up too badly—I did owe him a favor. I just wasn't going to hand my head on a platter over to a vampire in the process.

I stood and started for Artemis. If we wanted to reach Tokyo before it was too late—

Shiva stopped me, stepping into my way. In her hand was a small bag made of coarse canvas. She opened it for me to see. Inside was a finely milled powder, a mix of orange, pink, and dark yellow, swirling together. It was the powder she'd promised me.

She shoved it towards me but didn't let go.

"That device," she said, in a voice low enough for only me to hear. "It will work against him, but I caution you not to use it." Her dark brows furrowed, showing her more-than-human nature. "Magic like that—it has a steep price."

I took the powder and shoved it into my pocket, right beside the device. "Always does," I told her. "Artemis? Get ready, we're headed for Tokyo."

18

TOKYO NIGHT

Saturday. Twenty-four hours later: At Space Station Deluxe.

I sat at the bar, the red neon light shining through my Corona beer. It was a Friday evening, and Nadya's bar was uncharacteristically closed. In fact, the entire district of bars and nightlife seemed unusually subdued. Whether it was my imagination playing tricks on me or the supernaturals that had descended upon the city playing their own tricks, I didn't want to know.

Captain hopped up onto the bar and mewed at me. I swirled my beer, sending the reflected shards of light over the bar for him to play with. It seemed like a lifetime ago that I'd been spending my nights here with Nadya, planning heists and trying to stay under the radar of the IAA. Before Rynn, Mr. Kurosawa, and the rest of the supernatural world had come crashing down on my life.

Funny how things that used to seem so important felt so petty now. Especially as I watched Oricho's tattoos seemingly move under the collar of his shirt, as he sat across from me, Nadya standing across from us, on the mediating side of the bar, acting as referee.

"Rynn is already here," Oricho said. "My sources say he showed up at Gaijin Cloud a few days ago and has been in and out. He's getting more powerful."

"No kidding." I filled them in on his appearing act in Muziris—the very tangible version.

Oricho listened, then nodded. "He may be able to use his minions as conduits. It is a power I have heard of before, though never witnessed."

"Fantastic." New and unusual powers. Not what we needed.

"And we still have our opponents to deal with," Oricho said. "Our negotiations with them to broker a peace, however tentative, have deteriorated, not improved."

"What he's trying to say," Nadya offered, "is that they've been moving their forces in."

"How many? Twenty? Thirty?"

"Try hundreds," Nadya said. "And all stripes."

I frowned. "You mean Tokyo is overrun with monsters and what? No one cares?"

Nadya shrugged. "Everyone is still just . . . pretending. Plus, let's face it, this is Tokyo."

Meaning that a couple of extra monsters running around wouldn't necessarily come across as anything more than a blip on the city's already richly eccentric scene.

"Regardless of how blind people want to be, they won't be able to keep the wraps on this for much longer." I searched around the bar. "And where the hell is Artemis?" He'd come to the bar ahead of me but he'd said he'd be here . . .

"Artemis is meeting with Mr. Kurosawa's opponents in an attempt to broker a temporary truce—until the Electric Samurai is dealt with, that is."

"I'm having a hard time seeing how it's even an issue," I said. Rynn's current brand of chaos wasn't good for anyone, and I couldn't believe that the Malcontents, as Alexander had called them, didn't believe Rynn was a threat.

"They believe Rynn is a threat, but some of the younger ones are willing to gamble that he will give them an edge. The older ones are not so arrogant."

"Haven't they seen what he can do? They can't think they're immune."

Oricho inclined his head. "It is more complicated than that. Some of the older supernaturals believe the Electric Samurai is a powerful threat—but others? Some are unwise enough to believe themselves immune, but the majority simply believe all they need to do is outwait or outlive us. They are wrong."

No kidding . . .

A phone rang—one that wasn't one of mine—and Oricho took his phone out of his pocket and glanced at the screen. "My informants," he said, excusing himself.

Nadya hesitated as Oricho disappeared out the front door, likely onto the stairs that led to the club. She pursed her lips, looking as if she was deciding whether to follow him or broach another topic.

"What?" I said. When she hesitated, I added, "Look, whatever you have to say can't make things any worse than they already are."

She made a face. "It might." She made up her mind and opened her laptop, turning it so I could see the screen. "It's about the device," she said.

I swore.

"You want the good or the bad?"

"Bad—always the bad, Nadya."

"I've found out more about it. On one of the older servers in Moscow, one that doesn't get checked very often. It was buried amongst some old texts from the Renaissance period—a Russian Illuminatus's notes that hadn't been scrubbed."

"How come I get the impression that's not a good thing?"

She pursed her lips once again. "Alix, I think it drains the user."

The user? I opened my mouth to protest, but then I remembered that it had removed the corruption that Rynn had imposed on the vampires, both Charles and Alexander. I'd thought that was because it was healing them somehow or resetting their powers—but what if it was because it had been draining them? Draining away the extra power Rynn and the Electric Samurai had forced on them. It made frightening sense.

Shiva's warning that the device elicited a price came back to my thoughts.

It also complicated my plans. The powder would immobilize Rynn, but that didn't mean we'd be able to get the armor off him. Da Vinci's device was my backup plan.

"I have an idea," Nadya continued, than hesitated.

I waited, watching my best friend. Nadya wasn't usually this hesitant—or shy.

Whatever struggle was going on in her own head vanished with a shake of her neon red wig. "Get Artemis to use it," she said, meeting my gaze.

I lowered my head. "You can't be serious!" But from the expression on her face, she was. "You are! Jesus, Nadya, I'd expect that from Oricho, hell, I'd expect it from Artemis, but you?"

I needed some air, but she stopped me before I could leave, grabbing my arm. "As a backup, if we can't get the armor off Rynn," she said. "Artemis is not a good person—supernatural. Remember what he tried to do to you."

I stood there, shocked. More so as I realized I would have thought the same thing a week ago. I frowned at her. "You've been spending too much time with Oricho, Nadya, or you'd know the answer to that already."

She looked as if I'd struck her. "I'm looking out for you is what I'm doing!"

"I'm not throwing anyone under the bus!"

It was her turn to narrow her eyes at me. "You were the one who told me it was only a matter of time before he stabbed you in the back."

Well, yes, I had said that—numerous times—but I realized I didn't believe it—not anymore. Or maybe I did—I didn't know. "That doesn't mean I want to adopt the same goddamn tactics he uses."

Nadya frowned at me. "And you wonder why you always end up on the bottom."

I stared at my best friend. It was as if I were staring at a completely different person. "What the hell has gotten into you? Nadya, you're usually the voice of reason. You're the conscientious one."

A dark look crossed her beautiful features. "Maybe I've had to grow up as well in the past few months."

I was starting to think I shouldn't have left Nadya in Tokyo with the monsters for so long. After I fixed all the other problems, I was going to have to rectify that.

Nadya let out a breath and shook her head. "Just forget I said anything. It was an idea. If things come to the worst. Let's leave it at that—a suggestion."

Nadya took the empty bottles from the bar—there were a few; I'd needed them as the others had updated me on the situation in Tokyo—and headed into the back.

I turned my phone over, still reeling from Nadya's admission. There was a new message from Lady Siyu . . . and a text . . . and an email. Shit, I'd pushed the idea of dealing with her to the back of my mind. It was a simple message—only a few words long and very to the point: "We have been made aware of the da Vinci device. Return with it or do not return to us at all. You have been warned."

All of them were the same. I swore and considered my options. First off, there was no way in hell I was giving the evil dynamic duo the device—no way, no how—but I wouldn't be telling them that either. Lady Siyu was itching for a reason to kill me. I pushed that thought aside, though.

I heard the door open as Oricho reentered.

I sighed, abandoning any idea of trying to mollify Lady Siyu over email. I'd deal with it once we'd gotten Rynn out—or died. That was a distinct possibility . . . today's supernatural threat to my existence, not tomorrow's . . .

"Please tell me there are no more imminent supernatural disasters on the horizon," I said, putting the phone away.

Oricho inclined his head. "You can ask them that yourself, as you will have a chance to meet a representative from the other side. Artemis has succeeded in arranging a negotiation."

I didn't know if I was optimistic about the idea of negotiating. The other side hadn't struck me as the negotiating type so far. "So they've actually invited us to a sit-down?"

Oricho inclined his head. "In a matter of speaking . . ."

I grabbed my jacket from the bar. "Come on, Captain—this I've got to see."

Of all the ideas that had run through my head regarding a meeting of supernatural powers, one that involved a scene this macabre hadn't even made my list.

I glanced up at the skyscraper once more, at the man sitting on the ledge. Emergency workers were gathered around, some of them trying to place a net in the best possible position while others attempted to talk him down.

I'm jaded, especially where the supernatural is concerned, but this was pushing it, even for me. "I thought the Kitsune drained their victims of life through work?" I asked Oricho. Nadya had warned me about the salarymen/-women deaths, but she—and the media—had made it sound as though they'd died of exhaustion and dehydration at their desks, not, well . . .

"Usually that is the Kitsune's preferred method of feeding—slowly, over a period of months or years," Oricho replied. "But like any of us, they also make their exceptions. This is their idea of making a scene."

I'll say. I shielded my eyes against the spotlights darting across the skyscraper. He had to be on, what, the thirtieth floor? I shivered, not immune to the tragic nature of the spectacle being put on. The guy didn't want to kill himself, not really—it was a result of the feeding that had probably been going on for weeks or even months now that was driving him. Neither had any of the other victims, for that matter. Funny how the details changed one's perception of what was going on. One suicide with a spectacularly promised exhibition caused more uproar than twenty quiet deaths by overwork. Or maybe it wasn't the quiet aspect at all; maybe it was the fact that death at a desk was more mundane, expected, ordinary—but someone jumping off a skyscraper? Spectacular. Like the difference between influenza and Ebola—Ebola might kill only six thousand people worldwide during an outbreak, but it did so spectacularly. The run-of-the-mill flu? In a bad year it killed up to fifty thousand people in the United States alone, but you didn't hear much about that. It was all a matter of jaded perspective—which led us back to this . . .

Captain, picking up on my mood, let out a forlorn mew. "You said it, buddy." Despite the crowd around us, he was not picking up any supernaturals. I turned to Oricho and Nadya, who had forgone her red wig for her natural brown hair and glasses. I tried to find Artemis, but either he'd decided he didn't need to be here or he'd decided to stay out of sight. "So where do we meet this representative, exactly?"

"I imagine they will find us," Oricho replied.

"Before or after the show?" Being forced to watch an execution being billed as a desperate plea for help wasn't exactly what I'd signed up for.

"Before," came a distinct woman's voice from behind us. The three of us turned to see a well-dressed Japanese woman with ombré hair, black at the roots fading to a platinum white at the ends, the very tips painted with a pink that matched her lipstick. She was beautiful, but it was the kind of beauty that's more frightening than inviting. And her eyes? A pale, watery gray.

"The invention of contacts has been a wonderful thing," she said, catching me staring. She offered me a smile that would have put most people at ease. Not me. It was all I could do not to take a step back and run away screaming. For all her mild-mannered appearance, this woman was likely one of the more dangerous supernaturals I'd met.

For his part, Captain let out a mildly warning bleat, peeking over my shoulder before hunkering back down. Great, one of the few super-naturals who scared my cat. That did not bode well by any stretch of the imagination.

She was standing out in the cold in little more than a wool blazer, though no one in the crowd seemed to take more notice of her than a quick glance, and those who did were more appraising and admiring than questioning.

The Kitsune held out her hand to shake mine. "No offense meant," I said, only staring at her delicate hand, fingernails painted white with pink cherry blossoms, looking so harmless.

Rather than take offense, she only gave me a knowing smile and placed her hand back into her blazer pocket. "None taken."

I saw her face take on a dreamy look as it drifted upwards, her lips parting to expose a pinker-than-normal tongue. Screams around us followed, and as I glanced back up at the ledge I saw that the man had edged farther out onto the window ledge.

She closed her eyes and took in a deep breath. "Delicious, isn't it?" she said. "You can taste the uncertainty and anticipation, so thick is the air filled with it."

"Yeah . . ." I said ironically. Her nostrils flared as she breathed in—or however it was she sensed. I knew that Oricho and Artemis had both said to stay out of the negotiations, but there was no way they could have imagined this spectacle. "A little messy, though?" I nodded at her suit. "I'd hate to see the dry cleaning bill for getting too close."

Her smile deepened, and for a moment her eyes took on a pinkish shade. "Oh, I believe it would be worth it. Just to watch the plunge." She turned her face towards me, feverish with anticipation. "Rather like one of your Western adages, isn't it? Watching pigs fly?" Her lips parted in a smile. "Like bacon—not healthy but very satisfying."

This spectacle was getting more sickening by the minute. I opened my mouth to say something to that effect, but Oricho interrupted. "You are here to negotiate on your party's behalf, yes?" he asked.

"Ah yes. That," she said. "Leave it to you, Oricho, to spoil all my fun."

The pleasant, dreamy tone of her voice vanished as she spoke, and she gave Oricho an unfriendly, critical glance, narrowing her expertly lined eyes. "And I would expect you to be more sympathetic to our side now, all things considering."

If her tone and address offended him, he didn't let it show. Instead he offered her a smile. "Ah. I suppose a supernatural of your stature would come to that conclusion."

"I'd forgotten just how boring you Kami were, Oricho." She glanced back up at her victim, still precariously balanced on the ledge.

"What is it you have been sent to barter today, Kitsune?" Oricho pressed.

With a sigh, the Kitsune turned her attention away from the salary-man to us, her features schooled back to pleasant indifference. I winced at the screams from the people gathered around us as the man on the ledge wavered.

"Look, maybe while we're negotiating, could you just— Ow!" Oricho silenced me with a squeeze to my shoulder. "Never mind," I said.

"Our offer is simple. A cease-fire, a truce, as it were—temporary, of course, but a welcome respite to allow both our sides to regroup while we deal with the incubus and the elves' trespass."

Oricho's brows furrowed. "That's a pleasant offer considering your previous reluctance. I would be remiss for not questioning your motivations—and the cost."

"Ahhh." She turned back to look at the man on the ledge. "The cost? Your side's word that for the duration of one month neither side shall interfere with the other. As for our motivation and the cost?" She arched an eyebrow. "They are one and the same."

Meaning that Oricho, Mr. Kurosawa, and Lady Siyu wouldn't be able to enforce their rules. For an entire month, there would be a free-for-all. It would be disastrous—there was no way they'd be able to hide the existence of supernaturals.

For the first time since the Kitsune had arrived, she let her pleas-ant mask fall, exposing cruel and rather ugly features. "Oh yes—and we expect the Electric Samurai to be removed from the game. Permanently, if necessary."

I opened my mouth to say that that was obvious, but a warning touch from Oricho stopped me before I said it.

"An interesting proposal," Oricho said.

The Kitsune's pink upper lip curled. "We know you have a way."

Now, how the hell had they found that out? Rynn had his suspicions, but them?

The Kitsune continued, "And although we have considered attempting to obtain it from you directly"—she leveled that cruel pink stare at me and flicked her pink tongue, which was now forked—"we have decided it would be more prudent to call a truce."

"And let us clean up your mess?"

Both she and Oricho turned their decidedly supernatural gazes on me this time. "Since it was elves on your side who thought it would be such a great idea to shove him in there in the first place, no?"

I counted to a slow three while she regarded me, calculating. "Regardless, he is a problem for both of us. And I'll wager that in the long run you care more about the outcome than we do."

I snorted. "You can't beat him. You created a monster, let it loose with no way of controlling him."

"Ah, such is the beauty of chaos." Her eyes narrowed. "I suppose that is one way to look at it. Though I believe you will accept our terms as they are."

"And why would that be?" Oricho said.

She gave a pretty-sounding sigh and glanced once more at the man on the ledge. "Because unlike yours, my side cares very little for the value of life beyond our personal enjoyment and fulfillment. Perhaps you are right and we have no way to deal with the Electric Samurai ourselves. Then again?" She closed her eyes and tilted her head towards the man, then drew in a breath and leaned back, balancing on her heels.

Even though the air was warm and clear, I made out the fog—like reversed warm breath on cold air—that she sucked in. For a moment the street seemed to hold still—the people, the air, the noise of the city. Then screams broke out and mayhem ensued as emergency workers tried desperately to place the net below the man who was now plummeting off the building.

The Kitsune still had her eyes closed, her head tilted up as if savoring every moment. "Such a bore having to feed off the wretched, deserving, and invalid. They have an unpleasant copper taste that always leaves me hungry. A virile adult like that? Absolutely delectable, so sweet and fulfilling."

I've seen a lot of horrible things in my life—violence, death—things that would make normal, well-adjusted people never sleep a wink again. I knew about the things that went bump in the night with a vengeance.

I couldn't look.

I cringed and turned my face away as the screams reached a crescendo, followed by the unmistakable sound of something organic hitting the sidewalk.

The screams were replaced by the roar of people trying to speak over one another and the din of shock and excitement at what had just occurred.

Finally, careful not to let them drift towards the pavement, I opened my eyes. The Kitsune was licking her fingers. "Jesus Christ, I thought you said you wanted a truce?"

She stopped what she was doing and arched an eyebrow at me. "Consider it a well-timed reminder. You have until midnight tomorrow to decide, Oricho." She turned and started moving through the crowd. She gave me one last look over her shoulder, throwing her black, blond, and pink hair to one side. "Oh? Yes, I suppose I did. And who says we don't have a way to deal with the Electric Samurai? I would wager that if we do, you would not like it. Rather like this evening's spectacle. Accept our truce."

With that she was gone, leaving us with the mayhem she'd wrought with the poor man now dead on the sidewalk. Once again, there had been nothing I could do about it . . . at all. I'd been completely powerless.

But there was at least one person here who hadn't been powerless to do something. I turned on Oricho. "What the hell was that?"

"A Kitsune."

"Why the hell didn't you stop her? And don't tell me there was nothing you could have done!"

Oricho's hands were clenched at his sides—he gave me a once-over, turning away from his survey of the macabre scene unfolding in front of us. TV crews mixed in with the emergency workers now; apparently dead people garnered more attention than ones in need of help who were about to kill themselves. I stopped that train of thought for the whole new level of anger it drew out of me—at the people, not the supernaturals, who had started this and used an innocent human with a life as a disposable pawn.

"My hands were tied," Oricho said, not looking away from the scene.

"Tied? Jesus, you didn't even try—"

I trailed off as he finally turned his gaze back on me. "Do not tell me what I could and could not do. Events were out of my control before we arrived. That man's life was forfeited well before this evening. She decided to use it as a spectacle."

"Because you provoked her!"

"No, it was to get under your skin." The three of us turned to see Artemis standing behind us, hands in his pockets. "And from the looks of it, she did a brilliant job," he said.

I crossed my arms. "And you? You didn't lift a damn finger either!" It wasn't Artemis's fault, I knew that, but I needed to vent my anger and frustration at someone—and he and Oricho were right there.

He frowned, probably at the sheer anger boiling off me, all directed at him—but if it bothered him, he didn't let on. "As Oricho already said, there was nothing either of us could do. That man was dead weeks ago, the moment the Kitsune got her deadly fingers into him. The only thing we could have accomplished was avoiding a spectacle."

"Which is likely what she was aiming for, knowing your particular reputation," Oricho added, as delicately as he could.

"What is that supposed to mean?" I demanded.

"It means you have a bad habit of making a spectacle of yourself in public view. That's likely what she was banking on," Artemis offered.

"Oh, come on." I turned to Nadya, but she kept her eyes on the ground.

Fine, I'd defend myself. "If my trying to save someone—"

Artemis leaned in and placed a finger on my chest. I just about punched him in the stomach. "It would have been replacing one spectacle with another. We would have lost what leverage we had." He straightened and took a step back, as if just realizing how close we were. "They aren't confident they can handle Rynn; otherwise they would be pressing the advantage. Rynn has been picking away at their foot soldiers, warping them into his own personal brand of fiends. As it is, we still have the upper hand."

I snorted. If the upper hand was watching someone throw himself onto the pavement from the thirtieth floor of a skyscraper, I wasn't sure I wanted it. I might be used to being the underdog in these supernatural scuffles, but underdogs were normally able to escape with their morals intact. Not like . . . this . . .

"Like I said, he was dead weeks ago. This was only the grand finale. A heart attack a week from now, a month." Artemis shrugged. "The other side doesn't just fight dirty, Alix, they dig the knife in and twist for fun."

"So I should just let it go? Be okay with them killing someone in front of me?"

Artemis narrowed his eyes at me. "No, what I'm saying is that you need to learn to suck it up like the rest of us and stop being such an entitled brat." That was it. I wound up, but Nadya caught my arm before I could plant my fist on his nose.

Artemis snorted. "Like I said, one spectacle with another. Now, if anyone would like to know what I learned while I was doing my *job* instead of playing the self-righteous hero, like who the Kitsune was with, find me back at the bar. I need a fucking drink." With that he turned and left, Oricho following with a nod. I could have killed both of them, but most of all Artemis—throwing the fact that I was the only one here who cared back at my face as if it were some kind of self-righteous crutch—

"Alix, you need to drop this," Nadya whispered in my ear.

"Don't tell me you agree with them!" There was no way—Nadya had an even stronger moral compass than I did.

She sighed. "No, I think they're so used to this particular battle that they've forgotten what it's like to try. Alix, I'm not saying it's right, I'm not saying I agree with them. They're stubborn and wrong, but we didn't have anything that would have changed things. We're not mercenaries and soldiers, Alix, we're thieves and part-time archaeologists—and that's the truth."

I wanted to argue, I needed to argue—but part of me knew she was right.

"We don't have to like it, but for now?" She glanced over to where Artemis and Oricho had disappeared into the crowd. "Unless you have a better plan, it's all we can do."

I didn't, and maybe that was the crux of it. And it was eating me up inside.

Cold certainty descended over me. As Artemis had said, I needed to suck up my precious morals and either play with the supernaturals on their level or go home. "Fine, Nadya," I said.

Her surprise was quickly replaced by disbelief. I shook my head. I was serious—and certain. "Artemis and Oricho want us to play on their level? Then let's play. We'll do it your way."

She looked taken aback. "It's just—you were so sure . . ."

I shook my head. "No, Artemis was right. It's time for me to grow up. There are no such things as rainbows and unicorns." Or maybe there were such things as unicorns for all I knew . . . so that wasn't the point . . .

Nadya knew better to argue when I set my mind on something. She only nodded. Funny, considering her insistence earlier that getting Artemis to use the device would be the best way, I could have sworn she was the one who'd change her mind.

"Are you two going to stand there with the fucking cat or open the bar back up so I can get a fucking drink?" Artemis shouted. Not one person in the crowd looked his way.

Of course no one else could hear Artemis. Goddamn it, and he thought *I* made a spectacle of myself.

Nadya made a rude gesture at him, both of us knowing better than to shout and draw any more attention to ourselves than necessary. I tried not to look at the body on the sidewalk. It was covered, but there was only so much a white sheet could do to hide that kind of unnecessary violence.

Artemis wanted me to grow up? Fine, I'd grow up.

"Can you convince Artemis to use the device?" Nadya asked.

I shook my head. As they kept telling me—grow up. "I'll handle Artemis." He was no Rynn when it came to reading emotions.

Captain gave a mournful mew from my backpack. I patted him on the head. "Don't worry, buddy, I know what I'm doing," I whispered, doing my best not to look at the body on the sidewalk.

It still made me sick to my stomach, beneath the cold and ice—but then again, maybe learning how to ignore that was another part of growing up.

We set off after Oricho and Artemis. The device burned in my hand, though that was more from my gripping it tight than any magical effect. We'd managed to cast our own spell of sorts, Nadya and I, and I wasn't at all certain it was any better than the ones the elves had cast on Rynn.

19

CHARLATANS AND THIEVES

*8:00 p.m.: Space Station Deluxe. The bar is empty, the lights are off,
and despite being here, I'm still not sure anyone's home.*

Back at Space Station Deluxe, I'd skipped the Corona and gone straight
for the tequila. I sipped it, savoring the burn as I turned the silver device
over in my hands. How the hell was I supposed to use the device without
killing Rynn, as had happened with the vampires and just about every
experiment da Vinci had ever tried?

And then there was the issue of what the device would do with the
corrupted magic of the armor. In theory, it would strip the magic into its
most basic components, separating the armor, the corruption, and Rynn
into their own pieces. But I couldn't be certain.

I was between a rock and a hard place—or maybe with a cougar
and a bear on either side of the tree I was up. That was more like it. We
still weren't entirely sure that the device would work against the magic
corruption Rynn was spreading. There wasn't a good choice. I sipped my
tequila. Maybe we'd get lucky and the powder would work.

Goddamn it, why did I always find myself in these kinds of situations? Why the hell couldn't things ever be black and white?

Captain, who had been sleeping on one of the bar stools, lifted his head, turning his nose up in the air. He'd picked up on something—supernatural, if his curious mew was any indication.

I heard footsteps crossing the floor.

I put the empty tequila shot down and swiveled my chair around. "What?" I said, despite the fact that there was no one there.

When there was no answer I added, "Artemis, quit it with the games. I'm not in the mood."

"Well, you got the supernatural right. I guess that sort of counts for something—you know, if we were playing horseshoes," came a male voice, congenial and definitely not Artemis's.

Oh, for crying out loud. I swiveled my chair back around to find none other than Hermes behind the bar, nursing a beer. The king of thieves himself. The problem with thieves was that you never quite knew where trusting them was going to take you—or when the tables would turn.

I so did not need for that to be tonight . . .

"Look, Hermes, no offense, but whatever reason you've decided to show up today—"

Hermes *tsk*ed and held up his hand. Initially I thought it was to stop me, but Captain decided it was an invitation to a pat and took him up on the offer. Hermes smiled, pulled another beer out from Nadya's fridge, and held it out to me.

I shook my head and, with no other option open to me, headed over and took it.

"Well?" I finally said, when Hermes didn't offer me any reason for his visit.

"Just checking in, seeing what you're up to, that sort of thing."

"Bullshit," I said before taking a long pull from the bottle.

Hermes shrugged. "Why do you guys always have to be so damn skeptical? I mean, is it really that much of a stretch to think the people around you are maybe, just maybe, concerned for you?"

My thoughts drifted back to Artemis, unwelcome. "If you believe that, I've got a great bridge to sell you."

Hermes shook his head and took a long pull from his beer. After a moment he added, "You know, you try to be nice—"

"—and end up wasting a lot of people's time. Get to the point."

Hermes shrugged. "Thieves," he said under his breath. "I'm in a generous mood and you've been having a rough week, so for once we'll do it your way." He glared at me over the bottle. "But don't think we're making a habit of it." He paused. "Have you decided what you're going to do?"

My guard went up as he went back to paying attention to Captain, who had decided that the attention he was getting wasn't nearly enough and was on the verge of knocking over Hermes's beer. "I make a lot of decisions—some good, some bad," I said carefully.

Hermes shook his head. "Your problem is that you've taken on your boyfriend's habit of thinking of things as good or bad."

"You think he's wrong?"

Hermes shrugged. "Not wrong for Rynn. He divides the world and people up that way—helps keep the sanity—but you? You don't."

I crossed my arms. "Is this another 'You damn thieves have no morals'? Because if it is—"

Hermes shook his head and finished off his beer. "It's not an insult, so stop taking it that way. It's the truth. You and Rynn don't think about the world the same way. No two people ever think about the world the exact same way. That's why humans—and supernaturals, I might add—never fucking agree on anything—or at least don't agree on enough to put down their guns and magic."

I was getting tired of this. I polished off a good portion of my own beer. "So everyone disagrees on something. Is that your point?"

"My point is that you're the only one here who can decide how you are going to act on your interpretation of the facts of life as you see them." Hermes deposited his empty beer bottle in the bin under the bar and shrugged on a red windbreaker—the color he always seemed to pick.

"So if I fail, it's my own goddamned fault. Gee, thanks." I was going to need another beer after this just to counteract the demoralization.

"It means that only you can decide what kind of person you want to be, Alix: underdog, tough guy, independent rogue for hire, thief with a heart of gold—you, kid, no one can do it for you, because despite popular wisdom, you're the one who has to live with your actions. Stop pretending it's everyone else."

He started for the door. "Just whatever you do, make up your mind whoever the hell it is you want to be before you do something you'll regret. Otherwise you'll end up like Artemis—maybe not today or tomorrow, but eventually."

"Like Artemis?"

I caught sight of Hermes near the door as he passed under the lights. "Someone who hates what he's let himself become but still has to live with it." The shadows created by the lights finally swallowed him up. I heard the door swing shut behind him.

I realized I was clenching my hands. Hermes had hit a nerve. I didn't know which nerve exactly. They were all raw right now.

I turned back to my laptop, where the information Nadya and Oricho had acquired for me was waiting. Something bad happened when the device had been used; that was clear enough. But what was the price, exactly? And was it worth it?

Despite what I'd tried to convince myself and Nadya of, the truth was that I wasn't so sure it was. And the guilt I felt along with that realization was eating me alive.

Hermes wanted me to decide what kind of person I wanted to be. The truth was that I really didn't know. The question before me wasn't one of right or wrong; that was part of the problem. If it had been, I would have been able to decide: good guy or bad guy, end of story.

But this wasn't that kind of decision; it was as if I had a series of lousy options, and each of them had its own personal nasty potential outcome.

"It's like an Eastern European fairy tale," I said to Captain, who was still sleeping on the red-LED–lit bar. The kind of fairy tale where someone died, regardless of what the so-called hero did.

"I always preferred those—it was more honest to children to tell them that someone was probably going to be eaten by the trolls—whether they were or not."

I turned to see Artemis leaning against a chair a few tables away, watching me darkly, hands in his pockets.

Shit, how long had he been there? Could he hide from Hermes? "What did you hear?"

He arched his eyebrows. "Him?" he asked, nodding towards the exit. "Nothing—I picked up his scent and kept my distance. Not worth meddling with him. I'd suggest you put distance between you and him, but knowing you, you won't take my advice.

"I pick up on emotions," he added. "Not as well as Rynn but enough to know you got surprised. How often does he do that?"

"Drop in uninvited? Surprisingly frequently, and no, he doesn't help—just muddies everything up."

"He has a reputation for that, much like you have a reputation for bringing destruction and disaster wherever you go. And me?" He paused. "I've got my own reputation, I suppose."

"What do you want?"

"I'm here to apologize," he said, then cleared his throat. "For not telling you why I was helping."

I didn't say anything.

"I'm not proud of it," he continued. "But I'd be lying if I said I wouldn't do it again, so take the apology however you will."

I glared at him. To think that a few days ago I would have given him a chance. Not happening this time . . .

Artemis cleared his throat again, except this time he sat down beside me, then helped himself to my bottle of tequila. "I think I understand what you two see in each other," he said, downing the shot he'd poured. "Neither of you is willing to look at the world outside your own damned narrow views."

Oh, for— I shut my computer. "What's so wrong with wanting to save someone besides myself?"

"Tell me honestly, Alix, are you upset about not being able to save the woman from the will-o'-the-wisp or the students from the skin walkers because of an obligation you feel deep down inside to do the right thing?" He made a show of tapping his heart. "Or is it because in your twisted view of reality, it makes up for the fact that you'd do it all over again to save Rynn? Don't bother answering that."

Goddamn it, what had started off as an apology had morphed into a fight. "Maybe that's true, but at least I *try* to do better than my natural inclinations. You?"

"Take a good look, Alix, because as long as you keep thinking that, this is what you have to look forward to."

I clenched my hands into tight fists. "Go to hell," I said.

The bar stool scraped loudly against the floor as Artemis stood. "Gladly. You and my damned cousin deserve each other," he said, and turned to go.

And to think five minutes ago I'd been defending him to Nadya . . . "Artemis!"

He stopped and frowned, as if he were trying to read me. "Like I said, the two of you deserve each other." With that he left, leaving me feeling unsettled and even more confused as to why I was unsettled.

I didn't have much time to ponder our conversation, though—or Artemis's failed apology. Nadya stepped around the corner, passing Artemis as he left. She didn't see him, though she startled at the disturbance in the air.

At least I'd gotten under his skin enough to rattle him. Somehow that mollified my own anger.

Nadya's frown deepened as she settled in behind the bar. "I heard yelling," she said, and searched the bar.

"Artemis being Artemis," I said, and waited until I was certain that he had to be down the stairs. I finished the beer and poured myself another tequila. I took a sip, the tequila biting at my tongue. "What you said earlier, about getting Artemis to use the device? What if I changed my mind?"

She gave me a wary nod. "I would say good for you coming to your senses," she said. "Because Oricho found Rynn."

I stood up, less steady on my feet than I had been moments before—though whether that was an effect of the tequila or of what I was about to do . . . "Where?"

Nadya inclined her head and picked up the TV remote. "Where else? Downtown Tokyo." A news-reporting duo filled the screen, their frantic expressions flickering soundlessly.

The sound was off, but I didn't need it. The scene was set smack in the middle of the Shinjuku entertainment district, throngs of people rushing out under the neon gate. The view changed to the middle of the district. Cars had stopped helter-skelter in the street, a few turned over. Fires burned where neon lights had crashed to the ground. And in the center of the street stood none other than Rynn, his warped and twisted collection of monsters fanning out, chasing people like bedraggled urchins that had graduated to terrifying.

Rynn, smack in the middle of ground zero of the running, screaming, neon-colored mayhem. He glanced up at the camera with those watery, cold eyes and seemed to stare right at me, daring me to do something about it. If Rynn was in there, I sure as hell didn't see him.

Shit. I dropped my tequila on the bar and grabbed my jacket. There weren't any bodies littering the screen—yet—but give it time. I had no illusions as to what was coming—especially if I didn't take Rynn up on his dare. I felt in my pocket to make sure da Vinci's device was still there, then started for the door.

Nadya swore in Russian and rushed to catch up. "Alix!" she called after me, and when I didn't stop grabbed me.

"We need to stop him," she said, simply and to the point. And carrying more weight than she could have known.

I swallowed. "I know."

She searched my face, then nodded. "I'll get hold of Oricho and tell him to bring Artemis." I knew there was another question on the tip of her tongue, but it'd have to wait. We had to get to Shinjuku and stop

Rynn and his ragtag army of misfit supernaturals before they leveled half of Tokyo. The silver orb was warm in my hand. I hoped my plans wouldn't unravel halfway through like they usually did—not this time. There was too much at stake.

I couldn't get the image of Rynn's watery, pale eyes out of my head as I rushed down the stairs, Nadya with her bright red hair in step beside me. The sound of sirens in the air reached us along with the sound of car horns. Somehow I didn't think it'd bode well for me. Or Rynn.

20

THE DEVIL'S IN THE DETAIL

10:00 p.m. Friday: Shinjuku district, Tokyo.

By the time the four of us reached the red-lit gate of the Shinjuku district, my nerves were frazzled from imagining how many people had already died. As I looked around the abandoned streets, I hoped that most of the people had gotten out in time. Then I worried where the hell Rynn's vampires were. Sirens still wailed but there were no people to be seen, not even peeking out from the corners of the storefront windows that lined the streets.

"For a weekend it's quiet," Nadya observed as we stepped under the gate.

"Sure, if you can filter out the collapsed neon signs, crashed cars, and fires." I stepped around a broken sign whose bare wires had spilled out the back, blocking our way. Captain sniffed at the air. He sensed that there was something out of place but wasn't quite able to place it. He settled for taking a tense perch on my shoulder, ready and willing to pounce.

It was as though every instinct in my body was waiting for something horrible to happen.

There had barely been a sound since we had exited the Shinjuku subway station, with the exception of a handful of panicked people racing to get onto the train as we exited it. Their eyes had been wide and they had shouted as they pushed their way past us. There was no mention of monsters or destruction, not even of a blond man with hostages in the square. Just shouts, footfalls, and the train doors swishing shut before the train raced away from the disconcertingly unexplainable event. And of course we were headed straight for it . . .

—ɯ—

"Well, looks like we found the place. Now where the hell is he hiding?" Nadya said.

Good question. It was much too quiet. "Oricho?" I asked.

Before he could answer, there was a loud clang ahead, followed by a snap of electricity that arched up from the neon gate. We stopped where we were and scanned the intersection ahead, none of us willing to speak, despite the unnerving and unnatural silence that surrounded us.

The four of us jumped almost in unison as something crashed behind us, followed by another electric snap that charged the air.

I tried to pinpoint the source of the sounds, my heart racing. Another sign had fallen, and a white-light case had fallen three or four stories a block away. I jumped as another crashed to the street closer to us, then another, the lights exploding as the light cases broke and the electricity fizzling like miniature lightning. It was like a path cut raggedly through a dangerous forest with a trail of pinecones—except that this forest was made of concrete and the pinecones of skull-crushing Plexiglas.

"I'd say that was our invitation," Artemis said, his voice echoing through the tense night air. "Let's follow the bread crumb trail of destruction, shall we?"

I don't know what I'd expected—screaming, running, mayhem . . . "Anything strike you guys as odd?" I asked.

"You mean the silence?" Nadya offered, her voice barely above a whisper.

"That—and the distinct lack of *anyone*." I kept scanning the restaurant windows we passed. There was no one. Not hiding under furniture, peeking out through shuttered windows, waiting for the coast to be clear. I'd seen them running on TV—so where the hell had they gone? Even in the worst disasters, there were always a few lingering souls who were more concerned with protecting their things than their lives. Or keeping their front seat at the disaster so they could film it for YouTube. If people willingly died in pyroclastic floods and lava, why the hell weren't there any spectators for the monster show?

Unless the monsters ate them already. I pushed the thought aside as we continued past another fallen sign.

"Please say the distinct lack of activity is you, Oricho," I said.

Oricho glanced at me over his shoulder, arching one of his dark eyebrows, the dragon tattoo on his face shifting in the lights. "I only wish it were."

Of course it wasn't. I swore. Captain let out a forlorn mew, as if joining me in his own curse of the electrical hurricane.

"Everyone has their powder on them?" I'd divided the Tiger Thieves' powder up amongst us, so that whoever ran into Rynn first could use it, rather than waiting for whoever held it to show up. There was a round of nods. We kept moving forwards, Nadya and Oricho in the lead a few feet ahead.

Artemis dropped back beside me. "Give me the device, Hiboux," he said, his voice too low for the others to hear, holding out his hand. "Before you're tempted to do something stupid."

"I won't do anything stupid," I whispered back, afraid to raise my voice in case Rynn had his denizens waiting for us—or Oricho or Nadya overheard.

"You've used it not once, but twice now. I trust you not to be tempted about as much as I trust your cat with a vampire."

I ignored him, paying attention to our surroundings instead.

He frowned at me. "Give it to me—this is the last time I'll ask."

"No! And back off, it's mine."

Nadya glanced back at us, and I shook my head at her questioning glance. I looked away, remembering her suggestion—and warning.

The hairs on my arm were bristling with static now, the air itself electrified. Beside me Captain let out a forlorn mew as the hair on his back lifted from the static charge. We had to be getting close now.

As if the universe were taking my thoughts and churning them into reality, we turned a building corner, and there he was. Standing in the center of the intersection, waiting for us, was Rynn. His black armor was electrified, statically charged energy dancing over its surface. The air around him buzzed with electricity, snapping when it contacted the debris and dust in the air. He stared at us, his cold eyes so pale now as to be almost white as they burrowed into me.

There was something else I noted, though, which was much more disconcerting: along the sides of his face were angry red welts—and they were smoking.

"The armor is burning him up—just like it did all its victims," I said. Meaning we didn't have much time left to get Rynn out. The Kitsune's warning came back to me: I could take care of Rynn, or the supernaturals would try it their way.

Rynn's smile was feral. "Alix, so happy you could join us," he called out.

Sure enough, I saw them—mercenaries, the odd shadow moving around the buildings, a burst of erratic light. I even thought I caught the scent of lily of the valley, but I couldn't be certain, the way a dry breeze stirred around us. I frowned. There was something strange about the air around us— I reached out and just as quickly pulled my hand back as a shock coursed through me.

"Well, the invitation kind of sucked, but you know me, not much else going on tonight in Tokyo." I nodded to the dark figures. "A little impersonal bringing your retinue, don't you think?" I added.

I don't know what I'd expected—for the Electric Samurai piloting

Rynn to get upset, lash out, yell like a spoiled two-year-old? He *tsk*ed at me, then turned his attention on Oricho and Artemis.

"Such a change from the last time I walked the earth," the Electric Samurai mused. "Humans have surrounded themselves with such wonderfully conductive cities." Making his point, the box lights above us exploded, forcing us to scatter out of the way. The buildings around us crackled.

"Keep your feet and hands away from the metal—everything in this square is electrified," Oricho warned. "He's turned it into an extension of the armor."

Meaning that there was no way in hell we'd get close enough to use the Tiger Thieves' powder. Goddamn it, we'd been worried about his minions, but he didn't need his minions if he could electrify everything around him into one giant weapon. Why the hell hadn't we thought of that?

Oricho inclined his head. "Perhaps there's something I can do—but I will need a significant distraction."

"How?" Artemis asked. "You saw that, he has the entire square booby-trapped."

"He will not, I think, be able to guard all four avenues to him—not if he is focused on you, Alix." He turned to Artemis. "Not if we both employ our powers."

Artemis snorted but regarded me and said, "It's risky, but you're right. Using Alix to unnerve him is the best chance we have."

Oricho nodded at me. "You'll need to distract him—I believe talking to him will suffice—you have a talent for infuriating him as you do most supernaturals."

I wasn't going to argue that one—not now . . .

To Nadya he said, "Can you cover the mercenaries?"

Nadya nodded and from her bag removed a firearm. I couldn't help but arch my eyebrows; things had certainly changed in the last few months if Nadya was carrying a gun around in her backpack. That was a conversation for another time, though.

She gave me a quick glance, as if asking me if I would be okay. I nodded, and she headed for the building across from us, one with a number of balconies.

"Artemis, if you could confuse Rynn's supernatural denizens?"

He gave me a slightly longer stare than Nadya had. Then, "Why the hell not? Chances are we're all going to die anyway. Might as well spend my last few moments pissing off my cousin—it's become a family tradition." With that he disappeared from my sight.

And then there were me and Oricho.

"I'm waiting, Alix," Rynn called out, but it was in the Electric Samurai's hollow voice. It was enjoying this way too much. "What is it going to be? Hide in the shadows or come and face me? If you do, I might even let your friends live. You won't."

"Keep him distracted," Oricho whispered. "Once I'm close enough, I'll signal you to get out of the way."

"Wait a minute, a signal—what signal?"

"You'll know it when you see it," he said.

And then there was only me . . . and Rynn.

Great, just fantastic. They were going to let Captain and me negotiate with the violent supernatural. Just how had this plan gotten so far without anyone pointing out the huge problem with that? Oh yeah, my pissing Rynn off was the plan. Oh yeah, there was nothing that could go sideways with this.

I brushed off my pants and stood, Captain beside me, warily eyeing Rynn and trying to resolve the conflicting smells coming off him.

Let's try not to start this off with violence . . .

"What do you want?" I shouted. There, that was nice and neutral.

That slow, cruel smile. "I was going to take your life, but after that show in Muziris, I'll take da Vinci's device first, thank you very much." He held out his hand.

God, I hoped Oricho knew what he was doing. Otherwise we were about to have a very pissed off Rynn. The device sat there, a warm pit in my pocket.

I glanced at the building windows and was convinced that I saw more than one piece of metal reflecting. "Ah—yeah, how about fuck off and try— Shit!" I dived out of the way as a streak of lightning shot out towards me and Captain, striking inches from my feet.

"That wasn't a negotiation, Alix," the Electric Samurai said. But there was a twitch of muscle, a quirk of his lips. Rynn—it had to be Rynn trying to get through. Maybe that was it? Maybe I was going about this all wrong. Maybe goading the Electric Samurai was the way to release Rynn—or at least give him a fighting chance.

"Hey, asshole, why don't you stop wearing my boyfriend like a cheap suit?"

The Electric Samurai laughed. "Oh, you'll have to do much better to get under my skin."

I shook my head and removed the device from my pocket. "Not really," I said.

Rynn frowned, the first sign of confusion on the Electric Samurai's face.

"You have any idea how fragile this thing is?" I said, holding it above my head like a tennis ball about to be thrown.

Rynn's face twisted in fury. This time I was ready for the lightning and was already running for cover. It struck the sign I skidded behind, sending up a shower of sparks.

There it was again—another waver in the Electric Samurai's carefully controlled veneer.

I saw it then, a red car careening across the intersection towards Rynn. Oricho was right; I was going to see his sign.

The mercenaries saw the car as well, and I ducked farther behind a fallen sign as bullets rained down. I was certain I heard fire returned, though I couldn't pinpoint from where. The Electric Samurai finally gripped back enough control to turn towards the commotion, but it was too late. Oricho was behind him. Faster than I could follow, Oricho was on Rynn. He forced him to the ground and gripped his head between his hands.

Then he crammed the powder down the Electric Samurai's throat. The effect was immediate: Rynn sunk to the street, gripping his throat and coughing.

The lights surrounding us sputtered, once, twice, then went out.

"Quick, get the armor off!" I shouted. Oricho began to pull frantically at the blackened pieces that had reverted back to their pre-feudal Japanese origins. I ran until I reached Rynn and tried to help get the armor off.

I yelped and pulled back my hands, my fingertips red and angry. The armor still burned.

I wrapped my hands in my sleeves and tried again. The armor wouldn't budge, not an inch. "Why the hell isn't it coming off?" I shouted at Oricho.

He shook his head. "It's bound to him—we're too late," he replied.

No, no, we couldn't be too late—shit! I launched myself at Oricho as he raised a long blade over Rynn's heart. "Sorry, old friend," he said before I crashed into him. I have no illusions about my martial prowess; the only reason I managed to dislodge him was the surprise.

Artemis reached us at a dead run just as Oricho reached for my neck. Artemis pulled me off, then restrained me as I went straight for Oricho's throat.

"I can't remove the armor—none of us can!" Oricho said.

"So we what? We kill him? Just like that? What kind of a dick friend move is that?"

"It's not a 'dick friend move,'" Oricho said, the words sounding odd coming from him. "It's a mercy—he wouldn't want to be left like this, enslaved by corrupted magic—none of us would!"

"What you need is to try harder to come up with something else!" I'm fairly certain Oricho was about to tell me the supernatural equivalent of "Go to hell" and "Fuck off" all in one, but instead, his eyes went wide at something behind me.

Shit.

I turned. Behind us stood the Electric Samurai.

And he looked pissed. He *tsk*ed. "I'm. Not. Going. Anywhere."

"Run," Oricho said—simple and to the point.

I did as Oricho asked, as did Artemis. Over my shoulder I saw Rynn stand up. Oricho didn't stand a chance.

Before Oricho could even get back within arm's reach, Rynn launched a shock of lightning at him. I heard Nadya shout, and two bullets struck Rynn in the chest. They bounced off ineffectually. Rynn turned his attention to where the bullets had come from, an evil look in his eye as he launched another shock of lightning.

"Nadya!" I shouted as the lightning struck one of the buildings, shattering the windows. Oricho was lying smoking on the ground; he'd barely crawled out of Rynn's range.

I needed to stop this—now, before someone, including Rynn, got killed.

It was time to do something really stupid.

I held my hands up in something I figured resembled a white-flag gesture and waved them over my head. "All right, Rynn, you win," I called out. "You're right, we're in over our heads."

A slow, cruel smile spread across his face. "You never were much of a negotiator, Alix."

He had no idea. Fists clenched at my sides, I started to rise out of hiding but Artemis stopped me.

"Give me the device," Artemis said. "I know what you're planning, remember, I was there in Muziris."

I stared at Artemis's outstretched hand. I'm not going to lie, I was tempted. Selfish, self-absorbed, and probably a million other self-adjectives you can come up with. And let's face it. I'm not what most people would consider a moral person. Most of the time I struggle with right and wrong; often it's not until I see an outcome that I know which would have been the better choice.

But then there are times in my life when the right choice is staring me in the face and the decision I'm left with isn't what's right or wrong but whether I'm willing to do the right thing and damn the consequences.

My hand tightened around the orb. I was done taking the easy way out.

I shook my head at Artemis. "This isn't one of those responsibilities people should pass off." With that, I bolted and ran for Rynn before he could stop me.

I hoped Nadya was right about the device separating all the individual parts out.

As I was just about to slice my finger on one of the sharp edges I stopped—or more accurately, I came to an abrupt halt. I couldn't move: my legs, my face, I couldn't even blink my eyes. Mere feet away from Rynn.

That put one hell of a kink into my plan.

Rynn covered the distance and gripped my arm, the one holding the device. He squeezed. Pale, malevolent eyes glared down at me. He kept squeezing my wrist until one by one my fingers opened. The silver device dropped into his open gloved hand.

Oh, this time my reckless abandonment and shunning of precise plans was going to cost me—in sweat and blood, if his grip was any indication.

"Did you really think I was clueless to your plan to get rid of me?" It was Rynn's mouth moving, but the hollow voice was all the armor's. If Rynn was still in there, I couldn't see him.

Whatever force gripped the rest of my muscles relaxed in my face. Well, rule one of Owl's handbook for dealing with hostile supernaturals: no matter what the cost, keep them talking.

I ignored the pain shooting up my wrist as best I could. "Well, to be honest, I kind of hoped you'd be a bit more clueless— Son of a—" I bit back a yelp of pain as he squeezed my wrist again.

"Rynn is adept at deception—I do have to give him credit for that. Squirreling thoughts away in the far reaches of his mind, thinking them safe from me." Rynn's/not-Rynn's mouth twisted. "I'll give you a hint. They aren't."

As I watched, the cold blue faded from his eyes, as if they were melting back to Rynn's own blue-gray. There was a trace of movement, little more than a microshift; his eyes widened, the rest of his face still cruel and impassive. It was easy to miss but I caught it.

Rynn was in there watching, but the armor was still in charge. The idea made me nauseous.

"I told you I was a fast learner," came the armor's hollow voice. He was close enough that I could feel his breath, hotter than it should have been, brushing against my skin, reminiscent of Rynn but with something rotting underneath.

"You should have listened." The cruel smile widened. "Come to think of it, I believe I've finally determined a way to break my wayward host."

A snap like a twig sounded down the street. For a moment I felt nothing. Then I felt pain shoot up my arm and into my hand as my wrist snapped. I screamed. And all the while, the Electric Samurai was making Rynn watch me. I'd like to think I braced against the pain, but that would be a damned lie. I howled like Captain dumped into water—louder, if the way Rynn's eyes widened said anything.

"Now, tell me what it is this device does, and maybe I'll stop forcing Rynn to watch me kill you. It's the least I can do."

I think there's something particularly painful about having a wrist joint broken—not just the pain but the fact that there's now a ton of things you might never be able to do again . . .

Through the pain, though, something important registered: the Electric Samurai still didn't know what da Vinci's device did.

I licked my lips and clenched my teeth through the pain. I'll take my silver linings where I can get them.

He shook me again. "A weapon? Magic meant to trap me once again?" He twisted my wrist, eliciting a sickening squeal from me. "I've been imprisoned for more than *six hundred years*, so you'll understand I don't take kindly to that."

Come on, Owl, lie like you mean it—enough to put something over on an incubus . . . the best lies are rooted in truth.

"It's a weapon," I managed.

He twisted again. I couldn't feel the pain, but the slick wetness told me that bone had gone through skin. I focused on the blood that was on the device. Mine. I really hoped I was right about this. If I wasn't—well, I wouldn't be around to worry about it. One shot—I'd get only one . . .

"What kind of weapon?"

"One that kills supernaturals—and for all I know, humans too," I said.

"How?"

"You press the button—"

Another shake. "Really?"

"I swear!" I screamed. "That's how it works. Blood, supernaturals, and press the damn button."

His eyes narrowed as he peered into mine. For a moment I held my breath, thinking he'd figured it out. After too long a pause he said, "I believe you. Now, what are you not telling me?"

Please don't pick out the lie. I hoped to hell he wouldn't be able to tell the lie from the pain and fear—both of which were very real. That's what Artemis had said, hadn't he? That there was a point where even a skilled incubus could be fooled.

Here went everything. Through clenched teeth I said, "It kills everyone except the one holding the device," I said.

The Electric Samurai clicked his tongue and glanced over to where Oricho and Artemis remained away from the Electric Samurai's sphere of influence. "Now, isn't that interesting," he said. I watched him as he mulled it over, looking for the flaws. Regardless of any suspicions he might have, I knew it was too tempting. I had him.

"You know what your problem is, Alix? You give up too easily."

I licked my lips and watched as he slowly, oh so slowly, wrapped his gloved hand around the device, over the silver button. The device was still covered in my blood. He caressed it, and for a heartbeat, I thought he might not press it. I was too afraid to hold my breath.

Come on, just press the damn button already . . . I willed him to press it with everything I had left . . .

The Electric Samurai might have Rynn's body and mind, but his imagination and self-restraint he did not.

I watched as his finger pressed the blood-soaked silver button down.

For a moment nothing happened, and then the air around us heated up. Out of the corner of my eye, I saw Artemis help Oricho to stand.

The Electric Samurai realized his mistake too late. He whirled on me, eyes blazing red. "You tricked me!" There was no attempt to ape Rynn's expression now, it was the unadulterated twisted rage of the armor.

"Yeah, and that's not all." I kicked him in the knee as hard as I could, as Rynn had once shown me. It caught him off guard, and he let my wrist slip. Despite the fresh new pain that flooded my senses, I managed to slip out of his grip. I stumbled back. The Electric Samurai reached towards me—and couldn't get to me. His hand slammed into an invisible wall.

"You tricked me!" he screamed, face twisting in fury.

"And I hope it rips every last bit of you away from the armor and my boyfriend." I took a step back from the Electric Samurai as it pounded against the invisible barrier the sphere had created. "Every last drop," I whispered.

My back hit something solid.

Shit. Sure enough, behind me was another barrier. I felt my way around, but it had encircled me as well.

Damn. I turned back to the Electric Samurai, who either hadn't noticed or didn't care that I was trapped as well. As I watched, the armor began to smoke. There are some points in life where right and wrong just aren't so clear.

The armor lost its modern guise, retreating back through the ages until it reached its ancient Japanese origins. Smoke poured out of it now, and Rynn's skin began to char a smoky brown.

Please don't kill him, I thought.

The smoke wound around him, licking at the armor and Rynn's skin as the Electric Samurai raged, screaming at me and the world. Thousands of years of anger and hate swelled against the barrier between us.

I don't know if the Electric Samurai knew its existence had come to an end. I don't know if it was capable of regret or sorrow. I do know it knew it was dying and fought every step of the way. It sunk to its knees and bared its teeth at me. "This isn't over," it said in that hollow voice.

I shook my head. "Yes, it is."

The last of the smoke swirled around the Electric Samurai's charred body. A piece fell off and turned to ash on the ground, then another, and another, until all the pieces laid burning around it, turning to ashes, not unlike the way it had left countless cities and people over the centuries. The last flicker of the Electric Samurai's existence was a final glare of hate before the pale eyes shut forever.

I breathed a sigh of relief, finally tuning into the sounds and shouts around me. We'd defeated the Electric Samurai. I might not be certain about a lot of things, but I knew it was gone.

And then the smoke flowing around the invisible barrier dived for me.

Damn it. I pressed my back as hard as I could against the wall, but it wouldn't give. The smoke flowed under and then around me. It flicked at my skin, as if tasting me. Goose bumps rose along my arms. A tendril licked at my face, then gripped it, coating me in milky gray.

"Alix?"

The voice was strained and quiet against the backdrop of noise—so much so I wasn't sure if it was real. I glanced up as the gray smoke snaked its way into my mouth and nose, forcing the breath I needed out.

Rynn was watching me through the barrier, the rage of the Electric Samurai having vanished, replaced by panic and terror.

"No!" He tried to push through the barrier and when that failed searched for the device. He found it on the ground, the symbols still glowing with magic and my blood.

I inhaled but felt no relief. Panic washed over me, a reflex from the lack of oxygen. Oh, that could not be good . . .

Still, the panic didn't overwhelm me. I'd stopped the Electric Samurai, I'd saved Rynn, and for a time at least I'd stopped a supernatural war from bursting into the human world. Despite what happened, regardless if I died now, I'd done it. Somehow that made everything easier to take.

I leaned my face against the barrier separating us. It felt like glass under my fingers.

"Alix, you need to stop it!" Rynn screamed.

We both knew that even if I could, I wouldn't. My vision was wavering now—that happens, or so I hear, when there isn't any oxygen . . .

"Alix, look at me!"

I did—or tried to. I placed my hand up against the barrier. Rynn did the same. At least I'd gotten the chance to see him before—

The last throes of the spell hit us in a burst of blinding light.

I was vaguely aware of flying backwards and falling hard. The blow of back meeting ground knocked the wind out of me, and stars were added to my blurred vision.

As Hermes had said, even if all my roads led to disaster, they were still my roads. Somehow that fact made whatever would come next that much easier to take.

21

AFTERMATH

Still in Tokyo . . . though the jury's still out on whether I'm dead . . .

I was cold. I hate being cold, as much as I hate it when Captain howls in my ear to wake me up—which he was doing right the fuck now.

My head hurt way too much for me to be dead . . .

I opened my eyes.

I was on my back in a street. Neon lights flashed overhead along with the flickering lights of emergency vehicles. Downtown Tokyo.

I groaned and tried to roll my head. It didn't work well. At least the different pains were canceling one another out now, my numb, broken wrist competing with the pain in my back and neck . . .

Funny how it hadn't been until I started working with supernaturals that I'd begun to see silver linings—a coping mechanism?

I was also way more familiar with passing out than I had any right to be.

Somewhere over the background that was my buzzing head I could hear Nadya, Oricho, and Artemis shouting—commands, directions, threats, take your pick.

I turned my head. Ooooh, that was going to smart tomorrow. It took a second for my vision to catch up, but I saw Rynn. He was sitting unconscious, like I should have been, slumped against a wall.

His eyes weren't open, but that didn't matter.

The armor was gone, a charred heap of rusted metal scraps and ash scattered around him. A breeze blew down the street, and I watched as the ash was carried away until it was no more. Somehow that struck me as a very fitting end and a long, long time coming.

Through my throbbing headache, I searched for da Vinci's device: another smoking piece of magic debris lying broken on the pavement, a crack around it. I didn't think I'd need to worry about it getting into the wrong hands ever again. Which, despite every ounce of pain in my body, suited me just fine.

I laid my head back onto the pavement. I was a lot of things, but stupid enough to try getting up was not one of them. I might have lain there with my eyes closed, letting the world spin circles around my brain, forever, but the throbbing, shooting pain in my arm brought me back out of my stupor. I lifted my head, ignoring the headache to see just how bad my wrist was, before momentarily passing out.

Oh man, I really wished I hadn't looked. It was bent at an odd angle, and I was pretty sure that was bone sticking out. I closed my eyes and bit back tears. I couldn't move my fingers.

Numbness was replaced with warmth and sensation in my fingers.

Artemis? But he was still back with the other disoriented supernaturals trying to get their bearings around the square they'd found themselves in, not quite able to remember what had happened and whether what they'd done was a curse or a gift.

I heard more commotion and Nadya's voice above me. "Alix? Alix?" I think there was a shake at my shoulder as she loomed over me.

I forced myself to sit up. The area around me was cordoned off with yellow tape, yet there was no one to be seen standing at the edges—Artemis's and Oricho's work, I wagered. I spotted Oricho nearby; he was blurry, but whether that was due to the flashing lights or the pounding in my head . . .

"Alix?"

I winced—definitely my head.

Nadya crouched beside me, a hand tentatively on my shoulder. I was definitely alive—things hurt too much for me to be dead. "Nadya, pretend I have a really bad hangover."

I wiped at my forehead before I remembered I'd injured my hand—or thought I had. I frowned at it; where there should have been a twisted wrist, it felt fine. "How does it feel?" I heard Artemis ask. I saw him looming a short distance away. He nodded at my wrist.

"I take it I have you to thank for my hand?" That was the only explanation—Artemis wasn't nearly as adept as Rynn at healing, which would explain why I was still in such goddamned bad shape.

"The armor?" I asked, my voice catching, worried that I'd somehow dreamed it.

There was a look on Artemis's face that I couldn't quite decipher—a mix of concern and— Son of a bitch, the degenerate rock star incubus felt sorry for me.

I tried to push myself up and head over to Rynn, but Artemis and Nadya both stopped me.

"Just—wait until your head settles," Artemis said gently.

I wasn't buying it; Artemis didn't do anything gently. I turned to Nadya, but she was frowning at me as well—and blocking my way.

I stared at her face—and his. Both of them just seemed so damned . . . concerned. Under the circumstances, it was irritating more than anything else.

"How do you feel?" Nadya asked.

I ignored her and tried to get up, but both of them held me down. Captain continued his nervous dance around me, twitching his tail and bleating—a begging, confused sound.

Like hell I was going to sit here and answer questions while Rynn laid there unconscious on the pavement . . .

I drew in a breath. Shit, what if the device hadn't worked? What if Rynn was still the Electric Samurai?

But Artemis shook his head, still restraining me. "He's free of the armor. Now answer her question."

I drew in a breath out of irritation more than anything else. "Rattled but fine." I held up my wrist. "A quarter patched up, apparently. Happy?"

The two of them exchanged a look. "I think it's better if you just stay there—" Nadya began.

But Rynn groaned and tried to sit up. That nullified any chance of my cooperating. I shoved the two of them aside and stumbled over to where he was slumped, a jumble of emotions mixed in with my pain and god-awful pounding headache.

I got close to him as he managed to sit up but hesitated a few feet away. What if we were wrong?

Rynn looked about as well as I felt as he took stock of his surroundings. He took in the destruction and general mayhem. His eyes narrowed as they found Artemis and Oricho but didn't linger—not until they found me.

His eyes were gray. Not white, not blue, not any other color except gray.

I covered the last few steps and knelt down beside him. I stayed still as he took stock of me. "Alix? I thought it was another dream, the armor trying to break me—I didn't think it was possible . . ." I figured Rynn would throw his arms around me; instead his voice trailed off and his eyes narrowed in on me. He stared at his hands, and his eyes went wide. "Alix, what the hell have you done?" he asked, his voice barely a whisper.

I could feel the trepidation as if it was my own. Then my own anger replaced it. "What did I do?" *Saved you—I saved everyone from you.* "I found a way to get rid of the armor, that's what I did. One that didn't end up with everyone dead."

I expected him to snap back to himself, touch me—something. I reached out, but he did something I'd never expected: he pulled back, pulled his face just out of reach of my fingers. I was so shocked that none of the things that coursed through my head made it out of my mouth. The thing that floated to the surface from the cacophony was Artemis's admonition, clear as when he'd said it what seemed a lifetime ago: "The question you should be asking yourself is will he still want you when he finds out what it will take to save everyone?"

Rynn shook his head and averted his eyes. My anger dissipated. He wasn't angry at me, just sad, so incredibly sad. "Your eyes, Alix," he said, and nodded towards a building where the glass was still intact.

I crawled over and took a look at myself in a window. It was me, with fewer scrapes than I normally had, but me—except for my eyes.

They were blue. A devastatingly bright blue—not human and not my own darker shade.

Artemis and Nadya came over to us from where they'd been hanging back, apparently deciding that now was a good time. I saw them in the reflection of the broken window—I couldn't look away from my eyes.

It was Nadya who touched me and finally turned me away.

It was Artemis who finally spoke. "Well, I'll be damned. That's what the mad old Italian meant," he said.

The three of us turned towards him.

"Da Vinci. He said the device had a cost, that it couldn't get rid of any powers. We all assumed it meant that it didn't work half the time."

It hit me what he'd meant. "That's how he became a vampire," I whispered.

Artemis inclined his head. Nadya only gasped, though she hid it well.

"Something resembling a vampire, at any rate," Artemis said, glancing at Rynn, who was watching us, before turning his green eyes back on me.

That was why the device hadn't done anything to Charles except clear his head. He was already a vampire; stealing the essence of other vampires only cleared his head, while it reduced the others to ash, stripping everything away that was keeping them alive.

I hadn't just deactivated the armor, as I'd been led me to believe the device would do. She'd been wrong.

"You took my powers. All of them." We all turned to where Rynn was standing now, balancing himself against the wall.

"So I'm what? An incubus now?"

"Something resembling one, at any rate," Artemis said.

I would have said something more, something to the point, but I didn't need to. I could feel it rolling off the three of them now.

Once again, it was Artemis who finally spoke. He let out a low whistle. "Well, isn't this an outcome no one expected."

I glanced up at Rynn, who still hadn't touched me, not once, not after everything. He narrowed his eyes at Artemis, then at me. "No, not in a million years."

I don't know if it was all the emotions swirling around inside me, overwhelming me, or if it was Rynn, but one thing did claw its way to the surface: that once again, despite my best intentions, I'd managed to replace one disaster with another.

"Try blocking it out, Alix," Artemis said, his voice oddly even and quiet.

I was only half listening to his advice. That was easy for him to say; he lived with this stuff. If I had known this was going to happen . . . *Big breath, Alix*, I told myself. I unclenched my hands and did the best I could to school my expression.

I had to sit down. There was too much going on, too many feelings, the majority of which couldn't be my own. I slid my back down against a wall and tried to wrap my head around everything, shut out the onslaught of sensory overload on my raw nerves, make sense out of everything that was going on in my head, try to piece together which emotions were mine and which were coming in from outside.

What made it through was an incessant buzzing in the background, constant and unforgiving on my raw nerves. It was the kind I couldn't ignore. I pulled it out, meaning to silence it.

I stared at the screen. Everything else faded away.

There was only one person who could make a message box appear on my phone like that. It was the same messaging program Carpe had used to contact me.

I'd seen that text box only once since Shangri-La, when it had been filled with a jumble of numbers.

Are you there?

I swallowed and stared at the screen, not entirely certain whether I should trust myself or what I was seeing.

Another message popped up on the screen. *Please, Alix— Just tell me if you can see this.*

A cold sensation crept down my spine. Carpe was dead and buried in a collapsed pocket universe. I was certain about that, that's what I'd told the elves . . .

Please?

I hesitated but only for a moment, my fingers flying over the digital keys.

"Alix?" Nadya said. I held up my hand and continued to type.

Who are you?

A moment later, words appeared on the small screen: *It's me.*

Not *It's Carpe*, not *It's the elf.* Ambiguous. *Not good enough,* I typed back.

Another pause, then *Inventory.*

I switched apps and opened my game inventory log. A new item had appeared amongst my items. It was a scroll. An extra-life scroll, but this one had been customized. That was rare with game items, but it was possible to attach notes to them—usually to hide something from other players. I clicked on it. On the back of the scroll was written, *I finally got Paul the Monk.*

I caught my breath but stoppered my hope. Paul had been our in-game teammate who had screwed us over, trying to kill both our avatars and make off with the loot, using his soccer-dad status as the excuse. Very few people besides Carpe would know about that wanted poster— he had been the one to set up the bounty. It still wasn't clear, it was circumspect, like a code . . . Why the hell couldn't he just come out and say it was him?

There was a link at the end of the message. What the hell did I have to lose? I clicked it. The screen went blank and for a moment stayed that way before flickering and taking me to another player's inventory. I recognized the name and avatar. It was Paul the Monk's private inventory. I shouldn't be able to see it.

That wasn't what had my attention, though. The inventory slots did.

Every item he'd ever had had been replaced by a small computer-generated chicken. Even the empty slots had been filled with them. There had to be three dozen chickens on the screen. Just like the ones Carpe had saved from a plane crash in Egypt.

Son of a bitch. It had to be him.

"Carpe? Where the hell are you?"

I'm inside—in here. I need to go before it finds me again.

With that, the screen went blank.

Son of a bitch. "Carpe? Carpe, you asshole, type back now and tell me where the hell you are!"

"*Alix!*" Nadya spun me around.

I shook off the spell that had descended over me while I'd been staring at the blank message box. I cleared my head as best I could to find out what Nadya wanted.

She pointed to the place where Rynn had been a moment before. He was gone. "Rynn?" I called out. There was no answer. I searched the scene but saw only Artemis and Oricho along with a handful of other supernaturals. There was no trace of him.

I looked at Nadya, but she shook her head. "One moment he was there—" she said.

"—and the next he was gone," I filled in for her. I stood there, the pain that engulfed my body replaced by hollow numbness. I'd spent months of searching, worrying that I'd lost him, and as soon as I'd thought I had him back—he was gone.

The moment the world starts to look up . . .

I don't know how long I stood there, searching the crowds, hoping, willing Rynn to step back out.

Another of Artemis's sentiments came back to me loud and clear: "I might forgive Rynn, but that didn't mean he'd forgive me."

I stood like that, watching the crowd, until Oricho and Artemis had left and Nadya made me move.

Epilogue

INTO THE LION'S DEN

November 10, 8:00 p.m.: The Lion's Pub, London.

I pulled my jacket tighter around me as I stood across from the pub with the Lion placard above the door. London was a lot colder in the late fall than I'd imagined, particularly at night.

The bar I was standing across the road from was situated in an older part of town, one that had avoided the architectural face-lifts that had turned entire streets into tourist traps. There were no advertisements, no menus, no pleas for people to stop in. There was an authenticity about the place—and a lack of people. I'd been standing here ten minutes and had seen only one person come out of the pub.

I warmed my hands with my breath, then rubbed them together. Head in or leave, Owl? I still had yet to decide . . . I'd made it this far and been so certain.

Now?

Captain mewed from inside my backpack. "Yeah, I heard you the first time. You're getting cold." If I didn't go through with this, I could always hit the British Museum. It had central heating, right?

I pushed myself off while I was still feeling brave. It was time I started filling in the blanks instead of ignoring my blind spots. I'd seen too many people die for no reason.

The slight sound of boots sliding against the old cobblestones was the only warning I got.

I knew he was there before he spoke on account of what I could read off him.

There wasn't much there, like a big, dark, nebulous pit.

That should freak me out a lot more than it did.

"So what is a thief like you doing in a place like this?"

I doubted very much that Hermes didn't know what I was doing here, but arguing would only delay me and I might lose my will to continue with this particular endeavor. "Padding my résumé."

Hermes seemed to consider my answer. "Interesting answer."

"Let me guess—the wrong one?" I asked. I was nervous enough as it was; I didn't need Hermes derailing my resolve.

But he only shrugged. "Honestly? It depends. Is this you running blindly towards your next imminent disaster, or did you actually think this one out?"

That was a good question, one I'd been asking myself a lot the last two weeks. I figured I'd thought this one through about as much as I could without taking the plunge. "A little of column A, a little of column B."

Hermes considered my answer, then gave me a once-over—a serious one, devoid of his usual smart-ass demeanor. He nodded. "Well, then, far be it from me to stand between you and a well-thought-out decision. I mean, those come what? One every five years?"

Asshole . . .

"So what was the fallout in Tokyo?" he asked, changing the topic.

I shrugged. "Surprisingly little, considering."

He arched one of his red eyebrows.

"Oricho strong-armed the IAA into doing its job, but between the online videos and conspiracy theories floating around"—I shrugged—"they're on borrowed time."

"And the boyfriend?"

Maybe it was the sensory overload, but I was having a hard time figuring out what my own emotions were—what with everyone else's roiling around my head. "No idea."

Despite Rynn's being short a full deck of supernatural powers, no one had been able to trace him. That shouldn't have surprised me. He'd had training it'd take me a hundred years to come close to.

"Give him time," Hermes said.

But how much? I didn't need Rynn's powers to know that for once, despite this not being my fault or a product of my own recklessness, he might not be able to forgive me. I think that hurt more than anything.

Hermes nodded at the pub. "I'm surprised the Dragon and Naga aren't throwing a hissy fit over this. They don't strike me as the sharing type."

"Call it a work vacation." I hadn't argued with Mr. Kurosawa when he'd suggested I take a few months off to recuperate—whether as a reward for stopping Rynn or punishment for working outside the lines of a coloring book was anyone's guess. I needed time away from the Japanese Circus; I'd needed it for a while now. I wasn't doing anyone any good sulking around. As Artemis had said, I was toeing the line with a death wish—and let's face it, if Lady Siyu and I spent any more time in a room together, Mr. Kurosawa would lose his thief for hire.

Instead of offering a glib remark, Hermes just rocked back on his feet and nodded. "No promises, but I'll see if I can keep the vampires off your trail—for a while." He shrugged. "Mind you—vampires are a testy lot when it comes to agreeing to anything. Chances are good it'll do as much harm as good. And as for the other thing, regarding the incubus?" He shrugged. "I'll see what I can dig up, but—"

"No promises," I filled in for him. Hermes would see if he could find a way to reverse what I'd done to Rynn and myself, but as far as esoteric magic devices were concerned, there weren't exactly certainties. But I hadn't signed up for certainties.

"Best of luck, kid. Whatever you do, don't let them push you around.

They might have you beat in the brawn department, but you can run circles around them in the supernatural department—and they know it."

Right. That was what I had to remember. They might have what I needed, but I also had something to bring to the table. Funny that I'd needed Hermes to remind me of that . . .

"And keep those sunglasses on."

As though I needed the reminder . . . still, I did a mental check that they were still on my forehead. "You know, Hermes, for a thief and supernatural you aren't half—"

I had been about to offer him something akin to a thank-you, but he was already gone. Vanished into thin air.

I shook my head. Of course he'd vanished. One of the few supernaturals I knew who preferred to stick to the shadows in anonymity. I, for one, certainly couldn't fault him for that.

I turned my attention back to the door across the road.

Come on, Owl, what are you waiting for?

I headed over to the pub. My hands shook as I placed them on the heavy wooden door. I should have had a second shot of tequila before coming here. It had taken me a while to track down this place, and I didn't know what kind of reception was in store.

Being me, I'd figured the best route was to show up at their doorstep. Easier to ask forgiveness than permission . . .

Let's hope it came across as endearing.

Time to gird your loins, Owl, and enter the lion's den . . . or would that be equine den? I pulled my sunglasses down. I hadn't quite gotten the hang of keeping my eyes, well, normal looking . . .

Before I could talk myself into stalling any more, I pushed the door open and headed inside.

Unlike a lot of the bars I'd found myself in over the years, this one was tame, in looks if not in nature: well lit, tables full of people minding their own business, but short of being packed to the hilt. It had an old-pub charm to it—cozy, even . . .

If you overlooked the fact that the majority of patrons had chosen spots where their backs were to the wall and they had a decent line of sight to the front door.

Nothing to be afraid of, Owl. I started for the bar, ignoring the looks I attracted. They weren't immediate or obvious, I gave them that. Initially there were only a few looks, glances that started to linger as I reached the bar until I figured most of the patrons were eyeing me. The emotions I could pick up off them told me as much. What was it Rynn had said? That they had ways of detecting supernaturals. I wondered how I fit into their equation. Technically I was still human, albeit with a not entirely wanted set of new borrowed tricks. The question was, did their sensors know that?

A bald man behind the counter returned my nod and came over, resting his large, bulky arms on the counter. He didn't bother hiding the fact that he was giving me the once-over. "What'll it be?"

"Beer. Whatever is light that you've got on tap." Figured this wasn't the time to ask if they carried Corona.

Keeping his eye on me, the bartender started filling a glass. "New, are you?"

"You have no idea," I said. I felt more than heard people coming up behind me, not yet violent but definitely going in that direction. The tension in the bar was palpable as the barman passed me my beer and took the bills I'd left on the counter. Not even Captain was willing to stick his head out or offer an opinionated mew.

The only warning I had was the shift of the barman's eyes towards the group of men I knew had left their chairs and were moving in behind me—not from any sound that gave them away but from the wariness and tension that had amped up in the room. Nothing overtly violent . . .

The bartender nodded at me before hurrying to the other end of the bar.

And then my head was rammed into the bar with a bang that silenced the remaining din in the room.

"Ow!" I shouted.

Two men on either side of me pinned down my arms while a third held the back of my neck.

Okay, so my reading of violence versus tension and wariness needed some serious fine-tuning . . .

"Your kind isn't welcome in here," whispered the man pinning my head to the bar, forcing my face into a position where I could see most of the people standing around the bar, including the bartender—every last one of them pretending not to see me but fixated on the proceedings.

At least that answered my question as to whether my borrowed powers would set off alarms.

"I'm not one of them—your sensors made a mistake—goddamn it!" One of the men holding my arm twisted my shoulder—painfully. I might be able to pick up on emotions, more or less, but much like da Vinci, I was woefully outclassed with regard to any of the other supposed perks. Like a cheap imitation . . . I could certainly have used Rynn's and Artemis's strength.

"Don't lie," the man holding my head said, and to prove the point wrenched my shoulder once again.

My old temper flared. "Well, that's going to be a real fucking problem since I just told you the truth and you told me to fuck off. Lying is kind of the only option you've left me with here."

That seemed to catch them off guard, whether because I was denying being a supernatural or because I wasn't responding like one was anyone's guess. The grip on my other shoulder and neck lessened, even if my shoulder was still wrenched.

"The sensors weren't clear, Ed. Maybe she's telling the truth," one of the men who hadn't been involved in wrenching my limbs said.

I didn't think Ed liked that, considering that he wrenched my shoulder further. But since two out of three were obviously questioning themselves I pushed on. "I'm looking for Captain Williams, the Zebras' head honcho. If he's not here, I'll leave; if he is, point me in his direction and I'll conclude my business and leave. Either way, I'll be out of your hair."

A pause. "Who are you, then?"

I wetted my lips. It wasn't every day—or ever—that I'd had a full pub audience. Oh, what the hell. It wasn't worth lying about now, not with the IAA scrambling to keep itself afloat. It had bigger fish to fry.

"Alix Hiboux. The Owl—maybe you've heard of me?" I hazarded.

The three of them let go. I stood slowly and turned around. Now there were three guns pointed in my face. I raised my hands. Note to self: honesty is not always the best policy.

If any of the weapons was graded for supernaturals, there was no way I'd survive them. I heard a safety click off. Survive the supernaturals and get picked off by mercenaries . . . I closed my eyes and winced.

"Edmund, stop being a dick," a voice boomed.

Everyone in the room turned towards the booming voice. It had come from a chair near the fireplace; its owner was one of the few people who didn't have their back to a wall. His back was facing the room.

"You going to vouch for her?" Edmund said, his gun still aimed between my eyes.

"Since I invited her here, yes. And she's telling the truth. She's not one of them. If you weren't using old technology, you'd have known that when we did."

One of the men at the fireplace table nodded at Edmund, confirming the analysis—one of the Zebras' techs, I wagered.

The other two men really didn't want anything to do with me now. They lowered their guns and backed away. It was the third man, Edmund, who waited an extra breath before lowering his gun.

"Careful," he warned me loud enough that everyone else in the bar could hear. "You've got a reputation for damnation and ruin. Keep it the fuck out of here." Without another word or glance, he headed back to his own table.

Well . . . that was a hell of a lot more attention than I'd expected.

I headed for Williams's table by the stone fireplace. The two men sitting with him got up, and one offered me his chair. I almost jumped when a beer was placed in front of me by the bartender. "No apologies, you understand?" he whispered.

"No hard feelings." I kept my eyes on Williams.

Along with his men, he stared at me for a long minute. Finally he motioned for me to remove the sunglasses. Not seeing much of a choice in the matter, I did.

"What on earth caused *that* misfortune?"

"It wasn't pleasant, and it wasn't intentional." I made a wager. "It's also how you got your wayward men back. The ones misappropriated in Shangri-La."

His brow furrowed. "Which is why I didn't let them shoot you." He glanced down at a tablet on the table. "So, to what do I owe this visit? Or were you simply hoping that throwing the Zebra name around might buy you a few extra breaths?"

Here was my big moment, the one I'd been waiting for, the basket I'd placed all my proverbial eggs into this last week. The smart money was on my turning back—but that would have made me a coward, and though I was a lot of things, I was not that.

"Is your on-the-job training and placement program still on the table?" I asked.

Williams glanced up again—interested this time, though wary. He placed the tablet on the coffee table and gave me a more thorough once-over. "I'm certain we could arrange a more formal discussion on the topic." He waved the bartender over and held up two hands. "Though I have to ask, what's behind this change of heart?"

Sometimes even I don't risk lying. "Let's just say I'm woefully lacking in some skill sets, and from what I gather, you and just about every other mercenary outfit in here could use an antiquities expert who knows her way around supernaturals. I'd say I'm more than qualified." For once in my life I believed it. "I'm the best at what I do—you know it, and they all know it."

Williams regarded me again. So did his other two men. "The Dragon?" he asked.

"Sabbatical."

He nodded, thoughtful.

A pair of tumblers arrived—scotch on ice. Williams picked up one, passed me the other, and raised his glass. I took a sniff. Good scotch. "Far be it from me to waste top-shelf booze," I said, and returned the gesture before downing it.

"Are you certain about this, Hiboux? If you sign a contract with us, it's not only legally binding."

Meaning that if I reneged, they had other ways of doling out retribution. I finished off the scotch and nodded. I'd done my research; so had Nadya. The Zebras were the best and fairest chance I was ever going to get.

Williams waved over his men, who rejoined us at the table. It was a testament to their professionalism that they didn't shoot me even a glance as they took their seats.

"Johan, get the paperwork ready. I've found you a replacement for Hans."

The man closest to me on my left narrowed his eyes at me. "Who do I make the paperwork out for?"

"One Alix Hiboux." Williams nodded at me. "Welcome to the Zebras," he said before getting up and leaving the table.

At least neither of the others asked about my eyes. I turned to Johan. "Who was Hans?"

"Our last archaeologist and supernatural expert."

"*Deceased* archaeologist and supernatural expert," his companion clarified.

Johan inclined his head and slid me the tablet. "Let's hope you fare better than he did. We haven't had great luck keeping our archaeologists alive—not for long, anyway."

"You'll see it all in the waivers."

"Special ones for your type."

Of course there had to be a catch . . . I skimmed through the disclaimers and clauses. The contract was refreshingly short and to the point. I'd be working for the Zebras as an expert on all things supernatural and archaeological. The chances were good that I'd be dead in a few months, but in the meantime I'd be paid very well. There was a space at the bottom for next of kin and a description of the generous condolence package that would be paid out if and when I kicked the bucket in the line of duty.

The two Zebras continued their discussion while I read and signed the documents. No responsibility for imprisonment, death, maiming, etc., etc. . . .

"Though it looks like you've already survived a few run-ins with supernatural sorts," Johan said. "It'll factor into the betting pool."

"Betting pool?" I was on the last page at the dotted line. The point of no return.

Johan answered, "We do it for all new recruits, a pool for how long you'll last."

"It's more of an initiation. We don't give you an ID until you've survived two jobs," one of the other men said.

"Consider it your audition," Johan said.

"And our entertainment."

I closed my eyes and leaned back in my chair. Yup, definitely a great big catch. What to do, Alix, sign or not sign? I stared at the last line, which was waiting for my signature via finger pad.

At that point Captain decided to stick his head out of my backpack and let out a loud, impatient mew.

Oh, what the hell. It wasn't as though I'd been living a safe, normal life before this. Besides, there was something refreshing about their candor. Not the bullshit lines the IAA used to feed me. Honesty I could respect.

I signed the dotted line with the pad of my finger and handed it back to Johan.

"Welcome to the Zebras, Alix Hiboux," he said, scrolling through the documents. "May you fare better than poor Hans." The two of them lifted their drinks and drank to that. I joined them—what else was I supposed to do? There was as good a chance as any I'd be at death's door again tomorrow—and this time without any friendly supernaturals to save me.

At some point I'll have to grow up, and if I'm going to keep playing with the big, mean supernaturals, I'll need to stop being so damned afraid and learn to deal with them on my own grounds. Human grounds. This was the best way to do that. Before something worse happened than my stealing Rynn's powers.

The maturity shocked the hell out of me too.

I'm Alix Hiboux, antiquities thief and newly minted Zebra mercenary for hire.

God help me—or, more accurately, them.

Acknowledgments

As always, thanks goes out to Steve Kwan, Leanne Tremblay, Tristan Brand, Mary Gilbert, and Pervez Bill who read each and every Owl installment. Your encouragement keeps me writing. Special thanks this round go to my cousin, Rachel, for the Spanish translations, and Cindy and Wally for helping me with logistics.

I also have to thank my agent, Carolyn Forde, who picked the original *Owl and the Japanese Circus* manuscript out of the slush pile; my editor, Adam Wilson, who makes Owl that much better and puts up with me; and Brendan May for his encouragement and handling logistics at S&S Canada. There are many other people who have mentored and encouraged me in my writing career—thank you all!

Finally, there is one nonhuman without whom this series would never have been written, and that is my cat, Captain Flash, on whom the character Captain is absolutely based.

About the Author

Kristi is a scientist and science fiction/fantasy writer who resides in Vancouver, Canada, with her spousal unit, Steve, and two cats named Captain Flash and Alaska. She received her BSc and MSc in Molecular Biology and Biochemistry from Simon Fraser University, and her PhD in Zoology from the University of British Columbia. Kristi writes what she loves—adventure-heavy stories featuring strong, savvy female protagonists.